REPLAY

AN OFF TRACK RECORDS NOVEL

KACEY SHEA

KACEY SHEA BOOKS LLC

DEDICATION

For my parents.
Thank you for everything.
I love you.

1

AUSTIN

IT'S JUST another Tuesday afternoon. Nothing out of the ordinary. I'm rocking out with my boys, creating something awesome while we practice for the big stage. Most of the time I don't overthink it, but there are these fractions of seconds, when the music comes together just right and my breath catches at the sound, that it hits me . . . I'm living the dream. My dream. Playing rock 'n' roll, the best mother-fucking music in the world, and all for a pretty paycheck. I'm one lucky son of a bitch, and I don't take any of this for granted.

Sweat beads at my temple, but I bounce on the balls of my feet, banging my head along with the rhythm as my fingers shred across the steel strings of my favorite guitar. The sound she makes is better than a woman reaching for her orgasm. Which is saying a lot because I fucking love that sound too.

My fingers chase the crest of the melody, keeping within the confines of the steady bass beat. One more wail across the threads, and then the crash of cymbals and roll of toms from our drummer perfects one of our most loved songs.

"Sick addition to the intro," I say as soon as the room quiets. I tip my chin at Leighton's practice set. "You bang those harder than a full-time hooker."

"Thanks?" The newest addition to Three Ugly Guys squints up and meets my gaze.

"Dude, too far." Sean chuckles and shakes his head as he plucks out a series of notes on his bass. We've been at this for a few hours, preparing before we head back out on the road in a few days.

"What?" I shrug. "It's impressive. That's all I'm saying."

"Let's go over "Broken Mirror" again." Trent switches to his acoustic before stepping up to the microphone. He's all business, probably so he can split early and spend time with his girlfriend. "I don't like the way we transitioned to "Whiskey Saturday." Too rough."

"Aww, but I like it rough." I pump my hips in a comic display of bravado as my bandmates gag and groan as if they're disgusted by my comment. They won't admit it, but they love it when I do shit like that. I see their smiles and barely contained laughter.

Rachel Kinsley, the new head of legal for Off Track Records and total fucking babe, pops her head into the practice studio. "Austin, I need to steal you a minute."

I glance at the guys, their expressions as clueless as mine, and just like that I'm back in middle school being called to the office. It was a regular occurrence, so the memory comes with no guilt or shame, only curiosity. I lift my chin and set down my guitar. "A minute? Give me some credit . . . you'll want at least an hour."

"He's joking," Trent apologizes, but she's already out the door. He catches my arm and bugs his eyes. "Dude, are you looking for a sexual harassment lawsuit?"

I mouth *Sorry* and make a goofy face because that's what I do. I'm *that* guy. The one who says what everyone else is thinking but is too chicken to speak aloud. Then I take it a little too far but get away with it anyway because of my stunning smile. Or at least, that's what I assume. If I weren't so charming, I'd have gotten the shit kicked out of me a thousand times over.

Or gotten fired from the band.

In all honesty, it's surprising I've lasted this long. *That's what she said.* A grin settles on my lips. Even my thoughts can't control themselves.

With long strides, I catch up to the sexy Miss Kinsley before she reaches her office at the end of the hall. Her pencil skirt and crisp white dress shirt do nothing to hide her banging bod. The way her hair is pulled back into a tight bun practically screams *Don't fuck with me.* If I were a betting man, I'd venture to guess that's not the only thing wound tight about Rachel Kinsley. As hard as I try to resist, I want to fuck her even more.

She waits for me to pass through her office door and then shuts it closed behind us. Her eyebrows rise expectantly as she walks around her desk.

Shoving my hands into the front pockets of my jeans, I'm sure to flex my arms because, well, all ladies love arm porn.

But she doesn't even take notice. Nothing. It's as if I'm not even here. *Fuck. Am I losing my game? Nah, that can't be it.* I shake off the disappointment and apologize because I don't need any problems, for me or the band. "I'm sorry about what I said back there. It was completely inappropriate of me."

"Yes, it was. Please take a seat." She gestures to the empty chair across her desk and then turns to pull open one of the long filing cabinet drawers that line the wall. I concentrate on not staring at her ass while she picks through the documents. It's a good thing, because she doesn't take longer than a minute to retrieve her file.

She drops it on the desk between us and sits back into her chair.

"What's that?" I nod at the file folder.

"Care to take a guess?" She raises one eyebrow.

I shake my head because unless she had the foresight to file a harassment claim for my earlier comment or internal thoughts, I have no clue.

"Open it." She leans back, crossing her arms across that ample chest, and waits.

Curiosity may have killed the cat, but this rock star is dying to know what earned me a one-on-one meeting with the sexiest lawyer to moonlight at Off Track Records. She's probably the only perk that came with the recent re-org after being bought out by World Music Industries. I reach forward and open the flap to flip through the contents. It's all legal jargon, most of which I don't understand. But the name listed on top, that's mine. *What the—?*

"Coy Wright is suing you," she says.

"Our former drummer?"

"Well, one of them."

"You've got to be fucking kidding me! How?" My gaze scans the pages, but it's as foreign to me as French.

"You"—she takes the document from my hands and flips through the pages until she finds a part to read from—"beat him to unconsciousness in his own home. Caused physical and psychological damage rendering him unable to work as a musician." She drops the document onto her desk and meets my stare. "The short of it is, you made him unemployable and now he's suing for damages."

I shake my head because that is not at all how it went down. Anger surfaces with the memory. "He was living in our house, as a guest. He would've beat the shit out of Jess and anyone who tried to stop him had I not stepped in. How's he going to prove any of this shit?"

"You hit him. Repeatedly. It's in the police report." She pulls a paper from the folder and lays it on the desk.

I can't believe Coy. The bastard has brass balls to believe he can get away with this. "He's just pissed 'cause no one will hire him. He's an asshole who gets off on beating women. No one cares whether he's a good drummer."

"Was." She lifts her eyebrows and shrugs. "He can't play anymore."

Annoyance bubbles in my gut. I glare and shove the papers back to her side of the desk. "This is fucking bullshit and you know it."

"Don't get your panties in a twist, Mr. Jones." She meets my stare across the table, and there's a flicker in her gaze that stirs my dick to attention. Her complete control over her emotions and take-charge attitude are attractive as hell. She licks her lips as if they're dry, or maybe it's because I can't stop staring at them. "I'm only the messenger."

"Oh, I'd say you're more than that."

"Now, now, Austin. Are you hitting on me again?" She leans forward on her desk. The dip of her blouse and mound of exposed cleavage are incredibly distracting. "As the head of our legal department, I have to advise you that's most unwise."

"And as a woman?" The words tumble from my brain and escape my mouth. "As the beautiful, fucking gorgeous, and clever woman you are, how would you advise me?"

"Oh, Austin . . . they warned me about you." She flashes a smile and lets loose a throaty chuckle. One that goes straight to my cock. "You've got quite the mouth on you."

"You have no idea, but I'd be happy to demonstrate. Dinner?"

She laughs again but rolls her eyes. "I can't go to dinner with you."

"Then dessert? Text me. I'll deliver."

She doesn't answer, not immediately, and the silence charges with excitement as I hold her gaze. It's a bad idea. Sleeping with anyone at work is, but I've never been one for wise choices.

She swallows hard and shakes her head. "I'm sure you would." She narrows her gaze and points at the door. "Go back to practice before you cause any more trouble. I'll keep you abreast of the litigation. We're fighting it, yes?"

"Oh, hell, yes," I practically shout.

She glances at me from beneath her lashes and just as I expect her to get all flirty, her gaze turns completely professional. "In the meantime, try not to do anything stupid. Or at least, keep it behind closed doors." She leans back into her chair, queen of her domain. So fucking sexy.

"Debauchery behind the door. Got it." I wink.

"Austin." She drags out my name with that serious lawyer face. The one that says we're over and done with messing around.

"Yeah, yeah." I wave her off and push up from my chair to leave. "I won't be a problem. And Rachel?" I level her with a stare of my own.

"Yes." She tilts her head to the side.

"Thank you. This guy really is a bastard." I think back to all the shit that went down with Coy. It was only a few months ago, but I thought we'd moved on from him. Guess not. "I don't want him to see one dime. Men who prey on women the way he does . . . they deserve to rot."

"At least we agree on that." The hardness of her features softens and she tips her chin. "And you're welcome."

I walk to the door, but before I open it, I glance back with my most charming grin. "So, was that a no or a maybe on dessert?"

"You can go now." Her lips press into a hard line and she raises her brows, daring me to argue. I almost do.

"Got it. I love it when you're bossy. Totally hot." I wink, but when she narrows her glare I pass through the door. "Going!"

On my way back to the studio, I consider telling the guys about this development with Coy. They're gonna lose their minds. Sean especially. *Fuck.* They'll learn the truth soon enough, though. And we don't have the luxury of wasting time. We're only in town for one week to celebrate the holidays and record a new single, and then it's back on the road. As much as I want to bitch about Coy, I don't want to ruin anyone's Christmas.

"There he is. We were beginning to think you weren't coming back," Trent complains.

"You've seen how hot our lawyer is, right? I was in no rush to come back to you ugly bastards." I pick up my guitar and slide the strap across my shoulder. "Where were we?"

"Seriously? Dish. What'd she want?" Trent lifts his brow.

"She wanted me alone in her office. What do you think?" I stick out my tongue, hoping the obscene gesture will get him to drop the third degree. I'm well versed in lying, or truth avoidance, but I have a harder time when it comes to people who are familiar with my bullshit.

Trent stares.

I let loose a laugh that says I'm as carefree as a fucking bird. That does the trick.

"Whatever." He rolls his eyes and tightens one of the strings on his guitar. "Picking back up on "Wandering Soul"."

I nod and glance over to Leighton, waiting for him to count us off.

Sean struts over before we start. "Everything good?"

"Yeah, man. Nothing I can't handle."

He nods, but his lips press into a thin line. Worried.

"I swear. I'm good. Really, our sexy suit has it all under control." I level him with a stare and it must work because he wanders back to his amp. I pray I didn't just tell a lie. I have faith in our shark of a lawyer. Hell, how much of a case could Coy have anyway? Everything's gonna be fine. It'll all work out. It always does for me. Mostly.

2

AUSTIN

IT'S the most wonderful time of the year. At least, that's what people say, and honestly, I shouldn't complain. My life could be so much worse. But there's something about the holidays that brings forth nostalgia and loneliness.

I miss things I shouldn't. I miss . . . people . . . I shouldn't.

The joint pinched between my fingers makes a lot of that go away. I inhale one last drag, hold my breath until my lungs burn, and snuff out the flame on my exhale. The party's in full swing inside; cheerful voices reach all the way out to my perch on the back patio. Normally, I don't envy others' joy. Hell, I'm living my motherfucking dream. But today I've been avoiding this holiday gathering with my bandmates. In one year everything's changed, and I've become a proverbial third wheel. Technically, fourth. The Three Ugly Guys have fallen in love, found their other halves, and I'm the lonely son of a bitch looking in from the outside.

Fuck, what's in this weed? I shake my head and blink my eyes to clear the negative thoughts that swirl in my mind. I don't begrudge my friends' happiness. They fucking deserve all of it. And I don't do relationships. I prefer my no-strings-attached bachelor status just fine. Staring at the skyline, I take in the gray clouds that paint the horizon for another second before I push off the ground.

If I stay out here much longer I guarantee Deb will send a search party. Trent's mom practically adopted me as a teen. Not like she had much of a choice with the number of hours I spent at their apartment, but now I consider her more of a mother than my own. She won't let me miss Christmas.

Throwing open the back patio door, I stagger a little as I cross the threshold. "Merry fucking Christmas!" I raise my hands, a wide smile on my lips, and walk into the family room.

Trent chuckles from where he sits at the edge of the couch and shakes his head. "Someone's already lit."

I press the little button on my sleeve and make the front of my sweater blink and glow. "Lit like a fucking Christmas tree. Only way to be, bro."

"Festive as fuck." Sean slaps my hand for a high five.

"You like the sweater?" I glance down and puff out my chest. "I have a matching one in my room if you want."

"I'm good." Sean chuckles, his arm around Jess's waist. "Glitter isn't for me."

"Tinsel. It's fucking tinsel, man." I shake my head, but stop because the room begins to spin a little.

"You okay?" Opal crosses the room, concern knit in her brow, and she rests her hand on my forearm. She's so damn sweet. Her little baby bump protrudes beneath the apron she's wearing. I'd hate Leighton for knocking her up, except he makes her ridiculously happy. That and he's a madman on the drums.

Fuck. I need to find a sweet woman for myself. "No one wants to wear my matching sweater," I mumble at the sad realization. The floor dips and causes me to lose my balance, but I reach for the wall and set myself straight.

"Aww," she coos but her lips lift into a smile. She pulls me toward the kitchen. "Honey, you need to eat."

"I need Santa to bring me a woman."

She laughs and hands me a cookie.

It's frosted, decorated in white icing and pink sprinkles. If I squint, it looks like a naughty cookie. "Scratch that. Ask Santa to bring me a tray of pink pussies." I shove the treat in my mouth and reach for more.

"And he's done here, folks." Trent catches my arm before I steal all the cookies. I try not to pout as he drags me backward into a chair.

"Drink." Lexi places a water bottle in my hand and I catch the concerned look she throws her sister.

Opal purses her lips together and frowns.

"Don't spoil your dinner," Deb chides and motions for everyone to join her around the kitchen island. "A toast before we eat. Then we'll do presents." Trent's mom raises her glass of wine, her fluffball of a dog held tightly in her other arm. "I'm so glad we're all here together. It's been a while. This year hasn't been easy, and to those who are no longer with us . . ." Her voice cracks and she blows out a soft exhale. "They're in our hearts. Always. But looking around this room—all the new faces—your young love—I can't help but be proud of the lives you've created. You boys were hellions, and I won't lie. I'm relieved to see you settled down. Well, most of you." She pauses to meet my gaze.

"Love you, too. Mrs. Donavan!" I blow her a kiss.

She laughs and shakes her head. "I haven't given up on you, Austin." She lifts her glass in the air and glances around the kitchen. "To another year. May it bring you each more blessings. More love. And all your hearts' desires."

I open my mouth, a smart and highly inappropriate retort on the tip of my tongue.

Mrs. Donavan glares.

I snap it shut. The woman's known me for over ten years. I can't get away with shit around her. Never have.

"To family," Trent's smile is broad as he looks at everyone in the room. Sean and Jess. Leighton and Opal. Lexi. His mom. Me. "You all are my family."

"To family," everyone echoes back, and then we don't waste another minute, grabbing plates we load up on the home-cooked heaven Deb and Opal spent the better part of the day preparing. The food is ten times better than any restaurant, and I swear to God I haven't eaten this good in years.

The mix of being high and hung over propels me back to fill my plate a second time. I don't know why I was so sad before. In this room, right here, are all the people most important to me. So I don't have a steady woman; maybe it's not in the cards. I have more than most. All the money I need. Playing music for a living. My life is good. And these people, they're my family, even if we're not bonded by blood.

"Feeling better?" Opal asks from across the table, her feet propped on the empty seat at my right. Everyone else buses around the kitchen, helping Deb clear the counter and wrap up leftovers.

"Yeah." I meet her smile and shove the last bite of bread into my mouth. "I don't know how Leighton lucked out with you, but he better appreciate." I nod to my now empty plate.

"Stay away from my girl, Jones!" Our drummer is some kinda boy genius and apparently also has supersonic hearing.

I lift my middle finger, all in good fun, and shoot a wink at Opal. "I mean it; the meal was delicious."

Her cheeks flush with my compliment. "Deb did most of the work." She's modest. I know she was in here all day working alongside Trent's mom.

"Present time!" Deb claps her hands and shoos everyone back to the family room.

I grab another beer from the fridge before heading into the next room. Leaning against the door frame, I watch my bandmates and their partners gather around the ten-foot artificial tree. I wonder if we'll even be here next year. This house is provided to us by our label, a massive three-story in the Hills, with a practice studio in the basement. But ever since our label Off Track Records was bought out by WMI, a giant mogul of a company, we've been riddled with uncertainty about the future. Under new management, we're just attempting to get through our commitments and this last leg of the tour before we reevaluate or make any life-changing decisions.

Hell, living in one big house has only worked because Deb stays here year-round and we've never needed more. When we were all single fuckers, this place was more like an animal house. I bet everyone's going to want their own place now, somewhere to play house now that they're in love. *Fucking love.* Ruins everything.

"Come on, man. Don't look so sad. I'm sure Santa brought you something." Trent bumps his shoulder against mine and motions for me to follow him over to the empty couch. Everyone's already busy passing gifts around. The rip of paper, joyful musings, and Nat King Cole serenading through the speakers is enough to make me nostalgic. *Christmas.* The most wonderful time of the year. Only is it?

"Austin. Trent. Come sit. Those are for you." Deb points to the couch and a pile of gifts gathered there.

I don't want to get emotional. I blame it on the day-drinking and the joint, but the presents, the love in this room, it's all too much. The goodness of the moment hits me square in the chest. I take a second to watch everyone while they're occupied with each other. Their joy is fucking radiant. I swallow down the impulse to cry and blink my eyes to clear the moisture.

Opal catches my gaze. "Did you open mine yet?"

I sniffle and discreetly rub beneath my eye. "No. Which one?" I say to the stack more than her.

"With the pink ribbon."

I nod and take the package, carefully undoing the perfect wrapping. Inside she's written a note I can't look at right now because I know that'll send me over the edge. Instead I lift out the chia pet. It's in the shape of a Bob Ross head. Laughter bubbles from my gut and a smile chases away my earlier impulse to sob.

"Thank you."

She grins wide. "You're welcome."

I make my way through the pile. A few are ridiculous, like the mermaid tail Snuggie from Trent. Some expensive. A Movado watch from Deb. All thoughtful and completely perfect. I get down to one remaining box and glance around the room. I have no clue who it's from.

"It came yesterday." Deb says as if she can read my thoughts. She probably can. "No card or tag."

I rip through the paper, excitement and nerves in the pit of my belly at the idea of who it could be from. A gift from a certain sexy lawyer would make this day nearly perfect. But inside the package is a plain white box. No wrapping. No card. *Strange.* I shake my head, pull out a smaller box, and flip open the lid. It's filled with rocks. Nope. Coal. And between several of the pieces is tucked a note card. I pull it out and try to process the words scratched in dark ink.

You think you can do whatever you want? Wrong.

I hope you have a merry Christmas, because payback's a bitch.

I laugh and glance around the room. "Okay, who was it?"

Their confused expressions meet mine.

"Ha ha. You got me." I laugh again, louder, but no one joins in. No one even smiles. My amusement falls and is replaced with dread.

"What is it?" Trent shifts closer so he can read over my shoulder.

"Really. Who was it?" I say, keeping the tinge of panic from bubbling up. It had to be one of my friends. The alternative is disturbing. *Who would send this?*

"Mom, when did this come?" Trent glances up at Deb, his eyes holding the same worry that sends my heart racing. "And do you still have the box?"

"Yesterday, when you were at the studio. I think the packaging is in the garage. It didn't have a return address, though. None that I remember. Why?"

"Because my guess is the cops are gonna want to take a look at it." Trent swallows and looks at me before pulling out his cell phone.

"Nothing says Merry Christmas like a visit from the LA Police Department, right?"

Shit. The last thing I need right now is to talk to cops. Especially if I don't want my friends to have to post my bail. My eyes go wide as I catch Opal's concerned gaze across the room. "You still have some of those cookies left?"

"Yeah," she says warily, chancing a glance to where Trent speaks into his phone, "Why?"

"Because I'm pretty sure I'm still high and drunk. And apparently we're about to have visitors."

"Fuck." Sean swears and rubs at his temples.

Trent shakes his head and lets loose a humorless chuckle as he pulls the phone away from his mouth. "Can't take you anywhere, man."

"In my defense I wasn't planning on leaving the house," I offer, but catch sight of Deb's disappointed glare. Fuck, this is a new low, even for me. Yeah, I'm the asshole who ruined Christmas.

She crosses her arms over her chest and her look of pity is even worse than the judgment.

THANKS to another slice of Deb's lasagna and Opal's tray of baked goods, I'm sober enough by the time the cops show that I no longer appear as high as I am. Any weirdness is written off as nerves, because holy fuck, who gets threatened with a Christmas gift? If that's not enough to make a man stop in his tracks and assess the status of his current life choices, I don't know what is.

Only thing is, I can't figure out who might've sent it. Everyone I know who'd send a practical joke are the people here in the room. Which is exactly what I tell the cops.

"You sure there's not anyone you can think of who might want to hurt you? Someone who feels they've been wronged?"

I wince because I realize I have to come clean. What I was trying to avoid and delay is now plopped in my damn lap. "Our former drummer. Coy Wright. He filed a lawsuit against me."

"What?" Jess brings a hand to her throat. Her wide, fearful gaze makes me wish I had killed her ex when I had the chance.

"The hell?" Sean doesn't even try to contain his outrage. "Austin?"

"I'm sorry." I chew at the inside of my cheek and shove my hands into the front pockets of my jeans. "I wasn't gonna say anything until after the holidays."

Trent's gaze is serious. "So, that's what the lawyer wanted to talk to you about."

"Yeah." I shrug and then turn back to the one this hurts most. "I'm sorry, Sean. Jess."

"It's okay. We'll be fine." Sean puts his arm around Jess's shoulders. I don't know whether his reassurance is more for her or himself. "I won't let him near you, baby."

"We all won't," Trent says. "You never have to see him again. Not if you don't want to."

"So, we filing restraining orders, then?" The cop blinks and blows out a sigh. I can't imagine any of this, or the report he has to type up about my cryptic Christmas message, is fun.

"No, sir," Sean pipes up. "We took care of that earlier in the year."

The cop glances at his partner. "Looks like we have all we need. One of the detectives from the station will be in touch. We'll do our best to find out who sent this, but more importantly, keep your eyes open, and if anything seems out of order don't hesitate to give us a call. We'll alert the private security on our way out."

"Thank you, officers." Deb produces a few plastic containers, no doubt filled with home cooked food. "These are for you. We appreciate your service, and the sacrifice of you being away from your families today."

They smile, appreciative, and offer thanks as she walks them to the door. With the food in hand they no longer seem put out. Thank God for Deb. She's the best.

"Now that's out of the way, who wants to go out?" I clap my hands once and then re-light my Christmas sweater so I illuminate the room. This stupid sweater is gonna be a hit with the ladies. It's why I bought it. Sure, they'll laugh and poke fun, but it's an icebreaker, and soon enough they'll be looking to light up more than my tree.

"I think we've had enough excitement for one night." Sean pats my shoulder and pushes off the couch. He grabs Jess's hand and pulls her up too.

"Yeah, we're calling it." Trent runs his hands over his face and meets Lexi's stare across the room.

Leighton nods. "Us, too."

"Fuck. Y'all are no fun. It's Christmas Day. We should be party-ing. Living life! Drinking drinks! Finding me a woman."

"I'm sure that's the exact intention of our Lord and Savior's birth." Deb pins me with a glare and scoops up her dog.

"Sorry." I cringe and then look to my friend. "You know what I mean, right, Trent?"

He laughs, shaking his head as he wraps his arms around Lexi's waist. "Don't drag me into this. I have everything I need right here."

"'Night, everyone. Love you," Deb calls out on her way to the hallway. "Don't worry about cleaning up. I'll take care of the rest tomorrow."

"Thanks, Deb!" we say in chorus.

Trent gives her a kiss on the cheek. "'Night, Mom."

I glance around the room, taking in the happy couples. "You know what? Love stinks."

"You should write a song about it," Sean says. "But maybe change the title, 'cause that one's taken." He and Jess wave goodnight, and with an armful of presents, head for their room upstairs.

"Hey, but seriously"—Trent leaves Lexi's side to clasp my

shoulder—"don't go out tonight, man. Nothing good'll happen if you do."

"Yeah, yeah, yeah." I wave off his concern and make a show of rolling my eyes. "Go upstairs, have a fucking good time. I'll be in my room masturbating."

"Now, there's the holiday spirit." Lexi punches me playfully on the shoulder. Trent takes the gifts from the edge of the table and they follow Leighton and Opal out of the room.

"You guys used to be fun!" I shout at their retreating forms.

"We'll party tomorrow night, after the show. Promise!" Trent turns, walking backward, and levels me with a pointed finger.

I wave him off and lay back on the couch. "Promises, promises." I blow out a breath and relax into the cushions as the glimmer from the lighted Christmas trees, the big one in the corner of the room and the other on my chest, lull me to sleep. Fuck it. I'm too tired to go out on my own. But I'm holding my friends to it. None of this turning in early crap. When we jump back into the last leg of this tour, we better party like the rock stars we are.

3

JAYLA

THE MURMURS of excitement rumble through the long line outside the side entrance to the Staples Center. I've been to dozens of concerts here, but never once have I splurged for these kind of tickets —ones that include a pre-show meet and greet experience. I told my girls it was my treat, a Christmas gift from me to them, but that's a complete lie. This is an entirely selfish want. I'm not here for the music, or to take pictures with my favorite band. I'm here to see *him*.

There have been so many times I've wondered. Wanted. And now it's really happening.

I resist the urge to flip my phone to selfie mode so I can check my makeup for the thousandth time. Nothing has altered my face or clothes since my girlfriends and I exited the Uber twenty minutes ago. It's a cold night for LA, even with it being winter, and my teeth chatter despite the suede jacket that covers my upper body. Yeah, it's the weather. Not nerves. Not because after years, regret, and count- less hours of anticipation, I'm finally doing this.

My stomach plummets with the thought of seeing him.

He's probably forgotten. Won't even recognize me, and he shouldn't. I'm not the young woman I was when I left Phoenix my junior year of high school. He's not the same boy. Obviously, what with his famous rock star status.

Still, I hope.

"Girl." Aaliyah steps in front of me. "What's up with you tonight? You weren't even listening to me."

"Sorry," I say and shuffle a few steps as the line moves forward. My stomach dips and dives knowing he's right around that corner. We can see the security guards from here. It's only a matter of minutes now. *God, why did I think this was a good idea?*

"You nervous?" Kalise eyes me suspiciously. I should have known better than to bring her along. She sees right through my crap.

"No." I shake my head and tip my chin as I straighten my spine.

"Liar." She laughs and turns to make a face at Aaliyah before settling on me.

"Shut up." I want to be offended but end up giving in to my smile at her wide do-you-really-think-you-can-lie-to-your-best-friend stare. "Whatever. You know I like this band."

"Yeah, you do. I can't believe we're missing Drake for them." Aaliyah rolls her eyes.

"You aren't missing Drake." Kalise lets loose another laugh. "He's playing halfway around the world."

"I'm just saying. If we weren't here, we could have flown to Japan to meet my man."

I roll my eyes and let out a rough laugh. "Drake know about your undying love?"

"If he checks his Twitter, hell yeah, he does." Aaliyah licks her lips.

"Tickets please," the guy working the line says and interrupts our conversation.

"Oh, right." I swipe open my screen and flip through each ticket for him to scan. I didn't realize we'd moved this far up in line. Any easiness fades as a tidal wave of nerves crashes and settles over me again.

"Jay, you work with celebrities all the time. Shake it off, girl. You look like you're gonna pass out." Kalise knocks her shoulder into mine as we step over the threshold and into another line.

I shrug out of my jacket and place everything I'm holding before the security guard to check before passing through the metal detector. I wait as my friends do the same and try not to allow my knee to bounce as the anticipation builds. I'm not sure what I'll say when we reach the head of the line, even though I've practiced this scenario in my mind more than I'd ever admit.

"Next." A woman standing in front of the hanging red drapes waves us over.

"Fuck," I mutter under my breath, caught between the need to rush through those curtains and the desire to run back to my apartment.

"How many?" the woman asks.

My throat goes dry and my mouth doesn't open.

Aaliyah steps forward. "Three."

"I don't know what your deal is, but these rock stars are nothing," Kalise whispers at my side and pushes me forward. "You're a fucking queen."

She's right. Entirely. I don't do nervous. I don't do timid. I own my life, and I live unapologetically. Have for years. I give myself a shake, push my shoulders back, and walk forward with all the confidence in the world.

Maybe I should play it cool. Or at least try to look at someone else first, but I can't help it. My gaze searches for his, and maybe it's wishful thinking, but the minute his cool blue eyes catch me staring, I swear they light with recognition.

"Please tell me there's free booze," Kalise says as we join another line, this one for a photo op with the band. It's the reason I paid an ungodly sum for these tickets; I wanted to get near enough to him so we could talk.

"Yeah, after our photo." I manage to sound normal.

Kalise glances around and at the sight of the bar in the corner, she

tips her chin. "This line isn't going anywhere fast. I'll be right back."
She takes a few steps and calls back, "You want something?"

Aaliyah laughs. "Hell, yes."

"I got you," she says and heads to the bar.

I focus on my friends and not tripping as we shuffle forward
every few minutes, but my eyes continue to drift back to him. Each
time I do, he catches me looking and his lips lift in a flirty smile that
does things to my insides. The room is loud with laughter and conversation. The band takes time with each guest before they move along.

"Girl, he's into you," Aaliyah hums low enough he can't hear.

"You think?" That flicker of hope in my chest grows a little
stronger. I hold my head higher. My fears subside. I don't know
whether he remembers me, or if he just finds me amusing, but either
way I have his attention.

"Can't stop staring," she says, and it's true.

"Back, bitches." Kalise grips three drinks in her hands and
manages to hand two off without dropping one.

"Thank you," I say, though my stomach is in knots and I can't
imagine drinking anything. Besides, I want all of my senses on
full alert.

"Just in time." Aaliyah grins and sucks back most of her drink as
the line attendant greets us.

"Ready to meet the guys?" she says with an enthusiasm and
familiarity that instantly strikes a chord of jealousy in my mind.

I brush off the feeling and walk forward, refusing to back down
now that I've made it to this moment.

"Hey, beautiful," he meets my gaze. His voice is all sex and bad
decisions, nothing like when we were kids. "How you doing tonight?"

"Not great." The old familiar pain strikes at the sight of him this
close after so many years. I'm tempted to throw the goddamn drink in
his perfect, smiling face.

As if she can read my mind, Aaliyah takes the glass from
my hand.

"Oh? That's a shame. Someone as gorgeous as you should be having a good time." There it is again. The innuendo. *Does that work for him? Does he think one smirk and all is forgiven?*

No. He doesn't recognize me. He wouldn't be this arrogant if he did.

I ignore the part of me that jumps to attention at the thought of taking Austin to my bed. Letting him worship me in the way I've fantasized too many times. I shake my head and draw in a breath. "You don't remember me, do you?"

"Shit," one of the other guys mutters, but I don't catch who. I'm too busy reading Austin's face.

"You look really familiar." he says with sincerity, and takes a step forward, closing the space between us.

I could reach out and slap him. Better yet, pull him to me and allow him to wrap me in his arms. Instead, my hands go to my hips and I tilt my head.

He takes a languid look down my body, obviously appreciating my full curves. Good. My efforts don't go unnoticed. As his eyes scrape back up and settle on my eyes I finally say what I came here for.

"It's me. Jayla." I stare and wait for the realization to hit him. It does. His eyes widen and for a second he drops the cool rock star façade, looking more like the boy I fell for all those years ago. Words stick on the tip of my tongue—ones that berate him and express the anger, isolation, and sadness I felt when he never called or tried to reconnect. I never wanted to leave Phoenix, but at sixteen I had no choice. He was the one who broke his promise.

"Jayla," he repeats my name, a whisper first and then louder. "Jay? It's really you?"

I nod and take in the joy that lights his eyes, the thrill that runs through my body at being this close to him again.

"Jesus." He opens his arms, taking one step closer, and doesn't wait for my permission before pulling me into his arms. His body isn't anything like I remember. His muscles are filled out where he was once all long limbs, and his chest is full and strong.

I resist the desire to sink into his warmth, his comfort, his masculinity. And after a beat longer than is appropriate, I step out of his embrace.

"God, it's good to see you, Jay. I didn't know." His eyes don't leave mine, and without glancing around the room, I'm certain we've garnered everyone's attention. His words rush forth with what I think is a mixture of disbelief and genuine excitement. "You're here? I mean you live here, in LA?"

"Yeah, I've been here." My fingers clench my bag and jacket. I force myself to hold his gaze and school my features. I came here to tell him off. To show him what he missed out on. But instead, I can't produce more than a stare and a few awkward words.

"Shit." Austin turns to his bandmates and it's then I meet Trent's friendly gaze. "Guys, this is a friend from high school."

"Jayla, I remember." Trent steps forward, holding out his hand. "How are you? How's your brother?"

"Good." I return his firm handshake and offer a smile at the thought of my older brother. "Desmond. He's good. Married and with two little ones."

"That's fantastic. Tell him I said hi."

"I will."

"Excuse me, Mr. Jones. Mr. Donavan," the woman in charge of the line interrupts. "We need to get to the next guest. Can we get everyone lined up for a photo?"

"Sorry," I begin.

But Austin turns to her. "We'll get to them. There's plenty of time." He zeros his attention back on me before she even leaves and it's Aaliyah who clears her throat behind me.

God. They're going to kill me. I force my smile to stay in place. "These are my friends, Aaliyah and Kalise."

"It's so nice to meet you." Austin gives them each a sincere handshake, and makes quick introductions to his bandmates. But while my girls shake hands and chat with the others, he turns back to me. "I don't want you to leave." His gaze holds no teasing or lightness.

"I think I have to." I raise my brows and point toward the door. "You have a show or something."

"I can't believe you're here." He ignores my comment and reaches out to touch my arm, almost as if he can't fathom it. "Thank you."

His words swirl in my mind, catching me off guard. "For what?"

"Always believing in me." And it's as if time stands still. Frozen. Him looking at me. Me staring at him. All the years we lost disappear and I'm with my best friend again.

"Aust, we really need to take this photo," Trent says.

"Sure. Sorry." He guides me by my elbow, his touch gentle and light, and leads me to stand between him and Trent. We turn, smiling to the photographer as she snaps three quick photos. I try to smile. I swear I do. I hope I manage to appear happy and not full of the tremulous thoughts that race through my brain. This is all so surreal.

"Tonight. After the show. Come out with us. The Sands. We'll get you on the list."

"Oh, I don't know." I back up, knowing he has to go, and not sure where this leads. I can't erase the last thirteen years as if they never happened. We're not friends anymore. We can't go back.

"Please. I don't want to say good-bye."

The next group walks forward, and the rest of the band turns their attention while Austin stares and waits for my answer.

"I'll try," I finally relent, and then Aaliyah and Kalise are at my side, walking my dazed self toward the exit and straight to the first ladies' room.

"Jay, girl . . ." Kalise pins me with a no-you-fucking-didn't look. "You got some explaining to do."

"What?" I turn to the mirror and reach up to touch my corkscrew curls, hating the doubts that come to mind. *Did he like my hair? I never used to wear it like this. Did he find me attractive?*

Aaliyah rolls her eyes and shoves me over a few inches. "You never said you were friends with a rock god!" She glosses her lips in a natural shade of pink.

"He's just a man," I remind myself as much as my friends.

"A very famous one. A man who's loaded. Girl, you need to get on that!" Kalise bugs her eyes and levels her stare.

"Then hook a sister up!" Aaliyah presses her nails into her chest and bats her lashes.

"I thought you were in love with Drake," I say.

"I am," Aaliyah says with conviction before letting a smile take over her face. "What the brother don't know, won't hurt him."

Kalise gives in to a smile. "You're ridiculous."

The muted sounds of applause and wailing guitars greet my ears. The opening act. Not one I'm that excited to see, but if it'll lessen the current inquisition, I'm game. "Let's go. Concert's starting."

Aaliyah shakes her head, but steps ahead and leads the way.

I follow a half step behind, with Kalise on my left as we make our way through the now crowded concourse and to our section. After showing the attendant our tickets, she leads us through the almost deafening music to find our seats.

"Don't think just because we're here at this concert that you get out of explaining," Aaliyah shouts as she takes the seat at my right. "Imma need to know everything."

"Details." Kalise nods. "Including why the hell you had to pay so much for these tickets!"

"Seriously. We should be backstage or something." Aaliyah shakes her head, and I just know it doesn't matter what I say, she won't let this go. "Hook me up."

"It was a long time ago. I didn't think he'd remember me."

"*Mmm hmm.*" Kalise stares across my body at Aaliyah. Together they exchange some kind of silent communication.

Aaliyah lifts her pointer finger and levels her manicured nail at me. "We're going to that club."

"What?" I say like I don't know exactly what club she's referring to.

"You heard me. You're gonna meet him tonight so you can get whatever it is you came here for."

Only, I'm not sure exactly what that is.

4

AUSTIN

"WE'RE BEHIND SCHEDULE. Sorry, they need you in the green room. Now," Jax, one of the tour assistants calls from the open doorway.

We wave good-bye to the lingering guests and staff working tonight's pre-show meet and greet. I follow behind Sean as we head toward the green room. These meet and greets are an addition since WMI bought out Off Track Records, and one of the few changes we've actually enjoyed. Face time with our biggest fans in a more intimate setting is an absolute joy. We usually have plenty of time after to hang before the show, though tonight we're pushing it.

"What happened in there tonight?" Jax lowers his brow and taps at his cell, his long strides setting a quick pace. "Did they sell too many tickets again?"

"I don't think so." Trent glances over his shoulder and briefly meets my eyes. "Just a few familiar faces."

Jax touches his earpiece and nods before he opens the door for us to pass. "The girls are already on stage left. We're cutting it close. I need you guys ready in fifteen. That good?"

Trent tips his chin. "Ready when you are."

"Be back in a few." Jax taps the door frame with his knuckles and strides out the door, barking orders into his headpiece before it fully shuts.

Leighton settles on a chair and pulls his sticks from his back pocket to bang on one of the end tables.

I slide past Trent and Sean to head straight for the bar.

We usually have a good hour before we have to be on stage. Time to chill, nurse a few beers, shoot the shit. Hang with Opal and often times Lexi, too. Not tonight.

Not much these days rattles my nerves or shakes my confidence. I can play the set in my sleep. But not tonight. My mind races and I can't get into my usual pre-show headspace. Anticipation thrums in my chest, making it difficult to breathe. I want to blame it on the tight schedule, but that's a complete lie. It's her. It's always been her.

I grab a beer from the bar and pop off the top before tilting it back to drain the entire bottle.

"Slow down, speed racer. We got all night." Sean wanders closer and snags a beer for himself.

"Why wait?" I force a smirk and shrug. "I say, party starts now." I reach for another drink but Trent snatches it out of my hand.

"Pretend you've done this before." He shakes his head and by the forced smile on his lips I can tell he's annoyed.

"No bailing now. You promised." I step around him and grab another beer, taking a swallow before he attempts to block me again.

"Yeah, yeah." He pushes his hair back from his face. "But that's after the show. Nothing good comes of getting shitfaced beforehand."

I don't appreciate his tone, or that he's acting as if I need hand-holding. But I shrug it off because I know the reason I'm feeling out of sorts has nothing to do with him. She's out there. *She's waiting to watch me perform.* I set the beer down and reach for a water instead. I need to be at my best.

You're such a showoff.

Her playful words and a memory from my youth hit me square in the chest. As a teen, I wanted nothing more than for her to like me. It was half the reason I took up guitar in the first place. I guess no matter how much time passes, some things never change.

"Crazy seeing Jayla?" Trent says, probably able to read my mind. "You two were close. Right?"

"Yeah." I swallow down the memories and feign disinterest. I don't feel like rehashing the past. Not now. Not right before the show.

"She wasn't wearing a ring." Trent shrugs and glances at Sean with a smirk.

I noticed the same. But that doesn't mean she's single, or even interested. Hell, she didn't want to date me then, so there's no indication she'd want to now. Fuck.

Trent lifts an eyebrow and tips his head at the door. "Come on, Mr. Bachelor. You really trying to tell me you didn't notice."

"I did."

"And . . ." He twirls his finger as if to say get on with it.

"You think she'd be into me?" I ask in a moment of clarity.

Trent's jaw drops open and he turns to Sean. "I don't believe it. Didn't know it was even possible."

"Maybe he's sick?" Sean glances at me with wide eyes. "Inhabited by aliens."

"What?" I glance behind to see who they're talking about, but then turn back to find both their gazes on me. *Shit.* I pat my hands over my body, thinking surely something must be out of place.

"The humility thing." Trent's lips lift in a slight grin. "It's strange."

"It's uncomfortable for me, too," I admit.

"Don't worry, man. Get on that stage tonight and play your heart out."

Sean slaps me on the back with a chuckle. "Yeah, some chicks really dig rock stars."

He's right. What am I so worried about? I'm a fucking god on stage; if anything's gonna impress a woman, it's me and my guitar. I straighten my shoulders and let the smile take over my lips. "You ugly fuckers make me look good."

"And he's back." Trent laughs. "Come on, let's get out there."

I'VE BEEN on a thousand stages. Played so many shows I've stopped keeping count, but the high of playing for a massive group of screaming, adoring fans never ceases to amaze me. Doesn't matter that we've been up here for two hours. If anything, the crowd's enthusiasm only increases. We long ago exhausted our usual playlist. This is our second encore. But the fact we don't have to hop on a bus or catch a flight until tomorrow propels us to play just a few more.

"I love you, Three Ugly Guys!"

"Marry me!"

Trent chuckles into his mic and points a finger across the stage at me. "Don't give up hope, because that guy's still single, ladies." He winks and the crowd erupts in cheers.

A grin pulls at my lips. The knowledge that I could ask any number of said ladies to spend the night in my hotel room and they'd say yes still baffles me. Not too bad for the skinny kid who couldn't get laid or hook a girlfriend in high school. "That's right, all you sexy, gorgeous, single women. Sing your heart out for me." I point out into the crowd, even though it's difficult to see past the first rows because of my spotlight. "I'm gonna come find whoever's the loudest."

"Yeah, brother?" Trent chuckles into his mic. "Then what'cha gonna do to the poor thing?"

I turn to him and flash a smile. "Oh, I think you know exactly what I'm gonna do." But it's all for show. There's only one woman on my mind right now, and I wish to hell I had the good sense to give her backstage passes. Then I wouldn't be staring out into this massive crowd, wondering where she is, if she's even there.

Shit. She must think I'm a complete ass. If I hadn't been taken by surprise, I would have given her and her friends the best seats in the house. *Fuck*. I hope I didn't screw up. She probably thinks I'm a pretentious asshole. God, I hope she shows at the bar. I'll make sure to set things right. Take care of her the way I should have.

Trent turns to Sean, his mouth on the mic. "I say we take it old school for this last one."

"I like the way you think, brother." Sean grins and walks over to Leighton. Back in the day we did tons of covers. They were crowd pleasers, and we always try to squeeze one or two into each show. No matter how big or famous we become, playing the bar scene is where we started.

Leighton counts off with his sticks and we break into a rocked out, grungy cover of "I Wanna Sex You Up." The crowd eats it up, and everyone goes wild with my added theatrics. Okay. Not everyone. Sean doesn't seem amused in the slightest. But hell, if thrusting my hips into my guitar is wrong, I don't want to be right.

As Trent belts out the lyrics and I join in the chorus, I can't help my thoughts as they wander back to Jayla. She looked better than I remember. Full curves in all the right places, natural curls where she used to wear her hair straight. But her eyes, always expressive, are the same. Her lips, thick and luscious, still call to my inner caveman, wanting to claim them as mine.

And she's here. Now. Watching me right this very minute as I strut my stuff and shred to impress. We were other people when we knew each other before. Young kids. Dumb. Well, I was mostly dumb. And yet, she's the one girl I continue to think about. Never stopped.

Maybe second chances really do exist.

I wonder if she's thinking about that, too. *Fuck*. I want to search her out in the crowd. Abandon my guitar and call her out on the mic, bring her on stage and beg her to give me another shot, but even I know that's ludicrous. It takes everything to keep my gaze forward and focus on the performance.

We make the "Color Me Badd" classic our own and then transition into our last number for the night, "Anyone But You." As soon as our fans recognize the hit that's been stuck on the charts for the better part of the last six months, their screams become overpowering. I can barely hear the music in my headpiece, and by the way Trent holds his hand to his right ear, he's having the same issue.

Guitar in hand, I make my way off to the side of the stage to find a tech. "Turn it up!" I shout and then tap my ear. He nods and relays the message as I run back to my place on stage. Trent shoots me a thankful smile and breaks in with the first verse.

Lifting my arm, I sink into the rhythm and wail on Lola. Yeah, I name my guitars, and this beauty hasn't let me down once since I bought her used from a shop off Sunset Boulevard in West Hollywood. Having her restored to her former glory was a pretty penny, but worth it. It's the same make Hendrix played when he recorded "Electric Ladyland," and while his fucking talented fingers never touched this one, I feel pride in knowing there's a connection to the legend.

I lose myself in the notes, letting the music bleed from my heart and all the way down to the tips of my fingers as they move with a practiced speed I don't even have to think about. The fans sing along to every word above the amplified sound, but that only adds to the magnetic energy. I jam out, dancing and singing along until the very last note. The applause is deafening, and as I turn back to smile at my bandmates. I know they feel it, too. This stage, this moment, it's what rock dreams are made of. If we could, we'd stay here all night.

"Thank you, Los Angeles! You're beautiful!" Trent calls out to the crowd.

Waving, I throw my guitar pick to a skinny teen crowded at the front corner of the stage. He catches it with a big smile, and as we head off to the green room I'd like to think that inspires him to pick up a guitar himself, if he hasn't already.

"Be careful with my babe," I say seriously before handing Lola over to Ben, one of the more responsible stagehands.

"Yes, sir." He admires the guitar appreciatively as he packs her back up.

"Fuck, did you see that crowd?" Leighton says as we head for the girls. Opal waits until he's within reach and then pulls him in for a kiss.

"See it? I could fucking feel it," Trent slings an arm around Lexi's shoulder. "We kicked ass out there."

"You sure did, babe." Lexi pushes up on her toes and meets him for a kiss.

"Hell, yeah." Leighton grins and it makes him look like a fucking kid.

I don't even have to turn around and look to know Sean's kissing Jess.

Fucking lovebirds. A tiny burst of jealously coils in my gut. I want a woman to kiss me when I walk off stage. Hell, not just any woman. I want Jayla. "Enough with the kissing. You promised me partying. Let's hit the showers and head out." I try for nonchalance but who am I kidding? I'm never this impatient to get going.

"Why the rush?" Lexi eyes me with curiosity.

"He's got a girl waiting on him."

"Just one?" Opal teases and everyone laughs.

"An old friend of mine. I invited her and her friends to go out with us. That's all." Again with the lies. I don't know why I bother hiding my interest, other than the fact Jayla is someone from my past. Worry gathers at the edge of my mind. Jayla knew me before I was famous, before I was a rock god. She might not be all that impressed with the person I've become. I might not be as different as I try to act.

"Better have Jax or someone call ahead and get them on the list. That place is crazy any night, let alone the weekend," Leighton says.

"Good idea," I say and glance around for one of the assistants.

"Old friend?" Trent eyes me with a grin. "From what I remember, you two were really close."

"Yeah. So?" I pretend as if my heart doesn't race at the thought of her.

"Ohhh." Lexi lets loose a low whistle.

"An old crush? I need to meet her." Opal rubs her hands together and gives me a stare.

"Wait? An ex-girlfriend?" Even Jess lights up. "This I have to see."

"No." I roll my eyes. "We weren't ever together." The lie tastes sour in my mouth. I shake it off and wave Jax over from across the room, but he doesn't notice. "Try not to be embarrassing."

"Are we embarrassing?" Trent gasps and presses his hand to his chest as if he's offended.

"Rich coming from the dude who shit his pants at last year's VMAs." Sean chuckles.

"Nearly. I *nearly* shit my pants." I throw up my hands and narrow my gaze. "And this is exactly what I'm talking about. No stories that make me look bad."

"Fuck, what are we even gonna talk about?" Sean deadpans and scratches his head. "I can't recall one story where you don't do or say something stupid."

"Fuck off." I shove him and finally give in to a laugh. "Just steer clear of the stuff that paints me as a level ten asshole. Okay?"

"So, we shouldn't mention all the random women you hook up with?" Lexi lifts her eyebrow in challenge.

I narrow my gaze. "If I didn't love you, I would hate you."

She shakes her head, and leaves Trent's side to grab my arm. "Feeling's mutual. Come on, let's go find Jax and get you a shower. You smell, and not in a good way."

5

JAYLA

GOING out to a club always sounds like a good idea until I'm there. If it were just my girls, and the guys would keep their hands and eyes to themselves, this would be enjoyable. I love to dance, and hitting the floor with my ladies brings a smile to my face. We've been here a few hours waiting on Austin, sipping drinks and rocking to whatever the DJ spins.

I'm having fun. Something I don't do enough of. It's a good time.

That is, until some dickwad slides his hands onto my hips. I step forward and spin around. "Not interested."

"You're looking good tonight." He closes the space between us and reaches for my body again.

My pulse spikes and I hate that I still hesitate, even a beat, before I push back. "I said I wasn't interested. Move on." I wave him off and turn back to Kalise.

"Hey, come on. Don't shoot a brother down so fast." He drops his chin and flashes me a smile, positioning himself between me and my friend. This man had the audacity to put his hands on me without my permission or encouragement. Now he can't take the hint to leave, even when I spell it out for him. I hate men like this. One who assumes a nice body and handsome smile are his ticket to whatever he wants. By the lift of his smile, he thinks he's got game.

I hold up my hands to keep him from coming closer and bite out my response, rude and forceful this time. "Not. Interested."

His smile transforms to a look of disgust, and he throws an insult loud enough I can hear it above the music. "Cunt."

My temper flares, anger clouds my better judgment. "Excuse me?" I practically scream at his now retreating form. I open my mouth, ready to give him a piece of my mind, but Kalise gets in my face.

"Let's go get a drink?" She holds my arm as if she's worried I might go after the asshole. "Yeah?"

"Fine." He's not worth it. *He's not worth it.* I repeat the phrase over and over until my pulse reestablishes my normal baseline and I don't feel the need to rebuke the man who feels it's socially acceptable to assault and degrade a woman he doesn't even know.

We walk over to where Aaliyah shamelessly grinds against a total stranger. It's probably best she missed the entire encounter, because her temper puts mine to shame, and I have no intention of getting kicked out of this club.

"Drink break!" Kalise shouts and it's enough of an excuse for Aaliyah to ditch her dance partner and head to our table.

We've been here for hours, and while our name was on the list as promised and we were given a reserved table, I don't know how much longer I want to wait around. As much as I want to see Austin again, I won't hang around like some groupie. Does he even want to see me? If he did, he'd be here by now. I don't know much about his life, or how the schedule after a show goes, but I can't image he has that much to do.

"It's after one," Kalise shouts above the music.

"I know." I swallow down the disappointment.

"What do you wanna do, Jayla?" Aaliyah asks. "We can stay for another drink, if you think . . ." she trails off, but I know she's wondering as much as me where the hell he is. Or whether they're even coming. Maybe he got tied up, but maybe he just forgot.

"No. Let's go. This is stupid. I'm sorry." I shake my head and try to not let the feeling of rejection sink into my thoughts.

"Girl, don't apologize. You didn't drag us here. Besides, not a complete waste." Aaliyah pulls a folded napkin from her wallet and raises it between her fingers with a grin. "I still got it."

"I'm telling Drake," Kalise chides.

Despite being upset, I let loose a smile.

The cocktail waitress who's been helping us all night comes by our high top. "Another round?"

"I think we'll just take the check."

She holds up her hand as I try to hand her my card. "Oh, it's been taken care of. Sure I can't get you one more round?"

I look at my girls, but they're as shocked as I am. "Excuse me?"

"Another round? Or maybe bottled water?"

"Who paid the bill?" Kalise asks what we're all wondering.

"You're guests of Off Track Records." She smiles again. "It's all taken care of."

There's something wrong with me because her words strike a fresh wound in my already crippled ego. He wants to pay for my drinks, but can't be bothered to show up? I dig into my wallet and pull out a twenty. "Thank you."

She holds up her hand, not accepting my money. "My tip has also been taken care of."

"Oh." I grate my jaw back and forth.

"Do you need me to call you a ride?"

"Let me guess, that would be taken care of as well?"

She grins. "Why, yes it would."

"No, thanks," I say at the same time my friends answer, "Yes, please!"

I glare at them. "We're good. We can get our own damn ride." I slide out of my seat, toss my jacket over my arm, and march toward the exit. I don't stop walking until I pass the bouncers outside the deafening club. Even with the late hour, a line of waiting patrons wraps around one side of the building. I step to the opposite side and pull out my cell to request a ride. The wind whips through the night air and my arms break out in goosebumps.

The front door opens and my friends approach from the corner of my view. I don't glance up from my phone, knowing they're not gonna ignore my outburst, but avoiding it regardless.

"Girl, what's your problem?" Aaliyah demands.

Irritated that it's gonna be a good twenty minutes before our driver shows, I shove my arms through the sleeves of my jacket and pocket my phone. "I pay my own bills."

"Yeah, yeah, yeah, miss independent woman." Kalise rolls her eyes. "We get it."

I lift my hands. "What? That's such a bad thing?"

"Of course not. I just don't see the problem with your famous friend paying our tab and ride," Aaliyah says. "What gives?"

I don't like the feeling. I belong to no one other than myself. I'm not someone who can be bought. And he didn't even have the decency to show up? "He wants to pay my tab so badly? Where is he?"

"I'm sorry, Jay." The tightness around Kalise's lips softens.

"Don't, okay? It's fine." I stop her before my anger grows, this time at myself. I'm bringing them down. This night was about time with my girls, and seeing an old friend. I did both. It's on me for hoping it'd mean anything more. "But we had fun tonight, yeah?"

Aaliyah shrugs. "No complaints here."

Kalise laughs and shakes her head at our man-eater of a friend. "How long till you call that boy back? I'm surprised you didn't invite him home."

"Oh, come on. We all know he was a fuck boy." She rolls her eyes.

At that I do laugh. "Then why were you dancing with him?"

"Boy had moves!" She fans herself as a sleek black SUV pulls to the curb, and not a moment later a second one rolls up right in front of where we stand.

The doors pop open and with it the face I've been waiting on all night. *Austin.*

"Jayla!" He meets my gaze and strides from the vehicle as his friends exit the rear door. He doesn't wait for me to open my arms, instead wrapping me in a tight hug. "You came," he whispers against my earlobe.

"Hey," I manage to say and step out of his arms.

"Did you just get here?"

Kalise laughs, but the sound comes out tight. "Ah, no. We're just leaving."

"Shit." Austin meets my gaze before turning to her. "I'm sorry. It took longer than I thought. There any way I can convince you ladies to come inside for one more drink?"

"I already called a ride." I hold up my phone.

"Oh." It's probably my imagination, or great acting on his part, but he almost appears crushed. He shoves his hands into his back pockets and rocks back on the heels of his boots. His friends gather off to the side, talking with the bouncers and line of people waiting to get into the club.

Kalise and Aaliyah turn away, pretending to talk to each other. I know damn well they're listening to everything I say.

"So, it was great to see you." I force a polite smile onto my lips.

"Can I give you my number?" He glances at me through his thick lashes and I swear my heart skips a beat.

I lick my lips and press them together once before answering. "I don't know if that's a good idea."

"Or you could give me yours." There's a mischievousness to his smile, and he looks every bit the bad boy he did on stage tonight. In so many ways, he is the same. His full lips, strong jaw, and expressive eyes that were forever my undoing. But in others, he is completely different. He's filled into his skinny frame, not a big guy, but his presence and personality fill every breath between us. And the tattoos.

Colorful ink inhabits most of his skin's real estate in a way that would make most people look unfriendly. On him it's the opposite, actually. It only enhances the beauty and openness of his eyes. Or is that a trick? It hits me that I don't know anything about him or the man he's become. He could be an asshole. A player. A user. Exactly like every other man. It's for that reason alone I should proceed with caution.

He steeples his fingers in front of his chest. "Please?"

I force a lightness I don't really feel to my voice. "I'm sure you have better things to do than call a girl you once knew in high school."

He cocks his head. "Would you believe me if I told you I didn't?"

"Not really." I bite at my lip, unsure whether I want to give him my number. My phone buzzes with an alert as a silver Prius pulls to the curb. I nod to the car. "That's us."

Kalise steps toward the driver and pulls open the door, but doesn't get inside.

"You honestly aren't going to give me your number?" His eyes widen as if he's truly taken aback.

"Honey, you can take my number." Aaliyah steps forward and inserts herself into our conversation. *See. I knew she was listening.*

"What about Drake?" I grumble, more irritated than I should be. She's only playing right now, not seriously hitting on Austin. At least, I hope so.

"What about him? This sexy rock star is standing right here." She licks her lips and gives Austin a suggestive stare before digging around in her wallet.

Oh. My. God. I can't believe she's going to—

"Here." She shoves a card in his hand. *I can't believe she just gave him her number!*

Austin studies the card and his eyebrows rise before he turns back to me. "You're in private security."

I glance at Aaliyah. She gave him *my* card. I can't decide whether I'm relieved or irritated. I cross my arms over my waist. "And that's surprising to you because . . ." I'm used to being met with blatant sexism when it comes to telling people about my job. Because I'm a woman I must not know how to fight, or shoot a gun, or have a fucking brain.

"I never knew what happened to you after high school. I never would have guessed." He shrugs and offers me a slight smile.

"I'm really good at my job." I hate that I sound defensive.

He shakes his head. "I have no doubt. You were always a badass. How'd you end up doing that?"

"She was a cop first," Kalise calls from the Uber.

"Thank you, Kalise. I'm standing right here and my mouth works just fine." I let loose a laugh and shake my head.

"There's so much I don't know about you." He holds my stare captive in his.

"Yeah, same."

"Can I call you sometime when I'm back in LA? Maybe take you to dinner?" There he is with that boyish grin again. The one that transforms me into a confused teenager.

"I don't know," I admit honestly.

"Or hire you to work security?" He holds up my business card.

"You'd be so lucky." If we were friends I'd slap his arm, but we're not and I clench my hand to resist the impulse.

"I would." He grins wide and without inhibition. He glances over my shoulder at the waiting car. The one I should be inside right this very second. If it were for anyone else, my friends would be giving me shit about standing outside talking with a man after being so adamant about leaving. They'll still do it, after we get in the car.

"I don't want to say good-bye." Austin's gaze turns serious and his voice drops as he takes a step forward. "Not when I've just got you back."

I hate what his words do to my insides. That he has this much power to twist me up, and after what? A few minutes together, talking outside a club. It's terrifying what he could do if I gave him more.

But even I don't want this to be good-bye. Not for another thirteen years. "Good night," I clarify and meet his gaze straight on. *God, those eyes.* "Not good-bye."

He opens his arms and steps forward, capturing me in his sure embrace. Normally, it would spike my anxiety, or at minimum spark irritation, but with him it's different. Maybe because my body remembers, or that he's always been a safe space.

"Good night then, Jay," he whispers close to my ear.

My body thrills and then stiffens. Crap. *No.* Not doing this right now. I will *not* have a panic attack in his arms. "'Night," I mumble into his chest and step out of his arms. Relief and longing war against each other at the loss of his warmth. God, sometimes I'm so fucked up.

I lift my arm and walk the few steps to our Uber, turning away to slide into the back seat when I'd rather be the one watching him walk away. I don't glance out the window until the car rolls forward, certain Austin's made his way inside the club or over to his friends. What I see not only surprises me, but fills me with a giddiness I haven't experienced since high school. He's still watching, his eyes on me. One hand lifts to signal his good-bye, and the other is tucked into the front pocket of his jeans. And now I can't look away, so I don't. Not until our car turns the corner.

"Girl . . ." Kalise says both amused and as if she feels sorry for me.

"Oh, honey, you have it bad," Aaliyah adds.

"What? No." My answer feels as flustered as my thoughts. I can't have a crush on him; he's practically a stranger, and I don't pine after men. It's simply old feelings, the residual of what I felt for him when we were kids.

"I didn't know you to be a liar. Kalise, you hearing this?"

"*Mmm hmm.* My ears work just fine."

"Shut up. Both of you. He's an old friend. Nothing more."

"That why you never mentioned him before tonight?" Kalise lifts an eyebrow.

My lips press together and I glance back out the window, away from their knowing stares. I don't have it in me to lie or even attempt to explain.

Kalise lets out a soft chuckle. "Homeboy is hella hot. Even if he is a skinny thing."

"Those tatts. That mouth. Dear Lord." Aaliyah fans her face. "Take me to church."

That's it. I can't stonewall either of these girls. That and they're completely right. "He's ridiculously hot, right?"

"For a white boy, yes. Yes, he is." Aaliyah bobs her chin.

"Speak for yourself. I'm all about equal opportunity." Kalise bumps her shoulder into mine. "Man's got it going on."

"Probably knows it, too," I roll my eyes and voice my greatest concern. When we were kids, Austin couldn't get a date to save his life, but I saw how the women salivated over him on stage. I don't blame them, either. Kalise is right. That man has got it going on.

"Oh, you know he does." She glances at me, a soft knowing smile on her lips. "Still only had eyes for you, though."

"*Mmm hmm*," Aaliyah agrees.

We don't talk about him or the concert for the rest of the ride, but I can't help but wonder about their observation. Is Austin really interested in rekindling our friendship, or maybe something more? More importantly, should I even give him the chance?

6

JAYLA

IT'S LATE in the afternoon when I finally roll out of bed the next day. I hate that my first thought goes to Austin, wondering where he is, or who he's with. I don't want to think about him. He's someone from my past. A past I've worked really hard to move beyond.

Then why did I buy the meet and greet tickets?

I've lied to myself, insisting it was only to support the boy who once was my neighbor, my classmate, a best friend through a few of the most awkward years of my life. Back then he wouldn't shut up about his dream to play music. He and his friends were going to start a rock band. They'd be famous. He'd get out of that shitty apartment. Buy a big house and support his family.

I don't know if he's gotten everything he wanted, but from the outside looking in, it seems as if he's realized all that and more. Last night I wanted to ask about his family, but I never got the chance. There were so many things I wanted to say, and as I replay the night in my mind, I'm irritated at myself.

He must think I'm an idiot. What did I think would happen? He'd see me, and what? Ask to be best friends again?

That this time we'd get a chance to fall in love?

Dumb. I'm stupid for even thinking it. I shove those thoughts from my mind. I don't know him. We're different people now. We're grown up. He doesn't have feelings for me, and why would he? We don't know the grown up versions of each other. And we won't get to, not when we have different lives. Besides, he has thousands of women at his disposal, and I'm sure he's not looking for a friend or girlfriend.

He probably hasn't thought of me at all since I left the club. It's that realization that forces me to push him out of my head. I've already given last night's reunion too much mental real estate. It's pointless anyway since I won't see him again. I need to move on.

I work tonight, a boring security detail for a regular that I'm not especially looking forward to, but that's not why an hour later I drag my feet out the door with more dread than if I were headed to the dentist. Today is Sunday, also known as my weekly dose of guilt and disappointment. Dinner with my Mama and the family. I'd like to believe we can make it through one meal without her highlighting my fails and shortcomings as a topic of conversation, but as far as I know hell hasn't frozen over.

"Oh, look who decided to join us!" my brother calls out as soon as I step foot in the door.

"Auntie Jayla!" My nephew Zac practically knocks me to the ground with his tight hug around my legs.

"Hey, little man." I crouch to his level to meet his face. He's got barbeque sauce lining his lips so I don't bother to ask for a kiss. "You eat without me?"

"Grandma said we didn't have to wait."

"And where's your brother?"

"Sleeping. He's such a baby." Zac rolls his eyes, and it takes everything I can not to giggle. He's almost six, and my other nephew, Josiah, turned two last month. They're both a handful.

"How about you go watch your show so Auntie Jay can eat?" My brother shoos his son back into the other room before turning to give me a hug. "Glad you made it. Mama was ten seconds from sending me out to get you."

"I'm not even that late." I step out of his embrace and head for the dining room. Mama and Desmond's wife Lina sit at the table waiting and glance up as we walk in. There's a clean place setting for me next to my nephew's half-eaten and deserted plate.

"I tried to wait," Mama releases an exaggerated sigh and I can tell she's holding back. We have a standing three o'clock meal at Mama's house, and most weeks I get here early to help her in the kitchen. After last night and getting home so late, I'm pushing my luck and her patience by arriving fifteen after.

"It's fine. I should have called." I wave her off and take my seat.

She doesn't say anything, but I know she's already forgiven me when she passes a dish and lifts the foil off for me to fill my plate. Food is her olive branch. At least, I assume until I take my first bite.

"Reverend Samuel asked where you were this morning."

"Mama," I groan around a mouthful of food. Her sole mission in life must be to harass me until I give in. That, and butter me up with her cookin'. "You know I don't come to church with you." It's a reminder she doesn't need. Since the day I left this house I haven't been back, but she's relentless. By the lift of her chin my answer doesn't grant me a pass. "Besides, I had to work." Great. Now I'm lying. It's like high school all over again.

"He still asked about you. He's a nice man, Jayla, and it wouldn't hurt you to come around some time. Everyone always asks where my daughter is," she accuses and the guilt flows as naturally as her words.

"Do they ask about your son too?" I lift my brow in challenge before glancing across the table at my brother. Crap. He's not gonna let that go.

"Working, huh?" My brother's glare is almost as hard as my mama's. "Lina didn't mention you were working this weekend. I could have picked you up. You know we don't like you taking the bus late."

My sister-in-law meets my glance with an apologetic grimace. I hate that my brother is dragging her into our drama. I know how much she dislikes taking sides.

"I forgot to mention it," I lie again. I didn't forget. I never do. But I refuse to feed into their overprotective shit. I'm a grown woman. They don't need to check up on me. Not anymore. "It was too late to call so I took an Uber." Finally, a truth to work into my story.

"Everything okay? You look tired." Mama stares and tries to meet my gaze. Probably so she can determine whether I'm being honest.

"I'm fine. Promise." I scrape my fork along my plate and take another bite, hoping that will help turn the conversation elsewhere.

"Makes me nervous. I don't see why you can't get a normal job. It's not safe, you walking around with a gun with so many crazy people in this world."

I don't remind her those same people are everywhere, in all lines of work, and she probably interacts with them daily. Or that I know how to handle a weapon and myself after serving on the police force for six years. "Mama. Everything is fine."

She relents, the grim frown disappearing with a nod, and she passes me the casserole. She might not love that I work private security, but she worries less than when I was an officer. "Eat. You're too skinny."

I'm not, but I don't dare argue with her. I take the dish and scoop a generous portion on my plate with the intention of not eating it all. Her cookin' has been and forever will be my downfall.

"So, you worked yesterday? And you work again tonight?" Desmond meets my stare across the table.

"Yeah." I drag out the word and meet my brother's gaze. He's figured out I'm lying, somehow, but I'll be damned if he outs me at the dinner table.

"A fancy event, or home security?"

I pinch my lips together. "You know I'm not supposed to talk about my clients."

"It's just strange. Reggie said he saw you."

Shit. Reggie, my brother's best friend from high school. The same guy I used to bring into the station at least once every couple of weeks on petty theft charges when I worked for LAPD.

"Desmond . . ." my sister-in-law chides.

"Yeah? I never saw him." I give my brother an accusing stare. He knows better than to rile Mama up with the third degree. I get they're protective of me, but I'm almost thirty years old. I don't need a babysitter.

"Well, that's funny." He meets my stare with a raise of his brow. "Because Reggie mentioned he saw you walk into your building at almost three in the morning."

"And what was he doing out at that hour?"

My brother shrugs off my question. "I'm just saying. I don't see why you'd be coming back to your apartment so late. Especially when I *thought* you had the night off."

"We've already established I was working."

"Sure about that?" My brother raises his brow.

I open my mouth to say something not nice and not at all appropriate for my mama's dinner table.

"Desmond! Enough. Leave your poor sister alone," Lina shakes her head.

He smiles, completely satisfied to have riled me up. Smug too, because we both know his interrogation will have Mama up my ass for weeks. She was bad enough when I first moved out. Doesn't matter that I'm twenty-nine years old, my mama would prefer I don't live alone. Better yet, she probably wishes I'd meet a nice man and get married. Only, that's never going to happen.

I love my job. Even more, I love that I can provide for myself and afford to live in the city I call home. I don't *need* a man.

"I wish you would at least get a roommate. Maybe one of your friends?" Mama offers between bites of food.

"I don't want a roommate."

"You're too isolated. You work too much. I can't help but worry."

"Mama."

"I'm right. You know I am. Look at your brother. Your cousins.

They've all found good wives. Desmond wouldn't have met Lina if she'd been working all the time."

Desmond wouldn't have met Lina if her mother and mine hadn't conspired after church to bring the two together, but I don't mention that. The last thing I need is my mama meddling in my dating life.

"I'm young. I have lots of time."

"You're not as young as you think, Jayla."

"Okay, so this was fun." I push away from the table, thoroughly annoyed that I was sucked into this conversation, and that somehow I finished my entire plate of food. "Anyone else have news?" I glance at my sister-in-law and shoot her a pleading look.

She smiles softly, glancing into her lap as though she's been caught. "Well, actually . . ." she glances over at my brother and it's then I notice his broad, proud smile.

I already know what she's going to say. They've made this exact announcement twice before.

"We're pregnant."

My jaw drops open and I hold back the impulse to comment. At this rate they're on track for an entire basketball team. My initial shock morphs into a sting of jealousy, but thankfully I'm forgotten in the celebratory chaos.

Mama shouts, her joy overflows as she pushes out of her seat and hurries around the table. "What? When? Another grandbaby! I'm so happy!" She pulls Lina into a long embrace, and then my brother.

"We're only a few months along, but we couldn't wait anymore," his mouth stretches with a wide grin, and he wraps his arm around his wife.

Lina smiles and touches her belly, though she's barely showing. "It's been so hard keeping this a secret." She flicks her gaze from my mama, and then over to me. "Exciting, yes?" Her smile wavers, as if she's unsure about my reaction.

Crap. I realize I haven't moved or said a thing. I force my lips into a smile and nod my head. "Very exciting. I'm so happy for you." Emotion clouds my tone and I have to fight back tears. I don't know why it hits me like this. I am happy for them. They deserve this happiness.

But I don't.

That's the harsh reality. I won't ever experience what Lina and Desmond are. I don't allow myself to get sad about it often. Most days, I rarely think about it. But this news blindsides me, and my initial reaction is pain. Sadness. Loss. Jealous longing for another normal moment I'll never have.

"I better get going." I wipe my lips with the corner of my napkin and push away from the table. "Mama, can I help you clear the table?"

The surprised and anxious stares that meet my gaze tell me I'm not doing a great job masking my feelings.

"You won't stay for dessert?" Mama asks, almost as if she's insulted.

I resist the urge to roll my eyes and bristle. She knows damn well I have to work tonight, and that I'm trying to watch my weight. "My shift starts in an hour."

"Let me wrap it up for you. You can eat it later."

"Mama." I stare pointedly and shake my head.

"So stubborn," she mutters beneath her breath, but we all hear. By the stern lines around her mouth, I'll be leaving with leftovers regardless. I don't know why I even argue. It's easier to let her have her way.

I take my plate to the kitchen and rinse it off at the sink, thankful to have a reprieve from their stares. By the murmurs through the thin wall they're talking about me. I get the feeling they talk about me often, and I try not to care what my mama or my brother think. I live the best I can. I dare anyone else to do better.

Using a dishcloth to wipe my hands of the soapy water, I turn and steel myself against the pity and judgment I'm sure to meet. I've put in a lot of work to get to this point. I won't let anyone take that away from me, not even my own insecurities.

"Lina." I walk straight for my sister-in-law and offer her the heartfelt embrace I should have earlier. "I'm so happy for you. Take care of this little one. And yourself." I step back, proud of the smile I've put on her face. "If you need anything, call me. I can come help with my nephews."

"I will," she says. "Stay safe tonight."

"Yeah, and call me if you get back late again." My brother echoes my mother's concern. "I don't like you coming home alone."

"I'm fine. Promise." I hug him and then walk over to Mama to do the same. "Thank you for dinner. It was delicious."

"I packed this for you." She grabs the tinfoil wrap from the edge of the table, and I have to hand it to her, she's gotten resourceful, having this all ready to go without even setting foot in the kitchen.

"Good night, Mama." I kiss her cheek, take the package, and grab my coat from near the door.

"Next week?" she asks, as if I could tell her no. Or as if I'd have any other plans.

"Yes, Mother," I call over my shoulder and step out into the apartment hallway, attempting to sound less like a sullen teenager and more the adult woman I am today. I love her. She means well. But hell, is she overbearing. I opt for the stairs to work off a fraction of the calories I consumed at dinner. As soon as I hit the street, my face stings with cold.

The bus stop is just up the street, and I hunker into my coat as I make the short walk. The office isn't far from Mama's, and with this weather I'm looking forward to picking up one of the company's sedans for tonight's detail. At the bus stop structure, there's an elderly man hunched into the corner, a lonely shopping cart holding his possessions and helping to shield him from the weather. My heart goes out to him, as it does most weeks.

"Sir, are you hungry?" I speak loud enough to rouse him from sleep.

He pushes his knit beanie up to meet my stare before reaching out to accept my offering of Mama's cookin'. He mumbles something that sounds much like, "You're an angel," and he doesn't waste another second, unwrapping the foil and peeling off a bite to gnaw in his mouth. "Bless you."

Gratitude for what I have—mental health, a job, a safe place to live, and food to fill my belly—overcomes my earlier irritation and sadness. I have a good life, more than most, and thanks to this man, I'm reminded of how much. "Bless you, too. Stay warm tonight, sir." My words are interrupted by the groan of a rumbling engine and the slow squeal of brakes. The approaching bus rolls to a stop and I lift my hand, waving good-bye to the man.

The long night of work ahead, missing Austin at the club last night, and even my mama's nagging seems inconsequential in this moment. A few words from a stranger with far less than I serves as a reminder of how blessed I am. As I scan my bus pass and find a seat a peacefulness washes over me, and for the first time all day I'm able to take a full breath without anxiety threatening to take over.

7

AUSTIN

WE LEAVE Los Angeles late in the afternoon, flying to meet the crew in Salt Lake for this evening's show. I'm exhausted. Spent. But there's no rest for the wicked and we have another ten weeks on the road before we head back to LA to record our next album. I'm glad we planned to have the buses drive ahead last night; otherwise, I wouldn't have gotten Jayla's number.

Speaking of numbers and burning holes in pockets, it takes every bit of my willpower to not pull out my phone and contact Jayla. Everything between us feels unfinished, unresolved, but that's probably all on my end. When she left Phoenix our junior year I never got to say good-bye. I've thought of her a thousand times since then, but after a while I gave up hope of ever seeing her again. Now that I have, there's an insatiable need to fill in all the years we missed. While I was making a name for myself, chasing my rock 'n' roll dreams, where was she?

But if I call her, what do I say? I'm on the road for the next two months, it's not as if I can ask her to dinner. I have a shit ton of money and I considered inviting to fly her out to meet me for a show on the road. Some women would be blown away by that gesture, but something tells me Jayla isn't one of those women. A strangeness settles in my mind as I try to foster a better plan. Uncertainty stops me from taking any real action. Doubt, it's a feeling I'm not used to experiencing, not when it comes to women. So, why now?

I don't want to blow it with her. That's the difference. Anyone else I've pursued was purely for pleasure, a temporary need to be satisfied. I've never wanted more. But with Jayla everything's different.

"What time's sound check?" Leighton interrupts my thoughts from across the aisle. The plane tilts with its descent for landing. "Opal's hungry."

"Again?" I bug out my eyes and she glares. It might be intimidating if her smile didn't begin to break.

"I'm eating for two, remember?" She tries to act put out but she's so damn excited for that baby it's pointless.

"Yeah, yeah." I wave her off. "The love child needs to eat. I get it." I glance at Leighton. "I'm beginning to think you're the one milking this baby thing just so we stop for food all the time."

Leighton shrugs. "I can neither confirm nor deny those allegations."

I turn back to the rows behind us and tap Trent on the leg. "You good with that? We go eat before heading to the stadium?"

He pulls out one of his ear buds and shrugs with a grim smile. "Not my call. Ask Lipchitz."

"Fuck." I cuss under my breath and brace myself as the plane lands. One of the changes since Off Track Records was acquired is the difference in management styles. We didn't know how good we had it before. Or if we did, we didn't fully appreciate the freedom we had. World Music Industries, WMI, has a different approach to managing their big money makers, and one of those is to stick a leech on us. Okay, so Casey Lipchitz isn't exactly a blood sucking parasite, but it sure feels like it. It's as if they pay him to suck all the fun from things, and I'd bet money he's already waiting outside arrivals for us to disembark.

A few minutes later my suspicions are confirmed. I raise my hand to bite back the desire to grimace as the man comes scurrying forward.

"Hiya, Austin. How's it hanging?"

Did I mention the guy says hiya? All one word. It's weird and too fucking chipper.

"Hey, Casey. Fancy meeting you here." Trent greets him with a handshake, and slides me a look.

"Good flight?"

"Slept like a baby." Sean shrugs. "Can't beat that."

"Jess back at work this week?" Casey asks.

"Yeah." Whatever was left of Sean's good mood evaporates at the mention of his girlfriend staying back in LA. If it were up to him, she'd join us for the entire tour. Her job allows her the freedom to meet up with us for a few days every week or so, and that's fine by me. It's bad enough Trent has Lexi, and Leighton's a package deal with Opal. At this rate we're gonna need another fucking bus.

"We're hungry." I slap Casey on his back a little too hard. "Let's grab a late lunch, yeah?"

"I don't know." He chews the inside of his lip and unlocks the screen of his cell as if he hasn't memorized our entire literary. "We have a tight schedule."

"Loosen up a little, man. Life's more exciting on the edge." I shoot him a wink and hike the strap of my bag higher on my shoulder.

"Okay, yeah. Sure." He blows out a long breath and surfs for options. "We'll stop on the way. Someplace fast."

Trent chuckles. "Come on, Casey. We're not stopping for fucking Subway."

Lexi lifts an eyebrow. "You too fancy for sandwiches now?"

"No." Trent shakes his head. "I pay attention. Opal can't have it. Listeria or whatever the fuck is bad for the baby."

"Aww, thanks Trent. But I can find something anywhere we go. Maybe work on the potty mouth instead?" Opal grins.

"No can do. Lexi likes my filthy mouth."

Lexi bites her lip.

Gross.

"Uh . . ." Casey clears his throat, glancing up from his phone. "There's a diner on the route. Good ratings and they have a private dining room. I'll call now."

"Car outside?" Trent asks.

"You know it." A proud smile spreads across Casey's face.

Trent nods. "Thanks, Lipshitz. You're the best."

Casey stills, opening his mouth as if he's about to say something else, but snaps it closed and marches ahead instead.

Trent chuckles and slings his arm around Lexi to follow. "What's his problem?"

I shrug. "No clue."

"He's probably pissed he's spending the next two months babysitting grown men." Lexi rolls her eyes. She's annoyed with the new label as well. They've been giving her a hard time for coming on the road with us. She's supposed to be working on her next album. Which she is. They'd just rather she set up in some studio.

The diner ends up being good, both with service and food, and we leave an hour later with full bellies. Our detour puts us behind schedule, and the fact we should be at the stadium running sound checks this very second makes Casey a ball of nerves. His knee bounces a hundred times per second and I want to tell him to stop acting like a little bitch, but it's not worth the pout he'll wear the rest of the night.

I close my eyes and go over the set list, visualizing my performance, the crowd, and even the few willing women I'll snag for entertainment after the show. Or at least I try to imagine it. My mind wanders back to Jayla. Her hard stare judges my fantasies. Fuck. I can't even get it up for two nameless groupies in my daydream with Jay's calculating stare in my head.

The SUV comes to an abrupt halt with the afternoon traffic, and without opening my eyes I know Casey's seconds from giving himself a coronary.

"What the ever-loving-fuck?" The alarm in Sean's voice grabs my attention.

"Is that smoke?" Leighton asks, just above a whisper.

My eyelids snap open and I crane my neck in the direction they're all staring.

Plumes of thick gray smoke rise in the distance beyond the bumper-to-bumper vehicles. A flash of red and blue lights whizzes past us and joins the gathering of first responders racing toward the massive building. And not just *any* building. The stadium we're supposed to be inside.

"Shit . . ." Trent drags out the word from the back seat of our SUV.

"Turn the car around," Casey demands to the driver from his seat at my right. "Sir, please turn the car around." His gaze bounces between his phone and the fire trucks and police cars in the distance.

"What's going on?" Sean turns from his seat up front to face us.

"Where to?" Our driver flips a bitch before we're stuck in the worst of the traffic.

"Um, just keep driving. Straight. Away from that," Casey directs, but he's distracted. There's something going on.

"You got it," our driver blows out a rush of air.

Casey's phone rings and I lean back in my seat to try and catch what the person on the other end says. Casey's "okay" and "will do" and "keep me posted" do nothing to alleviate my growing concern that something is very wrong. By the silence of my bandmates, I'm not the only one.

"Lipshitz. What's happening?" Trent demands from the back seat.

"There was an explosion." The words leave Casey's mouth in a rush. His hands shake from where they clutch his phone. "That's all I know."

"At the venue?" Opal says.

Sean's brows knit with concern. "What about the show?"

"There's not going to be a show," Casey responds and his gaze drops again to his cell. "Not tonight."

Trent shakes his head and grabs his phone. We all follow suit and as the madness behind us fades from sight, I search trending news for details as to what is going on. Lipshitz is eerily quiet, and his hollow cheeks grow pale. Worry and dread fill my gut.

"Was anyone hurt?" Opal's voice is soft as it cuts through our silence.

Fuck. I don't pray often, or much at all. But in our speeding SUV I offer a plea to the universe and its maker that no one is hurt.

"Lipshitz." Trent's stern and calm voice draws our assistant from his phone. "What's the plan here?"

"We're meeting at a hotel, after it's cleared. For now, we drive." He clears his throat and speaks to the driver. "Please keep us moving and away from downtown."

"You got it."

"Was anyone hurt?" Sean repeats Opal's earlier question.

"I don't know." Lipshitz leans back into his seat and draws a shaky breath. "But God, I hope not."

8

AUSTIN

IT'S hours before we're given the all-clear to head over to the hotel, but by the time we do, the news is sprawled across every channel and social media feed. *A dozen injured. Three of them in critical condition.* Twelve people too many.

We gather in the Presidential Suite, waiting. Minutes drown into hours, staring at the news coverage on the television screen. Helpless. That's how I feel, and it fucking rattles me. I itch for a cigarette, though I rarely partake in the vice if I'm not drinking. I can't believe this happened. And before one of our shows. What if the explosion had happened an hour later? Would I be in the hospital watching one of my best friends fight for their life? Or worse. We could be gathered in the morgue.

"We need to find out who did this." The demand leaves my lips with a vengeance that surprises even myself.

"They have detectives on the scene. They'll get to the bottom of this," Casey says from behind the screen of his cell. He's been on that thing all evening, and for once I'm thankful for the guy. He's kept us informed, and while I'm sure he's tasked with keeping an eye on us, he could have cut out hours ago. We aren't going anywhere. I think maybe he doesn't want to be alone either.

"What about our next show? Could this happen again?" Leighton voices one of the thousands of concerns that races through my mind. "Are we still driving on to Denver tonight?"

"WMI is sending out a team to deal with everything. We'll meet with them first thing in the morning," Casey says. "Local law enforcement too."

"And what do we do until then?" Trent runs a hand through his hair and pushing the locks back from his face.

"Turn that off." Casey waves to the television and pushes up from his seat. He stretches his arms overhead and lets loose a wide yawn. "Try to get some sleep. We'll tackle the hard questions tomorrow."

I rise to my feet. "I want to visit the hospital." The need is to be there, with the families. With those this affects more than anyone.

"Okay, and I get it." He meets my stare. "But you can't do that. Not tonight. Not until we get more control of the situation."

"Situation?" Sean scoffs. "People are fighting for their lives tonight."

"Fuck." Lipshitz squeezes his eyes shut and for a moment I think he's about to cry. He opens them and inhales a sharp breath. "None of us were prepared for this to happen. It's a horrible tragedy. I'm doing my best here, man."

"That could have been us inside," Lexi says. Her words bounce off the walls, and the stark truth of them cuts deep.

It would have been us had we not derailed Casey's precious itinerary to go eat.

"Try and get some rest, okay?" He sniffles and I think maybe he is crying, or about to.

The urge to do the same hits me square in the gut and I don't have the courage to answer him but for a nod.

"You too, man. Thanks for taking care of us today. I mean that."

Trent blows out a long breath before walking Casey to the door. "Come get us in the morning, okay? We want to be involved in whatever next steps there are. And let us know if there's an update . . . about those in the hospital."

"I will. 'Night."

The door shuts with a resounding thud and Trent comes back into the room looking exhausted, stressed, and on the verge of passing out. I probably look the same.

"Casey was right. We don't need to watch this." Lexi picks up the remote and silences the television.

"Anyone hungry? We could order food," Opal offers from her seat next to Leighton.

He nestles his face into the top of her head and drops a kiss there before hugging her close. "I can't right now."

"Me neither," Trent says.

The thought of eating makes me want to vomit. By the looks around the room, everyone feels the same.

"I'm gonna call Jess again," Sean says before he heads toward his room at the far end of the suite.

"I think we'll call it a night," Leighton says.

"Us, too." Lexi looks at her sister. "Make sure you eat something."

Opal nods. "I have some crackers in my bag." She stands, hugs her so tightly I have to look away. The thought of losing either of these women is terrifying. I can't imagine how Trent or Leighton feel right now.

While everyone wanders to their rooms, Opal hangs back and reaches her arms around my waist, not bothering to wait for me to initiate the embrace. "You okay?"

"I'm fine," I lie because she doesn't need to be weighed down by any more stress than she already is.

"Sure?"

"Don't worry about me, little lady. You just take care of that babe."

"I do worry about you. You know I love you, right?" It's a platonic kind of love. The affection a sister shares for her big brother. A gift I never expected. The power of her sentiment hits me unexpectedly and this time I do give in to the heaviness of it all.

"I could have lost you today," I croak out.

"*Shh.*" She shakes her head and then hugs me tighter. "Don't go there. I'm fine. We're all here. Safe."

We're the lucky ones. For whatever reason, fate spared us the untimely destiny, and instead we're left to soldier on another day. With my arms around one of my best friends, I let the tears prick my eyes and vow to make good with all the days I'm granted from here on out.

"Get some rest," she mutters into my chest before pulling away to study my face.

I nod. "Promise."

I DON'T QUITE KNOW when I pass out, but the morning comes like the blink of an eye. There's no rumble of the bus engine, or sway that comes with wheels rolling down the open highway. Sean wakes me with a shake to the shoulder, and it takes me a minute to remember where I am and what happened last night. "Come on, man. Get dressed. Execs are on their way up now."

"Fuck." I rub my hand over my face and glance around my darkened hotel room. "What time is it?"

"Almost nine, lazy ass." He chuckles on his way out the door.

"Fuck." I didn't expect to get any rest last night, or even fall asleep, but once my head hit the pillow, the day's events crashed down hard and I couldn't fight the pull of sleep. Apparently, I slept the entire night through. Making my way to the bathroom, I shower and pull on a clean set of clothes before joining the others. I can't get the image of smoke churning above the arena out of my head, or the clip of victims being rushed by gurney to the back of the ambulances. My stomach rumbles with hunger and I almost feel a sense of guilt for giving such a basic need priority given the current state of things. How can I think of breakfast when people are fighting for their lives?

"Austin, how nice of you to finally join us," Vincent, one of the top executives for WMI, and a total douche in my opinion, says from his perch at the end of the long dining table.

There's a spread to his left— muffins, bagels, fruit, and coffee—so I take my sweet time strutting over to fix a plate before pulling up a chair. I don't know why, but it gives me a simple sort of satisfaction to make him wait.

"Shall we get started?" He clears his throat while I shove a bagel spread with cream cheese into my mouth.

"Please." Trent blows out a long breath and Vincent makes introductions for everyone gathered in our hotel suite. Some super sleuth team this is. Mostly lawyers. Old. White. Male. All uptight motherfuckers, if you ask me. No one does.

"Where's Rachel?" I interrupt before Vincent can continue.

He levels me with a glare. "Miss Kinsley is in Los Angeles. We brought in our top dogs for this."

I appraise the old dudes in suits. Let's hope they come with energy drinks. Or maybe pacemakers. Either way, I have no clue how they'll be much help right now. "When can we visit the hospital?"

"We're not sure that's the best course of action. We don't want this incident to bring on bad press, or connect the band any further than it already is. We want you all back on a plane to LA as soon as possible." He levels me with what I assume is a disappointed stare, only I don't give two shits what this guy thinks of me.

"Really, Vince? You don't think heading to the hospital to hit on all the hot nurses would look good in tomorrow's headlines?" I shrug off his assessment with my go-to humor.

His stare hardens, not at all amused. "I'd like for you to not end up in jail. But we can't all get what we want in life."

I hold up my hands. "Only making a joke."

"This isn't a laughing matter."

"And I couldn't agree more." Now it's my turn to look pissed off. "Which is why I want to go to the hospital. Those people could have been us."

"We all want to go," Trent says.

Vincent glances at Lipshitz, his lips pinched with a sour expression.

"It's going to be a tight schedule, but I think we can work it in." Casey remains neutral in his tone. *Suck up.*

I resist the urge to roll my eyes.

One of the old dudes clears his throat. "We don't know if the package you received at Christmas is connected to the explosion yesterday, but it's an assumption we're going off of until the cops prove otherwise."

"Given the timing of the explosion and the proximity to the stage, law enforcement believes your band was the target," another one interjects.

"My God," Trent mutters. The news isn't a surprise, but to have it confirmed makes it all the more real.

"What's the long term plan here?" Sean glances from him to Vince.

"The security for the tour will need to be beefed up. Darren is out."

"Wait. Why Darren?" I can't believe they're firing him. He's been with us for years.

Vince's jaw locks and for the first time since he started talking, appears uncomfortable. "Darren was on site when this happened. He sustained burns to more than thirty percent of his body."

My stomach drops. The severity of this situation hits me with a new force. I don't know why, but my brain didn't automatically connect that these victims would be people we've known and trusted for months. "Who else?" I barely manage.

"Robbie and Leo suffered burns too. Not as badly." Both are

roadies who've been with us for years. "Adam, no burns but a broken rib and arm." One of our sound techs. "The rest are all employees of the venue. One didn't make it through the night. She was a concession worker."

The room goes silent but for a few shallow breaths.

"What was she doing backstage?" Opal asks but I can already guess.

"Hoping to catch a glimpse of the sound check," Vince confirms.

Hoping to see us. The realization guts me. Silence settles over the room and I slide my plate to the center of the table, my appetite no longer present. I can't even muster the courage to glance up at my bandmates.

"So, what's our next move?" Trent's voice is void of his usual bravado.

"We're looking into hiring someone, but that could take several weeks."

"Weeks?" Sean's brows shoot up and his gaze sweeps the table before settling back on Vince. "What happens between now and then? We won't risk our safety or our fans."

"Canceling at this point wouldn't be cost effective," one of the suits says matter-of-factly.

"Cost effective?" Sean ask incredulously. He narrows his stare on the suit. "How many people need to get hurt to make it worth your time?"

The suit glances from Sean to Vince, an unsure grimace wedged on his lips. "I can't tell if he's asking a serious question."

"We won't play without new measures in place," Trent states. Normally, he doesn't speak for us, but there's no doubt we all feel the same.

Vince tilts his head and raises an eyebrow. "Then you'd be in breach of contract."

"This is bullshit!" Sean slams a fist on the table's edge and it rattles the tableware.

"I think I have an idea." I clear my throat and raise my gaze. The room goes quiet. By their unimpressed expressions they aren't expecting much. It only makes me want to prove everyone wrong. "I know who our new head of security will be."

"This should be rich," Lipshitz mutters under his breath.

"Care to share it with the rest of us?" Trent's lips twitch with the trace of the first smile I've seen since yesterday.

"She's the perfect woman for the job." I meet Vince's unamused stare. "And diversity is something I value. Don't you?"

Sean groans and shakes his head. "We aren't hiring someone you fucked."

"Good thing I didn't, then."

"Austin." Trent squints up at the ceiling and pinches the bridge of his nose. I don't blame him, because most of the time my ideas are shit. Only, the more I think about it, this one's perfect.

"Trust me on this one." I stare him down until he meets me gaze.

He blows out a breath. "Trust you?"

"Yeah, this is about our band. The safety of our fans. I wouldn't fuck around with either of those."

"That's fair." Trent nods to Vince. "Let's hear him out. At least feel out this option. Beats the alternative."

"Okay, Aust." Vince taps his pen against the notepad in front of him. "Who is she?"

"A retired cop. Head of security for a private company." I'm stretching the truth now and making shit up. I have no clue whether she retired or quit, or what her title is, but it sounds more enticing this way. "Jayla Miller." A fucking gorgeous woman. A woman I would surely love to fuck. Throwing her name in the ring holds less than noble motives—motives that include charming my way into her heart and her bed—but beyond that I have a strong feeling she's someone we could trust to keep us all safe. I might be wrong about a lot of things in life, but I'm going with my gut on this one.

"I have her number, but maybe we should go straight to her supervisor?" I pull the business card from my pocket, because yeah,

I've been carrying it around in my wallet since the other night. I aim for an innocent smile, but by the sets of eyes staring me down, I don't think I've fooled anyone. Flipping the card toward Vince, I hope I haven't made the biggest mistake of my career.

9

JAYLA

THE CROON of Sam Cooke blares through my Bluetooth speaker, transforming my humble apartment to a 1950's club. I sway my hips to the rhythm and sing along as I pull the bed sheets up and smooth them out before tucking in the sides.

"Yeah." I can't help but sing along and let my body go as I arrange the pillows. "Yeah." There's something about the songs from this decade that speak to my soul. I can't be in a bad mood, not possible, with these classics streaming through my speakers.

I slide open the closet door and choose a crisp white blouse and dark dress slacks for work tonight. My phone interrupts with my reminder alarm as I'm still getting dressed. Crap. Time to leave. I had a harder time than usual pulling myself from the bed this afternoon. Too many night shifts in a row, overtime because of the holidays, and the concert on my only night off in weeks finally catch up to my body.

I slide my feet into shoes, button up my shirt, and grab my phone off the dresser on the way into the kitchen. Pulling the fridge open, I snag the snacks I packed earlier and toss them into a lunch bag with a few ice packs. My phone pings with an incoming message and I glance at it.

Aaliyah: You okay?

Why wouldn't I be? Grumbling to myself, I continue getting ready. I'll respond to her once I'm on my way to work, or maybe tomorrow. I don't have time to chat feelings. I don't even have time to think about them on my own. Tonight's a big job for an even bigger client, and I can't afford to be late. With over two hundred guests and managing a team of ten, I won't have much downtime.

I head into the bathroom, check my makeup in the mirror's reflection one last time, and sling my bag over my shoulder. As I reach for the doorknob, a knock from the other side startles me and my heart practically jumps inside my chest. I check the peephole to find Kalise standing outside. I pull the door open. "Hey."

"Are you seeing this?" She pushes inside and straight to my living room.

"I have to leave for work. I didn't know you were stopping by," I say, annoyed and confused at both her intrusion and lack of explanation.

"Where's your remote? How do you turn this thing on?" She points at the TV, and when her gaze catches mine I see the panic in her eyes.

"Kalise?"

"Just turn on the damn news!" She throws her hands up. "I swear, for someone up-to-date on current events, sometimes you live in your own cave."

My irritation morphs to concern. I shut the door and grab the remote, knowing she won't leave or explain until I do. I flip to my favorited channels and glance at her for direction.

"Any one. It's everywhere," she says.

I click on a national station, prepared to view one more headline and incident of blatant racism caught on film. Another random and violent act of hate is what I assume. I can't count the number of times Kalise and I have sat huddled together as we watch such events unfold.

But the images that play out on my television tonight aren't what I expect.

"My God." My hand flies to my mouth as I take in the scene outside the arena in Salt Lake City. It takes a second for my eyes to wander to the scrolling headlines, and then my vision blurs. "Is he —?" I choke on the question. I can't lose Austin, not now. Not after I finally saw him again.

"They weren't there." Kalise grips my hand in hers, her voice strong. "I'm sorry, I should have led with that."

"Yeah." I release an exhale and try to recover from the pit of dread that twists in my gut. "What happened?" I don't know why I ask. The headlines say it all. An explosion. Pre-show, thank God. I can't imagine the carnage if that venue had been full.

"Someone died."

"I can see that." The words taste bitter in my mouth. Senseless. These things are always fueled by hate, and bringing terror to what should have been a safe place. Accidents happen every day, and for that I've become hardened to most things. But this? This should never have happened. "They better catch whoever did this."

"Reporters say it might have been targeted at the band."

"This was last night?" I'm usually one to flip the news on before bed, but when I got back early this morning I was exhausted, both from dinner at Mama's, and then eight hours following a client as she flitted all over Los Angeles.

"Yeah, but I didn't know until it was all over Facebook today. I'm sorry."

The screen cuts to images from outside the stadium. The band, visiting the hospital and sitting with patients, the ones injured from the blast. I turn up the volume at the sight of Austin and the band.

"*Off Track Records, a division of WMI, declined an official press conference at this time, but that didn't stop all four members of Three Ugly Guys, and front man Trent Donavan's girlfriend Lexi Marx, from stopping by the hospital to visit survivors of the explosion.*"

They're all there, but my eyes only see him. He looks exhausted.

Worry lines etch his forehead and don't disappear with his smile. The impulse to go to him, to reach out, hits me with an unsettling power. Which is ridiculous on so many levels.

I regret my decision to not get his number when I had the chance, because I want nothing more than to check whether he's okay. Of course he's not, but still. I'd let him know he's not alone.

"The band didn't spend much time with reporters, but what they did say reiterates the messages posted on social media accounts."

"We are devastated that something like this has happened and are working with law enforcement, our label, and contracted security to ensure the safety of our fans." Trent speaks and appears so much older than I remember him a few days ago.

A reporter shoves a mic at Sean Willis, which he graciously speaks into. "Our hearts are with everyone here and their families, especially Jessica Meeks, the concession worker who passed away from injuries she sustained."

Leighton, the latest drummer for their band, holds a young woman to his side. "We've personally committed to covering the medical care for what happened last night. We don't want that burden to be a thought in anyone's mind. Many of these people we consider family. They should be focused on fighting for a full recovery." It's the right thing to do, and I like hearing the commitment.

The feed cuts to Austin, and I can't help the way my pulse speeds at the sight of him. "We apologize to our fans. You guys have been amazing. We don't want to cancel shows, but we refuse to put anyone else in danger. Know that we will make it up to you, and reschedule as many shows as it takes."

"Are you saying this isn't an isolated incident? That you expect other venues to be targeted on this tour?" a reporter calls out.

Austin's lips pinch together and he appears seconds from going off.

Trent shakes his head. "We aren't speculating on anything. We are letting law enforcement do their job." He puts an arm around Austin.

The camera cuts out and pans back to images at the arena, but it's Austin's voice they use for the sound bite. "This won't happen again. I can personally attest that we're hiring the best security personnel possible."

Kalise clears her throat. "I should have called, but I was already so close and thought I could catch you before work."

"Shit. Work." I dig my cell out of my bag and dial the number to my boss, Larry, the owner of the private security firm I work for. Crap. He's gonna be pissed if I'm late.

Kalise reads my mind. "I'll drive you."

The line connects. "Just the woman I'm expecting to see."

"I'm so sorry. I'm on my way now."

"No. It's fine, actually. If you haven't left your house yet, don't."

Shit. He wouldn't fire me for being late this one time, would he?

"I'll be there in ten minutes. Fifteen tops." I turn the television off and signal for Kalise to follow me out the door. "I promise this won't impact tonight's client or the security detail."

"Jayla." His tone is forceful. "Don't come in. I'm calling you off."

"What? Why?" Key in the deadbolt, I freeze as my mind struggles to play catch-up. *Is this about me being late? Or something more?*

"We signed a contract today, and I need you. In fact, they requested you specifically, and it's in the terms of the agreement."

"I'm not a commodity you can trade." My pulse kicks up with how easily I've been put off tonight's gala. I spent the past month prepping for this job. No one knows the guest list or the venue better than me.

"Sorry, Jay. This is important."

"Bigger than the Vanderkamps?" I don't buy it. Larry and I have always been cordial, but it's hard to believe this isn't personal.

"Big time, baby. You're going on the road for the next six weeks."

"What?" We don't do travel. Our firm is small and it's not in the budget. My stomach fills with dread. "Who the hell has you sending me away?"

"Off Track Records. I'm sorry, I thought you knew. One of their clients had a security breach before a show, and their lead is out for the rest of the tour." He blows out a long breath. "Shit. I thought you knew these Three Ugly Guys. At least, that's what I assumed after talking with their legal team."

Austin. I let loose a groan. I'm irritated he didn't call or ask me before going to my boss. At the same time, I'm eager to see him again. After watching the news, I can only imagine what he's going through, as well as the rest of the band. That natural impulse to help, protect, and serve steps up at the chance. "Please tell me I at least get paid OT for this."

"Jayla, Jayla. Don't worry about it. I got you, girl."

"Larry, Larry. Don't make me hurt you."

"Fine. Time and a half."

"Double."

"Don't be like that, baby," he draws out the words and I refrain from gagging. I don't respond. He's a fool if he thinks 'baby' works on someone like me. "Time and a half, and when you get back we discuss your promotion."

My heart leaps with his offer. I don't know whether he's serious or just pulling leverage, but either way I'll hold him to it. "Promotion *with* a raise."

"Yeah, yeah." He chuckles. "You've got yourself a deal. Now turn around, go home, pack your bags. Find someone to feed your fish because they're sending a car at six a.m. tomorrow."

"I don't have a fish."

"Good. Makes it easier to leave." He clears his throat. "Don't screw this up, Jay."

"Yes, sir." I end the call and turn to Kalise.

She's been silent this entire time, watching me from across the apartment landing. She lifts her keys and dangles them. "We going or not?"

"Not." I drop my gaze, shaking my head a few times before I meet her stare. "I'm going on tour."

She lifts her brow in question.

"Three Ugly Guys." It hits me, suddenly and very real, what exactly I just agreed to. "I'm going on tour with Three Ugly Guys."

Her eyes bug out and then her face splits with a smile. "Oh, my fucking God! *Girl.* On tour? With that hot rock star boy of yours? Oh, honey, you are so screwed." She laughs like it's some joke.

And hell, I think she's right.

10

AUSTIN

SHE'S ON BOARD. I don't know how the suits pulled it off, but last night before we caught a plane back to LA, we were informed Jayla Miller accepted the position of temporary head of security for the remainder of the Three Ugly Guys North American tour.

And thank fuck for that. I don't see how I or any of the guys would have been willing to head on to the next show without increased safety measures in place. We can't take any more risks.

Visiting with the victims and their families last night was a sobering experience. That can't ever happen again. Not on our watch. Our security team before was obviously not enough. We were all naïve to think something like this couldn't happen.

I check the time on my phone before staring out at the horizon from my place on the patio. It's almost time to head out to Off Track Records for a few meetings, and I can't deny I'm looking forward to them, only because they involve Jayla.

I can't wait to see her again. I thought about calling her or texting, but held off because as much as our past connects us, she's a stranger. A stranger I trust with my life. With this band. I don't know why, but

I do. I know we've had years apart, but inherent goodness doesn't change, and Jayla Miller has always been a saint.

Doesn't surprise me that she's had a career in law enforcement or security. She always tried to protect me from the shit that went on at home, and school too. But I wonder what led her to such a tough profession. It doesn't quite fit the girl I knew. Her parents always expected her to go to college. They worked labor-intense jobs like my mom did, and were gone a lot of the time. But Jay's parents pushed her to do well in school, get good grades, whereas I was a lost cause.

The school thing never came easy to me, and my mom knew it. Honestly, the only reason I pulled straight B's my freshman and sophomore years was directly related to the girl next door. The one I was crushing on and who always wanted to study.

I delight in knowing I'll finally get to fill in the years we've had apart. I never stopped thinking about her. She was so much a part of my life, until she wasn't. We were latchkey kids, with big responsibilities and too much freedom. I never had to explain myself to Jayla. She always just knew. I always crushed on her, even when she broke my heart. But still, she never made me feel like an idiot, even when I embarrassed myself. It's weird, because I feel as if all of these crazy circumstances—her showing up unexpectedly at the meet and greet, the need to hire better security, all of it—have given me something I didn't realize I'd been hoping for.

A second chance. A replay. The chance to get to know her. Even more, the opportunity to win back my best friend. If I'm being real, I'm hopeful for more. Like a chance to prove to her my skills in the bedroom have improved exponentially since the last time we explored our sexual tension. I'm not holding my breath, because I know it's a long shot. But I have six weeks to charm my way back into her life.

Challenge accepted.

"Come on. Let's head out. Sean and Leighton left already." Trent stirs me from my thoughts and I glance up from where I lean against the patio wall. His gaze glances to the joint pinched between my fingers. "Really? Dude, we've got meetings all day."

"Don't be such a tight-ass." I snuff out the flame and tuck the weed on a decorative rack of potted flowers.

"You realize you haven't changed, like at all, in the fifteen years I've known you."

He's not wrong. I've been hiding joints from Trent's mom since we started hanging out in high school.

"And that's a problem?" I paste a grin on my lips and push past him, walking through the house and toward the garage.

"I guess not." He sighs but I hear it—the sliver of concern. I can't hide from Trent. Drug and alcohol use, as recreational as it is, have become a behavior of concern, considering everything we've been through this past year.

"I'm cool. Swear." I turn and catch his gaze, holding his stare to convince him everything's fine. It's not. But I'm not spiraling out of control. This shit with the explosion has me rattled, and smoking helps me relax. I'm sure it's the stress of all that's happening, but every time I've tried to sit still since finding out that concession worker died—because she was hoping to get a closer glimpse of us—I can't stop my heart from racing.

Even sneaking down to the practice studio this morning didn't help. The room began to feel like a cage. Not a response I was antici-pating when music has always been my escape.

Trent finally nods. The corners near his eyes still crinkle with apprehension but his lips twist up with the hint of a smile. "You're a pain in the ass. You know that?"

"Yeah, yeah, you love me."

"Who does Trent love? And who do I have to kill?" Lexi comes around the corner still dressed in pajamas and holding a steamy cup of coffee in her hands. Despite the threat, her face holds no animos-ity. If anything, she's minutes from laughter. She trusts him. Any of the women I've slept with, and there've been many, would be jealous as fuck if we joked like this—rightfully so—but Lexi trusts that Trent would never cheat on her, and he feels the same. I suddenly ache for that kind of closeness. Trusting someone the way they do—it'd be nice.

"Aust does, but don't kill him because I don't think our band can handle the search for another musician. We've got enough problems." He places a quick kiss on her lips. "We'll be at the studio late. Dinner?"

"Yeah. Your mom's planning lasagna. Your favorite."

"No, I want to take you out. Just the two of us."

"Oh." Her lips curve up with her smile, and she glances to the floor before meeting his smitten grin. "Okay."

He kisses her once more.

I take that as my cue and make a show of dragging my feet loudly down the hall and out to the garage. I shake my head at Trent when he catches back up. "I don't understand."

"What? Love?"

"Stupidity. Why you gonna pass up a free meal and go through all the hassle of going out—paps, fans—all for a sure thing? Lexi doesn't need all that. She only wants you."

Trent meets my gaze over the hood of his car. "You're fucking clueless. She doesn't need it, but that doesn't mean she doesn't deserve it. I won't stop showing her she's important just because it requires a little planning and work. She's my girl. I want her to feel special every moment I can."

I open the passenger door and slide into the seat. "I get it. Sort of."

"I feel sorry for whoever you end up with." He brings the engine to life and checking his mirrors before pulling out.

"What? Why? I'm a fucking catch."

"Sure, man." He rolls his eyes and hits the remote to open the property's gate. "Sure."

IMAGINE MY DISAPPOINTMENT when Jayla isn't at the studio. From what I've gathered, mostly by flirting with the front receptionist, WMI sent her downtown to some meeting with local law enforcement and she won't be here till after lunch.

They've delayed the tour for the next three days. Apparently that's how long it'll take to put measures in place to safely get us back on the road, but I'm not entirely confident. Just because some team of analysts has weighed the cost versus risk assessment and spit out a benign number doesn't change a damn thing. I'd feel better if the detectives in Salt Lake found who left the explosive to begin with. I try not to let the heaviness of the situation ruin my mood.

Amid all of this, our label has us laying down tracks for a new single. WMI thought it'd be a good use of our time, since we're here in LA anyway. I think it's just another way for them to squeeze as much as they can out of our contract.

The song is one we wrote with Opal and performed during a few live shows, so it's easy enough to record. Only, the restlessness I've been fighting over the past few days is back in full force and rattles my nerves so badly I feel as though the walls are about to crash in.

"I need a smoke," I say to no one in particular, and shove to my feet.

Trent glances up from his phone, but doesn't pull the headphones from his ears.

Sean taps a pencil against the notebook on his lap. His legs are extended, resting on the small table in front of the couch he leans back into. "Want company?"

"No, I'm good." I'm not, but if he knows, he doesn't argue. "I won't be long."

"Don't go all mellow on me. You're up in fifteen," one of the studio techs says absently from the soundboard. He's a cool dude and I've joined him to hit a joint before, so his warning is nothing more than business.

"I'm kicking it old school," I joke, grabbing a pack of Camels and a lighter from the table.

He chuckles but hardly lifts his gaze, his focus on the fiberglass window where Leighton wails on his skins from the other side.

My strides are long and purposeful as I weave my way through the halls and out the back entrance. As soon as the crisp winter air and Los Angeles sunshine hit my face, I suck in a breath and exhale as if I've just run a mile. I don't know what's wrong with me, but it's fucking annoying. My stomach aches, almost as if my insides have been tied in knots and I'm just now realizing it.

I pull out a cigarette and light up, irritated that within a matter of days I've relapsed to a habit I'd all but kicked. I should go back to the patch again, get this under control before I completely fall back into old patterns. But I already know that won't be nearly as satisfying. It's not the nicotine I crave as much as the peacefulness of stepping outdoors, the slow drag of an inhale, an even slower exhale, and then the chill vibe that takes over my body. It's my form of yoga, or meditation or some shit.

"Oh, hiya, Austin." Casey comes around the side of the building.

And there goes my chill.

"Hey, Lipshitz." I brace myself for whatever crap is about to spew from his mouth. Even though I know he doesn't smoke, I stick my cig between my lips and hold the pack out to him in offering.

He shakes his head in the negative, but doesn't leave when I exhale a long breath of smoke.

I study my cigarette, wishing for a moment I had a joint instead. Best that I didn't, what with being up next in the recording studio. That, and I don't want Jayla to quit when she shows up this afternoon. Actually, that's probably why Lipshitz's out here pretending the smoke I blow into the air doesn't bug him.

I wonder if smoking is a turn off to Jayla. Not that I'm trying to impress her. Okay, maybe a little. I inhale a long drag and turn my chin to stare at Casey. "Sure you don't want one?"

"I don't smoke." He taps his hand against his leg.

"Out here for the ambiance then?" I glance at the line of commercial buildings. It's not much to look at, and the buzz of passing cars from the freeway a couple hundred yards over doesn't help.

"Nope." He tips his head to the black sedan turning the corner. "She's here."

She. He doesn't need to clarify; I know exactly to whom he's referring, and my body lights up with the promise of seeing her again. Of seeing her every day for the next six weeks. Traveling together. Sharing conversation. Wearing her down until she ties me to a bed and uses me like her own personal sex toy. Okay, that last one is a pipe dream, but hey, shoot for the stars and maybe it'll happen.

As Casey rushes past a row of parked cars and to the end of the building where a sedan pulls to a stop, I hang back out of view. Maybe it's curiosity, probably infatuation, but I want to observe everything about this woman. Including how she reacts to our overly zealous assistant.

"Hello, Miss Miller. I'm Casey. We spoke on the phone." He shoves his hand out before she's two steps out of the car. "How were your meetings? Traffic okay?"

"Fine." She gives him a curt shake and glances around. Her hair is tied back at the nape of her neck. Simple gold hoop earrings dangle at her neck. A neck that would garner my entire attention, if I wasn't so captivated by her full lips and big eyes, their gaze sharp and on guard. Even dressed in a simple white blouse and boring black slacks, she's gorgeous. "Thank you."

"If you'll follow me this way, the touring management is ready to meet with you. We brought in lunch."

The driver pulls her luggage from the back. One lonely roller bag. Damn. She packs light. I hope she understands she'll be on this job for almost two months.

"Can I carry that for you?" Casey offers with too much enthusiasm. Bastard better stop looking at her like she's his fucking queen. I get it. I do. But he's no match for someone like her. She needs a man who's the leader of his own pack. Masculine. Accomplished. One who would honor her strength and not be intimidated by it. Someone like me.

"I've got it." She meets his gaze and her face gives no inclination of how she feels right now. Damn, she's beautiful.

"Right. Well, this way," he steps forward.

That's when she turns her gaze and it lands right on mine. She sees me, it'd be impossible not to, but I swear to God she completely ignores me.

I lift my hand to wave, and my lips break into a smile as I pull the cigarette from my lips.

She averts her stare to Casey and nods at whatever he's saying as they walk together.

What the—?

Fuck that. I drop my cig to the ground, stub out the light, and reach them before they get to the door. "Jayla," I say and block their path so she can't ignore me. I don't know what her deal is right now, but I don't like it.

She pauses, and meets my stare with one of professional coldness. "Mr. Jones."

Mr. Jones. Fuck if that doesn't make me hard. "It's good to see you again," I say, meaning every word and open my arms for a hug.

She steps back and tilts her chin, eyes narrow and hand still clenched on that fucking travel bag. *She's not gonna hug me. What the hell?*

"Jay? What's with you?" I laugh and glance at Casey, who diligently studies the ground.

She raises her brows and clenches her jaw. "I'm here to work. Surely, you know that." Her voice is unfriendly, cold, and even my balls shrink back from her tone.

I shove my hands into my back pockets and rock back on my feet. "We really appreciate you taking the job."

She scoffs. "Don't worry. I'll do my job." She turns to Casey, and when he doesn't move she walks around us both. Her fucking roller bag nearly takes off my toe.

I glance up and meet Casey's stare. He looks as if he's embarrassed for me. Whatever. I don't give a crap what he thinks. I do, however, need to find out what Jayla's deal is today. I step in front of her and turn to walk backward. "Why do I get the feeling you're pissed at me?" Becoming a human barricade, she has to slow her steps.

"Because I am." She blows out a breath and props one hand on her hip. Her glare is enough to make most men run.

I raise my brows and give in to a smirk. "Tell me about it."

She sidesteps me, opening the front door to the studio and walking inside without another glance back.

Okay, then. There's probably something wrong with my brain, because her dismissal sure feels like a challenge.

"Shit." Casey swears under his breath and runs to catch the door before it closes.

"Thanks, man." I slap him on his back and push inside before he does. I need to find the sexy new head of security and prove to her exactly why she and I should work together. *Intimately.*

"Jay, wait up." I'm surprised by how far down the hallway she is.

She stops at my words and places a hand on one hip while I close the space between us.

"Hey." I run my hand through my hair, suddenly nervous and unsure of what exactly to say. "We're cool, right?"

"You should have asked."

"Huh?"

"This job. You strong-armed me into taking it."

"Oh." I shake my head. "Shit. I didn't realize. I assumed it'd be a step up, a big opportunity and pay raise—"

"Exactly. You assumed. What if I don't want to be here? What if you took me off a job that was important to me? What if I don't want to live on a bus for the next two months?"

My hopes drop into a big puddle, along with my ego. "Shit. Sorry. I didn't even think."

"I get it. Okay. You're not used to considering others. Or not getting what you want. But I won't be someone's pawn, yours especially. This is a job, and I'm here to work. Next time ask."

"Sorry. I will. That was an asshole move."

"There you are." Trent's voice calls from a few doors down. "Come on, man. You're up."

I glance back and give him a nod before turning back to Jayla. "I should go."

Her shoulders relax, but her lips pinch with an impassive twist. "I'll be seeing you around."

"Yeah." *Yeah, you will.* An awkward, thrilling feeling I haven't experienced since we were teens buzzes in my limbs and I'm at a loss for words. We both have places to be, but I don't want to be the one to end this conversation.

"Miss Miller, if you'll follow me, I can show you to the board room," Casey Killjoy interrupts.

"Yes, of course." She nods as he passes by us. She gives me one last look, and thankfully she no longer appears angry. If anything, there's a hint of joy in those deep brown eyes.

I turn back to the recording studio, my steps not so heavy, and my chest feeling lighter than it has in days.

"Hey, Austin?" her voice rings out, capturing my attention.

"Yeah?" I glance over my shoulder and meet her gaze.

"I'm really glad you're alive." Relief. It's there on her face. That she cares, that maybe she cares more than somebody I used to know.

"I'm really glad you're here," I answer, and allow the truth of my words to extend past my usual mask of confidence.

She turns and walks away, but not before I catch the smile spread across her beautiful lips. I wait until she's out of sight before I turn on my heel and head back to the studio, a definite pep in my step. I can't believe she's mine for the next two months.

Ours. *Not mine.*

Semantics. If I play this right, she could be mine in a matter of weeks. Women can't resist the rock star. And I get it. There's something sexually charged about being on the stage and stroking the strings of my guitar to thousands of screaming fans. Under the spot-lights I'm bigger than life, made to be an idol, a rock god—and I dare her to resist my charms after witnessing show after show, night after night.

I just have to prove I'm nothing like the scrawny boy from her past. I do that, and she'll be putty in my arms. Okay, she probably won't go down without a fight, but for the first time since I can remember, I'm excited for the challenge.

"Fucking finally." Trent laughs as soon as I step inside. "Is smoke break a euphemism for jacking off? Took you long enough."

I shrug and empty my pockets on the small table near the couch. Thoughts of Jayla, and how I can convince her to join me in my bed cloud my mind. I adjust my jeans before flopping down into the couch.

"Where's your head today, man?" Sean raises his brows and waves a hand obnoxiously close to my face.

"Huh?" I glance up to meet his gaze.

"We texted you like three times." He bugs his eyes.

"Sorry, I wasn't . . ." I glance over at the door. As soon as Jay stepped out of the car I lost track of everything, including the time.

"Yeah, we know." Trent clasps my shoulder, his voice gruff. "I get this is hard. We're all a little off. But we need you in this. Three Ugly Guys doesn't work without our lead guitarist." He's mistaken my lack of focus as a result of the explosion. Had I not seen Jayla, he would have been right. Shit. I'm a shitty person.

Shame fills me for being more concerned with my sex life than what's impacting our band. I force a smile and make a joke to lighten my conscience as well as their misplaced concern. "You mean, without its best-looking member."

"And he's back!" Sean shakes his head, but there's a lift to his lips as though he wants to laugh.

Leighton steps out of the recording booth, glancing around the sound room before finding my stare. "All right, ugly fucker. You're up."

I push off the couch and pretend to take a swing at the kid on my way into the booth. The chorus of *oohhhs* and playful banter that follows before I shut the door brings a genuine smile to my lips. My dudes are giving me shit and the security issue is being handled. I can breathe without teetering on the edge of a panic attack. Right now that's enough.

11

JAYLA

FOR TWO DAYS straight I meet with logistics coordinators, security task forces, local law enforcement, contacts from the FBI, and the top executives of WMI and their subsidiary, Off Track Records. I fly to Utah, visit the site of the explosion, and then catch another plane back to LA. My head is full, and I'm completely overwhelmed.

Doesn't matter that I've had years of experience in law enforcement and private security, nothing prepares a person for this level of responsibility. As much as I don't want to admit it, this isn't only a job assignment. It's personal. When I close my eyes to sleep each night, all I envision is the newsfeed from the day Kalise barged into my apartment and my initial devastation; the fear that I missed my chance to reconcile with Austin. It fuels my already workaholic ethic.

Ironically enough, I don't run into Austin again. I'm too occupied with planning, research, and meetings. God, so many meetings. Most of them could be cut in half if everyone would stop with the BS and get to the point.

The facts are simple: we still don't know who planted the bomb, or even if it was intended for Three Ugly Guys. Regardless, the prior security protocol was a joke, and it's up to me to ensure another breach doesn't occur. I have my own theories about why the band may have been targeted, and I want to get their input before I continue to follow leads with private investigators.

After spending the morning on a video conference with the staff of our next two concert stops, I leave Off Track Records in a chauffeured town car to meet with the band in their home, a property the label provides in the Hills.

It's strange to go from being the woman who drives the important people, to the one riding in the back seat. I don't exactly feel worthy of the position, but until I do, I fake the confidence. There's no time to wrestle with impostor syndrome when we hit the road tomorrow.

My knee bounces with impatience as the driver fights his way through traffic, then crawls up the curvy, sloping road into the private exclusive neighborhood. I'm anxious about meeting with the band. I am. But if I'm completely honest, I'm also nervous about working with Austin. He may not be my direct boss, but I'm being paid to protect him, his band, and his entire staff. My desire to reignite a friendship, and yeah, maybe more, doesn't bode well for my focus. I can't afford distractions, and there's something about that man that's always been able to deter me from my goals.

The car pulls to a stop outside a mammoth home and the driver lowers his window to request entrance. Not a minute later, the gate swings open and he deposits me outside the entry. Before I take two steps from the car, the front door swings open and the band's overeager assistant Casey rushes out. "Miss Miller! You made it."

Of course I made it. I don't have much patience for people who always feel the need to state the obvious. "Is the band inside?" I go with a dumb question of my own so he'll move and stop staring expectantly.

"Of course! Right this way." He holds the door and then steps ahead, glancing over his shoulder. "Traffic not too bad?"

"Fine." I shut the door and let my gaze roam the room. I already studied the floorplan, all part of the research and pre-work with the security team. The place is large, but the grand entrance makes it appear massive. There's a staircase that leads up to the bedrooms, and another at the end of the hall that leads down to the practice studio. But the house is different than I expected; warm colors paint the walls, and decorations make it feel like a home and less like a museum. As I take in the décor, my curiosity has less to do with business, and more with the man Austin's become. How he lives, what interests him, his sense of style. I wonder if any of this reflects him, or if it's been selected by someone else.

Either way, this place holds no resemblance to the simple apartments we grew up in. Another reminder that I know very little about the person he is now. Fame and money change a person. At least, that's what I've observed. It's a reminder I need to keep things strictly professional. We were friends once, but that can't cloud my judgment.

Boisterous voices float through the hallway and Casey prattles on, offering me a concise tour as I follow behind. We step into the expansive kitchen and most of the chatter stills. The band is here, along with two women I only know from studying the files and background checks on them.

"Everyone," Casey announces until all eyes land on him. "I'd like to formerly introduce you all to our new head of security, Jayla Miller."

I step forward, poised to speak and tell them a little about myself, and what I hope to accomplish this afternoon.

Lexi Marx, Trent's girlfriend and rock star in her own right, comes into the kitchen from another entry. "So, this is the *friend* you won't stop talking about?" She pokes Austin in his ribs and passes by to slide into the empty chair at his left.

Austin grins confidently as his gaze rakes over my body. "Yeah, she used to be a cop. I told you that, right?" The presumption that he knows me and my past career sends irritation down my spine. That, along with the bold way he's checking me out. Maybe in another situation it'd feel nice, but in this moment it comes across hollow and rude.

I huff out a breath and it takes everything inside to not roll my eyes.

"Can we get everyone's attention please?" Casey clears his throat. "I apologize, Miss Miller."

"I spent three years on the beat in Compton. I can handle a chatty rock star." I narrow a stern gaze at Austin, one a mother would give a child, but it doesn't do any good. If anything, his eyes grow more heated. I avert my gaze when he grabs his crotch and adjusts himself in his chair.

"Well, then, I'll let you take over." Casey walks to one end of the table.

I clear my throat and glance at everyone in the room. I've studied their files, know more about them than I probably should. Sean, Jess, Trent, Lexi, Leighton, Opal, and of course, Austin. I wonder if it bothers him that he's the only one without a girlfriend. I can't lie, I was happy to learn that bit of information when meeting with the PI firm we contracted for this job, though I have no right to be. After his greeting today, I don't care as much.

"I've been briefed by the legal and security teams, and met with executives—" Uncomfortable to be the only person standing, I grab a chair from the table, cringing as the legs scrape when I pull it out. I sit, crossing one leg over the other and straighten my spine. "We resume the tour tomorrow and I'm confident in the new security measures. However, I'd like to know who the hell decided to try and blow you up so I can make sure it never happens again."

"I like hot cop." Trent nods to Austin. My guess is he's trying to embarrass or tease his friend, but if it's to undermine my authority, we're going to have a problem.

"We need to address all possible threats. There's a chance the explosive was placed by some random psychopath; the more likely theory is it's someone you know." My tone is even and my words straightforward, but my heart . . . it gallops inside my chest.

The gravity of this position, and all the responsibility that comes with it, settles on my shoulders like two sandbags I can't shake off.

Sure, I've been training for years for something like this, but it's a shit ton of responsibility to ensure the safety of a famous rock band, their staff and crew, and oh yeah, the thousands upon thousands of fans who come to listen in a new city each night. I push back my shoulders in an effort to exhale the tension, but it's in vain.

"Someone on our staff? No fucking way." Trent shakes his head.

"Maybe. Or a disgruntled former employee. An ex-girlfriend with a point to prove." I tilt my head and shrug. "It's imperative we leave no stone unturned."

"What do you need from us?" Sean asks, triggering murmurs of agreement around the table.

"To start? A list of anyone you've dated."

Austin chews the inside of his cheek. "Define date," his lips twist with humor.

"You really need me to spell that out for you?" I say snappier than I intend. If anyone notices, they don't react.

"Kinda." He scrubs a hand over his face. "I mean, is it only women we've had a relationship with, or ones we fucked too?"

Involuntary, I squeeze my thighs together and hate that my body reacts to his crass words.

Trent shakes his head, but he doesn't laugh. "Can't you do anything like a normal person?"

"Define normal." Austin winces and then gives in to a megawatt smile.

"Fuck, Austin, this isn't a joke," Sean groans. "Stop pissing off the woman who's here to protect our lives."

Austin has the nerve to look offended. "I just want to make sure I get the instructions right."

"A list." I school my features and refrain from glaring at him when I say it. "Of those you've been intimate with. Can you do that for me?"

"Uh . . ." He makes that same stupid goofball face and winces like he might actually be embarrassed by his next words. "First names are fine, right? I think I can remember most of those."

I lift my brow, and try to contain my disgust. That why he's single, he's become a ladies' man? "You sleep with that many women?"

"Hey"—Trent holds up his hands—"it happens on tour." He grunts as Lexi jabs him in the side. "Used to happen. As in past tense. I meant that I can understand where he's coming from." His gaze goes to hers, almost pleading she understand. Though by her hard expression, I don't think she gives him a pass.

I glance at Leighton and Sean. "Either of you have trouble remembering the women you've slept with?"

Leighton shakes his head in the negative.

"No, ma'am." Sean answers and then chances a glance at his bandmates. His lips quiver with the hint of a smile. "But that's because I'm not a whore like Aust."

"I thought you were against slut shaming!" Austin pretends to be put out, but his smug grin never fully leaves his lips. "I get no respect."

"We love you, Aust, but even you have to admit you take it to the extreme," Opal says, her voice light and innocent. She doesn't look old enough to be a mother, but her baby bump says otherwise.

"I love women." Austin chuckles, and his gaze brushes over my body again. "If that makes me wrong, I don't want to be right."

I swear everyone in the room holds their breath, as if they're unsure of how I'll react to his blatant perusal of my body, or his immature words. They don't realize it takes a lot to scare me off. As disappointed as I am by his behavior, my personal opinion of Austin or his sexual history have no bearing on my work ethic.

"Look, I'm not here because of Austin's inability to keep his dick in his pants. Or, at least I hope not, because I am not getting paid enough." I lift my brow at Austin, and he has the decency to appear embarrassed. A few people let loose a chuckle, but I continue reaching into my bag to pull out a stack of blank paper and a handful of pens. "So, if you'll please jot down anyone you can think of who might have something against you. Anyone you've wronged.

Anyone who might have felt jilted by a sudden absence of attention."

"This is stupid. We all know this was Coy," Sean grates out through a clenched jaw.

"We actually don't know that," I say. "He has an alibi. It checks out."

Austin shakes his head. "Then he paid someone. He had to. The guy's ballsy enough to sue me, he's crazy enough for this."

"Look. Maybe it's him, and he's not off my list, but I want to exhaust every possibility. We don't have the luxury of being wrong."

"What about the show tomorrow?" Trent hands me his list. It's short, which makes sense considering he and Lexi have already been together a year. "Are we sure the fans are safe? That we're safe? I love this band, but I'm not about to get killed over live music. Maybe we should cancel."

"You'd be in violation of your contract," Casey pipes in. He's been silent for most of this meeting and it draws suspicion since the guy can't shut up otherwise. He's the only person on WMI's payroll.

"That's bullshit and you know it." Sean points at him. "You were there in Salt Lake. You sat in that room and watched the news with us. Don't tell me you'd be able to risk it for the fine print in some contract."

Casey glances down at his hands, clenching them together and pulling them apart. "I'm only stating facts, not my opinion," he mumbles, not meeting Sean's glare.

"I am fully confident we're good to resume this tour," I say, willing my voice not to waver. I can't guarantee it. That's the thing about crime, about life; nothing is certain. "Chances of anyone who's not authorized getting into the arena tomorrow is slim to none, and quite frankly, I don't think we're working with a mastermind."

The stares that meet mine reflect the same fear and concern I've seen a thousand times. They want to trust my words, but they've experienced the darker side of humanity and it's still fresh in their minds.

"If Jay says we're good, then I believe her." Austin's voice breaks the silence. "She's the most honest person I know."

His words, God, they do something to me. My stomach clenches with anticipation, for what I don't know. My body heats under the warmth of his stare. His compliment is unexpected, and yet it's the only thing he's said since walking in this house that reminds me of the boy he used to be. Maybe fame hasn't completely stolen the person he was.

"You think we'll be safe on this tour?" he asks, catching and holding my gaze. "The fans too?"

Ignoring the way my pulse races at the trust he's putting in my hands, I nod. "Yes, I do."

"All right, then," Trent slides a sheet of paper toward his friend. "Better start writing. It may take all night."

The proud grin that spreads across Austin's lips tramples any goodwill I was beginning to feel. I can't let my guard down around him. I can't afford to let him distract me, not when he's obviously a player. The type of man who gets whatever he wants—*who*ever he wants. He thinks he can flash that grin and I'll bend to his will. He's about to learn a hard lesson, because he won't have me. No fucking way.

12

AUSTIN

CATCHING a plane to meet back up with our tour bus feels like a bad case of déjà vu. We just did this a week ago, but since then everything has changed. Nerves invade our ride to the airport, the usual banter and conversation gone. We're all afraid of the looming unknown. Sure, it's no different than any other day. Bad shit happens all the time. Accidents happen. Life is temporary. But ever since the explosion, those thoughts sit in the forefront of my mind. Same as with my bandmates. Same as the entire crew.

Fear is a controlling bitch, and I refuse to let it sour this day.

"Today feels like a good day to not blow shit up. Don't you think?"

Everyone in the SUV groans, but it no longer feels as if we're on our way to a funeral.

"What? Something I said?" I glance around, a smile playing on my lips. I'm the guy who cracks jokes at the most inopportune times. Why stop now? I'm determined to lighten the serious scowls. By the time we touch down in San Antonio I'll have everyone, including the team of security, cracking a smile.

"Just don't yell *bomb* before we take off," Sean warns, but there's a lift to his lips, as if he's fighting back a grin.

"But after is cool?"

Trent chuckles. "You're gonna get us detained."

"If that includes a full cavity search, I'm game."

"You're a sick bastard." Leighton laughs.

A smart retort dies on my lips as our chartered SUV pulls to the curb at John Wayne Airport and I spot Jayla among the team of security. *Hot damn.* Decked out in what I will forever refer to as *Sexy CSI*, her breasts press against the buttons of her crisp white shirt, and the thick leather belt that wraps around her waist only accentuates the curve of her hips. God, I love how feminine she is, even in her gender-neutral power suit. Dark mirrored shades hide her perpetually calculating eyes, and her glossed lips pinch into a firm line. She appears every bit the boss of this brigade, and pride fills my chest knowing I made this happen.

I allow my bandmates to exit the vehicle first, hanging on to the freedom of these last moments to drink her in without being caught. Once I exit the car, I have some serious groveling to do.

"Come on, Aust. Don't make us late," Trent hollers from outside the vehicle.

Jayla's gaze flicks to the open door. She's waiting for me, too.

A grin pulls at my lips and I slide toward the door, jumping out onto the curb with a wide smile in place. Only, she's no longer looking my way. In fact, she makes a point of turning away completely.

"Let's head inside. The plane is ready," she says to the security team and turns, removing her sunglasses and allowing her gaze to linger on each of us as she scans our small crowd. Except me. The second her eyes tilt in my direction, she walks away. I swear, if I didn't already feel ten inches tall, I do now.

Jayla was not impressed with my list of sexual partners when we met at the house yesterday. Not that I expected her to be. I wasn't exactly sure how she'd react, but the fall of disgust that took over her features wasn't it. Actually, if I'm honest, I was embarrassed handing over my list. If she were anyone else, I'd have zealously shown off my conquests like a proud peacock, but this was Jayla. I didn't want her to know I'd gotten my dick wet in almost every major American city, and some international, all because I wanted to blow off the post-show high with some pre-departure coitus.

The burn of her indifference as she scanned the paper that held predominately first names hurt the most. It's something I never considered. All these times I've been living my best life, hooking up with whomever I wanted, no strings attached, not imagining I'd someday have to come clean.

If there was any chance of her wanting to hook up, I pretty much killed it with that list.

Taking a few long strides, I catch up to Jayla and match her quick pace inside the airport concourse. Her shoulders tense, but she doesn't slow as I approach. If anything, she picks up speed.

"Hey." I chase after her like a kicked puppy. "Jay, wait up."

She ignores me.

Fucking blows me off.

Challenge accepted. I don't give up easily. I speed walk alongside her, not saying a word. She wants to ice me? Two can play at that game.

Her gaze takes in everything as we pass through the private gate. She's cold. Calculated. And fucking hot.

"I don't remember you walking so fast." I break, because hell, if there's anything I suck at, it's keeping my mouth shut.

Her lips pinch, as if it's work for her to suppress a smart retort. Of course, that only fuels my desire to elicit a reaction from her.

"There's a question I've been wondering all morning," I say, hoping she'll bite. The silence drags between us, the rest of the band trailing a few yards behind. "I know you're not a cop anymore, but did you happen to pack a set of handcuffs?"

She acts as if she didn't hear. Ignoring me. As if that'll make me stop.

It's like she doesn't even know me.

"Because I'd be into that."

"Stop. Just stop." Her nostrils flare, and she raises her hand, holding it in the air between us. She comes to a halt and I almost trip when I realize she's not walking anymore.

"What?" I flash a smile and glance around like I didn't just hit on her.

"I cannot believe that works for you."

I stare blankly.

She rolls her eyes and resumes her long strides. "You seriously think I'd let you handcuff me after a bad pick up line? Jesus."

"You can cuff me instead. I'm very open minded when it comes to sex."

"Don't." Her gaze trains forward and her lips pinch together. "Don't do that with me."

I hold up my hands, the poster boy of innocence. "What am I doing?"

"Making this a big joke. Diminishing my role. Expecting sex. If you hired me so I'd sleep with you, you must not remember who I am. Or yourself." She lets out a snarl of disgust and shakes her head.

Fuck. That's what she thinks? My feet falter and I nearly do trip. "Shit." I regain my balance and break into a jog. "Hold up. Jay! Wait!"

"What?" Jayla stops, heaving a forceful exhale as she meets my stare. "We have a plane to catch. I have a job to do."

My throat constricts and I swallow. "I'm sorry."

"Okay." She stares over my shoulder.

"Shit." I shove my hands into the front pockets of my jeans. "I'm an idiot most of the time, and I make jokes. Because that's what I do."

Her chin lifts, and her gaze meets mine. "I thought you played guitar."

"Yeah. I mean, sure." I rock back on my heels and shrug. "But I'm the guy who lightens the mood when things get too intense. I don't have a filter. At least, I've ignored it for a long time."

"Well, I don't think you're funny." She crosses her arms over her chest.

"Yeah, I'm getting that vibe." I should win an award for self-control because I don't allow my gaze to drop from hers once, even though her tits must look fantastic pressed together by her arms.

"Then why say shit you know is gonna piss me off?" She lifts a brow and I swear there's a slight hint of a smile.

"Because you're hot when you're mad." I chew the inside of my cheek.

She blinks as if I'm stupid. "Really?"

"It's true! I'm not even kidding. It's kind of a turn on how badass you've become." I hold up my hands, because I'm being completely honest. "Can we have a re-do? I'll try not to be an asshole, and maybe sometimes you can smile."

She rolls her eyes, but her tone is light. "You really think that's possible?"

"I mean, sure." I wink and give her my most charming grin. "You're totally fighting it right now. Come on. I know you wanna smile."

"Oh, Austin." She glances up at the ceiling and only then gives in to a grin. She shakes her head and meets my gaze. "What am I going to do with you?"

"I'd prefer something very, very dirty. But"—I quickly amend before she quits on the spot or punches me in the balls—"I want to get to know you again. I missed you, Jay. You were my best friend." The best one I've ever had if I'm completely honest. I don't say that, though. She doesn't need to know I'm more like the pathetic loser I used to be in high school than I'd like to admit.

"I missed you, too," she admits softly.

I resist the urge to sling my arm around her shoulder, pull her to my side, and walk us the rest of the way to the gate. Our party is catching up, and I'm not quite ready to share her company, so instead I tip my chin to the waiting flight attendants and begin walking in hopes she'll follow. "So, let's start over. How about you tell me what you've been up to? How you got into law enforcement and private security." I want to know everything about her, but that makes me sound like a creep. I can't ask her the questions I really want. What makes her come undone? How many sexual partners she's had since our baffled attempt at losing our virginity? My gaze rakes down her body and I clear my throat. "You can tell me about the kind of music you like."

"Music?" She stares as if she doesn't believe me. I both hate and love how perceptive she is. "You want to discuss my music preferences?"

"Yeah. I mean, besides Three Ugly Guys and Beyoncé." I tilt my chin to catch her reaction. "What's on your heavy rotation?"

"Beyoncé? That 'cause I'm black?" She raises her brows.

"You're joking, right?" I laugh out loud. "Don't think I forgot all the times you made me listen to Destiny's Child."

"I've changed a lot since then. Maybe my music tastes have too."

"Have they?"

"No. Beyoncé is queen." She laughs out loud, really laughs, and my God, it's the most beautiful sound. Like something I didn't realize I've been missing, I want to hear it again. I want to be the reason for it.

"So, can we talk on the flight?" I turn to her and hope my face communicates my sincerity. "I'd like to call a truce."

"That I can do." She tips her head toward the rest of band. "After we get everyone on this plane."

"Deal." Pathetic as it sounds, I've never been so excited to step foot on a plane. Jayla's giving me another shot, and this time I won't fuck it up.

13

JAYLA

THIS IS IT. The reason I'm here. From the moment the chartered plane hits the tarmac in Texas, through the entire pre-show bustle and concert, to the minute we get everyone safely back on the bus, I don't have a second to sit. I can hardly breathe, and it's almost as if I'm holding my breath. We've done so much prep work to ensure everyone's safety, but now it's go time and the variables are out of my control.

Despite the nerves that tighten in my chest, everything goes off without a blip or any major issues. One night down. Only twenty-three more to go.

Relief. It's clear in every face I meet as we load up and prepare to roll out. The equipment and sound crews follow behind, but Brian, my right-hand man and assistant for this tour, promises to keep me informed and report any issues. The roadies move fast, quicker than the band, and I don't doubt they'll hit the road within the hour.

I'm assigned to the fancy bus, the one with all the talent. I even have my own sleep bunk to show for it. Which also means I'm never off the clock.

It'll be fine. I can do this. It's only six weeks. Besides, I will have a few breaks as the tour includes a few overnights at five-star hotels. Too bad we can't stop for hotels every night. I'm already looking forward to them, to letting my guard down and not being in a constant state of 'on.'

I don't know how I'll handle the complete lack of privacy. Or Austin and his playboy ways. He agreed to stop hitting on me, and we actually had a nice conversation this morning on the plane after he apologized. However, I'm not thrilled about the women he's sure to drag to his bedroom, especially on the nights the band is booked for after parties. I don't know that I can stand by and watch. Yet, it's exactly what I'm being paid to do. One of the responsibilities in my contract is to clear any 'personal visitors' of band members. I shake my head, thankful we won't have time for any of that tonight.

Double checking with the security team, I finally board the band's bus and check in with the driver. "Hey, Ace. You good to go?"

"You know it, Miss Miller."

"Please, call me Jayla."

"Sorry, habit." He reaches for the gear shift. "You sleep well tonight. And get some of that food before those animals eat it all."

"Thanks, Ace."

"Hey! There she is," Austin calls, and maybe I imagine it, but there's a hint of pride in his voice.

"Hey." I lift my hand and give a polite smile.

Most everyone is gathered around the table in a long booth, and the aroma of Italian food fills the space. I make my way to the kitchen, pulling open the refrigerator and searching inside for the ingredients I asked to have stocked. Finding the freshly cut lettuce and cleaned veggies, I pull them out to set on the counter.

"Jayla, eat. Please. There's plenty." Trent points at the take-out trays as I turn around.

"I'll have the salad. Thanks." I grab a big bowl from one of the cabinets and fill it.

"That's enough? You won't be hungry?" Sean asks as he slides out of the bench seat and joins me at the island. He makes quick work of filling two plates with what appears to be seconds.

"I don't know how you guys do it, eating like this. I'd be a thousand pounds." I already feel like a whale next to these girls. Lexi's at least a foot shorter, but she's built like a pixie. I don't think she clears a hundred pounds soaking wet. Even Opal, who's five months pregnant is smaller than me.

I've always had curves. Those I've made peace with for the most part. But it's the extra weight I've put on since I stopped daily running that I can't kick to the curb with diet, try as I might. Maybe being away from my mama's cookin', it'll finally happen. At least, that was my intent when I filled out the request for stocked food a few days ago.

A pang of ridiculousness hits me for even worrying about such things when I have the safety of the band and concert venues to prioritize. I open a container of sliced veggies and stab a cucumber, sans dressing, with my fork and shove it in my mouth.

"Careful there, tiger. Save the stabbing for the bad guys." Austin grins, stepping to my side and filling his plate full of baked pasta and piling on several slices of garlic bread.

"I don't stab people." I glare, holding his cocky stare. I'm annoyed that he picked up on my anger. I work hard to hide my emotions; I don't need him peeling back the layers. I'm here to work. That's it. "Besides, I prefer the Taser."

"Fuck, you're hot." His voice rumbles and I look away.

"Austin—" Sean groans from across the kitchen island and then levels his stare on me. "I'd say he's not always like this, but I think we both know that's not true."

"Not cool. You're supposed to be on my side. Bros before—"

Sean slaps a hand over Austin's mouth. "Point proven. Now, please don't quit."

I laugh. "You think his filthy mouth will scare me away? I've worked the beat all over LA. Then private security for more than one asshole client. This is nothing."

"You must have some good stories," Opal says.

Sean scoots in next to her and Leighton at the table.

"I wouldn't call them good, but yeah." I tip my chin to Austin. "This guy is harmless compared to what I'm used to."

"Ouch." He rubs his chest as if it stings. "That hurts."

"And he does have a heart! We knew it was in there." Leighton grins.

"Fuck you. You're only pissed your girl likes me better." Austin blows a kiss at Opal, but she hardly takes notice. Her eyes never seem to leave Leighton.

I stare incredulously. "How do you still have a nose?"

"Huh?" He reaches to his face and rubs across the bridge as if to make sure it's there.

"The bone structure. It should be a mess by now." I chuckle and shake my head. "I don't know how you haven't been punched in the face more."

"Ha. Ha." He rolls his eyes, and then lets a grin spread across his lips. "Who says it hasn't?"

"He's right. There's only so many times you can push your luck," Sean says from his end of the booth, his fork poised in his giant plate of pasta. "His mouth is the reason for at least a dozen bar fights. If we weren't famous, it'd be more."

"What you're saying is that your life would be boring without me." Austin bats his lashes and then adds a few more spoonfuls to his already loaded plate.

I repress the desire to roll my eyes or laugh at his joke, instead focusing back on building my health-conscience meal. The aromas of pasta, sauce, cheese, and fresh bread beg me to abandon my measly meal for something more satisfying, but I won't give in. My hips will thank me later. Besides, as salads go, this one is packed with all my favorite things.

"What the fuck is this?" Austin stares at my bowl and inspects it with mock disgust. He even makes a choking noise at the back of his throat for added measure.

"A salad. Vegetables. You've heard of these things before, I hope."
I toss a few peppers into the mix, then close up the containers to keep
in the fridge for later.

"I have. I just don't understand why you'd eat them." He
reaches across the small island and nabs an artichoke from my bowl,
holding up to the light while his face scrunches up as if he tastes
something sour. "Seriously? This looks like it should still be in the
ground."

"Stop. Touching. My. Food." I move my bowl out of his reach.

His gaze snaps to mine, brows raised, and his eyes sparkle with
mischief. *Crap.* "Oh? Do you not like it? Afraid I might have cooties?"
He moves to grab a cherry tomato.

I beat him away with my fork. "I'm not afraid of you, but you
keep touching my salad and *you* should be afraid." I pick up my bowl.
It's safer for my salad, and my sanity, if I relocate. I hate it when
someone touches my food, and he's just annoying enough to keep
this up.

He chuckles, rubbing his hands together from across the island.
"Yeah? I remember you used to get like this about something else . . ."

Oh no. *He wouldn't.*

"Don't play." I take a step back and then to the side, my food
cradled protectively in front of my body. "You'll regret it."

"Oh? Will I? You still as ticklish as I remember? I think I should
check to make sure."

"You fucking touch me and I will take you down," I threaten.
Someone touching my food? I loathe it. But tickling? I lose my shit.
I've always despised it. And he always did it anyway.

"Take me down?" Austin laughs, casually advancing, which only
pisses me off more.

"Do it." Sean grins, his eyes catching mine from where he sits.

"This is the most entertaining thing ever." Lexi leans forward in
her chair, her eyes wide with interest.

Trent holds out his phone, most definitely recording. "I've got ten
on Jayla."

"You're betting against me?" Austin scoffs and shoots a glare at his friend.

I take advantage of his momentary distraction and set my salad safely out of range of the battlefield. I can take him down—I will if he pushes this—but I don't want to end up hungry at the end of it.

"Just going with the likely winner. Sorry, bro." Trent laughs heartily. "Kick his ass, Jayla."

"It's better if you let me eat my dinner." I give Austin one last warning. My gaze trains on his hips in case he decides to lunge and take me by surprise.

"Sure." His lips widen, showcasing his white smile. I swear, even his eyes are laughing. "After I tickle you."

"Your loss," I bite out just as he moves forward. I have to hand it to him, he's quicker than I anticipate, but the fool doesn't come close to hitting any of my ticklish spots. I have his arm over my shoulder and plow him down flat on his back before he realizes what hit him.

"Ohh!" Everyone cheers like this is an actual wrestling match.

"Damn, kid," Trent shouts. "You're getting your ass kicked."

Working my leg over his body, I straddle his hips and keep him pinned to the ground. From beneath me, he bucks to flip me over, but it does no good, not while I have his arms pinned against his head at an unnatural angle. If I used my full strength I could choke him out, or break his arm, but I have no desire to do either of those.

He struggles even though it's a lost cause.

"Sorry yet?" The words spill from my lips more breathlessly than they should. I'm suddenly aware—*very* aware—of our bodies, and how close they are. My breasts press into his heaving chest. My legs squeeze as they straddle his waist. His strong, hard muscles strain against my curves.

"Not even a little," he whispers and lifts his hips, pressing another hard part of him into my body. Our grappling excites him. *Fuck.* I don't want to like it, but I do.

"Don't touch my food. Or my body without permission," I add, but my words lack conviction. I wonder whether he can hear in my voice how much so. "Got that?"

He swallows, his body tense and eyes excited as he whispers, "Yes, ma'am."

My breath quickens. The room heats to a thousand degrees. Everything about this moment feels intimate. I should climb off of him. Release his arms and go back to my salad, but I don't, not immediately, and I swear he senses the desire in my hesitation.

"Lexi, I think we should wrestle later. *Damn*." Trent waves his hand, exaggerating as he fans himself and sets down his cell.

Shit. I practically jump off of Austin, my feet tangling as I climb away from his warm body. Embarrassment washes over me at the unprofessionalism of my actions. That and the fact I'm keyed up and turned on in front of an audience.

Grabbing a water bottle from the fridge, I twist open the lid and drink in vain to cool off. I can't bring myself to meet any of their gazes, most of all Austin's.

"Dude, she kicked your ass." The mirth in Trent's voice is clear. "She kicked it good."

Opal's slight drawl holds astonishment. "I didn't even see you go down."

"You and me both." Austin releases a soft chuckle. "Jayla doesn't play."

"I sure as fuck won't be going near her food!" Sean snickers.

"Jay? Grab me a water, too?" Austin says, drawing me back into the group. "Please." His lips tip up, and for once it doesn't feel as if he's making fun. If anything, his stare holds more respect and admiration than I've ever witnessed from him.

I ignore how that one look makes my stomach flip, and get him a water before re-joining the group. I take the empty chair and dig into my salad.

"Send that to me?" Austin tips his chin at Trent.

"Why? You gonna add it to your spank bank?" Trent jokes.

"Maybe." Austin smirks, drawing a roar of laughter from his bandmates.

"Ignore these idiots. There a lot to take, but you get used to it," Lexi meets my gaze across the table.

"We're like a bad case of chlamydia. At first it stings, but eventually you learn to live with us." Austin grins.

Leighton balks. "That's a horrible analogy."

"It's rather fitting, actually." Trent lifts his beer to his mouth.

Lexi shakes her head. "Comparing yourselves to an STD?"

"Well, you can't get rid of me, so yes?"

She rolls her eyes, but I don't miss how she doesn't appear put out by the idea of being stuck with Trent. They've only been together a year, but from what I read in the file, they are making the celebrity couple thing work. She swipes a slice of bread off Trent's plate but meets my stare again. "It's nice to have another woman in this circus." She takes a bite. "Helps even out the testosterone."

"Plus, I love boobs." Austin leans back into his seat at my right. Without looking, I feel the heat of his gaze on my body.

"Seriously? You can't say that. To her or anyone else." Lexi throws her hands up, and then after a short silence, "I'm with Jayla. I don't know how you still have a nose."

Austin grins. "It's my face. How can you think of hitting something so beautiful?"

"I can think of a few ways," I grumble.

"See! I love her." Lexi's laughter joins with everyone else. "Welcome to tour life, Jayla."

"Thank you. I'm happy to be here." I sneak another glance at Austin and throw him some shade. "Mostly."

It's enough to earn smiles around the table, and for the first time since I started this job, I decide it might actually hold some fun. I anticipated I'd be babysitting pretentious assholes. Famous divas. But these people act like family. Slightly crazy, but still family. I like the guys, and their girlfriends too. It almost feels as if I belong, and that's something I didn't expect.

14

AUSTIN

WE'VE ONLY BEEN on the road a few hours and yet I've watched the video over a hundred times. Stalker-ish even, and yet and I can't help myself as I cue it up again and revel in the way Jayla not only tackled, but flattened my ass to the floor of the bus as if I weren't a grown man. *Shit.* That's not only hot, it's impressive as hell.

There's one thought on my mind, in a constant loop, and it's figuring out a way to get her to do it again. Preferably a naked version, but even I'm not stupid enough to proposition her for such a thing.

Yet.

Then there was her threat. The one she leveled at me before we both became acutely aware of an audience and our circumstances. *"Don't touch my food. Or my body without permission."* The implication of those words doesn't sit right in my gut. The possibility of her consent being violated is enough to drive me mad. The thought of anyone touching her without her permission fills my chest with a surge of anger and an impulse to protect. Illogical, since she's the one who laid me out flat with her skills.

My mind wanders to the other women in my life whose path might have ended much differently had they been equipped with the same skillset and confidence to fight off unwanted advances. Lexi. Jess. My—

No, I won't go there. I squeeze my eyes shut and shake the past from my head, focusing on the now. I can't live with regrets. I refuse to.

But every woman should know how to do what Jayla did. If they had those skills, how many unwanted advances, how much abuse, could be prevented? I'm sad that's even a thought in my mind. If people wouldn't use intimidation or abuse power—physical or psychological, then self-defense wouldn't even be a need. At least in a perfect world.

Jayla has the knowledge.

I have the eager fan base.

Maybe together we could make a change.

That, right there, conjures the impetus to a brilliant plan. I'll get her to make more videos with me. Voluntarily, even. Seriously, how have I not already thought of this? It's a win-win. I'll get to spend even more time with her, and we'll do a hell of a lot of good in the process.

From inside my sleep bunk, I immediately get to work. By the hum of the engine and soft snores, everyone else on board is asleep, but I can't think of rest, not with the idea playing out in my mind. This is going to be huge; I feel it in my bones. It'll go viral. I can't see how it won't.

An hour later, I re-watch the video one final time. My eyes burn with fatigue, but I can't look away. I edited this version to include cheesy sound effects as well as freeze frames of the different moves Jayla swiftly and expertly executed, marked from my research.

Satisfied with how it looks, I turn on the light inside my bunk and flip my phone to selfie mode to record the final clip. I run a hand through my hair a few times and adjust the angle of the lens so the tatts on my bare chest are as much a focus as my face.

"If you enjoyed this video and would like to see more, please tag a friend, share, and let me know. I'm ready and willing to happily volunteer my body as tribute—for teaching purposes, of course." Keeping my voice low and hushed, I know the fans will eat this up. I wink and allow a grin to spread. "If you'd like to see us demonstrate more self-defense moves, make some noise in the comments. And of course, I'll also give you an exclusive, inside look into how we stay entertained on the road." My lips curve suggestively and I end the recording, making quick work of attaching it to the video.

"Here goes nothing," I mutter to myself and post the damn thing to all my social media accounts before settling into my pillow for a few hours of sleep.

It's a long shot. Aren't they all? But something tells me Jayla's competitive enough to rise to the challenge if this thing goes viral. And I have a feeling it will.

THE FAINT SOUNDS of familiar voices, arguing and harsh with tension, register somewhere in the thick, sleepy haze of my mind.

I snuggle into my pillow, pulling the sheets over my body as I turn, but before I drift back to sleep, my curtain is thrust open and light assaults my space.

"Dude, what the fuck have you done?"

I rub my eyes and in my state of half-consciousness it takes a moment before I realize where I am—on the tour bus—and who's pulling me from rest—Trent.

"What time is it?" I scrub a hand over my face and squint toward the light.

"Time to wake the fuck up." He grabs my pillow out from under my head and holds it to his chest, drawing my full attention. "Did you post that video on purpose? Or were you sleep walking? Please tell me you don't have a death wish."

The video. *Right.* Ignoring my bandmate, I fumble around in my bunk until my fingers make contact with my cell. I don't need to unlock the screen to know what happened. The sheer number of notifications says it all. That, and Jayla's rants from across the bus.

"I am going to hurt him. I don't care if I'm paid to keep him safe, I am going to hurt that man and not for show!"

"So, Jayla would like a word." Trent levels me with one last insistent look before shoving my pillow back into my bunk. "Make this right."

"I will, I will." I reach up and pull my curtain shut but he's already walking back toward the commotion. With a brief moment of solitude, I check the stats on the video. My eyes widen and I rub them once more to make sure I'm not dreaming.

Holy shit. Over a million views in what's got to be less than six hours. *They love her.* I had no doubt they would.

And now she wants to talk.

Interesting.

Exciting.

Arousing.

Shit. This is not the time nor the opportunity to sport a woody. I adjust my junk, count down from ten, and think about starving children and poisonous snake bites. By the time I get to one, my erected state is barely visible from the outside of my sleep shorts. It's go time, baby.

Jayla's still ranting, though her exact words are inaudible through the sound barrier of my sleep shade and the hum of the bus. I don't need to hear them to know she's hella pissed, and a sick part of me can't wait for the pleasure of being on the receiving end of her tirade.

Isn't that why I posted the video without running it by her first? I knew she'd probably shoot me down without a little outside pressure, but I also couldn't wait to get a rise out of the woman I'd love to spar with, physically and otherwise.

I climb out of my bunk, stretch my arms over my head, and strut out to meet my fate with more eagerness than I want her to see. "Morning, sunshine." I grin and lift my eyes to meet her glare.

She's goddamn gorgeous, her hair a mess of curls and her legs wrapped in a pair of those black stretchy pants that hug her curves almost as much as her fitted tee. The scowl on her face doesn't detract from her beauty; if anything, it highlights her full lips and sharp gaze. "*You.*"

"Me? Did I do something?" I point at my chest, satisfied when her gaze stutters briefly as it skitters across my naked chest.

"I can't believe you posted that!"

"Not bad, huh?" I feign nonchalance. I nod at my bandmates, Lexi, and Jess, who might as well have a tub of popcorn with the way they're watching us from the table's bench seat. I return my attention back to Jayla. "My editing needs work, but a million views before breakfast isn't bad."

"I am not part of some publicity stunt." Her tone is sharp, but she's not unleashed. She withholds her full wrath, and I hope it's because she doesn't totally hate what I posted. "It's bad enough you twisted my arm with this job." She glances around at my friends and her features soften as if she didn't mean to say that part to an audience. "You can't expect me to jump because you post some clip."

"It was a finely produced educational video," I exaggerate to get a reaction.

Bingo. "My butt takes up the entire frame!" she all but screams, closing the few steps between us.

My lips pull wide, because yeah, she's got a fine booty. "Your ass is the source of most of these comments." I swipe across my phone and it only takes seconds before I find one to read aloud.

"Don't," she practically growls.

Maybe I do have a death wish, because I can't stop myself. "That-Guy22 says, 'This girl can bring her milkshake to my yard any time. I vote for more videos and less clothes.'"

"I hate you."

"You love me, and look, there aren't just perverts watching. Here." I take the time to find a more encouraging comment, and clear my throat. "'Now, that's what I'm talking about! Thank you for putting him down like the fool he is. More women should feel empowered to not put up with bullshit. Teach us how!' Paints me in a bad light, but her heart is in the right place."

"Why did you post this?" Her voice is low, and oh, so frightening. I can't decide whether I should lean in closer or cover my balls.

Instead I go with humor, because it's worked for me this far. "Because I thought it'd be fun. You teach self-defense. I can be the dummy."

"That won't be a stretch," Trent calls from the peanut gallery.

I'd glare but I'm more concerned with convincing Jayla to agree to my plan. "I'm serious, Jay. Want to take me down and let someone else videotape us?"

"Leave it to you to make it sound kinky," she grumbles.

I want to agree with her, let her know the feelings I have for her—and about rolling around on the floor with her—are very much sexual, but that won't work. She won't agree if she thinks I'm getting off on it.

"Please." I bat my lashes once and hold her gaze.

"Stop. Don't make that face."

I have her. Puppy dog eyes work more than most will admit. "What face? This?" I do it again, not caring one bit that the guys will give me shit for weeks, if not years.

"You're a grown man." She casts a sideways glance, but I can already see the hint of a smile form. "Don't beg."

"Do it for the girls." I wink.

"You've lost your damn mind." She does laugh this time. Soft and throaty, and fuck if my dick doesn't stir at the sound.

"I'm serious; hear me out. I've done my research. Women are attacked and victimized at alarming rates. We could be the reason someone fights back, or knows how to fight back. We could make a difference."

She blinks and opens her mouth, then hesitates before snapping it closed.

I've got her. "Eighty percent of my followers are women."

"I'm not sure that's a stat you should be proud of."

"Manwhore," someone coughs. Probably Trent or Sean. I can't even be mad because I'd give them the same shit.

"Come on, Jay. It'll be fun. Do this with me. Please?"

Her gaze flicks to my friends, and when she speaks her voice is too low for the others to hear. "I didn't come here for insta fame."

"I know. That's why I want you. Besides, we both know your ass looks better in the camera frame than mine."

"I don't know why I'm even considering this."

Come on, Jay. I'll be your personal snuggle fuck buddy for the remainder of the tour? I almost speak it aloud. Instead, my mind conjures a stroke of brilliance I know she won't turn down. "I'll owe you a solid."

Her glare softens, the nostalgia working its magic. Growing up, I never had money. Neither did she. So we used to trade favors—a solid —even though she never really needed to. If she told me to jump off a bridge, I would have. I know before she opens her mouth that she'll do it.

"Fine. But no takebacks."

"I wouldn't dream of it. Any time. Any place. You can cash in and I'll do whatever you need."

"This just got interesting." Lexi claps her hands, her laughter joining with Opal's, but I can't see anything other than the woman before me. She's so much more than the girl I used to trade favors with, and yet the root of who she is—her inherent goodness—proves she hasn't allowed life to change her. Not where it counts.

15

JAYLA

AS SOON AS I AGREE, Austin stares, almost in admiration, and before I know what's happening he's by my side, his phone held out and camera flipped to capture us in a selfie.

Scratch that.

He's gone and lost his mind.

"What are you doing?" I ask the question, but I already know. We're live. On Facebook or Instagram or one of his other channels and I'm fighting the urge to either kick him in the balls or run off-screen because holy hell! I'm not wearing enough makeup for this and I certainly haven't fixed my hair.

"This woman right here"—he waggles his perfect eyebrows and flashes one of his panty melting grins—"just agreed to make my dreams come true."

"I'm gonna kick your ass if you don't stop filming me." I try to shove the phone away but he only holds it out of reach and laughs.

"That a promise?"

"Damn straight."

He steps away and I exhale a sigh of relief. I don't like being the center of attention. I can't believe he got me to agree to do this.

"You heard it here first. The beautiful and slightly terrifying Miss Miller is going to help you learn some sick moves." He glances over his cell, eyes twinkling with mischief as they meet mine. The lazy smile that stretches across his lips causes my stomach to flip. He's way too handsome, and entirely trouble. "She's gonna use my body, and I'm gonna get one of my bandmates to record so we can bring you weekly videos. A series, if you will." He pivots, his back to me, and holds out his phone so we're both on camera.

"A series?" I repeat, irritated at myself for agreeing without setting better terms. I'm not doing this forever. A few lessons, tops. And only if he keeps it educational and respectful.

"That's right. Self-defense 101, rock star style." He stares at the cell and laughs as hearts and scrolling comments burst onto the screen. "See, they already love the idea. What do you say, Jayla? We put together a series of tips and tricks for all the ladies? Keep those thwarted advances at bay. Teach them all to be a badass like you."

"Stop sucking up. It's unnecessary. I said I'd do it."

"Because you like me."

"Because I like kicking your ass." My lips twitch and I consider giving in to a smile.

"See." He stares at the phone. "My sexy head of security is gonna give it to me good for you all to witness." He winks and clicks a button before stuffing his cell into his pocket.

"You don't get told no often, do you?"

"On the contrary. I get rejected all the time. But I don't give up. Not when it comes to something I want."

I've never been one to respond to possessiveness. If anything, it sends me running in the opposite direction. But there's an undertone to Austin's words that stoke a fire I'd long but snuffed out. The desire to be cherished. The hope of being loved. My retort dies on my lips and instead I drop my gaze to my hands.

"If you really don't want to do it, you don't have to. It's your choice."

"Oh, right." I roll my eyes. "You kind of backed me into a corner. If I back out now I'll look like a coward. Everyone will be pissed."

"Everyone?"

"Your fans." I clear my throat, needing the reminder that he's not doing this for me. He's doing this to gain notoriety. A publicity stunt.

His brows shoot into his hairline. "You think I'm doing this for them?"

"To get them to buy your music. Concert tickets. Merch. Yeah, I do." He has to be. What other motivation does he have?

"Then you, Jayla Miller, are sorely mistaken." He almost looks put out.

I narrow my gaze. "Why, then?"

"You really wanna know?"

I lift my chin in a slight nod and he drops the teasing. It's a look I haven't seen him wear and it takes me off guard.

"Because there are too many men who don't understand the concept of consent, and too many women who aren't prepared to fight back."

My initial urge is to look away. The way he's staring, the depth of his gaze, it pulls forward memories I'd rather not recall. *Maybe he knows?* Maybe this is why he's pushing my hand.

No. *Impossible.*

I've worked too damn hard to build myself into the woman I am today. One who faces ugly with power and strength. A woman who fights for what's right. It's for this very reason I agreed to his stupid videos. "Thank you."

"Come again?" He holds his hand up to cup his ear dramatically and just like that, the glimmer of serious Austin is gone. "I think my hearing must be going because I swear you just thanked me."

"Is everything one big joke to you? Because you don't have to do that with me." I raise an eyebrow in challenge.

He raises his back. "Nothing about you and me is a laughing matter."

"I'm going to enjoy beating your ass. I hope you're ready for this."

"I can't fucking wait." He bites his lip. Fucking bites his lip, and a surge of lust pools right between my legs.

"So, do we get to watch?" Trent leans back against his seat, his arm draped across the back of the built-in booth. "Because I want to witness this go down."

"I'll tape y'all," Opal volunteers with a bright smile. I can't tell if she's poking fun or genuinely excited, and just like that I feel every bit the hired outsider I am.

"You gonna script it, or go on the fly?" Leighton asks.

"I don't know." Austin opens the fridge and pulls out the carton of milk as he fixes himself breakfast. "We have plenty of time to figure it out."

"Well, I think it's a great idea." Lexi meets my stare a beat before her eyes flick toward Austin. "Even if it was an asshole move to post that without asking Jayla."

"Thank you for not quitting." Leighton steeples his hands together. "I feel like we say that a lot."

"That's our boy. He likes to make things complicated." Sean pats Austin on the shoulder as he gives up his seat and heads toward the back of the bus. As he passes by, he meets my gaze and lifts his lips with a faint smile—as if he knows exactly what's going on between Austin and me. As if this is more than a simple publicity stunt. That maybe it's also more than helping the masses equip themselves with the ability to fight off an intruder. That he knows I'm attracted to his friend.

And fuck me, because I'm beginning to think he's right.

16

JAYLA

I NEVER PUT much thought into what goes into a concert, let alone a six-week tour across the United States. But holy hell, do I know now. The next eight days fly by in what often feels like heavily orchestrated chaos. I do everything I can to stay on top of security breaches between the miles of stretching highway.

The suspicious backpack in Dallas.

A fire alarm during sound check in Oklahoma.

None of which yields an actual threat, only accidental mishaps that give me and the rest of the staff near heart attacks.

I don't want anything bad to happen on my watch. It's no different from when I was on the beat, or working security at a party. I feel personally responsible for every single person who walks into a show, from the concession staff to the roadies to the talent themselves. Yes, the crazed and obsessed groupies deserve their safety, even though they are a pain in my ass. There hasn't been one show that they don't try to flirt, scheme, or buy their way past the guards. Everyone wants a piece of the band. In particular, a shot with the elusive last single Ugly Guy. *Austin.*

Against my expectations, he doesn't pay these overtly forward women any attention outside of the shows, meet and greets, and post-concert parties hosted by WMI. I don't know why this pleases me, but it does. I expected him to be a player. Especially after that ridiculous list he gave me before we left on this tour. Maybe he was exaggerating? No. If anything, he was embarrassed. I don't know what sparked a change in his manwhore ways, if it happened long before or whether my presence has anything to do with his sudden interest in a chaste lifestyle.

I'm lying. I hope I have everything to do with his behavior. Which is totally unprofessional and inappropriate. It's not as if *I'm* planning to sleep with him. I wouldn't do that. It would be a colossally bad idea. Yet the thought of him being intimate with anyone else makes me livid.

"What's wrong?" The man at the center of my thoughts pulls me from my musings. He jumps from the parked bus with a hop to his step and struts over to where I stand in the shade.

We pulled into Kansas City an hour ago, way ahead of schedule. Most everyone is still asleep on the bus, tired from the late show and grueling pace of the tour.

I straighten my shoulders and try not to notice how good he looks in his tight jeans, or the tattoos that paint his arms, or how that cocky grin makes his lips look incredibly kissable. "Why does something have to be wrong?"

His lips pull up as if he can read my thoughts. He nods to the bus. "You want to bail on the video?"

Yes. "No." The past week has been too busy to record content for our 'series,' but today we have hours to kill before the pre-show prep begins. Which means I have no excuse. "Let's get this over with."

"What every guy likes to hear before heading to the bedroom." He winks.

"Good thing we're not, then." I cock my head and lift my brows.

"Actually, I was thinking it'd be a cool concept. We have the room in the back, and it's as clean as any other space in the bus. I mean, we'll change the sheets after we kick Opal and Leighton out of there."

His words flow from his lips with ease, but my body tenses as I realize where he's going with this. "We could demonstrate how to fight off an attacker from that scenario."

No. No bed. No. No. No.

My stomach bottoms out. My heart stops. I swear to God, I can't force myself to suck in air, even though my mind knows it's crucial to breathing.

"Shit. Jayla!" His arms come around my waist.

Instead of leaning against his solid frame I shove him away.

His eyes widen.

I can't find my voice. My heart hammers in my chest so fiercely I'm certain it's about to explode. My fingers curl into tight fists. The nails dig into my skin and pain, real and on my terms, is what brings me back to the present.

"Jay?" My name's a question. His face is full of concern. *Because he doesn't know.*

I never wanted him to witness one of my breakdowns, but the shitty thing about panic attacks is I can't control them. It's only as my feet move, a stumble before they transition into a fluid stride, that breath fills my lungs. I pace the length of the parked bus until my pulse steadies. I dig deep for the courage to meet his gaze.

He stares but doesn't ask questions, and I can't settle on whether I should be relieved or disappointed. I don't want to explain. It's easier to not, but I also can't believe he'll let me get away without breaking down what just happened.

"So, how about we film out here? Maybe over by the arena? The entry kinda looks like an alleyway." He shoves his hands into his front pockets. "I mean, if you're cool with that?"

"Not all bad guys hide in dark alleys." The retort flies from my mouth snarkier than I intend.

His steady gaze doesn't make me feel better about my jab. His eyes hold a compassion I don't want to face.

I study the ground and kick my shoes against a stray rock from the pavement. "But yeah, that works."

"Jayla."

"Yeah." I lift my gaze to his.

"What do you need?"

What do I need? It's the most unnerving question. Almost as if he sees beyond my bullshit. Past my shield. I don't know what to do because no one has ever been brave enough, or stayed long enough, to see me like this. No one asks me what I need. *Ever.*

"I . . ." Words catch in my throat. I can't even answer because I don't know what makes this better. I only know how to avoid triggers, to mitigate my reaction with coping skills. But the damage has already been done. My history can't be erased. I close my eyes, take a breath, and face him with renewed determination. "I want to get this video done. The loading dock for the arena will work. Let me go fix my hair and makeup." I move to walk past him, back to the bus, but before I can pass he reaches out and gently brushes his fingers at my wrist. It's enough to make me pause.

"You don't need it. You're beautiful."

I tilt my head and deflect his words with lightheartedness. "Such a charmer."

"Yeah, well, I can't help it." He grins. "But about this I wouldn't exaggerate. You're gorgeous."

I am not used to compliments. Not like this and not from him, and I can't stop the smile that works its way onto my lips. "I'll be ready in fifteen."

But that's a lie. I don't think there's enough makeup or hair product in the world to prepare myself for one-on-one time with Austin. He's not only tearing off my masks, he's obliterating the walls to my heart.

———

FOR THE SEVENTH time in the past hour, Austin pins me to the concrete wall, his forearm across my throat the way I instructed.

My move is second nature; I transfer his weight off me with a palm to his face, at the same time shoving his arm off my throat. "Don't be shy. Hit him in the face hard. Go for the eyes. Use your fingers. Whatever it takes to get the pressure he has on your body to slip." I speak clear and loud enough that Trent can catch my words from where he records.

Not a second later, I grab Austin's arm and slam him back into the wall. I thrust my knee into his general groin area. I miss, on purpose. Okay, so I didn't miss the first time we ran this scenario, but that was an accident. I'm not used to practicing moves without my opponent wearing the protection of padding, headgear, and a cup.

"Get off me!" I scream and dart away before turning to face the camera. "You yell, you run, and you get to somewhere public and safe. You aren't trying to beat him to a pulp, you're only creating enough space that you can escape."

I glance back at Austin. He leans against the wall, posed like a fucking model and looking just as good. He shrugs before facing the camera. "I'd chase her, but I like my balls."

I can't help it. My gaze drops to the front of his jeans. *Damn.* The tight fabric leaves nothing to the imagination. I've seen Austin's dick before, but that was years before I could appreciate it, and our one-time fumble hardly rated as a pleasurable sexual experience. I'm sure he's long since learned how to use that appendage to its full and more than adequate purpose.

"I need a cigarette." Trent coughs and shakes his head. He stops recording and hands back Austin's phone.

Austin glances at his friend. "You don't smoke."

"Yeah . . ." Trent laughs, a deep, low chuckle before sneaking a glance at me and then Austin. "I think my work is done here. I'm going back to bed."

"Thanks, man."

"No problem."

Austin stares at the screen of his phone, flipping through the video clips. He worries his lower lip between his teeth and it draws all my attention. I don't know whether he realizes he's doing it or if it's a nervous habit, but it's as distracting as it is sexy. I can't find it in me to look away.

If I'm being real, I haven't stopped looking at Austin since we started working on this video. Being so close with our bodies pressed together feels intimate, and more than just acting out a play-by-play of how to push off an attacker. Out here, without the bustle of work or the tour as a barrier, his hands on me and mine on him . . . it's personal. And I like it.

Besides my initial reaction when he suggested the bed, I haven't freaked out. I can't tell whether it's because I'm in control or I know that nothing will happen between Austin and me. Either way, it's a new sensation, being touched by a guy without wanting to puke. I almost feel normal.

My eyes train on his fingers and the ink that decorates them as he swipes across his cell. Those same fingers play guitar with skill, strength and precision. I bet they'd be just as talented at eliciting pleasure.

"Hey." Sean bounds down the stairs of the bus and brings his hand up to shade his eyes.

I glance away from Austin, feeling as though I've been caught.

Sean tips his chin toward Austin. "Mind if I steal your girl?"

"I'm not—" I start.

"She's not . . ." Austin blurts at the same time. His gaze lands on mine, holding me captive with the lack of humor I find there. His next word leaves his lips a whisper. "Mine."

"Yeah," Sean draws out, glancing between us before catching my stare. "Anyway, you said we can't leave without a bodyguard. I was sort of hoping you'd be up for a run with me?"

A run sounds perfect. I need to clear my head. I need a second away from this tour, the band, and Austin with his entrancing fingers. "Yeah." I check the time on my watch. "Let me check in with Brian first."

"Already taken care of." Sean smiles proudly. "He said he'd come watch the bus in ten minutes. That give you enough notice?"

"Oh, sure." I don't like that he went behind my back to arrange it, but the need to gain some clarity and space supersedes my ego. "Let me change my shoes and grab my headphones."

"Cool," he walks over to Austin.

I don't waste any time making my way inside the bus to grab my things. I should probably use the bathroom too, but a soft moaning from down the hallway stops me from going any further. It could be coming from either the bathroom or the bedroom, I'm not sure which. But as the entire bus begins to rock and the sounds increase in volume, I shove in my headphones and shoot a quick text to Brian before getting my ass outside as fast as I can. Sex is completely natural, more so between couples, but it's not something I want to listen in on. I guess I should count myself lucky up until now they've kept it behind closed doors, considering the lack of privacy and number of couples on board.

Sean smiles as I step outside. "Ready?"

"Yeah." I stretch my arms over my head, then hold the bus with one while I grab my ankle and stretch out my quad. I glance at Austin, whose gaze drinks me up as if I'm more satisfying than a glass of water. I clear my throat and force a casual smile. "You wanna join us?"

"No." He chuckles and shakes his head. "I'm good with keeping my dignity intact. I remember how fast you were in high school. I don't need to embarrass myself today."

"Suit yourself. But you may want to find some earplugs." I scrunch up my face, and when he gives me a curious glance, I explain, "When the bus is a rocking, don't come knocking."

Realization dawns on his face and it only makes me laugh.

Sean joins in too, his chuckle low and deep. "Told you there were benefits to exercise!"

"Fuck! Are you serious?" Austin scrubs his hand over his face but shrugs in defeat. "Still doesn't make me want to take up running. Headphones it is. Thank God for whoever invented noise canceling."

"Like you're one to talk!" Sean chuckles while bringing his

knee up for a stretch. "I can't even count the number of times you've subjected us to a loud fuck. You always pick the screamers, too!"

I clear my throat and avoid Austin's stare. I don't want the specifics. I don't want to hear about any of the women he's been with. The impulsive need to hurt them, and him, flares in a jealous anger I can't explain. Thankfully, Brian's form emerges from the roadies' bus across the lot.

"Enough tea time, let's hit the pavement," I say.

"Yes, ma'am." Sean follows my lead with his long strides toward the end of the lot. He points up the street and jogs in place once we're out on the sidewalk. "I mapped out a five-mile route, but if you want to shorten it we can just double back."

"Five miles is good."

The burn of my muscles as they stretch and move with purpose is exactly what I need. My mind zeros in on my surroundings and I find an easy rhythm with my strides. Sean doesn't attempt to make conversation and I'm comfortable with that. There aren't a ton of people out at this hour what with it being a business district and if there were, I doubt anyone would recognize Sean as the famous bassist he is.

It isn't until the end of our route with the stadium back in sight that Sean clears his throat and catches my gaze with a tap to his ear. "So, you and Austin?"

I pull the headphones from my ears and shove them into my pocket, still keeping pace. "We're just old friends."

His brows rise. "You guys never dated?"

"No." We never had the chance. But I'm not about to fill in the blanks or leak details about the few times we crossed friendship boundaries. That was a long time ago and we were curious, horny teens. Austin got me, and I understood things about him because we were neighbors.

"That's surprising."

I don't ask why. I don't want to hear the answer. I don't want to hear about Austin's sexual prowess, not when that version of him is nothing like the young man I remember.

"He's different with you."

I lift my stare from the pavement to catch Sean's gaze. "Yeah?" His comment catches me off guard, and as much as I shouldn't pry, I suddenly want to know more.

"Yeah, he cares about you." Sean trains his gaze on the road, slowing for a stop light.

I stand at his left and press the button, waiting for the crosswalk signal to light up, trying my best to not read more than he intends into his comment.

Sean grins as if he can sense my train of thought. "We're all glad you're here, but it was Austin who pushed for you. I know he's a lot, but he's a good guy." He wipes his brow with the sleeve of his shirt. "Especially when it comes to the stuff that counts."

I nod, pondering how true that must be. "I read the reports, about your girlfriend's ex."

Sean's eyes seek mine. "Yeah, like I said. His heart is in the right place. Most of the time anyway."

"Good to know."

The light changes and we resume our run. Sean doesn't speak again and I don't ask questions. What little he said is enough to process for now.

Did Austin put Sean up to this? I doubt it.

And yes, his words stir up feelings I've been fighting back ever since the meet and greet in LA. *Is Austin interested in a relationship? Could I even handle one?* I didn't take this job for more than a paycheck. Hell, I was pretty much cornered into accepting.

But somehow this assignment has become more than protecting fans and a group of rock stars. It's an opportunity to set things right. Make up for lost time. Unearth old feelings, and yeah, maybe start something new. Maybe.

17

AUSTIN

I CAN'T BELIEVE how smoothly this tour is going. I knew Jayla would kick ass directing security, but she makes it look effortless. She's everywhere. All the time. And never once does she look tired. The guys love her. Opal and Lexi, too. And I know when Jess flies up for tomorrow's show, she'll love her, too.

On tour, it's always been the show that gives me my next high. Performing on stage and being adored is addictive. But now I find myself more excited for the next video Jayla and I make. Because having permission to touch her, even if it results in her hurting me, has become the highlight of my day. I realize how lame that is.

We're not even two weeks on the road and every day my feelings for her expand. With anyone else that'd be enough to send me running, but with Jayla it does the exact opposite. I'm acutely aware of her, and still, it's not enough. The friendship we shared during our teens is being repaired one conversation, joke, and interaction at a time, but the attraction I feel toward her grows by leaps and bounds.

I'm not only lusting, I'm crushing hard. Even with the good and likely possibility that'll come back to bite me in the ass, I don't want to fight it. I like Jayla Miller. I want her. In my bed. My life. Anywhere she'll have me.

Hell. If she asked me right now to escort her to the DMV, I would jump at the opportunity. God, I'm pathetic.

"You've got a good hold on those nuts."

"Huh?" I glance up at Opal, and find her eyes twinkling with laughter.

She points at the pistachios I'm fondling. "I don't think they're made for that."

"I wanted a snack," I mutter lamely, and shove the nuts into my mouth so I won't embarrass myself further at being caught in my own daydream. One of many that stars Jayla, of course.

"Yeah, I can see that." She pats my back and laughs. "Don't go far, we have that call with Vince in five."

I nod and lean back into the leather couch, not looking forward to hearing what the executive wants. He's probably pissed that we didn't wear the corporate sponsor's T-shirts on our radio interviews this afternoon. With sound checks done and Trent off to hair and makeup, I'm content to relax in the green room until it's our turn to take the stage.

"How's my baby girl doing?" I reach over and place my hand on Opal's belly when she joins me on the couch.

"It could be a boy." She raises her brows. "You know we're waiting to find out."

"I was talking about you." I tap her nose, frowning as I notice the dark circles under her eyes. I hope she's getting enough rest.

"Dude, I'm right here," Leighton calls from the craft table. "She's my girl. Get your own."

Working on it. I almost grumble the words aloud, but thank fuck they don't leave my mouth. After all the shit I've dished, there's no way my band would let me live it down if they knew how hard I was crushing on Jayla. I'm surprised they don't give me crap as it is. "But you're not working too hard? Getting enough sleep on the bus?"

"I'm good. Promise." Her lips pull wide with a soft grin. It fades as soon as Casey steps in the room.

Phone in hand, his voice raises to an all-time suck-up level. I know instantly he's talking to Vince. "Just give me a few seconds here, Vince. The guys are stoked to chat with you."

Sean takes the chair to my right, raising his brow as he whispers, "Stoked?"

I bite my lip to contain a snicker.

"I'm putting you on speaker, Vince. The guys are all here except Trent. Opal's here, too."

"Where the hell is Trent?" Vince barks from the device Casey holds out.

Before he can answer, the green room's door opens and in walks Lexi, Trent, and Jayla.

"That's my mistake. Gang's all here, boss." Casey manically waves them over.

"Hey, Vince," Trent pulls up a chair to join the rest of us. "To what do we owe the pleasure of this call?"

"Can't I just check up on my favorite band?" Vince goes for a joke, but it's hard to contain the eye rolls. We know we're a pain in his ass, even with as much money as we bring WMI.

"Well, we're just fabulous. So, I'm guessing that's not the only reason you want to chat."

"Yeah." Vince clears his throat. "Austin, there's something we need to discuss."

Everyone's eyes dart to me, and I race through the possible reasons he'd want to speak to me. An update on the lawsuit from Coy, maybe? But that'd likely be a call from our lawyers. I've been on my best behavior since we left LA. "Don't leave me in suspense," I joke when he doesn't continue.

The sound of papers shuffling from his end fills the silence. "Casey, can you bring Jayla Miller on the call with us as well?"

I glance up from the cell to where Jay stands a few feet away. She clearly heard him and her eyebrows lift as her gaze meets mine. I shrug, having no clue what he wants.

"I'm here. How are you, Vince?" she asks.

"Honestly, I've been better."

She rolls her eyes at his response and I bite my lip to hold back my amusement.

"We've been following these little videos you've been making." He *tisks* and his disapproval is clear. "Not good."

"You mean my YouTube channel?" I hold back the sarcasm in my tone, just barely.

"Our self-defense tutorials? What about them?" Jayla quickly amends.

"I'd hardly call them that. Each one ends with Austin on the ground."

"And that's a problem?" The playful smile on her lips does something to my insides. *Why is she so damn beautiful?*

"Well, yes." Vince's tone is hard. "You see, people don't pay hundreds of dollars for a concert ticket to be inundated with your feminist agenda. They want a night of entertainment."

What the hell? I glance at the guys and they all looked as bowled over as I feel.

"I don't know, Vince." Sean chuckles. "The videos are entertaining as fuck if you ask me."

I nod and smile, thankful for his attempt to lighten the tension.

"We need you to stop," Vince says.

"Stop?" I laugh, but when he doesn't continue I realize he's not joking. "You're serious?"

"Yeah. No more. I get that you don't realize the ramifications, but 3UG has never been political. You don't address issues. You play rock music. And Jayla isn't here for the spotlight. She's supposed to be keeping this tour safe. We're not paying her to empower women. Or black people. Or whatever this is."

"Wow," Jayla says, her eyes wide and blinking. She looks about two seconds from telling him off.

I can't have that, because then she'd get fired. "I'm sorry, Vince, and maybe I'm dumb. . . but how is the two of us demonstrating to others how to protect themselves a bad thing?"

"Come on, Austin. Tell me you watch the news. The 'me too' movement. All this 'black lives matter' stuff. Whatever you want to name it, we don't want the band taking sides. It could impact ticket sales." He clears his throat. "No more videos. Have I made myself clear?"

I open my mouth to argue, but it's Jayla who answers first.

"Yes, sir," she says.

"Fuck that." I shove to my feet and reach for Casey's phone, intending to take this asshat off speaker and tell him where he can shove his ticket sales. But I'm not quick enough.

Jayla grabs Casey's cell out of reach, and brings the speaker up to her mouth. "There won't be any issues. Good-bye, Vince." Her words are clipped, the tone professional. She doesn't wait for a response before ending the call and handing the phone back to Casey.

"What the hell?" I hold my hands out and stare.

"Austin, it's fine." She crosses her arms over her chest.

"It's not. Not even a little. And guys like Vince don't get to make these decisions. That's *my* YouTube channel. I'm not taking the videos down. They can tell me where to play and what to record, but they don't control the content of my personal media accounts."

Casey raises his hand. "Actually, they do."

"Fuck off, Lipshitz." I glare until he looks away.

"Austin, it's fine. Let it go." Jayla shakes her head. "It's not that big a deal. Not worth getting yourself or the band into hot water with your label." She smiles tersely at the rest of the guys, not meeting my glare before turning her back and walking toward the door.

"But—" I step over Opal's legs and jog to catch up with Jayla. She's out the door before I can close the space. I glance back at the guys, but they're already on to something else, laughing and joking as if our management isn't the devil incarnate.

I swing open the door and find Jayla a few yards away in the open corridor. "Hey! Wait up."

"What?" She spins, hand on her hip and expression annoyed.

"You're going to pretend that didn't happen. Act like you're okay with being told what to do, even if it's unjust?"

"Sometimes it's not up to me to determine." She shakes her head. "I have to follow orders, even when I don't want to."

I can't believe she's so quick to lie down for this. "That's rich, coming from you."

Her brow rises and she juts out her hip. "What the hell is that supposed to mean?"

I should take it back. Or apologize, but I can't believe she doesn't care. Or that she's so quick to give up making these videos. Sure, we've only done a few, but I thought she enjoyed the time with me. I take a step closer and lower my voice. "It means I never pegged you for a spineless soldier."

She rears back as if I've slapped her. "You know nothing about me. You think that was bad? You have no clue." Her eyes narrow but I can't help but notice how they also fill with unshed tears. I hate that there's hurt there.

"Enlighten me," I all but demand.

"No, thanks." She straightens her spine and steps forward to leave.

I block her path. "Don't. Don't push me away." I grip her shoulders and stoop so she can't avoid my gaze. There's no one in the hallway but us and a few hired security guards, yet I whisper my next words so they're only for her. "Don't force me away and carry it all."

"You'll regret it." Her words lack conviction, and even her shoulders slump under an invisible weight.

"Lay it on me." *Trust me.*

"You want to know what it's like to be a black woman on the force? You want to know how many names I've been called, or how many people have tried to humiliate me? Why I left?" She lifts her chin with challenge and there's venom in her words, as if she thinks that'll scare me away.

"I do. I want to know. I want everything you're willing to give me." I want the opportunity to prove I won't run.

She pauses to scrutinize the truth in my eyes. At long last there's a shift in her expression and I know she sees me, the Austin she always knew.

"The worst were the supervisors," she says. "The co-workers. The people who were supposed to be on *my* side." She swipes a tear from beneath her lashes before there's a chance for it to fall. Her body radiates strength, but her voice shakes. "That's why I quit. It wasn't the shitty low-lives I arrested, or served to protect, it was the men I worked with. The ones who were supposed to have my back."

"I'm sorry." And I am.

"I don't want your sympathy. But you wanted to know. Now you do." She takes a step back and crosses her arms over her chest. She's done. Closing off. But I don't want our conversation to end.

"How long were you on the force?"

She presses her lips together and I wonder if she'll push me away again. To my relief she doesn't. "Six years. It was my ticket out of a life going nowhere. I couldn't afford college, and my grades weren't that good. Not after moving to Cali, I was working retail to help with rent after my dad left. But then I saw an ad. LAPD was hiring. Looking for diversity."

"That's the only reason?"

"I wanted to protect people like me. I could be a part of the solution." She opens her mouth as if she wants to say more but instead glances away.

"What changed?"

"Chief Benson." She blows out a harsh exhale. "He came on and everything changed. All of a sudden I was partnered with the most racist guy in our squad who thought I went through the academy for the sole purpose of filling out his paperwork and picking up food. Anytime we had a race-fueled protest, and those happen weekly, I got assigned to work security. I was no fool. The only reason they wanted me out there was because it looked good for them on the five o'clock news."

I swallow hearing her truth. "That's horrible."

"It was the beginning of two very long and agonizing years. I thought I could stick it out because giving up my career, everything, felt like the ultimate failure. I didn't come this far to quit." Her jaw works back and forth and she doesn't quite meet my stare.

"What changed?"

"During my last review, I asked if he would refer me to the detective training program, or how I could work toward that, and you know what he said?" Her eyes find mine, and the hurt I find in her gaze cuts as badly as her words. "He said, over his dead body would a black woman get promoted under his command."

Rage. It's all I see. The need to hurt this idiot and make his life hell overcomes me. "What's his name?" The anger in my question is unmistakable.

Her lips pinch with disapproval. "No."

"What's his name?" I lift my brows. "I want to talk to that son of a bitch. See what he says when a civil suit is slapped in his goddamn face."

"Austin. He's not worth it." She shakes her head.

"You're worth it." *You're worth everything.*

"Stop." She drops my gaze.

I lift her chin with my fingers until her proud gaze is locked with mine. "You know that, don't you? You're worth it."

Her breath quickens but she doesn't avoid my stare when I drop my hand back to my side.

"Someone like him should never be in a position of power."

"But he was," she whispers.

"Was?" My pulse races with the use of past tense.

"He died of a heart attack last year." The words leave her mouth void of anger or bitterness. It only exemplifies the character and strength this woman has.

"Good." I can't help myself.

"Yeah."

"Could you go back?" *Is that what she wants? Did me bringing her on this tour take that opportunity away?*

"He wasn't the only racist, sexist man in the department, Austin." The light chuckle that leaves her mouth is humorless. "I was way too optimistic to think I'd make the difference."

"That's why you ended up in private security?"

"I ended up working security because I needed to pay my bills." She rolls her eyes. "But my passion project is an after-school center in LA. I started volunteering there, teaching self-defense classes, mentoring. It's how I make a difference. Well, did. Now I'm stuck on this tour with your ugly face." Her lips twist with a smile.

"I'm sorry you had to go through all of that." *I'm sorry I wasn't there for you. That I didn't protect you when I could. I can't make up for not being there, but I want to anyway.* If I could take this from her, I would.

"I don't need you to apologize for someone else's poor behavior." She shakes her head and glances over my shoulder, but there's nothing happening right now. It'll be another hour before this stadium is full. "It doesn't do any good re-hashing this."

"No, but it helps me understand."

"You'll never understand what it's like to be me." She's right.

"But I can empathize. You can let me in. Help me understand. You shouldn't have to carry all of this on your own." I reach my hand out to hers, and risk the possible rejection of her not holding mine back. "I'm sorry for what I said to you about Vince. About the videos. I was wrong. You're the strongest woman I know."

She slides her hand in mine and squeezes once. "You're not the worst when you drop the act, you know that?"

"What act? I'm a fly motherfucker twenty-four-seven."

She shakes her head. "I see we're back to making everything a joke."

"Hey, Jayla?" I try not to fixate on how good her hand feels in mine. Or that I never want to let it go.

"Yeah?"

"Thank you. For trusting me with your story."

"It's just a small part." She pulls her hand back and balls it into a fist.

My gaze stays on her hands, watching them contract and release, like a nervous habit. "Another part I missed." I don't know if I'll ever get over the guilt of it.

"Hey, Austin?"

I lift my gaze. "Yeah?"

A phone pings, and she pulls her cell from her back pocket. After glancing at it briefly, she offers me a smile. "Never mind. It's nothing."

"No." I shake my head. It's never nothing. "What were you gonna say?"

"Why didn't you ever call or write after we moved?" Her gaze drops, almost as if she's embarrassed to ask. "You promised you'd never let us drift apart."

Her comment takes me back to that day. Back to when we'd been spending so much time together. With her dad out of work, her parents fought all the time. And my mom's latest loser boyfriend didn't want me anywhere near the apartment. Every day, we snuck onto either her balcony or mine, out of sight, and found escape in each other. But then one day she was gone. I knew the moment she didn't show for school there was something wrong. I never could have predicted her family would just up and leave. But they did.

"I didn't know where you went. How to get hold of you. Fuck, I didn't even know if you were okay, or still in Phoenix. Everywhere I went I was always looking for you. Your hair. Your face. I called out your name to strangers. I drove myself crazy wondering why you'd just up and leave without any way for me to contact you."

Her gaze hardens. Eyes narrow, and it's almost as if she's analyzing not only my words but the truth of them.

I lift my hands at my sides. "Jayla, what the hell? You were my best friend. The girl I fantasized about every night. And you just . . . disappeared."

"You're lying. You have to be," she accuses, but her words come out unsure with disbelief.

"What are you talking about?"

"I wrote you letters." She points her finger at my chest. "You were the one who moved on without me."

"Letters? When?" If this is a joke, it's not funny. My stomach coils with dread.

"All the fucking time." She shakes her head and pins me with a glare.

"I never—" My jaw clenches with the realization of another thing my mom and one of her stupid fucked up boyfriends ruined. If things were bad when Jayla lived across the building, they became desolate after she left. My mom's live-in boyfriend at the time spent more time getting high than anything else. And when Mom wasn't working, the two of them went out partying, leaving me to play babysitter on the weekends he had custody of his kid.

He never liked Jayla. Never liked me. I'd bet money he made damn sure those letters never made their way into my hands. Hell, it could have been my mom. My jaw hardens with the onslaught of memories I rarely visit.

"Austin?"

"Sorry, I—" I run a hand across my face and push the rage from my voice. "I can't believe you wrote. They never gave me your letters."

The hardness on her features soften with understanding. She was there enough to know. "Your mom?"

I shrug. "Or her boyfriend."

"Are they still together?"

"No." I swallow the anger and guilt. "I don't really speak to anyone." Not since the big blow up. Not since leaving home. Running away. At the time, it was the only way I knew to survive, but looking back I realize how utterly selfish it was. If I had been there, then maybe—

"I'm sorry." Her apology cuts through my spinning thoughts.

"No, I'm sorry. All this time . . . I thought you forgot about me." I step forward. Wishing, wanting to pull her in my arms, but knowing I have no right.

Her gaze seeks mine. "I thought the same."

"Miss Miller?" A deep timbre pulls her attention away.

"Yes?"

"We're ready to open the doors. Brian said to get you first."

"Yes, I'll be right there. Thank you." She brings her gaze back to mine, hiking a thumb over her shoulder. "I better . . ."

A grin pulls at my lips. I don't know why, but the knowledge that all these years she didn't just walk away, that she cared, it changes everything. "Yeah, go do your thing. We'll talk later."

"Good luck tonight." She backs away, but there's a reluctance to her steps, as if she's not ready for this moment to end. Her lips mirror mine with her smile. "Break a leg. I can say that, right?"

"Jayla, you can say whatever you want." My face hurts, that's how big my smile grows, and before she turns, her laughter echoes off the walls and it's my new favorite sound. The pit of my stomach bubbles with a sensation akin to excitement and nerves before a big show, something I haven't felt in years. The source is clear, though, and it has everything to do with Jayla and the fact she's in my life for good—or at least for the remainder of this tour.

18

JAYLA

I THINK about Austin for the rest of my shift. *No.* Obsess is more accurate. We had moved back to California to be near family when Dad hadn't been able to find work and Mama couldn't support us on her own. Only everything that transpired that first year in Cali broke down what little was left of their marriage, and our family fell apart. I wrote Austin often at first. It was my way of holding on to our friendship and surviving my new life in spite of the hundreds of miles my parents forced between us. In all the years, I never once considered he hadn't received my letters. Eventually, I lost hope in everything, including Austin.

But now, everything is different. He never read my letters. He didn't ignore me, or move on. Not the way I imagined. All the anger I've directed toward him for years is no longer justified. In its place grows a seed of interest. Now more than ever, I want to know him.

While running the security team, I can't help but sneak a few glimpses of the show. They're fantastic performers, all of them, but my eyes seek out Austin every time. Everything about him screams sex on that stage. His confidence; the way his hips rock with each strum of the guitar; his lips as they part against the microphone to serenade for backup vocals. Most of all, those long, nimble fingers. Sweet Jesus. They're my undoing. I wonder what it'd be like to have him touch me the way he caresses those guitar strings.

Unprofessional. Wrong. Not a good idea. I remind myself over and over, but the more I repeat the reasons, the more they feel like excuses. Given his current revelation, they seem insignificant. I need to live in the moment. Get to know Austin as the man he is today. We missed out on so many years, and I won't allow myself to waste more time worrying about what might or might not happen. Besides, I don't even know whether I could handle being with him. I don't enjoy being touched intimately by anyone, and as amazing as Austin is, he won't be able to erase my load of emotional baggage. If we were to cross that line, I'd have to explain things I'd rather leave in the past. I'm not sure I could do that, even for him.

Straightening my shoulders, I turn away from the stage to focus on the most important task at hand, getting through the rest of the concert. I'll have plenty of time to mull over my feelings once we are back on the road again safe and sound.

MY EYES BURN against the brightness of the laptop screen, and my body aches for the comfort of my sleeping bunk. From the driver's seat, Ace hums along to the song in his head, steering the bus along miles and miles of dark highway. We left Omaha a good hour ago, and after scarfing down the dinner Opal arranged, everyone settles into their nightly routine.

Austin's in the shower. Opal and Leighton retreated to their bed a while ago. Lexi strums her guitar from her spot on the floor, her deep, soulful voice crooning lyrics I've never heard before. She stops every few minutes to jot down a note, or hit record on her phone. Trent snoozes beside her. He always tries to stay awake, but the exhaustion of performing catches up to him. Lexi catches me staring and lifts her brow. "The boys can't hang."

"You like to work at night." Not a question, just an observation.

Her lips twist with a hint of joy. "It's as if the entire world stops. The stillness helps me focus, and the parts of the song that have been hanging out in the back of my mind just click into place. Feels like magic." Her passion for writing is clear.

"You love it."

"Makes me feel alive, you know?" She strums her guitar, tuning the sound before buckling it into its case. "But I'm ahead of schedule on this record so I'm gonna call it a night."

"You don't have to," I say, worried she's turning in because of me or that I've interrupted her process. "Once I finish these reports, you'll have the space to yourself."

"He won't go to bed until I do." She rolls her eyes, but when her stare lands on Trent it's full of admiration and affection. "He needs his rest. This tour has taken a lot out of him. All of us." Her lips press together and she lets loose a long exhale before meeting my gaze. "There weren't any security threats tonight?"

"No." It's almost unsettling, really. I expected this to be more challenging. Not that my job is easy. It's just, given the explosion before I came on, I anticipated more problems and security issues.

"Good. Thank you for being here. For keeping my boys safe," she says. Before I can answer, she's pulling Trent to his feet.

"Wha—?" He rubs the sleep from his face. "Did you get enough done?"

"Yep. I'm ready for bed."

"'Night, Jayla." Trent waves and slings his arm around Lexi's shoulder on their way to their sleep bunk.

I exhale, pinch my eyes shut, and rally the focus I need to finish up my work too. But the sound of the bathroom door opening followed by footsteps steals what attention I have left. I glance over my laptop as Austin struts into the space. Shirtless. Freshly showered. The ends of his hair still dripping.

Well, that doesn't help me. Every intelligent thought scatters at the sight of him. Damn. Just. *Damn.*

"Jayla." Austin tips his chin.

"Hey," I manage to get out without sounding like an idiot. My eyes fall back to my computer screen and the three lines worth of letter V's I've added by accident. "Shit," I mutter, and highlight the text to delete it.

Austin's soft chuckle registers and I can't tell whether he's laughing with me or at me. Regardless, my body comes to attention at the sound.

I try to look busy, at least until he climbs into his sleep bunk, but he doesn't make his way there, instead plopping onto the bench seat at my right. His presence crowds my solitude.

"You gonna be up awhile?"

"Yeah." I lift my gaze to meet his and it takes every bit of willpower to not let it rove over his body. The ink covering his skin practically demands for me to stare, but I'm not that woman and I won't be caught ogling him. I have too much pride for that.

"Cool." He flashes a grin, then settles his gaze on his phone. "I'm going to edit our next video."

My brows pull with my frown. "But WMI said no more videos."

"Yeah, well. If they don't like it, they can fuck off."

"You think that's a good idea?"

"Probably not." There's that smile again.

I should reprimand him. Convince him to shut it down. But the rebellious nature of his words pulls my own lips into a smile. I tear my gaze from his and back to my laptop, and we settle into a comfortable silence. Him on his cell and me working my way through the list of questions and security protocol. I finish the reports but decide I'd better check into preparations for tomorrow's show. We'll be staying overnight in Illinois, sleeping at a hotel. It adds extra work, but the promise of a night in my own room is one hundred percent worth it. The label is sponsoring an after party at the same hotel following tomorrow's show, and clearing the guest list of one hundred with background checks is of the upmost priority. No easy task as the list changes daily.

"Done!" Austin sets down his phone with a satisfied smile.

"Already? That was quick."

He squints and scrubs his palm across the scruff of his chin. "Oh, but I can take all night when it's important."

"Oh." I bite my lip, not exactly intending to bring up our one very awkward experience as teens, but considering everyone else is asleep, I may as well address it. "I guess you've cleared up that issue since high school."

He stifles his laughter with the back of his hand. "I knew you were going to bring that up."

I lift my eyebrows in challenge. "You don't look embarrassed."

"Hell, no. I was a sixteen-year-old kid. You were letting me put my dick in you. Of course I blew my load right away."

"Technically, you didn't put it in me." I cringe, remembering our one and only attempt at having sex. My brother had football practice, so after school Austin walked me home the way he had dozens of times before. Both my parents were still working, and I'd invited him over to study.

Our hormones were at an all-time high and we'd been flirting for months. It was a natural progression, I suppose. He was my best friend. I found him attractive in spite of his awkwardness, and when we got to talking about sex, or more like our shared inexperience, I asked if he'd take my virginity. Heavy petting and kissing commenced, followed by him suiting up in a condom only to ejacu-late less than a minute after he rolled it on.

"Yeah, that's my only regret." Austin chuckles and scrubs a hand over his face. "And you avoided me for like two weeks afterward."

"I didn't know how to not make it weird." My defense brings another soft laugh.

"I apologize for being the worst sexual experience in your life."

Not worst. I almost tell him, but then it would ruin this light comradery we've rediscovered. Instead, I reach for the nearest truth, my face a mask of easygoing normalcy. "It was certainly the quickest."

"God." He glances up and his chest shakes with the laughter he can't hold back. When his gaze lands on mine he looks so much like the boy I left behind. "I really screwed up. Blew my chance with you. Literally and figuratively."

I don't know what to say to that, so I glance back down at my laptop and check for a response from my last email. My neck aches. My back too, but I might as well power through a few more minutes of work.

"Anyway, check this out." Austin slides his cell across the table. His finger glides alongside mine as he transfers the device over. He smiles proudly. "I think it's the best one yet."

I can't help but smile and press play. In another life, I think Austin could've been a filmmaker. He has a talent for knowing just how to string clips together. It's funny, smart, and the smile at my lips grows knowing how many people it will reach.

"You like it?" he says as I push his phone back into his hands.

"It's really good."

"Practice makes perfect." His lips curve up knowingly. *Practice.* The way the words drip from his mouth make them sound sensual. He's had plenty of practice since we were kids. Hell, he gave me his list. And while his sexual promiscuity is a turn off, the knowledge of his practiced skills in the bedroom shoots a thrill down my spine. I press my legs together and my arms cover in gooseflesh at the thought of *practice* with Austin.

His gaze catches mine before landing on my arms. He notices my body's reaction, and that only turns me on more. I don't want him to know. I don't trust he won't take advantage, and I need the upper hand. Always. It's how I maintain control. I won't show him my weakness. I can't.

I play it off as exhaustion and sore muscles, stretching my head to the right, and then to the left. It's not a lie. My entire body aches. I consider myself in shape; for the most part I live a healthy lifestyle. But the number of hours I've spent on my feet standing or walking through venues only to sleep in a less than comfortable bus has my muscles strained in a way I'm not accustomed to.

That, along with the pressure that comes with each and every tour stop. We've had no threats, no breaches in security, and everyone is safe. *So far*. I can't help but question whether it's a result of luck more than planning. If someone is dead set on hurting these guys or causing terror at a show, they will attempt to abolish the safety measures I set in place. It's a probable situation and one that weighs heavy on my mind, especially these late nights while we roll along miles of empty freeway and my thoughts have the freedom to wander.

"Neck hurt?"

"A little." I reach back to work the tightness from my muscles.

"Here, let me." He's up from his seat and behind me before I open my mouth to argue. His thumbs knead my skin, firm and with solid pressure. "You're tense."

I resist the urge to moan, because holy hell, his hands are amazing.

"It's this job, isn't it?"

"Yeah."

"I'm sorry. It's my fault for coercing you into accepting."

"Yeah, well it's on your conscience when I'm subjected to a lifetime of acupuncture, chiropractic care, and prescription drugs for these stress headaches and back pain."

"Shit." His voice is low and throaty through his chuckle. "I don't want that. I'd have to get my own medical marijuana to deal with the pain of ruining your gorgeous body."

"You already have weed."

"I do?" His hands still a moment, then resume with the escape of another laugh. "Busted."

"Good thing I'm no longer a cop." I tip my chin up, letting my head fall back against his stomach. I catch his grin and let my own lips curve up playfully. Or at least, it starts that way. Under the heat of his stare and with his hands still moving across my shoulders in deep, sure circles, my body tenses for an entirely different reason.

His touch feels intimate.

The way he's studying me from beneath those dark lashes is intense. He doesn't look away, and I couldn't if I tried. "Honestly, Jay, what can I do? You shouldn't carry all this stress."

"I—" *want you to touch me.* The words catch in my throat and hammer in my chest. My pulse gallops and I press my legs together as the need between them—the need for him—obliterates any rational thought.

I almost say those words aloud.

By the heat in his stare, I wonder if he feels it too.

"Jay," he whispers. My name on his lips is full of the same tortured longing I feel down to my core. We barely scratched the surface of this sexual tension when we were teens, both too young and too naïve to fully understand the power of it.

Now. Right here. I swear those same feelings have multiplied and grown. It's overwhelming. Terrifying as hell. And yet . . . I can't help but arch my back even more. I delight in the way his gaze drops to the neckline of my shirt.

His eyes zero in on my chest and his touch becomes feather light as his stare takes in the hard peaks of my nipples straining against the soft cotton fabric. I want him to touch me there. To haul me off this chair and into his arms. I need to taste his lips as they press against mine. Crave it.

"I have an idea," he whispers so softly that if I weren't watching his lips I would have missed the words.

"Yeah?"

His hands brush along my arms, down to my elbows and then back up, his fingers so close but not touching the swell of my breasts. "It's selfless on my part, because you know how giving I am." He's teasing. Joking. But it doesn't kill the chemistry that swirls between us. If anything, it only adds charge to an already building momentum.

His hands feel good, but they're not enough.

"Your idea?" My gaze waits for his.

"I want you, Jayla."

"Oh." Heat pools in my belly. My skin feels flush. And my body, my body wants this and everything he wants to give.

His hands slide up the length of my neck, then still as they cup my face. "I'll make you feel better. I swear." He tilts my chin up and my back arches in response. His body leans down over mine, slowly closing the space between our mouths.

"I don't think that's a good idea," I murmur, completely fascinated by the heat in his stare, and the way his tongue swipes across his lips.

"Let me kiss you at least?" He lowers his mouth, his intent as clear as his words. "I've been dying to taste those lips. To see if they're still the same."

"Um . . ." I should feel caged in. Between the chair and the table, his hands near my throat and his body behind mine, I expect my anxiety to ruin this moment. Only it never comes. Instead, desire and attraction so powerful flood my veins. I almost reach up and grab for him.

"One kiss?" He bends, closing the remaining space until there isn't more than shared breath between us. All I need to do is close the space, to nod my consent, and his lips will crash on mine.

Thrilling. Terrifying. I can't settle on which emotion rules.

But I don't have to. A melody bursts from his phone. An interruption, and instead of pressing my lips to his, I chicken out, dropping my gaze to the phone.

What I see on his screen kills any ounce of desire.

He reaches out to swipe the phone from my gaze, but it's too late. I already saw. I don't even attempt to mutter an excuse, and he doesn't stop me as I push out of my chair, stalk down the hall, and lock myself in the bathroom.

You should know better, I chastise my reflection in the small mirror. I'm not anyone special to him. I'm just convenient. All the time we've spent together—the videos, the conversations—it's all blinded me to the truth.

Once a player, always a player. Shame on me for imagining otherwise.

19

AUSTIN

MY FUCKING PHONE. Worst cock block ever. The second Jayla's eyes drop to my screen I know I'm screwed. Why the hell did I think it'd be a good idea to program, "Fuck Me Heels Lawyer" as the contact? *Fuck me* is right.

Jayla races to the bathroom and I reluctantly swipe across the screen, holding the cell to my ear. "Hey."

"Is this a good time?" Rachel Kinsley says in her all-business tone. "I know it's late with the time difference, but I just got to my computer."

"It's fine." It's not at all. I'd like to tell her off for sending Jayla running, but it's my fault for the misinterpretation. Truth is, a few weeks ago I would have jumped at the thought of a booty call from Rachel Kinsley, but now it does nothing for me. She's not the one I want. "Everything okay?"

"Not really." She clears her throat, and I can't tell whether her pause is for dramatic effect or she's just distracted. "Sorry, okay, so the preliminary hearing is set for next week. You don't need to be present, and I'll request the judge dismiss the claims. However, I'm going to be honest with you. There's a good chance it'll go to trial."

Coy. The mere thought of him causes my jaw to grate. "But there's a chance it won't?"

"We've been assigned to Judge Hallstorm, so I'd say that chance is slim to non-existent." The wariness in Rachel's voice isn't something I associate with her, and for that alone the seed of worry in my gut begins to grow.

"Should I know who that is?"

"No, I hope not." She sighs. "I went to law school with him and let's just say, he won't make this easy."

"Damn." I rub my temples, wishing this mess would all disappear. Coy caused enough damage for one lifetime. He has real balls to come back for more. "I wish this could just be over."

"Funny, I was hoping you'd say that." There's a smile in Rachel's voice.

"Why's that exactly?"

"Because there's another option. We can still settle."

I bristle at the suggestion. "Pay him off? Fuck no."

"It'll end up costing the same. And we'd require an NDA to his acceptance of any settlement monies. This would keep you and the band out of the press."

My jaw tightens with the influx of stress.

"Austin. My advice, which you pay for, is that you let me do my job and work a deal with this lowlife. We have enough to win, but his lawyers are gonna spin the circumstances and quite frankly, you aren't completely innocent. You did hurt him. He can't play anymore. That doesn't win you sympathy votes. They're gonna go for the jugular. They'll drag out any skeletons in your closet. Your bandmates' and Jess's, too."

I don't want to give him a penny, but I'm not the only person this affects. The band, sure, but there are others. I should talk to Jess. She deserves a say in this. "Can I think about it? When do you need a decision?"

"We scheduled the hearing for next Thursday, so the sooner the better. If you don't give me a few days to negotiate, I can't guarantee they'll settle."

"I'll let you know by Monday."

"If I don't hear from you, expect another call." Rachel is no-nonsense, one of the things I've always loved about her. That and pushing her buttons.

"So, what else did you call to chat about?" I try half-heartedly with a need to lighten the mood. Usually when I razz our lawyer, it's because it gets my dick hard. Movement from the corner of my vision steals my attention. Jayla climbs into her sleep bunk without a single glance in my direction.

"Did you get into more trouble?" Rachel's irritated reply does nothing for me.

Tonight, my cock is otherwise occupied. Hell, for the last two weeks it hasn't wanted anyone other than Jayla Miller. "No." Jesus. "It was a joke."

"With you, I can never tell. We'll talk Monday. Goodbye, Austin."

I set my phone down and stare at Jayla's bunk, willing and wishing for her to open the curtain, or better yet, invite me in. But I killed that chance the second my phone rang. I release a groan of irritation and scrub a hand over my face. I came so close to kissing her, I can almost taste her. My body tenses and my dick throbs with desperation. I was so close, but now it's not gonna happen. Jayla isn't the type of woman to overlook that type of behavior.

I fuck up everything good.

As if the universe doesn't want me to forget, my phone pings with an incoming text. My stomach lurches when I check the screen. It's from the discreet private investigator I've been in contact with since last year. The one I can never tell a soul I hired. I've screwed up so much in my life, but even I know how bad it would look if this comes out.

More profiles for review. Let me know if they're what you're looking for.

I glance at Jayla's bunk. It's not as if she can read my cell from there, but wariness sets into my bones at the thought of her discovering what I've been up to. It would be a relief to come clean. To tell her, or someone, but that's only selfish talk. This is my cross to bear. My wrong to right. I glance around the bus once more to be sure everyone is sound asleep before reaching for my laptop and slinking into the far corner of the booth to power it up.

Shame and regret wash over me as I flip through the photos this PI collected. I have to give it to him, I don't know how he finds them. These women—no, they're just girls—caught in the most desperate of situations. My pulse races, the anticipation and hope of finding a familiar face amongst this new collection of photos pushes my gaze across the screen with near manic devotion. But by the last photo, my heart rate slows and disappointment pools in my gut. *She's not here.* I'm left with another failure. Another fuck up. One I can't seem to make up for.

I delete the email. Clear my browser. Slam the laptop shut with more force than necessary, and bite back the urge to cry. Most days I pretend just fine. My selfish nature pushed me toward greatness, success, and the life I have now. But at what cost? Will I ever be allowed to repent for my sins, or will they continue to eat at me from the inside? I wish I could forget. Or move on. I've tried that, but no matter how far we tour, I can't escape the guilt.

With my cell balanced in hand, I type out a reply, waiting for it to send before deleting all evidence from my phone.

Keep looking.

No answer comes, but I don't expect it to. The guy I hired has as much to lose as I do. I can imagine the headlines now. *Three Ugly Guys lead guitarist, Austin Jones, hires PI to collect child porn for his personal collection.* No, I can't tell Jayla, or anyone else for that matter. I'm not sure any explanation would be justification for what I'm doing. This would only give her another reason to push me away, and the thought of Jay walking back out of my life is about the worst reality I can imagine.

I glance at her bunk, not sure what I hope to find there. Nothing but the low hum of our driver Ace singing along to a song in his head and the steady rumble of the coach's engine meets my ears. Resolve blooms from the feeling of helplessness in my gut. I refuse to accept this fate. I won't give up. Not on myself. Not on the need to right my wrongs. And especially not on a future with Jayla. Yeah, I fucked up, but chances are it won't be the last time.

An idea hits me and I grab my phone, taking it into the bathroom with the determination to wriggle my way back into her good graces. There's something important I need to tell her, and while she probably won't listen to me right now, she might with a little outside pressure.

It's an unfamiliar feeling, having to work to gain someone's attention, but hell if it doesn't feel more important than anything I've ever done. I'll become the kind of man she deserves. It may not come naturally, but I'm stubborn enough to get there. For her, I'd do just about anything. She's worth it.

20

JAYLA

THE NEXT MORNING, I wake to the muffled sounds of people moving around the bus. Their hushed voices tell me I've slept longer than I should have. I like to be the first up and last to sleep, but the schedule we've been keeping, it's wearing on me. The glide of a moving bus tells me we haven't pulled into our next stop yet. I reach for the privacy curtain, but the memory of Austin's late night call flashes through my mind and I hesitate.

Masking my face with an expression of indifference, I slide from the sleep bunk, but only find Trent, Sean, and Lexi in the kitchen. "'Morning," I say and pour myself a cup of coffee.

"'Morning, Jayla." Lexi grins.

"How does it feel to be famous?" Sean meets my gaze and then moves from his seat at the table, setting his cell on the counter between all of us while he refills his mug. He tips his chin to Lexi. "Check the stats again."

She drags his phone closer.

"Six million views. Fucking hell." Trent's brows shoot into his hairline and he glances at me with wide eyes.

"Jayla, have you seen this?" Lexi hands me the phone as the

pieces click together. The video Austin edited last night. He must have posted it.

"I can't believe he posted another video." Trent slings an arm around her shoulders, his grin wide as he flicks his gaze to Austin's sleeping bunk. "Our little rebel is trying to get us on the shit list."

As if he'd been waiting for the mention, Austin whips open his sleep bunk and stumbles out. I try not to stare, really I do, but his shirtless form and the low-slung sleep shorts hugging his hips do nothing to hide the span of tattooed, muscled chest. He looks half asleep, his eyes hooded, and that only adds to his sex appeal. He reaches down to his crotch to adjust his junk, and it's only then I glance away.

Lexi meets my gaze and catches me staring, but doesn't humiliate me by addressing it.

My gaze darts back down to the video and my eyes widen as I take in the screen. Six million views. "Wait. Are those the comments?" I stab my finger at the number.

"Yeah, all ten thousand of them." Trent chuckles, shaking his head. "Crazy, huh?"

Austin struts to Trent's side, his gaze wide and alert.

"This." I glance down at the phone, my mind and verbal skills temporarily suspended at the numbers. His hand curls around one end of the screen, and I allow him to brush his thumb along my fingers before meeting his stare. "You." Unreal. I can't even process it.

"I posted it last night." He swallows, his expression void of its usual teasing.

Last night. After his call with the lawyer he wants to fuck. Or has fucked. I yank my hand away from the phone as if holding the device a second longer might burn.

"I added something extra at the end."

"Oh," I say lamely. I don't want to discuss this video. Not when I can still taste my stupidity. I was seconds away from kissing him last night. No. I wanted more than just a kiss. I wanted so much more with him. I turn away from everyone and open the fridge, digging around until I find a container of yogurt shoved to the back. I close the door and reach for the drawer filled with cutlery.

Austin gently grips my arm above my elbow before I pick up my spoon. His voice is low so only I can hear. "I did it for you."

He did what for me? I shrug off his touch, but he's already gone. Anger flares in the pit of my belly. Damn him. He can't just whisper in my ear and expect me to forgive him. If we were alone, I'd call him out. But I won't embarrass him, or myself, in front of his friends. And what's with his cryptic message? Now I have to go on a treasure hunt, watch the video again, and what—? Expect he left a message for only me on a video blasted to millions? *Please.* This woman wasn't born yesterday, and he better not take me for a fool.

"Vince is pretty pissed about the video. He keeps calling." Trent's voice pulls me from my thoughts, and I turn to meet everyone's stares. I open my mouth to apologize, but Trent cuts me off. "We're sending him to voicemail. He can chew us all out in person." He chuckles and shrugs.

Sean tips his chin, a smile of his own in place. "Don't worry about Vince. We've all got your back."

"Thanks." I dip my spoon into my yogurt and let his words sink in. In spite of whatever is going on with me and Austin, these guys and their girlfriends have welcomed me into their fold. I have no doubt they mean what they say. It's unexpected, and something I didn't ask for, yet their concern and protection bring forth a sense of security I haven't experienced in years. I won't allow myself to get too comfortable though, because life has also shown me that the same safety gets snatched back without any warning.

I'M WATCHING THE VIDEO. So help me God, I don't know why. Curiosity killed the cat, and yet here I am lined up for the punishment. At least I have the good sense to wait until the band is on stage for sound checks. It's embarrassing enough I'm watching this damn thing. There's no way I'd give him the satisfaction too.

Everything is the same as last night; that is, until the screen fills with Austin's face. I recognize the location. It's on the tour bus, in the bathroom. As I turn up the volume I wonder whether he recorded this last night or pulled it from another time.

"So, I hope you learned something new, and you feel a little safer the next time you have to walk out to your car alone, or you're walking into your building. My friend Jayla is a badass, am I right? But I have something I need to admit."

He signals to the camera, his finger moving in a come hither motion. "I'm an idiot. Because I don't know how I got so lucky to have a woman like her on my side. She doesn't just volunteer to kick my ass for these videos. She keeps our band safe—our staff, the roadies, the concession workers, everyone who comes to a show, it's all because of her relentless leadership." His eyes pierce me with their sincerity, and I hold my breath waiting on his next words.

"She's the best thing to happen to me in a long time, but I keep doing stupid shit around her. She's already way out of my league. Obviously." He flashes a grin. "But somehow she still puts up with me, and the rest of the band, and I've never been so thankful as I am to wake up each morning and discover she hasn't quit."

His face drops the smile, the hint of humor, and I swear he might as well be right here with me as he says his next words. "Don't give up on me, Jay? Not yet, okay? I know I have a lot to prove, to make up for, but I swear I'm in this thing." He blinks and clears his throat, the smile back in place as his tone loses its intensity. "And you don't give up, either. Find a friend, a sibling, a parent, someone who will practice these moves until they're second nature. It's a crazy world out there, and it doesn't hurt to add a few skills to protect yourself. Until next time . . ."

The video collapses as the next one in line pops onto the screen as it loads. I close the app and hold the phone to my chest. My heart races with his plea. *Don't give up on me, Jay? Not yet, okay?* It's those words alone that want me to forget and forgive him for every wrong he's ever done.

It's unsettling how strong the impulse is, and of their own accord my feet push my body toward the music. I slip inside the stadium but stay off to the side, watching the band perform from behind one of the cement pillars. I'm caught off guard, though, when it's Lexi at the microphone and not Trent.

She dances around as the guys rock out, and I realize I've heard this melody before. It's the one she was working on last night. She steps up to the mic, her rough and deep voice cutting with strength through the crash of guitars.

"It was never me. Innocence lost.

It was never me. Childhood stolen.

It was never me. Not me you broke."

Her words fill my feet with a heaviness that settles throughout my entire body. My chest tightens, and my breath is shallow, but I can't tear myself from her performance or the lyrics that hit too close to home.

Her gaze travels over the empty seats in the arena, and before I can shrink back into the shadows, her eyes find mine. She doesn't look surprised or shaken at all, and I guess she wouldn't. She's a rock star in her own right and plays for crowds as big as the guys'. I expect her to turn or look away, but instead she holds my stare through the next verse.

"So long I wanted you to hurt.

But it was only me bleeding from those wounds.

Hurting myself gave you power, the power you stole,

And now I'm just done, unable to stand on my own."

I suck in a sharp inhale, my body trembles, and my vision clouds with the onset of unshed tears. *I won't cry. I won't.* But no matter the number of times I repeat the command, hurt—real and fresh—slices through my chest with the tragic beauty of her song. There's an openness to her stare. One that says she sees everything I hide, she knows everything I've been through. *She knows.* I don't know how, but she does.

Before the song ends, I hurry back into the corridor of the arena, away from Lexi's perceptive gaze and Austin's heavy presence. I walk through the mostly empty passageways, attempting in vain to slow my racing heart. I'm tired, worn down, and I need to clear my head so I can focus on getting through tonight. At home I'd throw myself into work, but that doesn't bode well as a diversion here. Not when work centers around the one man who sparks a desire I never thought I'd know. But he's a part of my past, and every time we're together I'm confronted by other memories. They're a distraction I can't afford, not with the welfare of everyone on this tour at stake. Now isn't a good time to fall apart. *When is it ever?*

My phone rings and I half expect it to be another call from Vince. My finger readies to send him to voicemail as I've been doing throughout the day, but I pause when Kalise's name pops up on the caller ID.

"Hey, girl."

"So, you are alive," she smarts with a laugh. "How's everything going? How's the rock star?"

"Good. Fine." I glance down the corridor to see Austin, Trent, Leighton, and Sean talking off stage with Casey. "It's been good."

"I haven't heard from you." There's accusation in her tone.

My gaze trains on the guys. I can't hear them from this distance, but by their furrowed brows and pinched lips, they don't look happy. "Yeah."

"What the hell kind of answer is that?" Kalise snaps.

I turn away from the guys. "Sorry. Distracted."

"Sure you aren't dick-stracted? You leave LA, become this viral sensation, and all of a sudden I never hear from you." Her tone is as harsh as her words. "Aaliyah, either."

"That's not fair and you know it. I've been working nonstop since I got put on this job." I sling my words but a tiny wedge of guilt seeps into my mind. I'm a crappy friend. I should have checked in with them both. "It's a lot of responsibility. Pressure to make sure nothing happens at these shows."

"At least tell me you're getting some." Her words lack their sharpness. She's already forgiven me.

"Oh, my God!" I laugh out loud and shake my head. "Would you stop?"

"So, that's a no on bone-town?" She digs for details.

"You're ridiculous." I roll my eyes and laugh again.

"You miss me."

"I do. I'm sorry I haven't called." I blow out a long exhale and kick my shoes against the ground. "This tour . . . it's a lot."

"I take it you don't mean dick."

"No. Unfortunately," I admit, because this is Kalise. It's pointless trying to hide my attraction to Austin. She witnessed it for herself.

"I don't understand you. You have access to perfectly good man candy, and yet you resist the temptation. You hold your moral ground like someone who's afraid an earthquake is about to hit."

What she doesn't understand is that if I don't, I risk losing my mind. I follow rules because they hold everything together. They make sense. The minute I start breaking them, I risk losing more than my footing. I risk the peace within I've worked so hard to find.

A voice clears at my back and I turn to find Austin eating me up with his eyes. He crosses his arms over his chest, leaning against the corridor wall. He looks delicious as hell. *Man candy*. Damn, Kalise got that right.

"I gotta go. I'll call you more often. Promise," I say into the phone and hold Austin's gaze. A thrill shoots down my spine at his pointed attention.

"You better." She draws out the warning and I make a mental promise to not let weeks go by without checking in. "'Bye, Jay."

"'Bye, Kalise." I end the call and pocket my cell. "Hey." I tip my chin in greeting.

"Hey." He pushes off the wall and closes the space between us in a few long strides. He doesn't invade my personal space with his body, though. "You watched." Not a question but a statement, and by the intensity of his stare, I can't tell whether he's talking about the video or the sound check.

I nod and swallow. My mind races with conflicting feelings. The lustful attraction for him battles against the simultaneous need to push him away and protect my heart. He's unearthing feelings I'm not prepared to deal with. When Lexi was singing, she saw right through me. Does Austin see too?

"I never slept with my lawyer," he twists his hands together in a nervous movement.

His admission is the splash of water I need to find my voice. Anger surges with the knowledge Austin's been with lots of women. That he's able to have sex without panic taking over. That he has a healthy—albeit leaning toward excessive—sexuality, and I'm nothing close to normal. "Yeah, I remember. She wasn't on the list." I bite the words out and give no other indication he has the power to shake me. I don't like feeling weak, but somehow Austin pulls it out of me.

"That's fair." He nods but his gaze never leaves mine, as if he's searching for something. "I just want to be clear. We good? Because I feel like we're not."

"Everything's fine." But it's not. Not even a little. It doesn't matter whether I want him or not. Or that the message meant for me in our latest video melts the shield around my heart. I won't be able to do anything about it—not without being completely vulnerable, and that would shatter what control I've gained. My mental health is more important, and I won't put that at risk. Even for him. I shove my hands behind my back so he doesn't see them shake.

He stares, waiting, but when I don't give him more he finally nods, his disappointment as clear as his gorgeous green eyes. He doesn't say a word, simply turns and walks away. My rejection to his proffered olive branch steals the lightness from his steps.

I did that. But instead of satisfaction or a sense of security, I'm left with the fear that maybe I pushed too far. I lived without Austin's friendship for thirteen years, but something tells me I'll be forever changed after this tour. I won't survive without him this time. Even now as I push myself through the routine of pre-show security, it's lonely as hell without the warmth of his smile or jabs of humor. I wanted to protect myself by not allowing him to get too close, but there's a good possibility I already fucked that up.

Why am I still fighting this force of attraction between us?

I already know the answer, and it's one I don't like to think about or dwell on. I don't get the luxury of having a normal relationship. I freak out when someone touches me wrong, or when a memory slams into the forefront of my mind. Guys don't want me. I'm damaged goods. It's deceiving because my scars don't show on my body. They're woven into the facets of my mind. Even I have the good sense to understand that as interested as he seems, there's no way in hell Austin's prepared for what that entails.

21

AUSTIN

I'M DYING HERE. Hard up and rocking a case of blue balls that puts all dry spells to shame. I need to get off before I lose my goddamn mind. I *need* to sink my dick into Jayla's slick, tight pussy. No, her mouth. Fuck, I'd be happy if she stroked me. Or better yet, I could stroke my dick while she gets herself off.

But none of that is going to happen. Not tonight. Probably never. The stress of trying to be a better man or to be celibate for a woman who doesn't return my affection is pointless. And I can't keep running off to masturbate like a horny, pathetic teen, not when it doesn't offer much relief. The minute I clean myself up and tuck my dick back in my pants, my entire body goes back to aching for her.

I'm acting like a pussy-whipped loser, and I am not that guy. No one finds that guy attractive. Jayla isn't going to give me a medal, and waiting for her is pointless since she's made herself perfectly clear. She doesn't want me. Not in that way. After the video I posted last night and practically begged her to watch, I expected *something*. A kind word. A smile. Hell, I'd settle for a look in my direction. But if she's watched it, she's not impressed. It's almost as if she's actively avoiding me, going out of her way to be nowhere near me tonight.

Which, frankly, is all the answer I need. It's time to move on. Stop pining after a woman who wants nothing to do with me.

So, tonight I'm resolving my problem the best I know how. I'm finding a consenting woman to fuck.

It shouldn't be difficult. This post-show party is packed with groupies, industry professionals, and the *It* list of Chicago's social media influencers. There are plenty of hungry-eyed women who want to leave with a rock star. It's their lucky night, because I'm in need of a warm body. All I need to do is pick one, lay on the charm, and presto, my temporary vow of chastity will be gone.

Only, they're all wrong. I scan the crowd of women searching for something to spark my interest but come up short. Sure, their skin is beautiful, but it's the wrong tone. There's no tempting dark chocolate, the kind I've come to adore. I look for curves, but all I find is flat asses and skinny legs. There're no plump lips spouting fiery words, or eyes sharp with skepticism and truth, or hair as wild as it is beautiful. Right now, I couldn't get it up for any of these women.

That's it. My dick is broken. Fuck my life.

A hand clamps down on my shoulder. "Why do you look like someone pissed in your beer?" Sean tips his chin, raising two fingers to the bartender before turning his attention to me. Our other two bandmates are off in the crowd, mixing and mingling with their girl-friends, the lucky bastards. Jess's flight is scheduled to land soon if it hasn't already, but considering Sean's next to me and not upstairs in his hotel suite, my guess is she's not here yet.

I take a long swallow of my beer and exhale the bad news. "My life is over."

"What?" Sean lets loose a chuckle, takes in my serious expression, and hands me a fresh beer from the bartender before leaning his back against the bar. "Tell me all your troubles, bro."

"I don't want to fuck any of these women," I admit begrudgingly, and lift my drink to my lips.

He lifts his brow along with his lips. "Yeah? Me, neither."

"That's 'cause you're love drunk."

"What's that exactly?"

"Stupid, head over heels, committed to Jess. Which I respect, but that's not my issue."

"No? What's your problem, then?"

Jayla.

"Come on, motor mouth. Cat got your tongue?" he goads, and it's the truth. I don't have problems spilling my thoughts, or telling it how it is. He bumps his shoulder against mine. "Not that I'm complaining; it's just a rare sighting. I'm not sure how to handle it."

"I'll drink to that," I mutter and lift my beer, feeling even more confused than before.

"It's her, isn't it?" There's amusement in his tone, as if he finds this funny. As if he finds it hilarious my dick can't get up for a beautiful stranger and he knows exactly why. *Asshole.*

"Who?" I turn to face him with a carefree expression even though I know damn well there's only one woman he could be referring to.

"So, it's gonna be like that, is it?" He laughs and then tips his chin over my shoulder. He leans in close, motioning me to do the same as if he's about to drop a secret. "She's here, you know. Just walked in."

My entire body lights up with the news. My chest puffs up, my body tenses ready to make a move, and my dick throbs like it hasn't spent the last hour in voluntary hibernation. But I need to play it cool. Fuck me, I can't let her see how she's gotten under my skin or stolen my game. I have my man card to protect.

"You wanna look, don't you?" Sean waggles his brows.

I shrug, feigning nonchalance, and bring my drink to my lips, pretending for a moment they're pressed against her warm skin and not a cold glass bottle.

Sean laughs, but it dies as his stare comes to a halt at something across the room. For a second my pulse thuds with fear, but it's quickly rectified.

"And I'm out. Later, man."

"Wait, what?" I call after him, but he's already pushing his way through the room. He's like an animal claiming his prey, and good luck to any idiot who tries to stop him. "Some friend you are," I grumble to myself as I watch Jess's gaze find him stalking toward her. Her entire face lights up as if she's just won a million dollars or been given the gift of her dreams, and I guess that's basically the same thing. They're disgustingly romantic as he sweeps her into his arms, kisses the hell out of her, and then practically drags her back out the doors she just came through. Thank fuck we have our own rooms tonight. No way do I wanna listen to them banging.

"What's a guy like you doing alone in a party like this?" a smooth and candy sweet voice croons at my right. It's the wrong tone, nothing like Jayla's, but I turn to take her in regardless. Gorgeous long legs, toned and tanned. She's blonde but not from a bottle. No, she's actually beautiful and yeah, she wears makeup, but not so much her face appears fake.

"I'm not alone. I'm drinking with fifty of my closest friends." I tip my bottle in the air. I should ask her if she wants a drink, or call over the bartender, but my eyes catch Jayla's staring from across the room and I can't find it in me to care about anything else.

This beautiful young thing doesn't slink from my coolness, though. She only laughs, and surprisingly it's not an annoying sound. It's warm, inviting, and I dip my gaze to hers for another moment.

"I'm Destiny."

Of course she is. Old me would ask if her destiny includes joining me in my bed. But those aren't the words that come out of my mouth. Apparently my mouth is as broken as my dick. "I'm Austin."

"Yeah, I know." She laughs again, the sound throatier this time. She leans forward, and I'm granted a very generous view of her cleavage.

I look, because I can't not, but my gaze snaps back over her shoulder searching for someone else. Only this time Jayla's not looking. Her back is planted against the wall next to one of the guards, and her attention is solely on him. He talks to her with a too friendly grin on his lips and I suddenly feel the urge to punch it off of his face. *Who the fuck does he think he is?* He better not be hitting on her.

"Austin." Destiny inches closer, her lips practically on my ear now. She doesn't seem to care that I'm not fully invested. Or maybe she thinks I'm playing hard to get. "How about we get out of here? Spend a little time in your hotel room. I'll let you do dirty things to me while I play with your cock."

Well, that gets my attention. Or at least my dick's. He's not totally broken. *Phew.* That's a relief, but it's short-lived, because as this woman pulls back, a Cheshire grin forms on her lips and I just know I can't go through with it. Not with Jayla on my mind.

"I don't think so. Not tonight." As soon as the words leave my lips, my dick fully retreats, and I'm not sure whether he's more upset at this turn of events, or relieved we're not gonna pretend Destiny is Jayla.

"You sure?" Destiny's brows rise and she's shocked at my refusal. In all honesty, so am I. She's supermodel gorgeous, and I doubt she ever gets turned down. Another night and I'd be salivating after her like a little puppy. But I only have eyes for one woman . . . and said woman is glaring daggers into the back of Destiny's head at this very moment.

Interesting. Either this lady hitting on me is a real threat to security or Jayla doesn't like the idea of me hooking up with her. Jealousy is a powerful tool, one I didn't think to use until this moment.

I lean forward to drop a chaste kiss on Destiny's forehead and flash her a smile. "Sorry, I'm not interested."

Destiny's eyes widen wildly at the finality of my words. *Shit.* They came out arrogant and more asshole-ish than I intended. She flips her hair across her bare shoulder. "Your loss."

"I'm sorry, I—" The excuse dies on my lips. *I'd do you, but I'd have to pretend you're someone else.*

Her brow rises and the hardness in her gaze challenges me to continue stuffing my foot in my mouth.

"Sorry." I sound like an idiot. I feel like one too. A month ago I wouldn't have apologized to any woman. A month ago I would have hauled this girl over my shoulder, slapped her barely clad ass, and had my wicked way with her.

"Whatever," she says, annoyed and put out by my rejection.

"It's not personal." I try for nonchalant and shrug, but clearly that's wrong.

"Yeah, and karma's a real bitch." Her hands ball into fists as though she's holding back her impulse to strike out physically. I almost wonder whether she will, but she must think otherwise and turns, walking all the way across the room and out the main doors.

My gaze searches the room, wanting—no, needing—to find Jayla, if only to observe her reaction to the spectacle I caused. But she's not here.

"Looking for someone?" Trent saunters up with a beer in his hand. "'Cause your lay for the night just left in a huff. Not sure that you noticed."

"What?" I say, more irritated that I can't find Jayla anywhere.

"Oh, right. You didn't notice the seething unicorn who just left the building. The one talking to you?" He laughs and slaps me on the back. "What did you say to her? It had to be absolutely horrid because she was totally into you otherwise. I thought for sure you'd be taking her back to your room."

"Why are you still talking?" I glance over his shoulder, but only find Lexi chatting with her sister. "And where the hell did Jayla go?"

"Dude. No." The smile falls from Trent's lips and he shakes his head. "Don't."

"Don't what?" I bark back more irritated than I should.

"No fucking with Jayla. Not when we've just got things going good again."

"Jayla doesn't want to fuck me." I hate the truthfulness of the words.

"Wow." His eyes widen and he pushes his hair back from his face. "I don't believe it. I never thought I'd see the day."

I scan the crowd again, but I lost her. Jayla is gone. My gut clenches with disappointment. So much for my attempt at provoking jealousy. I finish my beer with one last long pull and rub my temples after I slam the bottle back onto the bar. "What the fuck are you yammering about?"

"You like her. You *like-like* her. You turned down a sure thing because you only want Jayla."

"Fuck you." The fact he sees through my bullshit leaves me rattled, that and he's exactly right.

He laughs and I swear Lexi hones in on the sound, circling up to our spot at the bar with Opal and Leighton in tow.

"What's so damn funny?" Lexi grins.

"Austin. And the fact he's being cock blocked by his own head."

"Wait, what?" Lexi leans in close. "This I need to hear."

"You are all fucking idiots." I stare at their expectant gazes. The fact I'm talking to two happy couples only irks me further. "You think you have it *so* good with your person. All the support, and love, and fucking 'how was your day?' crap."

"Bro, how much did you drink?" Leighton chuckles.

"I bet you pity me, don't you"—I should walk away, or shut up, but now that I've started, I can't seem to stop—"with your whispered little love secrets? Look at him. Poor guy. Doesn't have anyone to share his hopes and dreams."

Trent just raises an eyebrow.

"Well, fuck y'all anyway!" I throw up my hand and then pound my chest to drive my rant home. "I'm the smart one. I've got it all figured out. Last man standing. I should get a fucking award."

"More like last one to fall," Leighton mutters but we all hear him clearly.

"It's a long way down from where you're sitting." Lexi crosses her hands over her chest, her brows raised incredulously. "I hope you brought a parachute."

"I'm standing." I widen my stance. "And I'm not falling for anyone."

"*Mmm hmm.*" Opal takes a sip of her water, but she won't meet my eyes.

"Keep telling yourself that." Trent slaps his hand on my shoulder. "Might even make it true."

"Whatever." I push off the bar, not willing to be their entertainment for the evening. "This is bullshit. I'm out."

"Oh, come on, lonely boy!" Trent shouts. "Don't bail. We're just having fun."

I flip them the bird but don't turn back. I'm tired of this party anyway, and Jayla isn't here. I wish I knew where the fuck she went. Isn't that her job, to keep us safe? How the hell is she gonna do that if she's nowhere to be found?

I walk out into the hotel lobby and when I don't find her here, a sliver of worry that something bad happened works into my mind. That's the reason I pull my cell out to text her. At least, that's the lie I tell myself.

Me: You okay?

I walk to the bank of elevators, my stride lazy and my gaze on my screen.

"Mr. Jones. Heading up to your room?" Ray, I think that's his name, says low and rough as he hits the call button for the elevator. He's on the security team and though I've never said more than two words to the guy, he always nods in greeting when we pass.

"Yeah," I say, remembering how Jayla asked we all request a security escort before heading back to our rooms. Fuck that. I'm not a baby. I don't need anyone to witness me slinking back to my bedroom alone—like a loser—so early in the evening only to report my actions back to Jayla later. How pathetic. "Forgot something in my room. I'll be back down."

He nods, holding the door open for me as I step inside. "Terrance is walking the halls if you need him. Or if you decide to stay in."

"Thanks, man," I say, but I don't like the way he hints at me staying in, as if he sees through my bullshit but won't completely call me on it.

I step into the elevator as my phone buzzes.

Jayla: Working. What's up?

I don't want to sound like a whiny bitch, but . . . fuck it. I step into the empty elevator and lift my room card to the sensor before pressing the top floor.

"Hold the door, please!" Before the doors shut, two women race to step inside. Ray stops them, but one of the woman shoves her ass against the open door, halting it from closing. Great. They giggle, talking in hushed tones to Ray, but I can feel their eyes on me. Normally, that'd be enough for me to lift my gaze and smile. Maybe flirt. But I'm most interested in why Jayla left the party and where she's working.

Me: I didn't see you leave. I didn't get to say good-night.

Jayla: Didn't realize I needed to check in with you.

She doesn't, but I can't deny I'd rather she did.

"Excuse me, Mr. Jones, would you rather these two ladies wait for the next elevator?"

I lift my gaze to find Ray and the two women staring. They look completely harmless, and I shrug, glancing around the empty lift, not caring one way or the other. "There's room in this one."

Ray's lip pinch and he gives a stiff nod. "I guess it's your lucky night." He allows them to clamber inside. "You get up to your rooms safely."

They giggle again, but my attention is back on my phone.

Me: What's your room number?

Jayla: Bye, Austin.

Me: Maybe I can tuck you in later?

Jayla: Good. Night.

I imagine she gives in to a smile even though she tries to fight it. It's probably better she doesn't share her room number. I'd be tempted to wait outside like some pathetic fool. Fuck. I shove my cell into my back pocket so I won't message her again. The guys were right for giving me shit. I'm pussy whipped, but without access to her slice of heaven.

The elevator stops and with a glance up at the number I realize it's my floor. The two women are still inside, coy smiles on their lips. And now that my face isn't buried in my phone, I notice how gorgeous they are. And how drunk. If eyes could fuck, that's the look I'm getting.

My bruised ego puffs up at their attention. I tip my chin and give in to a grin. Before the door slides shut, I step forward, my body blocking the sensors. "You ladies look like you're up to no good."

They giggle. The sound strokes my confidence, but it's nothing like Jayla's.

"Need help to your room?" one of them offers.

I pause, considering her proposition. They're both pretty, and I have no doubt they'd be up for a threesome. I imagine fucking one from behind while she eats out her friend. My dick full-out retreats with the idea. *Fucker.* The bastard can't think of anyone other than Jayla, too.

"I think I'll manage on my own tonight. Thanks."

Their gazes fall with disappointment, but I don't stick around to ease their rejection. I have one of my own to deal with, and I'm fully prepared to sulk in my room for the remainder of the night.

Fucking hell. How much of a loser am I? I'm a motherfucking rock star, and here I am turning in early on the rare night we don't have to ride a bus. I walk the distance to my room and slam the door behind me with more force than necessary. I'm pissed at myself for not being desirable enough for Jay. For not taking a random woman to my room. For overall sucking at life. I flip on the lights, going straight for the bar but not bothering with a glass as I split the plastic seal to the tiny Vodka bottle with a twist. I down it all within seconds, but the burn does nothing to dull the cycle of negative thoughts racing through my mind.

Sweat gathers on my brow. My clothes stick to my skin. What the fuck kind of liquor is this? I check the label and then realize it's the room that's too hot. As if maybe the air hasn't been running. I peel off my shirt, tossing it across the posh sitting area and then kick off my boots and socks before walking over to the thermostat.

"Fuck!" I shout to no one as I fiddle with the controls. The damn thing is off, which means it's probably not working. Just great. I'll be tossing and turning in my own sweat all night. Thankfully, the damn unit finally clicks on after some reprogramming, and as cool air blows out, I exhale my own frustration.

Nothing is going right. Nothing.

Because all I want is her.

She consumes every facet of my mind, like a skipping record. *Jayla. Jayla. Jayla.* I can't get her out of my head. Maybe it's only because she's on this tour and I'm forced to see her every day. Or maybe it's because I'm not accustomed to working for a woman's affection. But no. It's more than that. It's that I've never felt this kind of connection to one person. That combined with the fear that she doesn't return my attraction, that she doesn't want me in the same way I want her . . . it's maddening.

Knock, knock, knock. The sharp raps at the door startle me and I glance around, not sure exactly what I'm looking for. It's almost one in the fucking morning. I know it's not housekeeping. It's not my bandmates. And wish as I do, I know it's not Jayla, either. The probability of it being some hopeful groupie looking for a fuck slows my steps as I walk toward the door. Before I reach it, though, a white envelope slips through the bottom crack.

I squint, and lean into the door to view out the peephole, but it's completely dark. Strange. The beam of light beneath the door tells me the hallway lights work just fine.

Someone doesn't want me to see out. The thought hits me in the chest and I take a step back, my eyes trained on the damn letter as if it's a loaded gun, or a bomb ready to explode. My pulse races as apprehension prickles my skin. I think back to the girl from the party, the one who told me karma's a bitch, and wonder if I'm being served up a platter of that now. Or maybe this is connected to the package I received at Christmas?

I muster the courage to move closer and pick up the note, but there's another sharp knock followed by a shuffle of footsteps. *Fucking hell, stop being a pussy!* I'm not usually like this. I may not be the first to run into a burning building, but when it comes to the safety of those I love or defending my honor, I've been known to be a little reckless. I mentally slap myself for standing here like an idiot.

"Who's there?" I holler, proud of the strong and dominating tone of my words. But the only answer that comes is more wordless movement from the other side.

This is the scene in the horror film when the dude creeps toward danger, opens the door, and gets slaughtered. My mind wants to rationalize there's a perfectly acceptable reason for someone to be knocking at my door, but given everything that's happened, I can't bring myself to reach for the doorknob or retrieve the note. I'm too talented and young to die this way.

The paranoid sensation that someone has been watching and waiting to find me alone in this hotel scatters all rational thought. Fear, real and palpable, consumes my mind. I hate feeling scared. Hate being alone. It reminds me too much of my youth.

Fuck this shit. I don't need to do anything stupid like throw open that door, but I'm not gonna sit and quake under the covers, either. I slide my phone from my back pocket, my heart still hammering in my chest, and slink back to lock myself in the bathroom and call the one person who might actually kill me if I don't.

22

JAYLA

I STARE at the open exit door next to the hotel employee and try to not let my impatience and frustration show. This door, at the end of an employee-only corridor, has been propped open for God knows how long, and leaves the entire hotel at risk. "And you're sure one of the employees didn't do this? Maybe for a smoke break?"

"No, ma'am. We were all given explicit orders from your team to do nothing of the sort. Besides, our employees use the catering exit for smoke breaks."

I exhale a breath and kick out the brick before tapping my earpiece and speaking aloud to alert the team of a breach. "Unknown person, possibly several, may have accessed the hotel from an unmonitored door. No one gets in or out of that party until threat is cleared."

There's an audible chorus of groans in my ear at my words and I feel their pain. We went above and beyond, hired extra staff, and put every plan in place to ensure a relaxing and pleasurable party experience for the band and guests of WMI. And it's all for shit, because anyone could have come in through this door.

I turn back to the hotel manager. "This door was likely opened by a staff member. I need to know if anyone leaves early, goes home sick, or acts out of character." The guilty tend to grow a conscious after cash has exchanged hands.

"Of course. I'll check with each of the on-duty managers now."

"Thank you." I nod and walk back toward the main room. This exit doesn't offer a direct entrance to the party. Someone would have to either sneak through the busy kitchen unnoticed—nearly impossible—or walk out to the main lobby and then enter from there. "Manning?" I say into my Bluetooth. "Get tape of the front lobby and kitchen from the past hour, further back if needed. Our uninvited threat had to enter from there."

"On it, boss." He's running the intel on this event from his seat in one of the hotel rooms, and has an eagle eye view of the party, main entrances, and elevator bank.

My phone buzzes in my hand, an incoming call on the screen. *It's Austin.* I grit my teeth at the sight of his name as it scrolls across my cell. I am not in the mood for this right now. If he's calling because he's taking that blonde back to his room for the night, so help me, God, I can't be held responsible for chewing him out.

After his endearing little "Don't give up on me" speech to the masses on that video he posted, I started to consider his offer. I began envisioning an us—a future together—as more than just friends, or whatever it is we are. We have history, and obvious chemistry, and maybe, just maybe, I could trust him enough to lower my guard. He was asking for patience, after all, and I'd require the same in return.

But it was only an act. I should have known. Damn it, I feel so fucking stupid. He wasn't even willing to wait one night. At the party, he wasted no time finding another woman. I squeeze my eyes shut a second, remembering the way he checked out her flawless body. How he showered her with his complete attention while I looked on from across the room. I shake my head, angry at myself for expecting anything more from someone like him, a famous rock star used to instant gratification. I'd allowed our past and my own desires to cloud my good judgment.

Shame on me. It won't happen again. If he's calling because he needs me to do a background check on a one-night stand, I *will* give him a piece of my mind. Or be tempted to send her packing with a lie. I knew going into this it'd be part of my job. Clearing any person a band member requests to spend one-on-one time with, but hell if I'll do it with a smile.

"Please tell me this is important." I pick up before the call goes to voicemail, my reply dry with no hint of my inner turmoil. "Because I'm a little busy at the moment."

"So . . ." He chuckles, but it's an awkward sound. "I'm in my room right now." He pauses and clears his throat. "Actually, the bathroom."

I stop walking and pinch the bridge of my nose. He's going to ask me to clear that woman. *He's going to fuck someone else tonight.* A surge of jealous anger pulses through my veins and this time I don't attempt to contain my irritation. "And that's important to me how?"

"Er . . . uh . . ." He laughs again, but there's a catch to the sound and my body tenses with concern. "Someone keeps knocking on the door, and I'd check who, but I think they blocked the peephole."

He's in danger. My gut knows it, and I react immediately. My first impulse is to start running, but I settle for long quick strides, pushing past the kitchen staff to make my way to the employee elevator.

"Who else is with you?"

"I'm alone." His answer shouldn't deliver relief, but it does.

"I'll be right up."

"You don't have to. I just wanted to check-in, in case I get murdered in my sleep or something." He's joking. Fucking joking, but there's a glint of fear in his words he can't mask and it churns my gut with an extra layer of alarm.

"That's not gonna happen." I have each of the guys' hotel rooms memorized, and access to all of them. I dig into my backpack to retrieve the hotel card and as I step inside the lift, I swipe it on the sensor and press the button for the top floor. "I'm on my way up. Give me five. And stay in your room."

He doesn't respond right away and the silence that stretches only causes another wave of unease to wash over me. I open my mouth to say his name, to make sure he's still with me, but before I can speak, his voice, low and deep, interrupts. "Be careful, please. I don't know why, but I have a bad feeling about this."

Me, too. I reach for my holstered gun to touch the metal, a nervous habit from my days on the force. "Four minutes. Stay in that room. I'm ending our call now. I need to check in with my team."

"Be careful," he warns again, and I end the call.

I don't waste a second getting one of my guys on the line. "Ray?"

"Yes, ma'am."

"Please tell me you escorted Austin Jones to his room this evening."

"No, ma'am."

I blow out a breath, but before I can ask him why the hell not, Ray continues as if he's read my mind.

"Terrance? He's still on floor duty." His assignment was to stay on the same floor as the guys' suites. An extra security measure in case any of them decided to ride the elevator up without detail. "He checked in about an hour ago."

An hour? *Shit.* That timeline coincides with when I estimate the staff entrance was left open and unsecured. "Damn it." I should have hired more staff. Assigned each of the guys a bodyguard. Installed more surveillance. Demanded they cancel this PR event.

I watch the floor numbers light up as I ascend, but they move at a painfully slow pace. Seconds feel like minutes, but it's the adrenaline pumping in my veins mixed with the need to protect Austin from this unknown threat. I tap on my ear piece again, bringing everyone on the line. "Brian, you're lead until further notice."

"Yes, ma'am."

The elevator doors roll open and I step out cautiously, quiet, unsure of exactly what danger exists, but determined to clear the floor and get to Austin without problems. The heavy fall of sure footfalls approaches from around the corner, and my hand goes to my gun.

A familiar face turns the corner and his hands fly up as his gaze notices my stance. "Whoa, it's just me."

"Terrance." I heave a rush of breath. "Feel like taking a walk?" I motion toward the way he came.

His lips twitch with the trace of a grin. "Where you go, I go," he says and together we make our way to Austin's door. If I ran it'd take two minutes, but we stop along the way, clearing any area someone could be hiding—the staff storeroom, the vending nook, the small common sitting area near the elevator bank.

"Anyone been up here? Anything suspicious?"

"No, boss," he says. "Besides Mr. Willis and his guest—the girl-friend—it's been kinda boring."

There's nothing out of order. No evidence left behind of any wrongdoing or shady business—not that there needs to be, but the lack of chaos does loosen some of the worry and stress from my limbs.

"What about Mr. Jones?"

"What about him?"

That prickle of fear surges back, along with a dose of concern. "He's in his room. Did you not see him come up?" I gesture to Austin's door and immediately I notice the coating on the peep hole. I scrape it away with my nail, a simple white sticker coming off with ease.

Terrance lowers his gaze, a glimmer of guilt passing over his features. "Maybe I missed him?" He bites the inside of his cheek. "Might have been the same time room service came up?"

"Room service?" Jesus. Was everyone and their mother getting around our security measures? I pinch the bridge of my nose and shake my head. My hand flies up to stop his explanation. I swipe my card to unlock Austin's door and inch it open. Nothing seems out of place. Hell, the suite looks pristine but for the open liquor bottle on the bar. Terrence pads forward, clearing the large living space and attached bedroom with a quick sweep while I walk to the closed bathroom door. I give it a knock. "Austin? Everything okay in there?"

The door flies open. He stands there looking as handsome as earlier, if not more, and the moment his eyes lock with mine he wraps me in a bone crushing embrace.

A throat clears at my back. "Boss, um, everything is clear."

Austin's arms go stiff, as if he realizes how improper this must look to my employee, and he releases me from his hold.

"Thanks, Terrance." I turn and nod toward the door. "False alarm. You can go back to your station."

"Call if you need anything." He taps his earlobe and nods before heading out the door. The latch clicks into place, the soft sound feeling so much louder than it should in our silence.

My mind reels, connecting the pieces of everything that's happened, and how exactly I found myself here, standing in Austin's hotel room. The two of us alone. My body prickles with awareness, and yeah, attraction too. That's when it hits me. "There's nothing here." My eyebrows furrow as I turn to meet his gaze, but instead I catch him staring at my breasts. My pride flares with indignation. "There wasn't even a knock, was there?"

His eyes widen, and he almost looks shocked by my accusation. His chin jerks back and forth under my glare. "You think I made this up? Shit, Jay. I'm hard up, but I'm not that desperate."

I almost believe him. If I hadn't fallen for his expert manipulation before, I probably would. "Because this isn't some fucking joke. I'm not here for your entertainment." I take a step forward, my spine straight and tone hard.

"That's not—" He stops, runs his hand through the locks of his hair and tugs at their roots. He stares and meets my gaze with a steely one of his own. "I swear. Jayla, I'm a fuck-up about a lot of things, but I'd never lure you to my room under the pretense of a threat. I don't joke about the safety of my band."

His explanation holds merit and I find myself waver.

"I've heard you laugh off everything." I tip my chin to better hold his gaze.

"Not this. Swear it." He shuffles forward a step, bringing our bodies closer.

"Right now your word doesn't hold much weight." My words stretch between us. The memory of him hitting on that woman downstairs only an hour ago brings a sharpness I usually hold back.

"That's not fair." His jaw tightens and the tension winds tighter, like a band about to snap.

"No?" I challenge and lift my brow, begging him to argue.

"I've *never* lied to you. I never would." The gravelly scrape of his low tone sends a thrill up my spine and my body comes alive, not with adrenaline this time, but need. Desire. Want.

I don't dare open my mouth, even to argue, because I'm absolutely sure if I do, he will sense my longing. Besides, he won't change my opinion with words when it's his actions that garner my mistrust.

His gaze drops first, and then he practically shouts, "See!" His finger shoots out, pointing at the floor near the doorway. "That's what someone slipped under the door. And the air conditioner was off."

It is warm in here, but there's a steady stream of cold air pumping from the ceiling vent.

"I turned it back on," he says, as if he can read my thoughts, and shrugs in defeat before brushing past to retrieve the letter. "And the peephole was blocked. I wasn't making that up."

"It was a sticker," I grumble, and take the envelope from him. It's hotel watermarked and the flap is sealed shut. I peel it open, and inside is a note handwritten on matching stationary.

New set. 24-48 hours. Expect link.

I tilt my head and hand over the letter, having no clue what this means. But I want a full view of Austin's reaction in case he does and won't tell me.

His eyes widen for a fraction a second, and if I weren't staring critically, I would have missed it.

"You want to tell me what that means?" I tilt my chin and blow out a breath.

"No clue." He passes it back to me as if it's nothing.

"Really?" I carefully fold the letter and place it back into the envelope, choosing my next words wisely. He's hiding something. Or protecting someone? Either way, I don't want him on guard. If he senses my suspicion he might close off completely. "Maybe the hotel staff got the wrong door?"

"Maybe." He shoves his hands into the front pockets of his jeans and shrugs.

So, that's how he's gonna play this? Fine. I'll bring my own tactics. "Thirsty?"

His gaze shoots to mine with a stare so hot my lips suddenly feel parched. He lifts his brow. "You offering to help?"

I swallow hard at the innuendo and tip my chin to the bar. "You were drinking."

"Right." He nods and I swear he almost appears disappointed. *In me? In himself?*

"You left the party early." I don't know why I keep pointing out the obvious, but I can't seem to stop. Tension builds in the air with our silence. I don't entirely trust myself when it comes to Austin.

"Yeah, well." He rocks on his heels before flicking his gaze to mine. "The only person I wanted to hang with was unavailable."

My heart rate picks up, my pulse racing under the implication of his words. He couldn't be referring to—?

"You left," he blames.

"I was working."

"Was?" His brow lifts with challenge.

"Am. Still."

"But you're here with me now." He drags out the words.

My body does the strangest thing, tightening with hyper-aware-ness of how close we're standing, and at the same time straining to lean closer. "Because you were supposedly under attack."

His chuckle scatters goosebumps across my flesh. "I feel like an idiot." He smiles that damn smile. As if it's just for me.

"Why did you post that video?" The question flies from my mouth before I have the good sense to keep it in. I shouldn't care so much about his words and the disappointment he filled me with tonight, but I do.

"The one we made?"

I swallow and conjure a confidence I don't necessarily feel. I already brought it up, no use in backing down now. "The part you added at the end. The message for me."

He nods, evaluating me as if he's unsure of how to proceed, but he must settle on a decision quickly because he takes a step forward, his gaze steady and open. "I'm not sure whether you're aware, but I like you, Jayla."

I like you. What does that even mean? His stare leaves no doubt, but his behavior at tonight's after party? "You also liked that woman at the bar."

His lips tug at the corners and the trace of his smile appears. "I thought I could make you jealous."

I lift my brows and roll my eyes. It worked, and I hate myself for it. But I'm not interested in playing games. Spinning on my heel, I turn toward the door.

He catches my arm. "Wait. Jay. Stay." He moves in front of the door. "I was stupid. I am stupid. But if we're laying things out, being totally honest, I thought maybe I'd find a woman to bring back here tonight." He reaches his hand out as if he wants me to hold it.

I raise my hands in front of my body to ward off his advance, or maybe it's to push away the hurtfulness of knowing he intended to sleep with someone tonight. Someone who was not me. "Don't."

His eyes cloud with sincerity, and even his lips turn down in a frown. "Stupid idea, because like I said before, there's only one woman I want."

I stare, unwilling to do more than inhale a shaky breath. I won't admit how much his words stoke the hope building in my mind. I should walk out of this room right now. But my mouth must have other thoughts. "So then, why did you come back here alone?"

"You, Jayla. You're the only one I want." His declaration takes me by surprise, and next, his lips. The remaining space between us disappears in one long stride of his feet, and then his chin dips, his heavy lidded gaze holding mine right up until the second his mouth presses over mine.

My pulse races, my body heats, and then I'm opening my mouth to him, eager for a taste.

His tongue brushes across my lips, soft at first, and then dips inside, possessive and tangling with mine as if he can't get enough. He shuffles forward, his hands at my hips, and I let him lead until my back hits the wall.

Panic flares at the sensation, but damn it, I won't let my past steal this moment. My hands reach for his chest and I push. Maybe a little too hard, because he stops kissing me. Our breaths mingle together, ragged and out of control. My chest brushes against his with each deep inhale. His gaze searches mine, but I don't want to talk about why I freak out every time my body feels caged in. I want his lips back on mine. I need this. Need him.

I shrug my shoulders and allow my small backpack to slide off my arms until it hits the floor with a thud. Snaking one of my hands into the nape of his hair, I thread my fingers through his locks and tug his lips back to mine. He doesn't attack my mouth this time, probably still confused as to why I stopped to begin with. But it gives me the opportunity to set the pace, to lead, and my anxiety fades as my lips move against his. With my other hand, I press against his chest and move us until the backs of his legs hit the sofa.

"Sit," I demand, rough and low. The desire in my voice surprises my own ears.

Austin doesn't argue, or skip a beat. His butt hits the cushion. His hands skim up the backs of my thighs, his eyes searching mine as I stand over him. My hands settle on his shoulders for balance and I straddle his lap, my knees pressing into the cushions on either side of him before my mouth finds his again.

His hands skirt along my hips, then slide back to squeeze my ass. *No!*

Panic flares and I rip his hands off, gripping his wrists tightly and pressing them into the couch, a safe distance from my body. I expect him to question, or at the very least stop kissing me back, but instead he groans, releasing the most erotic sound. His hips lift and his hardness presses against the apex of my thighs.

He's into this.

This might actually work.

I resist the urge to sob, because fuck, it's been so long since I've had sex—good sex—and this is Austin, the man I dreamed about, the boy I once thought hung the moon, and if I'm honest, the guy who's consumed my thoughts since our lives became intertwined once again.

I suck his bottom lip into my mouth and nip it before resting back on my heels. I release his hands and resist the urge to grind down on his erection.

His gaze is molten, hot and heavy with lust, but he waits for me to make the next move.

"I like to be in charge," I say.

He doesn't even blink. "You have my full cooperation."

Fuck. That's hot. I reach for the hem of my shirt and peel it off, slowly, but it snags going over my head. My eyes fly wide open and I fumble with my earpiece. *Dear God!* I hope I didn't broadcast our make out session to the entire security team.

I'm weak with relief when I find everything still muted. I climb off Austin's lap and step away from his gaze to check in with Brian.

"Everything okay, boss?" he asks at my call.

Okay? *It's fantastic.* My gaze drifts to Austin, half-naked and notably aroused, sitting a few feet away, and decide for once in my life to throw caution to the wind. I don't do impulsive. I don't take uncalculated risks. But between the heat in Austin's gaze and the wetness between my legs, I allow temptation to lead. "I need you to take over for the rest of the night. Can you do that?"

"Sure. Yeah." Surprise tinges his tone. "You feel okay?"

It's a loaded question, but I reach for a bit of truth to justify my actions. "I'm fine. Just following up on a lead. If you need anything, or any issues arise, call my cell."

"Got it," Brian says.

"And remind everyone about the briefing tomorrow morning."

"Conference room, nine o'clock sharp. On it."

"Thank you," I say, and end the call. Austin's gaze trains on my body, and I swear he leaves tingles with each sweep of his eyes. I turn off my earpiece, remove my holster and gun, then kick off my shoes—all the while meeting Austin's stare. *This man.* He drives me to do crazy things. Things outside my comfort zone. The desire from one look emboldens me to ditch my pants too, before strutting over to him in nothing but my bra and panties.

"You're so damn gorgeous," he whispers, his gaze greedy but body unmoving. *Because he respects me? Because he's giving me permission to lead?* Either way, this moment between us feels safe. Sacred. He's mine—maybe not for long, but for this night—and for this fraction of time we're the only two people who exist.

"Take off your jeans."

He shucks them down his hips, kicks them out of the way, and leans back onto the sofa. His erection is obscene, hard and pressing to escape those tight boxer briefs. He's bigger than I remember. Or maybe the last time we were together I was too embarrassed to stare. That, and I had nothing to compare him to. Not anymore.

His lips quirk as I close the space between us.

"What's so funny?" I ask.

"Nothing. I like when you look at my dick."

"Yeah?" I release a soft laugh.

"Yeah. He promises not to embarrass himself this time."

"He?" I straddle his hips again, this time allowing my hands to run up and down his chest. "You refer to yourself in third person now?"

He shivers at my touch, his voice raspy. "No, my dick promises."

"Sure he can keep that promise?" I tease, reaching between us to stroke his length over his underwear. Wanting to feel him, I slide my hands under his waistband and wrap my hands around his hardness. I squeeze firmly, stroking him, and relish in the power I feel when he lets loose a groan.

Austin coughs out a laugh, and his entire body flexes as if touching him causes him pain. "Not if you keep that up."

I let go of his hard-on and find his gaze. "Sorry?" I murmur and lift an eyebrow.

"Fuck." He grins back. "Don't apologize for anything you're doing right now." His hands come up to cup my face, and he arches up away from the backrest to brush his lips over mine.

I kiss him back, but when his hands move to wander down my neck, I reach for his wrists and press them against the back of the couch. "Hands here," I murmur against his mouth.

"Yes, ma'am." His fingers dig into the upholstery.

We kiss again, and this time I allow myself to get lost in the touch of his lips, our soft moans, and the brush of his tongue inside my mouth. My sex clenches with each delicious movement, and the scraps of fabric separating us do little to contain my wetness or his hard length. Without meaning to my hips move, grinding myself along his cock in search of release from the pressure building deep in my core.

God, he feels good. So good, and I'm close. Closer than I've ever been. That is, if I don't count the times I've gotten myself off alone. Adjusting my movements, I grind down harder and my clit brushes against his pelvis to bring me closer with each swivel of my hips. My fingers leave his shoulders to tangle in his hair and tug at the strands.

He groans and his hips lift on a thrust to match my movements. *Yes, right there.* His fingers brush over my hip once before gripping my butt.

I shake my head, grab his wrist and pin his damn arm back to the couch. "Keep touching me and I'll use my cuffs." My threat comes out harsher than I intend, but I can't contain my frustration at being pulled from the moment, especially after being so close to orgasm.

His face lights with desire, and the lust in my veins amps up at his gaze alone. Even his length hardens further against my center.

"You want me to tie you up"—I cock my head and study his reaction—"don't you?"

He holds my gaze—so damn serious, a rarity for him—and then nods. He likes it. Or at least the idea.

My colleagues used to brag all the time about using their cuffs on their sexual partners. Their wives and girlfriends liked being tied up and at their mercy. That'd be a hard no for me, but I'm not like most women. Guys joke about wanting to play with my cuffs, but that's only because they imagine getting to act out some low-budget porn where the bad guy fucks the cop. I consider telling this to Austin, but there's something in his gaze, a vulnerability that makes me believe he's not joking. He actually wants this. And if he's restrained, I don't have to worry about him touching me. About the ghosts of my past barging their way past his fingertips and painting my skin with shame and disgust. I could let go. Totally.

"Okay." I nod, still holding his stare. "Don't move."

His gaze widens, as though he didn't anticipate I'd take him up on the offer. But it's full of excitement, not fear, so I climb off and grab my bag from the floor.

I walk over to the bar, needing space to calm my racing pulse. The anticipation of what we're about to do, of my own excitement, is almost overwhelming. But I want this. Him. And that's all the confirmation I need to unzip one of the pockets and remove the metal handcuffs. I turn to him and take in my fill of his body. Sexy. Masculine. Ink sprawls over his skin like paint on a canvas. He's a work of art.

"Take off your underwear," I demand.

Again, he follows my directions without argument or verbal sparring. This version of Austin is different. But his dick bobs as if it can't wait until I return to shamelessly rubbing myself against him and chasing my release.

I can't wait either. Reaching around my back, I release the clasp of my bra and drop it to the floor.

"Oh, fuck, yes." Austin groans, watching intently as I return to him. His eyes shift between my naked breasts and the restraints dangling from one of my hands. In the depths of his irises I find my own desire reflecting back.

Standing before him, I bend over to reach for one of his hands and stand to circle the metal restraint around his wrist. He offers me his other hand with total trust. The sharp click of the cuffs practically echoes off the walls as I slide and lock each one into place.

We should move to the bed. It'd be more comfortable for him. But I don't want to break this spell we've created or chase another freak-out on my part, so instead I raise his arms over his head and help him settle onto the couch so his head rests on the sofa's arm and his body lies stretched out across the cushions. His long legs don't have much room, but he makes it work by bending one and hanging the other off the side with his foot on the floor.

"Please tell me you have the key." He chuckles, a low and throaty sound as I discard my panties and straddle his thighs.

"I lift my brow. "Already backing out?"

"Fuck, no." He almost groans, and we both glance down at his bobbing erection. "I just don't want to be stuck here forever. I do have a show tomorrow."

"They're not too tight?" I climb over his body, my fingers caressing his skin from his chest to his shoulders, and then the length of his arms to slip a finger between his flesh and the metal cuffs.

"Perfect," he mutters, his face pressed between my breasts. Before I can sit back, his mouth captures one of my nipples and laves his tongue across the sensitive flesh.

My sex clenches and a groan escapes my lips.

He continues to suck my nipple, only releasing it with a pop when I sit back on my heels.

Taking his length in my hands, I stroke the soft skin over his hard flesh, determined to drive him insane with need. To bring him to the same crazy lust I feel inside myself. His hips attempt to buck off the couch, but without the use of his arms, my thick thighs hold him in place. The head of his cock beads with precum and I gently brush it away with the pad of my thumb. My actions are meant to drive him wild, but my own anticipation builds with each touch of his skin. The wetness of my desire grows with each sexy groan that falls from his blessed mouth. The need to have him inside me overcomes my intention to keep this controlled.

"I want to taste you," he says, his gaze zeroing in on my pussy.

Jacking him with one hand, I use my other to dip two fingers inside my core. He watches. I love his eyes on me. Love how he stares as though he can't get enough, or I'm doing something so captivating that it's the only thing that matters. I pump my fingers inside myself a few times, the wetness filling the silence. His eyes practically roll back into his head on a groan.

"You want a taste?" I don't know what comes over me, other than the surge of power that comes from this position, from the sense of control I've never experienced before this. "Ask me for it."

"Please let me taste that pussy. Please, Jayla."

My fingers slip from my wetness and into his mouth. My entire body lights with need as he groans around my fingers, sucking and licking the taste of me away.

His dick thickens in my hands.

"Austin Jones, I didn't realize you had a kinky side." My voice comes out husky and deep.

"You have no idea."

A thrill goes up my spine and my body comes alive with another wave of desire. The air is heavy with the scent of my arousal, the smell of sex. I blame that for my next words. "Do you want me to touch your cock now? Suck you off?"

"Yes," he grunts out, staring at the space between our bodies. To where I go back to fingering myself with one hand and wrapping around his erection with the other. "No." His gaze flies to mine and swims with something I can't define.

"What?" I swallow. I want him to trust me enough to voice whatever it is he's holding back. "What do you want?"

"You." His lips part and he exhales on a rush. "I want you."

I want him, too. It's the first thought I have before I rub the head of his cock against the wetness of my folds. "I'm clean," I whisper, captivated at the erotic sight of our bodies so close together.

His body jerks, as if it's suddenly hard for him to not be in control. His eyes shine bright with heat. "I am, too."

"I know." It's in his report. "Unless you've been with someone since."

"I haven't been with anyone. Not since—" He swallows as if reconsidering what he was going to say. "The tour."

Of course. When would he have? We've been together every stop, and he hasn't invited anyone onto the bus. There've been no groupies in the green room. But his gaze holds more tenderness than a man who's excited to get laid.

My heart races, and this time it's from fear. Fear that I can't handle whatever it is he wants. "This is a fuck. You get that, right?"

His smile spreads. "Who has the dirty mouth now?"

"Austin." I drag out his name, but I can't seem to tear my fingers from his shaft. I like how it feels in my hands. I love the way I feel in control. I want to press my hips forward and take him in, every delicious inch.

"Do you want me to beg? Because I will. I have thought of nothing but—" He stops to swallow, pausing as if he's unsure whether he should continue.

"Tell me. No bullshit. Not now."

"Sinking inside your pussy. Those tits in my face. I want you to touch me and fuck me and most of all . . ."

I wait. As much as it frustrates me that I even care, I want to know every single one of his desires.

"I want whatever you're willing to give me."

My mouth suddenly feels as dry as the desert. I draw in a breath and lick my lips, as if that'll help.

"But Jayla? If we're gonna fuck . . . put my dick out of its misery soon. Please."

"Just fucking," I say, but it comes out more like a warning because I need to set the rules. I can't risk being out of control, even with Austin. I sink down his shaft, groaning at the blissful fullness he brings. "This is what I want," I whisper as I ignore the emotion pressing into my chest. Inch by glorious inch he disappears inside me, our bodies connected, this moment finally happening.

My throat feels thick and my eyes rapidly blink. Oh, my God. No. I am not crying.

But the impulse to do that hits me square in the chest.

"So damn good," Austin murmurs, and it only causes my eyes to fill further. *This is good for him, too. He thinks I'm good.*

Forcing a slow exhalation, I try to get hold of my emotions or at the very least, calm my racing pulse.

"Touch yourself." Austin's strangled plea brings me back into the moment. His gaze is hotter than his words. "Please. Touch yourself for me."

I nod and focus on his desire. On my needs. My hands brush over my breasts to play with my hard nipples while I rock my hips. He's big and hard, but my body adjusts to the fullness, and soon my clit is aching for stimulation too.

"That's it," Austin pants between shallow breaths. "You are so damn sexy. Fuck." His whispered encouragement spurs me forward without shame or inhibition. "And beautiful. Keep going. Don't stop."

I watch him watching me until the heat of his gaze practically sets my skin on fire. I stop thinking, give in to the sensations, and allow my eyelids to close. Skin on skin. Hard and soft. Breathy moans. We connect mind, body, and soul. I forget where his pleasure begins and mine ends.

I crash over the edge before I even see it coming. My release moves through my body with so much force my toes curl, legs shake, and my thighs squeeze against Austin.

"Fuck, yes, baby. I'm coming." A throaty groan erupts from his lips, and his muscles tighten with tension. His elbows bend, back arches, and hips lift as he comes inside of me. He exhales a few ragged breaths before lifting his gaze to mine.

Our eyes lock, and I swear the rapid beating of my heart stills. A pang of longing presses against my chest to have this—him—always.

23

AUSTIN

MOST FANTASIES in life a man eventually gives up.

Like riding a unicorn. Or owning an ice cream shop for the convenience of eating mint chocolate chip every day. Finding the pot of gold at the end of the rainbow. Or one of my long time favorites, jamming out in a practice studio with the legendary Jimi Hendrix.

But there is one, and as far-fetched as it may be, I've always held out hope. Only when it finally happens, reality blows my imagination out of the fucking water.

That's how it is when Jayla offers to cuff me. I won't lie, it's been a dream of mine for many, many years. But longer still, probably as long as I've understood the desire to sink my dick in a woman, is the fantasy of being with Jayla. I've imagined fucking her in all the ways, but this, her restraining me and getting us both off? *Fuck.* I've never experienced sex this good. Ever. And for as much as I've had, that's saying something.

Then again, this is Jayla. Everything with her is better.

"Good?" I ask, looking up into her big brown eyes. Her legs straddle my hips and our bodies still connect as we catch our breath. The need to touch her pulses through my veins. I want to tug her body down to mine and hold her close until I'm ready for round two, but unfortunately, I can't do any of those things. Not with my hands still bound together.

"Yeah," she answers, and with that one word it's as if she disappears. She avoids my gaze, looking a million miles away, and climbs off my body. "I'll just . . ." She stares down at me, then the cuffs, before glancing toward the bathroom.

"Take care of yourself first. I'm good." My lips lift in a grin and I waggle my brows in an attempt to put her at ease. "As long as you don't leave me here all night."

"Yeah." She tries for a smile, but it doesn't quite reach her eyes, and then she retrieves her clothes on the way to the bathroom without a backward glance.

Shit. She doesn't regret being with me, does she? It was good for her, I swear it was. The second I felt her falling apart, her inner walls squeezing my cock, I let myself go too. But fuck, maybe I was overeager? That would be embarrassing. I no longer have the excuse of being a fumbling, inexperienced teen. Failing her twice would be a nail in the coffin of any chance of a future relationship or coupling.

What the fuck? We screw once and now I want her as my girlfriend? I don't *do* relationships. Only, the thought of having Jayla as mine forever doesn't sound bad. Not bad at all. In fact, it sounds glorious as fuck.

Damn it.

When Trent fell so hard for Lexi, I chalked up his obsession to weakness on his part. I mean, she's a cool chick, but if this is what it feels like? If this is—dare I say it—*love?* Hell, I get why each of the guys toppled easier than a row of dominos.

The sound of the toilet flushing and the sink running pushes me to sit up on the couch. I'm making a mess all over these cushions, but I can't even feel bad about it. Cupping my junk in my hands, I push to my feet.

I love her. I love Jayla. I always have.

The realization beats steady in my chest, filling me with a joy I can't contain.

Jayla emerges from the bathroom seconds later. *Fully dressed.*

My excitement over my newly discovered feelings dulls at the sight of her reaching for her shoes and walking over to her bag. "Hey," I say dumbly. "Where are you going?"

She digs into her bag and produces a set of tiny keys. "Back to my room." She dangles the keys and presses her lips together. "But first, I'll let you go." She closes the space between us and I just stare, searching for some sign she's bluffing. She doesn't want to leave, does she? I don't want this moment to be over. Not when we're just getting started.

Her hands trail over my arms, caressing the skin around my sore wrists and scattering goosebumps in their wake. With two twists of the key, the metal restraints release and she drops my hands. I immediately mourn the loss of her touch.

"My bed is better," I blurt out. It's a ridiculous argument, but it's the first that comes to mind.

Jayla's gaze lifts to mine. "Austin, I can't stay here."

"You're worried about the label finding out?"

"No." She shakes her head once, and then nods. "Yes."

"Jesus, Jay. You're making me feel like shit. Was it—" I cup my junk again, all of a sudden feeling underdressed for this conversation, and maybe also a little inadequate. "Was it not good for you?"

"I just . . ." She exhales in a rush before meeting my gaze. "I don't want to confuse this with what it is. We hooked up. Fine, we're both adults. But we work together, Austin. Things are complicated enough."

So, the sex was good. *Thank God.* "Because I swear you orgasmed first. I could have held off longer—"

She cuts me off with a short laugh. "Austin."

"What?" I shrug. "I promised you a better performance than last time."

"It was good." She glances at my body and her eyes blaze with desire.

"Just good?"

"Best sex of my life."

"Hold up. Let me get my phone so I can record it when you repeat that." A shit eating grin stretches my lips.

She laughs heartily. "Oh, I'm never repeating those words."

I hope she realizes the gauntlet she just laid down. Challenge fucking accepted.

"I need to go," she says, and I can read the resignation in her eyes. As good as this was, she doesn't want to stay here with me now. Fuck if that doesn't hurt a little.

My mind races with a thousand ways to convince her how good we'd be together, but even I know that argument is better left for another day. Right now, I just want to be with the woman who rocks my entire world. "Stay for a while? We don't have to sleep. I just don't want you to go yet."

She's wavering. I can see it in the way she no longer eyes the door.

"Please."

"I don't know if I can." The way she mutters those words . . . an irrational surge of protectiveness overcomes me.

"Why not?"

She swallows hard and glances at the floor. "Nothing. It's nothing. I'll stay." The defeat in her features puts my entire body on edge. It's not nothing. It never is.

"Come on." I hold out my hand to her, relieved when she clasps it. I lead her into the adjoining bedroom, and then I let her go just long enough to retrieve a T-shirt from my bag and a pair of sleep shorts for me. "This'll be more comfortable." I hand her the shirt.

She holds it up, a laugh bursts from her lips. "I am *not* wearing this."

"What?" I lift my brow; a surge of pleasure runs through my body at her laughter. "It's a true statement."

She scrutinizes the 'I spent a night with Three Ugly Guys' graphic tee. "People actually buy these?"

"One of our best sellers." I grin.

She blows out a breath, rolls her eyes, and shakes her head, but in the end she ditches her shirt and slacks for the soft cotton. The fabric of my shirt hugs her curves and those fantastic breasts, but my favorite part is how it's not long enough to cover her ass. I'm treated to a nice view of her butt cheeks, her sexy boy short underwear doing nothing to contain the luscious curves.

"Better?" I ask and plop down on the sheets. I prop the pillows at my back and then pat the empty space beside me.

She nods and climbs onto the bed.

The urge to hold her pushes my hand out to reach for hers. I smile when she doesn't pull away. Turning onto my side, I study her gaze. My thumb traces soft circles over her hand, memorized by the contrast of my pale inked fingers against her dark skin. We're opposite in so many ways, but we fit perfectly. "So, if the sex was good and you don't totally hate being around me"—I lift my gaze to hers —"why'd you try and run?"

Her body stiffens. "I wasn't running."

"You know what I mean." I go back to tracing patterns on her skin, letting the silence stretch between us.

"I don't do sleepovers."

But there's more. She's holding out on me. Protecting something or someone and I want to know. I want her to trust me enough to share. The vulnerability in her gaze is locked behind a fortress. By my guess, most leave before they make it through.

"Jayla. No more bullshit. Tell me. Why?"

Her jaw locks, and she pulls her hand from mine to wrap her arms across her chest. I wait her out, knowing she'll explain when she's good and ready. More minutes pass and my gut churns with fear. I won't push her, but I won't let her shut me out. Not anymore.

"It's really hard for me to talk about," she admits barely above a whisper. She pulls her knees to her chest, her back straight against the headboard. Her body is armed like a shield. But I can't tell what she's trying to ward off, me or something else.

"I'm right here." I sit up, moving in front of her to sit cross-legged on the mattress.

She lifts her gaze. "I don't want you to look at me differently. I don't want your pity. This doesn't define me. I've moved on. Done a lot of work to get to where I am."

"Jay, you're scaring me." I hold out my hands and open my palms, hoping she'll take them.

After a quiet moment, she does. "Don't stop looking at me the way you have been."

"And how's that?"

She blinks, emotion thick in her voice. "Like I'm perfect."

Like it's possible she could be anything but.

"Jay, I swear to you right now, I won't ever stop looking at you like you're perfect, because you are."

She cringes at my words.

"You're perfect to me. Always. It's okay. Whatever it is. You can tell me."

She takes one long look, as if she's gauging me with a bullshit meter, and I must pass. When she finally glances away, she opens her mouth. From her beautiful lips she spills her secrets. Confesses everything in a voice so soft if I weren't this close I might miss the words. In the safe space of this hotel suite, in the quiet of the night, she trusts me with her pain, her nightmare, her excruciating sadness, and I never stop holding her hands. I refuse to let them go because if I do she might realize she's breaking my heart.

24

JAYLA

MUSIC PLAYS, and my uncle swings his wife around the kitchen while the rest of the women laugh and cheer. My other uncle and his friends sit outside the open window with my dad. The small apartment patio makes the perfect place for them to smoke. The thick, humid air from early today is long gone, and the breeze cools the sweat along my neck. My cotton shirt sticks to my skin no matter how many times I pull it away.

"It's late. Time for bed, Jayla." My mama dismisses me from the room.

I longingly glance to where my older cousins crowd around the table with my brothers. Dealing cards, trading jokes, and having all the fun. After helping my aunt and Mama clean up from dinner, I hoped to join them.

"Can't I stay up a little longer?" I all but beg, though it's pointless.

Her lips tighten and form a thin line, the wrinkles at the corners of her mouth more prominent with her scowl. "No. It's late. You need sleep for that test."

My SAT scores are my ticket to a college scholarship. At least that's my plan. Dad still hasn't found work, but even when he does, it won't be enough to pay for college. And after high school I need to do something that offers us a better life. I don't want a future like my parents', one of arguing, a mountain of debt, and having to move around so much. Mama and Dad haven't stopped fighting even though we've been staying with my uncle's family for over a month. I don't understand why we even moved. Things were supposed to be better here, but they're not. I miss my friends. I miss Austin.

"Fine." I give off just enough attitude to let her know my dissatisfaction, but not enough that I'll pay the consequences later. She's right. I've studied too hard for the SATs and I can't afford to fail. Begrudgingly, I stomp down the hall, sticking out my tongue, childish as it is, as my older brother Desmond grins. Boys have all the fun. He has to work early, but Mama won't send him to bed for hours.

I change into clean underwear and a lightweight tank and shorts. It's too hot for anything else, and in the room I share with my brother I'm not allowed to open the window more than a few inches. The neighborhood isn't that safe. I dart across the hall to the bathroom, using the restroom and brushing my teeth before padding back to my room. I leave the door cracked, not because I'm scared or anything, but so I can hear down the hall.

I climb into bed and throw the covers off my body. Voracious laughter reminds me I'm missing out on all the fun. Stupid test. Stupid Mama. I'm not a child anymore. I'll be seventeen next month, but, that doesn't matter because they'll always regard me as a little girl. That's what happens when you're the youngest.

The fan by my bed squeaks, the rhythm familiar, and despite my irritation and the party outside my room, my eyelids close with the heaviness of sleep. I don't know how long they stay shut, but a prickle of unease pulls me to consciousness. The sounds of merriment down the hall mute as my door latches with a soft click.

There's someone in my room.

My first reaction is to feign sleep. I can't say why, other than I'm a little curious which of my relatives snuck into my room. Maybe it's my brother? With my eyes closed, I focus on keeping my breathing even. I *wish I weren't sleeping on my stomach, or that my face wasn't smooshed into the pillow. I'd be able to peek and see who it is.*

My sense of hearing heightens but there's no movement in my room, no sounds. I strain to listen and the click of my bedroom door lock practically slams in my ear. The same unease that woke me surges full force and sends goosebumps across my flesh. Desmond wouldn't sneak into his own room. He certainly wouldn't lock the door.

Get up! My mind commands, but my body doesn't obey.

Not when the bed dips, and not when the weight of a hand presses against the back of my thigh.

It's my leg. It's his hand. It shouldn't feel weird, but it does. I don't know how, but I know it's not my brother's, or my parents' either. The bed dips again. My heart beats hard and fast in my chest, so much I wonder if it might shake my entire body.

Whoever is here brushes my hair to one side. Breath, heavy and warm, blows across the back of my neck. It's all I can do to not shiver. A body presses against my side, longer, bigger, stronger than me, but still doesn't say a word. My neck grows hot from the stranger's breath, and then a pair of lips presses down. They're moist and move up toward my earlobe.

If I open my eyes I could make out his face. But I don't. Instead, I hold perfectly still. So damn still. As if it'll somehow stop this, or maybe I'll wake up even though I know this isn't a nightmare.

The kisses continue, and his body presses onto my back. I can feel his hardness. His arousal. I think I might be sick. The hand on my thigh skims higher, under my pajamas.

Get up! The command is loud in my mind but my muscles don't move. He doesn't go away, and I keep pretending this isn't happening. Panic fills my lungs, making it almost impossible to breathe. His hands explore with sure movements. His touch is assertive, as if he knows exactly what he's doing, and it only confuses me more. Why would he do this?

Scream! But my mouth doesn't move. My eyes won't open, either. I can't bear to see his face.

Disgust coils in my gut, boiling and churning with each of his touches. But he doesn't know. He can't hear my thoughts, and he doesn't stop. The pads of his fingers brush against my most private areas. My nipples harden, and the flesh between my legs grows wet. As much as I don't want it to, my body reacts.

Shame. Heavy and thick, it douses my thoughts. Why can't I push him away? I want to. I hate what he's doing. I hate him for doing this, and all I want is for it to stop. But I'm mute.

I clench my eyes and block it all out. His breath. His touch. The audible squeak of the fan blades. I don't want to be here anymore.

"Jayla," Austin says.

In the safe space of this hotel room, I'm so caught up in reliving my nightmare aloud it takes the scrape of Austin's voice to jolt me from my past.

"Don't, okay?" I pull my hands from his, needing the space. "I don't need your sympathy. It was a long time ago. I'm no longer that girl." But that's not entirely true. It's why I don't bring this up. Why I don't ever talk or think about what happened. When I was telling Austin, it was as if I was back there again. Sixteen, frightened, and confused as my cousin assaulted me while my family celebrated unknowingly down the hall.

"I'm sorry for what you lost." Austin swallows and the Adam's apple of his throat bobs as if he's fighting with his emotions. "What he took."

"I didn't fight him." I brush off Austin's concern with a whisper. I don't want it. "I never said no."

"No. Don't do that. Don't diminish what you lost." His voice is rough. "You were a child."

"He was only a few years older." I swallow, my throat thick with the truth.

Austin levels his stare right in my face so I can't miss his concern. "He didn't have your consent."

I nod. Because that right there, it's my why. It's why I shut men out. It's why I became a police officer. It's why I agreed to making those damn videos with Austin.

"Did you tell your family?" He reaches forward, the pad of his thumb wiping a tear from the corner of my eye before it falls from my cheek.

I get a lockdown on my emotions. I don't cry, not about this. The bastard who took my choice doesn't deserve tears. He doesn't deserve a second thought. I won't give him that power over me, not anymore. "No. What could I say? They wouldn't have believed me anyway."

Confusion crosses Austin's features. "Why? I thought you were close with your family."

"Because"—I swallow the bitterness—"he was my cousin."

Austin's jaw tics with strain and he blows out a long breath. "Your cousin did that to you?"

I nod and recite the information I've long ago memorized. "Most sexual assault abusers are a friend or family member of the victim." I clench my hands into fists, the pain of my nails as they dig into my skin keeping my mind in the present. "One in three girls and one out of every seven boys will be sexually assaulted by the time they turn eighteen." It's a sickening statistic. One I'm a part of, though more than likely it's undervalued because most don't report or tell. Like me.

"I'll kill him," Austin practically growls. His body is tense, muscles tight, and he's obviously upset. His threat comes out more like a vow, and though it's completely insane for him to commit murder for something that happened to me, a tiny part of me sighs in relief at not being the only person outraged about this.

"Hey, now. Don't go making death threats with a former cop as witness." My joke doesn't bring even the hint of a smile to his lips.

"So, you what? Smile and give him hugs at Christmas?"

"I did. For several years." The shame I've worked so hard to overcome threatens to berate me again. As a trained police officer, and someone who's been through years of counseling, I'm all too familiar with the psychological elements resulting in abuse. I know my reaction is natural, as well as misplaced.

"Please tell me he met a painful and untimely death." His hands reach for mine and I let him peel open my clenched fists. He threads our fingers together. "That way I don't have to track him down and commit first-degree murder."

"My parents' marriage fell apart. Everything fell apart after we left Phoenix. He was a cousin on my dad's side, and since Desmond and I lived with Mama after the divorce, I never had to see him again."

"You never told your mom?" He seems surprised.

I get it. Because my mama and I were always close. At least when we lived in Arizona. Things changed when we moved away. She was torn up, and just trying to survive those first years without Dad. I don't even think she noticed the change in me. Or if she did, she blamed herself. "She had enough to deal with, and I didn't need to add to the drama."

"This isn't a little gossip, Jayla. It's abuse."

"I know, Austin. You don't have to tell me." A laugh escapes my lips but it holds no humor. "But if I don't let this go, it eats me alive. I choose to let this go."

"And make sure it doesn't happen to other women." His eyes widen with the realization. "That's why you agreed to the videos."

"Yeah."

"You realize this makes you even more attractive, right? You're already drop dead gorgeous and a complete badass, but now . . ." His gaze is hungry, but it's full of so much more than lust. Admiration maybe? It's the last thing I expect to find, and yet it obliterates the apprehension I had about sharing this part of myself with him.

"Now what?" I whisper. It's a loaded question.

With my hands still tangled in his, he brings them to his lips and places chaste kisses across my knuckles. His gaze never leaves mine. "How am I going to stay away?"

My breath catches in my throat. The intensity of his stare eats right through the last of my defenses. My soul is cracked open and vulnerable, ripe for his taking. I should retreat. I should shut this down. But for once I give in to the tiny whisper of my heart that begs for safety, for love, for home. "I'll kick you in the nuts if you get too close." The retort flies from my lips, though it lacks any real malice.

Austin's lips curl up with his smile. "I'm surprisingly okay with that."

Moving to my knees, I close what little space is left between our bodies and straddle his waist to sit on his lap. His hard abs flex and he tips his chin up to meet my gaze. "This won't be easy. I'm not like most women. I have to have control. I understand if you want out." On one long exhale I spill the rest of my truth. "But if you're gonna walk, do it now. Don't fuck with my heart."

"I'm not going anywhere," he says. "I swear."

My pulse races with his promise, but I still can't trust myself to be swayed by pretty words. "Don't make promises you can't keep."

His finger brushes along my jaw and down the length of my neck. His gaze grows heavy, and I feel the hardness of his arousal press between my thighs. But his touch is tender as the scruff of his cheek rubs against my skin, up the column of my throat and down again, pressing sweet kisses as he moves. His touch is more worship than greedy, and I have to resist the urge to melt into him completely. My body comes alive under his sure and steady moves.

I can almost picture him laying me down. Moving on top of me. Me enjoying the weight of his body. Being intimate without fear. He makes it feel possible. This. Us. Everything.

My pulse speeds. My breath catches. I can't deal. My hands press against his pecs and I shove so he lands on the mattress. I have control again. My chest heaves with each inhalation, but I'm no longer over-whelmed. "Hands here." I press his wrists into the bedding, a few inches from where my legs straddle his waist.

He doesn't hesitate or fight my request. His fingers grasp for the sheets, and it's the most erotic sight. His arms flex, his body tight and hard beneath me. I press my hands onto his chest and scoot up his body so our most intimate parts align perfectly before leaning forward to capture his lips in a kiss.

"Be sweet," he whispers against my mouth as our lips brush. "Please."

If he hadn't already stolen my heart, he captures it now. My eyes pinch shut, a vain attempt to hold back the surge of emotion that threatens to escape with tears. A part of me wants to fight this. But the other part wants to give in to his simple request. To at least try.

I leveled him with my dirty secrets. He didn't run. Even before, when I shared my body, he took only what I was willing to give. I trust Austin. I do. This time as we come together I offer him more.

Sensual. Connected. Dirty and sweet. His hands never release their grip on the sheets, and I give in to the pull of desire that builds and explodes between us. There are no words this time, only mouths, tongues, breath, bodies—two people reaching for delicious release. Sweaty and intense, we're the only two people in the world, or at least that's the way it feels. This time is as good as before. No, it's better. The buildup is slower, the coil of nerves at my sex tightens, edging me closer to release until I can't hold off. Our bodies move together, still on my lead and on my terms, but this is no longer just sex. No, it's very much like making love. This time when my orgasm hits, I give in completely because I trust without a doubt that Austin will catch me if I fall. And damn, that feeling alone is life altering.

25

JAYLA

I FELL ASLEEP.

I can't believe I fell asleep. After sex. In a bed. With a man. *Not just any man.*

Austin.

This is messy, I know, and maybe it was stupid to cross lines last night. *What are we even doing?* We never hashed out details. I don't know what I want, or how this works. But no matter how many times I replay last night in my mind, I can't find it in me to regret being with him. My muscles ache with that delicious soreness that only comes from a night of sex, and for once in my life I don't feel shame or bitterness the morning after. I gave him everything, and he took it all willingly. My soul feels lighter, more free than it's ever been, and if I could hold on to this forever I would.

Austin's rhythmic breathing keeps me rooted to this bed. I really have to pee, but I don't want to break the enchantment of this cocoon we created to hide us from the world. Once I get up, the day begins and everything will change. My gaze drinks in the sight of his sleeping form, and I unabashedly study the ink on his skin. He's so beautiful. He's strong. He's all man, and for last night, all mine.

Something changed between us. The invisible line we drew between us is now non-existent. I can't go back to work today and pretend last night never happened, but I'm no idiot either. He has his career, and for now I'm paid to protect him and the band. No doubt there would be consequences if we were to date publicly—if that's even what he wants. Or what I want.

Maybe last night was merely a hookup for him. Does he even want to date? What would the band think? The label? I could get fired, and if I wasn't on this tour, we'd be forced to do the long distance thing. Could I trust him on the road? Would he have issues staying faithful?

"Keep frowning and you'll get wrinkles."

My eyes fly up to meet his. "You aren't sleeping."

He chuckles, his voice still thick with sleep, and it sends tingles down my spine. He rolls onto his side to face me. "We pointing out the obvious? Because you're beautiful in the morning."

Wrong. He's the one with the unfairly perfect bed hair. His locks are just a little too long and my fingers itch to run through the curls. Instead, my hand goes to my own head and I cringe imaging how bad I must look.

"Beautiful." He draws my hand away and any smart retort gets caught in my throat under the heat of his gaze. My body thrums to life. I already want him again.

"I need a shower. I should go." I drag my gaze from his and climb out of bed. I also really need to use the restroom.

"Funny." He sits up in bed, watching as I move toward the open door. "My room has one of those."

My hands go to my hips. "But I need my things."

"We'll have the concierge bring them to my suite," he says so simply. It hits me just how much our lives differ, and how much money he must have. Add it to the list of the many differences between his reality and mine.

"No, we won't." I gather my clothes from last night and head to the restroom before he convinces me to stay. We still need to talk, but

I also don't want to get caught sneaking out of his room. Last night we came together perfectly, but the harsh light of the morning sun illuminates all the ways this is wrong.

I avoid his gaze until I'm safely locked in the bathroom where I relieve my bladder, dress in my clothes from yesterday, and pull back my hair the best I can until I'm back in my room with my conditioner and comb. My feet drag as I head back out to face Austin, confliction bubbling in my gut and slowing my retreat. I should stay, at least long enough to talk and sort this out, whatever it is between us. But I'm battling the impulse to run, to protect myself from the vulnerability that makes me feel more naked fully dressed in this hotel room than I did last night.

"Hey," Austin says with a slight grin when I finally emerge from the bathroom. A pair of sweats hang low on his hips, and he holds out a cup of coffee while another brews from the single-serve machine behind him. *Fancy.* Hotel suites have all the good stuff. "I thought we could talk." The smile he wears almost looks unsure. Hopeful. As if he's worried I might reject his offering.

"Thank you." I take the mug and take a long sip, glad I'm not the only one unsettled about where we stand.

"I like you, Jayla."

"I know." My lips pull into a teasing grin.

He rewards me with a megawatt smile. "Yeah, and I think you might like me, too." He scrubs a hand over the scruff of his face. "Last night was . . . incredible. Amazing. Fucking hell, I can't even put it to words. But thanking you feels stupid, and also not enough, because being with you felt more significant and real than anything I've ever done."

My cheeks heat at his word vomit and all the compliments he throws my way.

"Say something before I make an idiot out of myself." He grips his coffee and brings it to his lips.

I do the same and lift my brow, teasing because I can't help but love this unsure and fumbling version of Austin.

"Okay, *more* of an idiot." He chuckles, setting down his coffee. "Please, put me out of my misery."

"I like you, too."

"Yeah." His lips curve up until the grin takes over his face.

"But how does this work?" I signal between us.

His smile turns absolutely dirty.

"Not that!" I roll my eyes. "I think we figured out how that works just fine."

"Maybe we give it a go once more to be sure?" He steps toward me like a man on the hunt. Like he can't wait another moment to touch me. Kiss me. Taste me. I feel the same. His lips meet mine in a possessive kiss, one in which our mouths battle and bodies spark with lust.

"Coffee," I mutter between kisses, because I don't want to spill the hot liquid on him or me. The way this is going, that's a likely consequence. His lips leave mine and he takes a step back, grabbing my mug and setting it on the counter in a rush.

Before he can claim my lips again, our phones go off, simultaneously buzzing with incoming calls. *Shit. The time!* My security team meeting! *God, how irresponsible am I?* I should have checked in last night. This morning too. Guilt, thick and suffocating, edges my thoughts as I scramble for my cell. I exhale a rush of relief when I find it's only seven—I haven't missed the meeting with my team—and it's only Trent calling, not one of my security staff.

Austin holds up his cell, frown lines etched in his brow. "It's Sean. Stay. I'll take this in the bathroom."

I don't have a chance to tell him Trent's on my line—or wonder why two of the band members are calling so early—because I need to answer if I don't want this going to voicemail.

"Hi, Trent." I turn and walk back into the bedroom so my voice won't carry to Austin's conversation.

"Jayla. Hey, sorry to bother you so early."

"It's no problem. What's up?"

"We have a problem." There's a long pause. "Do you think we could meet and uh, talk in person? Privately?"

My heart rate jumps and races. "Um, sure." He couldn't know about Austin and me. *Could he?*

"Good. We're all in my suite. Well, almost all of us. Sean's still trying to track down Aust."

I breathe out a sigh of relief. Of course he couldn't know Austin and I hooked up last night. This is about the band. "Give me thirty minutes?"

"Thank you. Oh, and Jayla? I hate to ask, but can we keep this meeting between us. I'd rather it didn't get back to the label. At least not yet."

My stomach clenches with his request to keep this from my boss. Not because I don't want to, but because I feel more of an allegiance to Austin and the band than I do my actual employer. My priorities are all wrong, and that's something I haven't felt since leaving the police force. "Yeah. We'll talk when I get there. See you soon."

"Thanks, Jayla."

Austin steps out of the bathroom as I end my call. He holds his phone up with a frown. "I take it you got called into the trenches also."

"Yeah, is everything okay?"

"Doubt it. They wouldn't call a meeting this fucking early for nothing."

"You're worried?" I wonder whether this has anything to do with the note the hotel staff delivered yesterday. I want to ask him, but more so I want him to voluntarily explain what it meant.

"No. Yes." He runs a hand through his hair and tugs at the locks in frustration. "I am, but that's not why I'm upset."

"No?" My stomach churns with uncertainty.

"I was hoping to convince you to stay for morning sex." He bites down on his lip.

As if by some invisible thread, my sex reacts to the sight and clenches with need. "Oh?" I ask breathlessly.

"Yeah. I mean—" his lips tug into a grin and he waggles his brows —"I am the best lay of your life, after all."

I groan and roll my eyes. "I'm going to regret telling you that."

"No takebacks." He steps forward, closing the space between us, and brushes his hands up my arms.

"Humility. You should try it sometime," I say, but I can't hold back the laughter as it escapes my lips.

"Not the first person to tell me that." He winks, holding me loosely in his arms. "Hey, Jayla."

"Yeah?" I tip my chin up.

"I know I said I wouldn't, but thank you. For last night."

I bite my lip so I won't thank him, too. I've had sex a handful of times over the years and it was good enough, but I've never climaxed during the act. Never felt anything remotely as enjoyable as what we did last night. I thought it was because I was broken. My mind so damaged that I physically couldn't orgasm with a partner. But Austin proved me wrong. Sex like that could be addicting.

Austin drops a chaste kiss on my lips.

"I'll see you in Trent's suite." I sigh, wishing I could stay longer, but we're running out of time. I step back from his embrace to grab my bag and reach for the door handle.

"We'll continue this conversation later"—he moves between me and the door, this time brushing his lips against mine with more pressure, more promise—"and pick up where we left off."

I hope I don't have to wait all day until he delivers.

26

AUSTIN

"WHAT'S WITH THE FIRE ALARM?" I push into Trent's suite and meet the grim expressions of my bandmates and their girlfriends. A sense of foreboding settles on my shoulders when no one responds. I brush my hair back, the strands still wet from my shower, and plop next to Opal on the couch. "Seriously, what's going on?"

Trent's gaze flicks to Sean and then over to Jess. She studies the tips of her shoes, her face etched with worry. Opal rubs her hand over her belly in slow circles. Everyone is being weird and that knot of concern in my gut grows.

Lexi meets my stare and breaks the silence. "Maybe we should wait for Jayla?"

I laugh to ease the tension. "This better not be an intervention. I promise I hardly get high anymore." And I don't. Not unless you count the woman I am completely addicted to.

Trent rolls his eyes, but there's a hint of a smile on his lips. "Not everything is about you, dumbass."

"But it should be. Speaking of, I hope to God you ordered break-fast for this impromptu meeting. I'm hungry."

"There's bagels, fruit, and orange juice," Opal says. "Let me make you a plate." She presses her hands into the couch and moves to stand.

"No way, little mama." I reach for her elbow and halt her from moving any further. "I should be getting you a plate. You want something?" I stand and take a few steps backward.

"Bring me an apple?"

"You got it." I wink, mostly because it annoys Leighton. I have no interest in Opal, but I do like fucking with him.

As if on cue, he frowns.

I just laugh, strutting across the suite to make a plate and brew myself a cup of coffee. I have a feeling I'm going to need several more to get through today. I didn't get a ton of sleep last night, not that I'm complaining. I'd gladly trade rest for more sexy times with Jayla, but we have a full schedule on the agenda. Interviews with local radio and news stations. Sound checks. Luncheon with some sponsors. Then a meet and greet before tonight's show. It'll be past midnight before we roll on to St. Louis and do it all again.

"You're in a much better mood this morning." Trent stands next to me at the bar and snags a grape off my plate, popping it into his mouth.

"Yeah, well. New day. New dawn." *Jayla and I fucked and it was amazing.* The urge to brag is there, but for once I don't let it out. Not because I'm embarrassed, or because he'll give me shit about sleeping with her. No, it's bigger than that. Last night was everything I'd hoped for, and all I needed. More than I ever expected. It was more than sex, and special, and I don't want to share that with anyone.

"You got laid," he deadpans.

"What?" *Is it that obvious?* I've been a miserable SOB this week, sure, and even now when I know there's something big going down, I can't keep the slight smile from playing at my lips, or the lightness from my step.

He shakes his head and rolls his eyes. "Shameless. What did you do, chase down that chick from last night? All because we were giving you a hard time for crushing on Jayla."

"Something like that," I mutter and mix cream into my coffee.

"Wait. You didn't fuck—?"

The door swings open with a sharp knock, and Jayla struts through wearing her badass CIS pantsuit and self-confidence like she runs this show. Which isn't far from the truth. *Damn. This woman.* I can't help but stare.

"Jayla." Sean stands from his seat next to Jess. "Thanks for coming."

"Tell me what's going down," she gives a curt nod, and settles herself onto the edge of an empty armchair.

I grab my plate but pause at Trent's gaping stare. *He knows.* About Jayla and me. Shit. It's probably written all over my face. He's come to the truth by his own conclusion and if he asks I won't lie, but by the nervous bouncing of Jess's leg and the anxiousness in Sean's eyes, this isn't about me right now. I leave him to ponder and rejoin Opal on the couch.

"Coy is harassing Jess," Sean says plainly.

"Wait, what?" I practically roar.

Jess shoots me a pleading look. I don't know if it's meant to calm me down, but my mouth clamps shut regardless.

"Explain," Jayla says. "The more details the better."

"It started with a few texts." Jess's voice is soft. "I didn't know for sure it was him, but I deleted them anyway."

Jayla leans forward on her elbows. "When was this?"

"The first week of January. After the tour restarted."

"What did they say?"

"They were mostly nothing. Just a lot of 'Hey, girl,' and 'Can I see you?' that kind of stuff." Jess waves it off, but it's obvious this isn't nothing.

Jayla nods. "And you think it was Coy?"

"That's what I think now. About a week ago, he started showing up at work."

"Fucker," Sean mutters under his breath. I concur.

"You work at a clothing boutique, right?"

"Yes." She says. "Paula Sorrento's shop on Rodeo."

"Did he approach you?"

"Not at first. He just came in, browsed, and then left." She visibly shivers. "Then I caught him waiting outside a few times."

"He's stalking her." Sean's arms flex with agitation. "That's illegal, right? We have a restraining order."

"Good. The restraining order is good." Jayla's demeanor is calm, her voice firm. Her presence alone settles our room as everyone looks to her for guidance. In this one moment I can see that she must have been an amazing cop. "Jess, did you ever call the police when he came in? Or say anything to him?"

"No. Should I have?" Jess bites the inside of her cheek and presses her hands together. "I didn't want to cause problems for the shop, or make a scene. But now, I think maybe that only encouraged him."

"None of this is your fault. You know that." Sean rubs the small of her back.

"What happened next?" Jayla encourages.

"He followed me to school. I'm taking classes at the community college. I didn't see him approach. Like at all. One minute I was grabbing a soda from the vending machine during a break, and then next he was there, right in my space."

My head pounds with rage and I'm overcome with the impulse to beat the shit out of Coy Wright all over again.

"That must have been terrifying," Jayla says.

"It was. I wanted to scream. Or run. But I felt stuck. I just kept flicking the tab of my soda back and forth while he begged me to fix things. He said I owed him, that he would take me back." She shakes her head and bristles. "Like I'd ever go back to that monster."

"Did he touch you, or hurt you?"

"No. He didn't get close enough. Once the shock of seeing him again wore off, I excused myself and went back to class. I thought he might wait for me, but he wasn't there when I came out."

"And when was this?"

"Yesterday." Jess blows out a breath and leans into Sean's side. "Before I flew out for the weekend."

Jayla taps her fingers at the knee of her pants for a quiet moment before she speaks again. "Do you know what he meant, for you to fix things?"

"He kept saying I ruined his life. That no one would hire him. That I broke his heart." Jess's gaze flicks over to me briefly. "And that my new guys made it impossible for him to play."

No.

My gut fills with dread.

This is my fault. Mine. I'm the reason Coy is stalking her. Harassing her. Why the fuck did I think it was a good idea to fight his lawsuit? I could settle. I should have sooner. A bastard like Coy doesn't just go away. Of course he'd reach out and try to hurt the people I love to get what he wants.

"This is all my fault," I blurt, unable to keep the crush of guilt to myself a second longer.

All eyes in the room swivel from Jess over to me.

"I'm sorry." Sean chuckles but it's filled with annoyance. "How do you have anything to do with Coy the douche canoe harassing my girlfriend?"

"The lawsuit." I swallow my pride. "He's coming after us to make us hurt."

"That's his choice. Not yours." Jayla levels me with a serious stare. "You can't take responsibility for someone else's circumstances." By the undercurrent of her words, I feel as if she's talking about more than Coy. That she's giving me absolution for not being there for her when she needed me most.

"But I told Rachel I wouldn't settle." I swallow another wave of responsibility and send a meaningful glance in Jayla's direction.

"That's why she called the other night. That's why Coy came after Jess. It has to be."

Jayla's brown eyes give nothing away. I can't tell whether I convinced her my lawyer's late night call meant nothing, or if she's forgiven me, and I wish we could go back to my room to work all of this out.

"Austin." Jess waits until I meet her gaze. "You have done nothing but protect me. This is not your fault. Besides, what makes you think Coy will go away, even if you pay him off?"

"We have to try," I say immediately.

"How much?" Jess's lips press into a nervous line.

"Doesn't matter," I say, because it doesn't. If it buys her safety, it's worth it.

Jess shakes her head. "I can't let you do that. I'll pay you back." Jess doesn't have money, but she's also someone who won't take hand-outs. She fights Sean every time he insists on paying for things, and they're together. The woman is incredibly resilient and strong despite her outward appearance.

"You're not paying him back." Sean shakes his head and lets loose a chuckle. "I know for a fact he has the money."

I wink at my friend. "That's right. I'm a fucking baller."

Sean groans with a roll of his eyes, but I can tell he appreciates the diversion. "Scratch that. I'll pay for it. I can't have you holding this over me."

"Coy's suing me, not you." I shake my head. "I'll pay."

"You guys can argue about who's flipping the bill later. For now, I think it's best we come up with a plan to keep Jess away from Coy." Jayla turns back to Jess. "You're not flying back until we get to Ohio, right?"

"Right."

"That gives us a few days. I'll arrange for private security when you get back. I also have some connections with a few guys on the force who owe me. I'll ask them to check in on Coy."

"Is that necessary?" Jess rubs her hands up and down her arms.

"I'm probably overacting because of my past. He didn't do anything other than try to talk to me."

Sean opens his mouth to argue but it's Jayla who lays down the law.

"Yes. We won't take chances. He hurt you before, and he'll do it again if given the chance. I don't want him feeling comfortable enough to approach you anywhere, ever."

Jess nods, and despite her earlier bravado, her features soften with apparent relief.

"We got you, Jess," Lexi reassures. "You're family. You don't do this alone."

"Thank you," Jess says.

Not wanting to waste another minute, I pull out my cell phone and fire off a text to Rachel. I should have done this days ago. Thinking of how Coy hurt Jess, how Jayla was hurt by her cousin, how I've let down the important women in my life time and time again, spurs me to action. There's a good chance Rachel won't get my message until Monday, but it's better to get the ball rolling as soon as possible. Thankfully, Jess is here with us for the next few days and safe until then. As crazy as Coy is, he's a fucking coward too. I don't think he has the balls to approach her with all of us around.

"Thanks, Jayla. I appreciate your help on this." Sean scrubs a hand over his face, the worry not completely gone from his features, but eased. "We don't want the label involved. This is a personal matter. But we also don't want to put you in a situation you aren't comfortable with."

"Oh, yeah." Jayla straightens her shoulders and presses her lips together. "It's fine. I understand." She doesn't meet my gaze.

"You've been a total professional since you joined this tour," Sean continues, his hand rubbing circles against the small of Jess's back. "We trust you. And we don't want to force you into an ethical dilemma."

Jesus. He's pouring it on a little thick. Jayla appears as uncomfortable as I feel. Fuck, Sean. He's going to make her re-evaluate spending the night together, and probably cock block me from ever enjoying that again.

I glare daggers at my bandmate, willing him to shut the fuck up, but it's in vain. And pointless, because not a second later, a sharp rap of knocking pulls everyone's attention to the hotel door. We all glance at each other, no one making a move to see who it is.

27

JAYLA

I RAISE my brows with a tired sigh. "I take it none of you ordered room service?" My stomach knots with anticipation as well as a touch of alarm. I don't know what lies on the other side of the door, but if it follows the way my morning's been going, it's probably not good.

"We did not."

"Trent, this is your room, so you should open it. Everyone else stay here." I motion for him to follow me to the door. A glance out the peephole reveals a giant bouquet of roses. I don't miss how the arrangement hides the face of whomever is holding them. Convenient or happenstance? Either way, my entire body tingles with suspicion.

"Did you order flowers?" I whisper to Trent.

He shakes his head in the negative.

"Who's there?" Trent shouts and glances through the peephole.

"Delivery for Mr. Donavan."

Trent's gaze darts to mine and he gives a shrug as if asking what he should do.

I nod to the door, signaling for him to turn the handle, and then stand to one side so our intruder won't see me once it's open.

Trent drags the door open a few inches. "Can I help you?"

"Mr. Donavan. These came for you," the man holding the bouquet says.

"No, thank you. I'm not expecting them."

"Sir?" the man asks, confused. "I got the request a little over an hour ago from corporate. Security gave special permission."

I never gave permission and I've heard enough. I step in front of Trent before he can take the arrangement. "I'm sorry, there's been a mix up. Can I please see your ID?"

"Miss Miller," the hotel employee says, clearly surprised at my presence. I recognize him from the meetings we had yesterday to go over procedure. He jostles the arrangement from one arm to the other before finally setting it on the floor. He hands over his identification.

I study the card. "So, Mark. Want to tell me what you're doing? We talked about no outside deliveries to hotel rooms. I'm pretty sure we went over the protocol until everyone was blue in the face."

He tilts his head, confusion etched into the furrow of his brow. "But I was told to bring these up."

"I never spoke to you."

He swallows and glances from me, to Trent, and then to the flowers. "I'm not trying to start trouble. Just following orders."

"Who gave you the orders?"

"Mr. Vincent Collins." Head of operations for WMI. *Why would he send flowers to the band?* "Your security team said you were off the clock. Some guy name Brian searched these before I came up. I swear."

Now it's my turn to swallow. I wasn't in my room last night or this morning. Did someone try to get hold of me? Is this guy telling the truth? "Okay." I pull out my cell, notice the time and almost blanch. My security team meeting started five minutes ago. *Fuck.* One night with Austin and I'm already distracted to the point I can't do my job. I pull up my contacts and click on Brian's name.

"Morning, Miss Miller."

"Hey, sorry I'm running late. I'll be there in five, but did you okay a flower delivery for Mr. Donavan's room?"

"Yes, sure did. Vince called this morning and said to expect them."

"Huh." I cradle my cell between my shoulder and ear and eye the bouquet in the hall. Turning to the bellhop, I mouth a thank you and he leaves, clearly relieved. I stoop next to the arrangement and pull out the card. Looking at Trent, I hold it and he signals I should open it. I skim the note inside, feeling both relieved and ridiculous at my overreaction.

"Thanks, Brian. I'll see you in a few," I say, ending the call and handing the note over to Trent. "I think you'll want to read this."

I grab the bouquet of flowers and he holds the door open for me to pass.

"Everything okay?" Austin asks.

"False alarm." I feel stupid even saying it. I hide my embarrassment by finding a spot on the counter for the flowers and then meddling with the arrangement. I feel so off my game right now. I'm the woman always one step ahead. I plan. I stay in control. Had I not spent the night with Austin, I would have known these flowers were being delivered. As head of security for this tour, it's my responsibility to know things. I just had a mini-heart attack and put the band through the same, and all for freaking celebratory roses.

"Fuck, yeah!" Trent whoops as he reads the note and rushes to pull Lexi into his arms. "Baby, we're gonna be king and queen of this year's Grammys!"

"What?" She smiles, shaking her head with confusion until he hands her the letter. She processes the words and I think this is the first time I've ever witnessed Lexi Marx rattled with emotion. "Oh, my God! This is amazing! They want us to perform. Together?"

Everyone cheers and offers congratulations to their friends.

"Hey, what about the rest of us?" Austin complains.

"Find a girl with the voice of an angel who is also a rock goddess, and maybe they'll ask you next time," Trent teases before returning his adoring gaze to Lexi and capturing her lips in a heated kiss.

"This calls for a toast." Sean stands from the couch and walks over to the refrigerated cabinet below the bar. "They've gotta have champagne or something good in here."

Austin's stare finds mine from across the room. The way he's looking at me, like he'd love to kiss me right here in front of everyone, warms me from the inside. It's an unfamiliar feeling, and while the impulse to bolt lingers in the back of my mind, for the first time in my life I consider fighting to stay. What would a life with Austin entail? Am I woman enough to handle the playboy rock star? Is he man enough to withstand my insecurities?

I don't have time to dig into these big questions because I'm already late to my meeting. Not wanting to break up the celebration, I quietly make my way back to the door. Austin's mouth falls with disappointment as I offer him a smile before slipping out the door. We still need to talk, but it's gonna have to wait. I've already let myself down, I can't afford to do the same with my team.

———

"HEY," I say as I push into the conference room. "Sorry I'm late." Everyone is already gathered, and their chatter ceases the moment I step inside. I'd like to think it's only because I'm the boss. Or perhaps it's because I'm a woman. But knowing I cut out on them last night to spend time with Austin floods my mind with guilt. It's so out of char-acter for me to put anything above work, or to bail early. I pride myself on my work ethic. It's the way I earn respect from my colleagues, and somehow I feel as though I've let them down.

"Miss Miller," Brian hands over a stack of papers. "These came in a few hours ago."

"Jayla," I say, reminding him for the thousandth time he doesn't need to address me so formally. "What are they?"

"Reports from local law enforcement in Salt Lake. Or what the

FBI would allow them to share with us. There was a local tip, and an arrest was made."

"They caught the guy who did this?" I flip though the papers at an almost manic pace. If they caught the person who placed the explosive, the fear that it'll happen again lessens.

"Woman, actually." Brian shrugs.

"Motive?" I ask, already knowing Brian can tell me faster than I can skim through the sheaf of paperwork.

"Claims she had affiliations with the band, but when you get a chance later read through the transcripts. More likely psychotic or on drugs, in my opinion."

"This is good," I say absently. "Isolated incident."

"Seems so."

"Then let's get down to business and make sure something like this never happens again."

"Uh, Miss Miller." It's Casey, or Lipshitz, as the guys call him. I don't know why he's here or why I haven't noticed sooner.

"Yes?"

"A word. Or rather, a minute please?"

"I need to meet with my security team."

"It'll only be a minute. Five tops. Promise."

"Go." Brian nods. "We'll start assignments and you can approve them when you get back."

"Thanks," I say and follow Casey out into the hotel hallway. "Is there a problem?"

"I, uh . . ." He fiddles with his phone, then holds it out to me. "Mr. Collins would like to speak with you. He's on the line."

I take the phone and hold it up to my ear. "Hello?"

"Miss Miller. You're a difficult woman to track down."

I inwardly wince at his observation. I've been avoiding his calls since Austin posted the last video. Sending his calls to voicemail was immature. Then I got caught up in the responsibilities of the job and never reached back out to him. I take a few steps down the empty hallway, away from Casey. "I apologize for that. It's been busy."

"Not too busy to make another video, though. Some might wonder whether you're more interested in a career in Hollywood than security with all the acting you've been doing."

"Pardon?" I twist to see Casey lean against the wall outside the meeting room. He whistles and taps his fingers as if he has no worries in the world. I'm pretty sure he's out of earshot, but I take a few more steps to be sure.

"Let's cut the shit. Yeah?" There's a condescending edge to Vince's tone that causes me to bristle. "Can I be frank?"

"By all means, please." I don't mask the incredulity from my voice.

"I don't like you."

What the fuck is this guy's problem? "Okay."

"I don't trust you. I would have never hired you if I hadn't been pushed into the decision."

"Please. Don't hold back now," I say at his sudden pause.

"I won't have you running this show. Three Ugly Guys are a dime a dozen. They make money for us because we know how to market them. How to pull the next top single and shove it down listeners' throats until they claim to love it. We set up the press events. We have all the connections. I could easily do the same with any other band."

I should bite my lip. He's an ass and I won't change that, but I can't help myself. "Sounds like you appreciate your talent. Respect them, too."

"Please." He drags out the word. "Don't act like you care. You're using that band like everyone else does, to get whatever it is you want. So, Miss Miller, what exactly is it that you want?"

"I'm so sorry to disappoint, but I have no ulterior motives." Not exactly true, but I'm not about to confess my feelings for Austin to anyone, let alone this asshole.

"Everyone has a motive."

"I think I've had enough of this phone call. I need to get back to my security team. The one that keeps your expendable band safe each night. Though maybe you don't care about that?"

"Don't be ridiculous," he chides as if I'm a child. "No one wants to buy concert tickets when there's a threat of being blown to bits. It's a public relations nightmare I don't want to repeat."

I want to tell this guy off, but this time I do bite back my retort.

"Anyway, if you insist on being difficult, that's better for me. One more video with Austin, or any of the guys, and you're off the job."

Off the job? He thinks he can fire me? I don't like the way the thought settles over me. I don't want to go back to LA. Not yet. I don't want to be apart from Austin. I like my work, and how every day brings new challenges. I like spending time with Austin.

"I have a contract."

"The one my corporate lawyers drafted. I'm aware." He chuckles through the line. "So, don't cross me, stay off the fucking internet, and you'll finish your contract. I'll even add in a little bonus if you make it to the end. Another grand? That's fair."

I don't want his money. I don't like any of this or how it eats away at the integrity of my position. But I can't seem to open my mouth, or form a decent comeback.

"I'll take your silence as agreement. Have a wonderful day, Miss Miller."

I don't bother muttering my good-bye because without even checking the phone's screen, I know he's already hung up. *Inhale. Exhale.* I try to calm my nerves along with my spiraling thoughts. I can't believe this is the guy Austin works with. Does he know what a horrible human being he is? Does he care? I shake off the questions and straighten my spine. I don't have time for this. Today's agenda is filled down to the hour, and I have a new hater to prove wrong. *Vincent Collins doesn't like me? Fuck him.* I'm being paid to do a job, and I won't give him a reason to doubt that I'm fully qualified or committed.

28

AUSTIN

A DAY that started out so damn promising—Jayla in my bed, finally in my arms, and working her way into my heart—quickly turns for the worse with the news of Coy's harassment of Jess. I can't believe that fucker came after her again. And yet I can. It takes a few hours, but Rachel Kinsley returns my message and I thank God she's a workaholic. She promises to get started on a settlement offer immediately so it'll be waiting for Coy's lawyers Monday morning.

That should set my happy-go-lucky attitude back on track, but my mood sours with each passing hour. I want Jayla. To myself. Back in my hotel suite where we can make up for thirteen years of pent-up sexual attraction. Yeah, it might be immature and I'm worse than a little kid going through separation anxiety with his favorite blankie. Only I'm a grown-ass man, and Jayla isn't some object I can lock away in my room.

Though, the thought of being locked in a room with Jayla sounds about the best thing in the world right now.

I don't like how our paths rarely cross today, but that's how it works out and when they do, it's all business. On the way to interviews. In a crowded room of fans. Mingling with sponsors. Even backstage before the show affords no privacy with my bandmates and their women in attendance. Pisses me off even further, because she's right there, not five yards from me, and I can't ask her the questions that've been racing through my mind alongside images of her naked and falling apart while we fucked.

When can we do that again?

Will you be mine?

I want you to be mine.

Won't you ride my dick, forever?

Fuck. I sound like a dirty version of the intro to "Mr. Rodgers Neighborhood."

"Hiya." Casey pokes his head inside the green room. "Twenty minutes till show time."

"Thanks, Lipshitz. You're the shiz." Trent lifts his chin to nod at Casey.

Casey's lips pinch together, his smiles falls, but he leaves before saying another word.

My body thrums with impatient anticipation. My knee bounces and my fingers tap along the black fabric of my jeans. I can't wait to get out on that stage to expel all this energy. I'd rather work it out with Jayla, but at this point I have no clue if or when that's gonna happen again.

My gaze finds hers across the room. She speaks into her head-piece, but her stare is focused on the tablet she carries around for most of the shows. She's working. The alpha leader and queen of her domain. I witness how the security team regards her with respect and trust. Each time I watch her work my chest swells with pride. She's doing her thing, and fuck if that doesn't make her even more attractive.

My phone rattles with an incoming text from where it rests on the small table at my side. A glance at the screen sobers my hopes regarding Jayla. *Another photo link.* Another chance to right a wrong, or more likely, another chance to fuck up everything good in my life. Every time I open one of these emails I put my place in the band at risk. If this ever came out, the guys might understand, but the public would never forgive me. It's why I pay the guy who finds them for me a fucking pretty penny for his silence. Part of me wants to tell Jayla, but I'm scared it'll give her a reason to push me away for good. She'd remember Brianna, I think. She helped me watch her sometimes. But I don't think she'd be okay with the desperate measures I've taken to try and find Bri. Something like this could obliterate all of the trust I've earned.

I pick up the phone and delete the text. It's sent from a burner phone, and I doubt anyone could decipher the meaning of the message, but after Jayla saw the note sent to my room last night, I'm certain this would spark curiosity on her part. As it is, I'm surprised she didn't push me about the hotel note. *Oh, right. That's because I distracted her with my mouth.*

My cell rings before I set it back down. I catch my mom's name on the caller ID and let loose an audible groan. I'm not in the mood for her shit. Not ever, but especially not now. However, she only calls when she needs something and she will keep calling until I eventually answer.

"Austin," she says, sounding surprised that I pick up. In her defense, I usually don't on the first try.

"Hey, Mom." I keep my voice low, but Trent catches my greeting and meets my stare with concern. He's the only one who understands the depth of turbulence when it comes to my relationship with my mother. Right now I can't handle his pity, or attention. Pushing to my feet, I stride past everyone, including Jayla, to take the call in the hall. "What do you need?"

"So, it's gonna be like that?"

"You're the one who makes it like that." I scrub my hand over my face, wishing she'd get to the point. She needs something. Most likely cash.

"You always were an ungrateful child." Her words shouldn't affect me, but even after all these years, they fire me up.

My jaw tightens. "Oh? What should I be grateful for? The times you left me to take care of your boyfriend's kid so you could go out and party? How about the times you said I'd amount to nothing? Told me I was an idiot for all the hours I spent practicing guitar? Or how about the times you kicked me out of the house?"

"You ever gonna grow up and let that shit go? You know I did the best I could. I put a roof over your head. We always had money for groceries. I even got you your first guitar. Remember that? No? You conveniently only remember my failings, not all the times I clothed and fed your ass."

She's right about one thing. I need to let it go. I shouldn't hold on to this stuff; it doesn't serve me to have one foot in the past. I shouldn't get this annoyed by her calls. She's always been the same woman. I can't expect her to change, and I shouldn't get so angry when she's already shown her character.

I should cut all ties. Leave the past in the past. Except I can't. Not when Brianna's still unaccounted for. If there's a chance she ever comes back, she might contact my mom, and my mom's just spiteful enough to not tell me.

"Have you heard from Bri?"

"Steve's kid? Why would I hear from her? I told you what happened." I remember. I'd been on the road. Three Ugly Guys was finally gaining success. We'd cut an EP that was blowing up the radio charts. I hadn't been home in years, not since I left my mom's for good. Steve liked to get high, so much so that he started dealing from the apartment. It wasn't safe. Not for me, a teenage kid, but even worse for his little girl. She spent half of her time at her mom's, and when she was with Steve, it was mostly me who looked after her.

The last day I saw Brianna, I threatened to call CPS on Steve if he didn't stop. She was six years old. Steve and I got into a fist fight that left my body and my ego bloody and bruised. I was going to move out when I turned eighteen anyway. Steve gave me the push to pack my shit and never look back. Only life's not so simple. I was the only one who protected Brianna, and after I left she must have felt so alone.

Two years ago my mom called in a panic after Brianna showed up out of the blue, claiming her dad threw her out. While Mom stepped out on the patio to call Steve and light up a cigarette, Brianna ransacked the apartment and made off with all the cash and what few valuables she could find. Steve and Mom had been long broken up by then, and apparently Brianna had been skipping school and hanging with a bad crowd. Local law enforcement found her cell in a trash can at the Greyhound station a few days later. Given her behavior leading to her disappearance, foul play wasn't suspected.

No one had heard from or seen her since, and from talking to a few of her friends, we think she might have made her way to LA. Which is why my mom reached out. Brianna had always looked up to me. But Bri never came to see me—if she even made it to LA. She'd be seventeen today, and the private investigator I hired to locate her is convinced she's one of thousands hiding in plain sight as a victim of human trafficking. That or another unthinkable possibility, but I refuse to believe she's dead.

"I'm just asking," I grumble into the line so I won't go off on my mother. I blame them for not being better parents, but mostly I blame myself. If I'd been braver, I would have actually called Child Protective Services on my mom and Steve. Then maybe this would have never happened. If I hadn't left, or had checked in more, maybe Brianna wouldn't have felt the need to run.

"That girl won't come here; her daddy and I aren't together. And she stole my jewelry and two hundred dollars too."

"Which I replaced."

"But she doesn't know that. And before you bite my head off, I'm not mad about it. Brianna was a good kid. It's the teen years that changed her. Shame too. Waste. She was such a pretty girl."

There's nothing I can say to that. I'm tired of this conversation, and the walk down memory lane.

"But I didn't call to talk about Bri," my mom snaps. I'm almost relieved for the change in topic. I already know why she's calling. It's the same every time. "I'm a little short on rent."

"How much?"

"Whatever you can spare. My hours got cut this month. It's been a struggle. Did I tell you Dale moved out?"

Dale? Last I remembered she was with Eric. Or was it Ron? I honestly can't keep up and stopped trying. My mom's co-dependence on men is something I've accepted. She attracts guys who are users—namely she supports them financially because she doesn't like being alone. Until she decides she deserves more, nothing will change.

"Three grand enough?"

"That's perfect, sweetie."

Sweetie. I roll my eyes. Pet names only roll off her lips when I send her cash. It's okay. I have the money. I'd set her up with more if I wasn't certain she'd blow it all on one of her conniving boyfriends.

"I saw you on the news. You're all over Facebook with those videos you're making."

"Yeah."

"The woman on there with you? She reminds me of your friend from high school. The one who lived across from us."

I can't tell if she actually recognizes Jayla or she's just generalizing that all black women look alike to her, but for whatever reason I don't tell her it's actually Jayla in the videos.

"Speaking of that"—I swallow a surge of anger—"did I ever get any letters? Back in high school?"

"In the mail?" She laughs. "Honey, how would I know? That was over ten years ago."

"They would have been from Jayla Miller. Our neighbor. After she moved."

"Jayla! That was her name. She had an older brother too, didn't she?"

"The letters?"

"Austin, I don't know about any letters."

"It's fine." But it's not. Whatever shortcomings my mom has, she's not much of a liar. I take a little solace from the fact she wasn't so hateful to keep Jayla's letters from me. It was Steve. I'm sure of it more than ever.

The green room door swings open and my bandmates emerge, along with the girls. Trent tips his chin toward the waiting carts ready to drive us through the concourse and onto the stage.

I hold up one finger to indicate I'm coming. "Hey, I've got to go," I say to my mom.

Jayla leaves the guys at the golf carts and struts over before I can end the call.

"Sure, of course. The money? Can you wire it Western Union? I don't know how much longer I can put off the manager. He's been leaving notices all week."

"Yeah. Sure." I don't care about the money. And as bad as it sounds, it doesn't bother me knowing my mom is struggling financially when I'm not. It doesn't matter how much I send, she'll always need more. "I'll send it tomorrow. 'Bye."

"'Bye, Austin."

I pocket my cell phone and breathe out in relief. She won't call for at least another six months.

Jayla catches my gaze and lifts her brow. "What was that about?"

"Nothing." I shake my head. A heavy cloud of guilt settles on my shoulders. I should tell Jayla about my mom. The call. Brianna. The private investigator I send way too much money each month to find lost girls. But I can't put any of this on Jayla, and I won't risk pushing her away now that we just found our way back. The pressing need to find Brianna, wherever she is, eradicates any regret I have about keeping all of this from Jayla. For now, at least.

"Nothing," she repeats, leveling me with a stare that calls bullshit.

I roll my eyes and paste on a smile that doesn't feel quite right. "Another sponsorship offer because of our kickass videos." The lie tastes bitter on my lips but I push forward anyway. I swing my arm around her shoulder and walk us toward the waiting carts. "Hey!

Why don't we tape a new one after the show? It's been a while and I can't wait to get my hands on you again."

She wriggles out from beneath my arm, a scowl hiding her beautiful features.

I stop walking. "Jayla?"

She clenches her jaw and shakes her head, holding one hand up between us. "We'll talk later, okay?" She keeps walking toward the carts.

I jog to her side.

"Come on, big boy!" Sean pats the open seat across from him and Jess. "You're gonna make us late."

I'd rather take a seat next to Jayla, but she jumps in next to the driver of one of the other carts. Begrudgingly, I climb in across from Sean. If he notices my sour mood, he doesn't comment on it. Probably because he's too wrapped up in Jess.

A few minutes later, our crew is deposited at the backstage entrance. The packed stadium repeatedly chants the initials of our band name. "3-U-G. 3-U-G." Sound techs wait to hand us the in-ear equipment. I slide the flesh colored buds into each ear and hook the battery operated receiver into my belt so it rests over my back pocket.

I should be thinking about the show.

About the opening song.

Anything to do with playing in front of thousands of screaming fans.

But there's one person on my mind right now, and I can't seem to drag my feet to the stage without being sure she's not pushing me away. So instead of lining up by the stage hand, I turn and stride over to where she's working.

"What's wrong?" she says as I approach.

"We're good, right?" I want to reach out and hold her hand in mine, but I hesitate because we haven't really established any terms to whatever it is we're doing.

"Focus on your show tonight." Her gaze softens as if she wants to release my worries. "We'll talk later. Okay?"

Surprisingly, it's exactly what I need to settle the seed of insecurity rattling my mind. "Yeah, okay. It's a date." I take a step back, wink, and aim my pointer fingers at her. I swear she fights back a grin, but I don't have time to stick around. I hustle back to the stage.

She wants to talk. That's a good sign. *Right?*

AUSTIN and I have to talk. If he thinks I'm avoiding him, I'm not. Today has been insane, and by the time we load up to head out to St. Louis, all I want to do is fill my belly and put my feet up. But I can't do either because I have reports to upload before tomorrow, schedules to approve, agendas to finalize, and time to squeeze in for a private conversation with Austin. All of which feels impossibly overwhelming.

"Jayla, come on. Ditch the salads for one night. This is Chicago deep dish," Sean tempts as I take a seat at the full table.

"I'm fine." I wave off his offer and stab a cherry tomato onto my fork. "Besides, there might not be enough."

"There's plenty," Lexi pushes the open pizza box my way.

My mouth waters at the sight of sauce over thick layers of cheese and toppings. I've been so good this far. If I had a scale to weigh myself, I bet I'm down at least five pounds. Most things I can resist, but after such a long day, it sure would be nice to overindulge. "Okay, I can't turn down pizza." I push my salad to the side to wrap up for tomorrow and grab a plate.

Austin deposits a piece onto my plate with a wicked grin. "Some things are irresistible."

I should roll my eyes, or glare, but instead his comment sends my mind down memory lane—back to his hotel room—and damn, he's right. My thighs press together as my body tingles with awareness. He was absolutely sinful, and I want another taste.

"We knew you had a weakness." Opal winks, and for a second I fear she read my thoughts.

I force a laugh when I realize she's talking about the pizza, not Austin. "Yeah, I've been sticking to my diet, but rules are meant to be broken every now and then."

Austin coughs, and quickly reaches for his bottle of water.

My face heats with the double meaning to my words, and I keep my gaze on my plate. The pizza is good. The best kind of cheat meal, and I can't find it in myself to feel guilty. I want a second piece, but I don't want to be bloated later, so once I'm done with my slice I finish off my salad too.

"Hey, I haven't seen any videos posted lately." Opal leans back into her seat and finds my gaze across the table. "If you need someone to hold the camera, I'm game."

"I was just saying we need to do another," Austin says through bites of pizza. He grabs his beer and takes a long swig. "What do you say, Jayla? Do we have time tomorrow?"

No! The response almost flies past my lips. Now is the perfect opportunity to tell the band about my phone call with Vince. But I don't want to create a rift between the guys and their new label. They've told me enough about their last manager and how he screwed them over to sell out, that I can't imagine Vince's threat to take me off this job would go over well. Deep down I also have to wonder if I told them everything, would they take my side or even believe me? I'd like to think they consider me more than an employee, but life has taught me to be wary.

"Hey." Austin lowers his voice, but we're all gathered at one table. Everyone hears. "You don't have to do anything you're not comfortable with."

Before I answer, Opal gasps. One hand flies to her mouth while the other holds her cell. Her hands shake as she drags in a breath.

"What's wrong? Is it the baby?" Leighton's eyes widen with a mixture of shock and fear.

Opal shakes her head. "No." She drops the phone at her side and says it again. "No. It's not that."

My spine prickles with alarm. She appears fine. It must have been whatever she saw on her phone.

Leighton runs his hand between her shoulder blades. "What is it?"

Her gaze lifts to mine, but she only holds it a second before turning to Austin. "Have you checked your social media lately? The YouTube channel?"

"No." He shakes his head and a puzzled frown draws his brows together. "Why?"

"There are"—she swallows and licks her lips before glancing back at me—"some very ignorant and hateful comments."

Oh. My stomach dips and I can't settle on whether to be relieved or disappointed. Opal's fine. Nothing is wrong. But I don't have to look to imagine the racist and sexist comments that people I've probably never met left on our videos. Sometimes I hate the world.

"What? Let me see." Austin whips out his cell phone.

Trent grabs it out of his hands. "No. Bro, you don't want to read that shit." He tips his head to Opal. "Can you delete the comments? Take them down."

"Of course. Austin, send me your logins and I'll take care of it."

Austin's jaw works back and forth before he blows out a long exhale. "Just take my phone."

"That because you don't remember your passwords?" Trent lifts a brow and passes the cell to Opal.

Austin smiles as if he doesn't want to but can't help it. "Maybe."

"Don't read that shit," Lexi says to Austin. "You know better."

He scrubs a hand down his face in frustration. "You're right."

"Of course I am." She grins smugly, and then turns to catch my gaze. "Words are toxic. They fuck with your head, but we aren't made of stone. I've learned it's better not to read what people write about me or the people I love."

I consider her words, and while I have no interest in reading the comments, I also have a different opinion on the matter. "Sometimes it's not enough to turn the other cheek, or look away and pretend it's not happening. I don't have the luxury of ignoring what's happening in the world."

She nods, still holding my gaze, and flips her lip ring as she presses her lips together. We couldn't be more different. Our skin tones are opposite. She's tatted, pierced, and in my everyday world, I'd never spend time with someone like her. But we're drawn together by this band, and if I'm honest, so much more. I respect her work ethic and talent, and she's always treated me well. "You're right. Sometimes it's important to acknowledge and speak out against injustice."

"That's why our videos are important," Austin says.

I don't comment because I'm completely torn on what to do with those. If we were free to do whatever we wanted, I'd want to make another. They are important. Yet, I don't want to be ripped from this tour. I don't want to be sent away. Not yet. I hate that it's a choice I have to make.

"Right." I nod to Lexi and don't restrain from holding back my point of view. "My friend Kalise says we have to bide our time and save our voice for the big things. No one listens to the person who complains about every damn thing. But people can't not hear the truth if you meet them at their humanity. We're all in this thing together. We're sisters and brothers. We love. Hurt. Hope. We all bleed."

"I like Kalise already." Lexi smiles. "I hide behind my music, but I bleed through my lyrics. Maybe it doesn't change the world, but it changes the world for those who need to hear my message." She holds my stare and I swear she sees my past. The assault. And it hits me why she knows. She experienced something similar. We connect on a shared pain. My respect for her grows.

I catch Austin staring with an expression I can't quite read because it's one I've never seen him wear. It's more than attraction. It's more than pride, too. He's looking at me as if he wants to hear more of what I have to say. My desire to have a relationship, a real and honest one, flourishes under his gaze and for the thousandth time today I allow myself to picture a future in which he and I are together.

"Comments deleted. Users blocked," Opal states proudly. "At least, the most heinous ones." She hands Austin his phone and he stops looking at me to take it from her. "I'll go through the rest tomorrow and make sure I didn't miss any."

"You're the best." He smiles and pockets his phone. "Thanks, little mama."

Jess and Lexi insist on cleaning up from dinner. The rotation of showers begins, and there's a steady stream of chatter and movement as everyone settles down from the post-show high. Opal turns in early. She's really showing now, and I can't imagine being pregnant on tour is comfortable, but she never complains.

I settle myself into the bench seat with a cup of coffee and my laptop. If I stay focused I can knock this work out in an hour. My mouth opens in a yawn so big my eyes water. The pizza was a bad idea. My belly is full and this coffee could use an espresso shot or two to revive me from the food coma my body wants to give in to.

Speaking of things my body wants to give in to . . .

"Hey." Austin drags out his greeting as he pulls out an empty chair. His gaze travels greedily over my body, lingering on my breasts until I'm certain he can see the hard peaks of my nipples pushing through my bra and T-shirt. I'd blame it on the air conditioning, but we both know it would be a lie. Self-conscience with everyone still up and about, I grab my laptop and pull it in to my chest.

Austin laughs heartily, drawing everyone's attention.

I narrow my glare. "Excuse me, but I have work to do."

"I think you should take a break." He flashes a smile.

"I'm sure you do."

"Good. We're on the same page. Besides, I have a matter that could use your attention."

I cock my brow at him and motion for him to continue. By the smug ass grin on his face, I doubt it's an emergency.

"It's a very pressing matter." He winks. "Hard. Might take two hands."

I roll my eyes. "That seems generous."

"It's my dick." He points toward his lap. "I'm talking about my dick."

My eyes widen and I snap my laptop closed. Leaning forward, I hiss with a whisper of a shout. "Everyone can hear you!"

"I know!" He throws up his hands. "My dick would be offended, but he likes you too much."

Without glancing around the room, I can feel the stares of Lexi, Trent, Jess, and Sean. Their pause in conversation could be unrelated, but given the clear enunciation Austin gives to the word dick, I highly doubt it. Even Ace stops humming along to his music from the front of the bus. I refuse to have this conversation with an audience.

"Austin. Could I have a word? In private." I push out of the bench seat and cross my arms over my chest to protect everyone from an obscene view.

"Yes. Private. That's what I'm talking about." He jumps to his feet.

I bite back the impulse to yell, because he's infuriating and not taking any of this seriously. I want to be with him, but he can't just come up and start talking about his dick when I'm working. Not when we haven't even discussed the terms to our relationship. I stomp toward the short hall that runs along the sleep bunks back by the only bedroom. If Opal and Leighton weren't sleeping, I'd suggest we go inside, but this will have to do.

I turn on my heel as he comes up beside me. "What is your deal?

You can't speak to me like that!" My voice is low, but holds all the anger as if I weren't holding back.

"Good call." He opens the bathroom door, steps back, and reaches for my hand to pull me inside. He slams the door and locks it. "Better now?"

I glance around the bathroom. There's a pile of towels in one corner and the air is still damp from the guys' earlier showers. "Not even a little."

"I thought you enjoy it when I misbehave." He takes one step forward, challenge in his stare as he crowds my body.

"Check yourself. Right now." I press my hand into his chest.

His eyes dance with delight, and that cocky grin grows. "Worried you can't handle me?"

"Oh, I'm the one you can't handle." I take a step forward and straighten my spine as I lift my chin.

"Yeah?" He leans forward so we're standing close and he invades my space with his breath. "Prove it."

Instead of closing the space between our lips, I press my hand between our bodies and grip the collar of his shirt in a tight fist. My other hand cups his erection through his jeans. I don't know what comes over me, other than I need to have control. That and he's totally into this. "This is exactly how you saw this play out. Isn't it?"

He holds my gaze, nodding yes, but the humor in his eyes is replaced with need. He wants me badly.

I want him, too. "Terms?"

"Huh?" For a man who never shuts up, he's at a loss for words.

"If we do this"—I squeeze him though his jeans and delight in the groan that leaves his lips—"I need rules. It's not a free-for-all."

"Whatever you want."

"Monogamy."

His nostrils flare. "Not an issue."

"I mean it, Austin. I find out you let anyone near this"—I rub my hand against him once more before releasing his hardening cock —"and I cut it off."

"What else?" His gaze holds steady, my threat doing nothing to deter him.

I can't believe I'm agreeing to this. Given our positions, he in the band and me as the head of security, a relationship between us comes with risk. And yet, I can't deny or ignore this chemistry between us. "No one gets to know."

His lips pinch with disapproval. "The press only reports what we tell them."

"Not just the press." I level him with my stare. "Everyone. The band. The girlfriends. My boss. Your label. No one can know."

"So, I'm your dirty secret?" He shrugs, but for a split second I see the hurt my insistence brings.

I feel bad, but it's the only way. "Can you handle that?"

His lips draw into a brilliant smile. "Only if you promise to tie me up again."

"Oh, that's a guarantee." I grab his wrists and turn us both so his back is to the door. My lips hover a breath from his as I press his hands behind his body. My breasts press into his chest and I take pleasure in the control. "We stick to the rules."

"So you keep saying. Worried about falling in love with me, Jayla?"

He doesn't know the half of it. I release his wrists and run my fingers along the stubble of his strong jaw. "Shut the fuck up and kiss me."

"Yes, ma'am." His lips crash to mine. Strong. Gentle. Urgent. He's all this and more. My body sparks alive with a yearning that's been building all day. Doesn't matter we just did this last night, or we don't have the privacy of a bedroom. I want him. Now. The desire to sink onto his cock and fall apart increases with every move of his mouth. I sweep my tongue into his mouth and release a moan.

"Jayla," Austin reaches for my waist.

On instinct I push against his chest to create space between us. My gaze finds his. The touch of his hands should've scattered the lust from my mind, but it doesn't. My pulse speeds under the understanding in his stare. He doesn't push. He also doesn't stop looking at me as if I'm his favorite dessert.

"I'm good," I whisper. I don't try to hide my vulnerability. "Don't stop."

He nods and a slight smile draws his lips up as he kisses me again. Before we get carried away he pulls back and catches my stare. "I want to try something." There's an unspoken question in his words. *Do you trust me?*

He waits until I offer a slight nod, and then tentatively grazes my hip with his hand. He moves, and with a shuffle of feet he moves me backward. My butt hits the sink's counter and before I can question, Austin drops to his knees.

His hands skim up the sides of legs, over my thighs, across my hips, and to the button on my slacks. His stare asks for permission, or maybe he's gauging my reaction.

My body heats with desire under his stare, and in them he must find what he needs. He removes my pants. My socks. My underwear. His movements are reverent, focused and measured, and with a gentleness that makes me feel precious. Next, he reaches back and pulls his shirt over his head with one hand.

I greedily take in the sight of him. He kneels before me as if he's ready to worship my body, and my pulse speeds with anticipation. I don't do this. I like to have control. I need it. And yet, the way Austin positioned us, I don't feel caged in or fearful.

His hand skims up the inside of my leg, and he presses open my thigh so his face is directly in front of my pussy. He licks his lips as his gaze flicks up to mine. "Is this okay?"

He's asking permission. He's asking for more. I don't know whether I'll be able to orgasm like this, or if I'll freak out, but I trust him enough to try. "I don't know."

He holds my stare, his own eyes reflecting back the same mix of trepidation and lust I feel down to my core. He lifts my leg onto his shoulder and I balance myself by gripping the counter. I still feel in control. He's on his knees and not dominating my body with his posture, but this is the most vulnerable of sexual positions I've ever experimented with.

"If it stops being okay—" He spreads me wide with his fingers. "Stops feeling good, tell me. Yeah?"

"Yeah," I manage to breathe out.

He inhales, a smile graces his lips, and then his mouth is on my body. Licking. Kissing. Sucking. He goes at it like a man on a mission, which is quite accurate. He only backs off enough to meet my eyes, a silent check-in to make sure I'm okay with this, and fuck if that doesn't turn me on more.

"I love how you taste," he says, more to my pussy than my face.

"You like it?" I bite my lip so I won't let loose a moan, and shamelessly thread my fingers through his hair to bring him back to where I ache for more.

"No." He shakes his head, all humor gone with the disappearance of his smile. "I fucking love it. I think I'm gonna quit the band and do this instead." He flashes his devious grin and I swear my sex clenches in response.

"There's a plan I could get behind," I reply just as cheekily. But my words are stolen as his lips suck my clit.

"Oh!" I pant and clutch the counter so hard it'll leave marks.

His tongue runs circles around the sensitive bud of nerves, and he presses my legs open wider. His fingers, first one, then two, slip between my slick folds and he fucks me with them. *Oh, yes!* That's it. I'm officially in love with this man's mouth. He never lets up; his fingers, lips, and tongue move together, bringing me closer and closer to the edge. The sounds of sloppy kisses and the wetness between my legs as his fingers thrust in and out fill the small bathroom. It's a heady, erotic soundtrack. I feel my orgasm approaching and my pulse speeds, my breath coming fast as I let go of the last of my control.

That's it. Fuck, yes! I'm so close. My thighs squeeze together but Austin holds them open, his mouth sucking my clit. My eyes slam shut and my orgasm hits.

"Yes!" I shout, and my body spasms with the aftershocks. Shamelessly, I ride his face and I almost feel bad except Austin doesn't look up once. His mouth greedily licks between my legs as he lets loose a groan of his own.

"Damn, boy," I heave out between breaths.

He lowers my leg to the floor and sinks back on his heels. His mouth pulls into a satisfied smile, his lips wet from my arousal. His erection presses against his jeans in an illicit manner. It's obscene, really. Probably painful.

I should put him out of his misery. My sex clenches with a 'yes please' before I come up with the best way to fuck in this space. The floor is out for so many reasons. But with his help for balance, this counter ledge will work just fine. Even though he just made me come, I want him inside me, and my body shivers with anticipation.

I crook my finger and bite my lip to contain my smile. "Come fuck me."

Austin's eyes heat with desire and he's on his feet in seconds, shucking his pants. He strokes himself and steps between my legs, lining himself up at my entrance as I hike my leg around his hip. He finds my gaze before he thrusts inside, and it's full of so much adoration, for a moment my breath catches. The world stills. It's just the two of us against it all.

Then he moves his hips and we become all about lust, pleasure, and chasing another high. His mouth moves against my throat, nestles into my neck, and deposits open kisses along my skin. His hips rock, and so do mine. We start again, building this crazy friction and reaching for gratification. Together our bodies keep rhythm, his kisses set the melody, and my moans become the chorus. What we had last night wasn't a one-hit wonder. No, this is the lovemaking of legends.

"Don't stop." I push my hips forward to meet his thrusts. My hands grip the counter. My clit throbs, aching for more friction.

"What do you need?" Austin pants, his jaw tight as if he's holding back. "I want you to come."

"More," I say, reaching for another release. "Give me more."

"Fuck," Austin swears on a strangled moan, and his palm

snakes between us until his thumb finds my clit. The groan of pleasure is all the encouragement he needs to rub tiny circles against my flesh, and that's exactly what my body needs to come apart.

My sex clenches and I release a cry before I bite down on my lip to rein it in. He gives a few more pumps of his hips and then he's right there with me, his body tremoring with his strength as he fills me with his release. His head falls forward and rests on my shoulder, his breaths heavy and rushed.

Not wanting him to pull away yet, I wrap my arms around his waist and hug him to me.

A bang against the wall surprises us both. "Oh, my God!" There's laughter in Trent's voice. "Turn on the shower! Or play music! Some of us are trying to sleep!"

"Or use a gag!" Sean yells. More laughter.

Austin meets my stare and then bursts into a laugh of his own. "I guess we're telling people."

"Oh, my God!" I press my hands to my face. What was I thinking, fucking Austin in the bus bathroom? *I wasn't.* "I'm so embarrassed."

"Don't be. I like that you're so vocal when you come undone." He leans in for a kiss.

"But we just agreed not to tell anyone." I groan.

"Hey, it's fine." Austin shrugs. "Besides, I'm pretty sure Trent figured it out this morning."

Trent already knew Austin and I slept together. "Ugh!" I push at his shoulder. "And you didn't tell me!"

"In my defense you seemed set on not telling anyone, and who was I to argue when I was about to get laid." His gaze drops to where our bodies are still connected, and I do the same. We watch as his cock slides out of my wet center.

"Fuck, that's so hot." He groans.

As much as I'd like to agree, I'm mortified to leave this bathroom and face everyone. Because they just heard us having sex. Because it's too much to hope they'll be okay with us being together. "This is bad."

"It's fine, Jay." Austin pulls out two clean hand towels from under the sink and wets them with warm water. He hands one to me, and cleans himself with the other. "They won't care, if that's what you're worried about."

"How can you be so sure?" I know how this looks. They don't know me. They don't realize our history. This band operates more like family than friends, and if they're protective of Austin I'd completely understand.

"Because you make me happy," he states as if it's as simple as that. And maybe it is. Hope blooms in the pit of my belly, along with another rush of longing. This time for something more than sex. I don't know exactly when it happened, but I'm thoroughly addicted to this man. I can't imagine my life without him in it.

30

AUSTIN

I NEVER THOUGHT I'd be the kind of man to fall in love. It's not who I am. I'm the guy who makes everyone laugh. Inappropriate jokes and shameless self-deprecation are my go-tos. The women who want me only do because of my money, fame, or rock star status. I never thought I'd find a woman who'd want to be with me when all of that other crap is stripped away. If I'm honest, the belief probably goes all the way back to my childhood. Being told you're not worthy, and being raised by a mother who didn't think she deserved a healthy, honest relationship does a number on a young man's head.

But Jayla is different. She always was. She understands my past because she was right there as a witness. She doesn't give a shit about my money or celebrity clout. She challenges me. For some reason I don't fully understand, she wants me, and I'm the lucky son of a bitch who gets to love her back.

The next week passes in a whirlwind. I've become one of those people I can't stand. I smile all the damn time. I catch myself singing in the fucking shower. Happiness and positivity radiate from every-thing I say and do—because every day is a good day when Jayla's in it. We spend our days working hard, and at night our bodies come together to work even harder. Though we have to be creative. The bathroom on the bus is my new favorite location to hook up, simply because it has a locking door. But sometimes if we're extra sneaky and everyone else is sleeping soundly, Jayla rides me on one of the lounge chairs. Sleep bunks are off the table. I don't even try, because being alone in one is uncomfortable enough. Given her triggers, I won't risk a setback.

But earlier today we rolled into NYC for two nights at Madison Square, which means hotel overnight stay. *Halleluiah!*

I'm about to make this stop one she'll never forget. And no, that's not some reference about my cock, though it could be. I pulled out all the favors to arrange a little surprise for my woman. She works so damn hard. I see how this tour wears on her with the long hours, responsibility, and work ethic she brings to keeping everyone safe on the road and at our packed shows. She's appreciated for her efforts, but I want to spoil her. Jayla takes care of everyone around her, but who takes care of Jay?

At the end of sound checks, I step off the stage and hand my precious Lola to Ben. "Take care of her."

He laughs. "You say that every time. When do I not treat your guitars like they're newborn babes?"

"And that's why you're my favorite roadie." I chuckle and pat Ben on his shoulder. "Thanks, man."

Trent taps his wrist and lifts his brows. "Almost go time."

Sean notices the movement and comes closer. "You still think she has no clue?"

"God, I hope not." I blow out nerves and the tiny sliver of doubt that she won't like me going behind her back. I had to recruit Brian's assistance to sneak Jayla away for a few hours. He thinks it's because Jayla's family is flying out to surprise her for her birthday, because that's the lie I told him. It's risky. But aren't all important things worth the risk?

On cue, Jayla and Brian appear from one end of the stage.

"You guys ready to head out? The interview starts in an hour," Jayla asks.

"Yep!" I say with more enthusiasm than necessary.

Jayla eyes me warily, but doesn't say anything as we head out to the waiting car.

Trent chuckles. "Don't blow your load, young grasshopper."

"We're the same age," I grumble. His warning hits too close to home. Fuck. If the guys ever learn the details to my first fumbling sexual encounter with Jayla, I'll never hear the end of it.

We all pile into the SUV and I bury my nose in my phone. If I look at Jayla, I swear she'll see right through me. Thankfully, the ride only takes fifteen minutes, most of which she chats with Brian, going over last minute changes for tonight's show. Our driver pulls up to the hotel where our fake interview is scheduled.

"This is our stop," Brian hustles out of the vehicle. He holds the door for Jayla, and then waits for me to get out.

Leighton pats my shoulder and gives in to a grin. "Go get 'em, tiger."

"Be back in three hours," Brian slides back into his seat.

"Wait, what?" Jayla pins him with a confused stare.

"Enjoy your birthday," he says and then slams the door. Honks of annoyance trill through the busy New York backdrop as the SUV pulls back into traffic.

Jayla spins on her heel. "Why did Brian just wish me a happy birthday?"

A smile takes over my face. "Because I told him it was—"

"And why would you—?"

"Let's go inside."

Her gaze heats with something other than annoyance. *Passion.* She's totally turned on right now, and for half a second I consider bailing on my plan and spend the afternoon fucking instead. But no. There's time for that. Today's about showing Jayla how much I care.

Inside the hotel, the concierge steps away from his desk and meets us in the center of the lobby. "Mr. Jones, so nice to meet you. I'm Cal. We spoke on the phone."

"Yes, thanks for your help." I reach out to shake his hand.

"It was my pleasure," he says. "Are you and your guest ready?"

"Let's do this." I grin, knowing it's probably killing Jayla not to know what it is we're doing. As we follow Cal, my hand itches to cradle the small of her back, but I refrain from the gesture. I won't put our new relationship at risk, and while the risk of paparazzi or an excited fan snapping a covert photo isn't likely, it's still a possibility.

We take a private elevator to the top floor, and Cal weaves us through a series of hallways before opening a secured door. "You two enjoy. I'll be back in an hour."

Jayla steps through first and once she realizes what I have in store, she whips around, her eyes wide, her smile growing. "Nails! I'm getting my nails done." The joy from her words is worth all the sneaking around to arrange this.

"*We're* getting our nails done," I say through my own grin.

"How did you—?" Her mouth falls open as she takes in the room. The spa is closed, but with money it's easy to convince a few techs to stay after hours.

"You said it's one of the things you missed most with being on tour." I shrug. "Well, that and your friends."

Her eyes go wide and she glances around. "You didn't—" Shit. She thinks I flew Kalise and Aliyah here. Damn it. I should have.

"No." I shake my head. "Fuck, that would have been a better surprise." I run a hand over my face and scrunch my nose. "Next time."

"Austin." She pins me with a glare. "Don't even. This is . . . so unexpected. It's too much."

"It's not close to enough, but I'm glad you like it."

One of the techs approaches. "I'm Amy, and that's Rhonda." She waves toward her co-worker. "Pick a color for your nails, then come have a seat when you're ready."

"Thank you."

I follow Jayla to the wall display of bottled polish.

She browses several minutes and picks out a few colors. She holds one out to me. "Here's your color. It's called Rockstar Pink." Her lips twist with her grin.

"Don't tease." I lean in close to whisper in her ear. "We both know your pussy is my favorite shade." Her body shivers and when I step back her eyes hold desire in their depths. My cock aches uncomfortably in my pants, but I remind him that's for later. "I think I'll keep my nails natural." I wink and nod toward the chairs. "You ready for our first couples' mani pedi?"

"Yes," she says as if she's surprised by her answer. "Yes, I really am."

For the next hour our nails are buffed—and hers polished—while we're treated to cucumber infused water and hand massages that pull actual moans from our mouths. It's not sexual in the least, and I swear by the time we put our shoes back on, I'm the most relaxed I've been all month. By the satisfied, blissed out expression on Jayla's face, she feels the same. I tip Amy and Rhonda generously for that alone.

"Thanks, ladies!" I say when it's time to head to the next stop of my spoil-Jayla-so-she-never-thinks-to-leave-me surprise.

"Come back and see us next time you're in New York!" Amy calls after us.

"Yes, and have a great show tonight!" Rhonda adds.

Out in the hall, Cal is waiting for us. He glances at me and then smiles at Jayla. "Did you enjoy the spa?"

"Very much," she says.

"Glad to hear it," Cal gestures for us to follow.

I fight the urge to hold Jayla's hand. This whole keeping our relationship on the down low is more challenging than I thought it'd be. It's a predicament because I find myself longing for this tour to be over. Once we get back to LA it'll be easier to date, and I'll be able to have my hands on her without hesitation. But once we're back home there'll be new challenges. Namely, how to spend as much time as possible together with two very different careers. From what Jayla's shared about her private security work, she often works weekends and late nights. When the guys and I are recording, we're done most nights by dinnertime. I'm sure there's no way I could convince her to be my stay-at-home girlfriend, but part of me wants to try.

"This was the best not-my-birthday surprise ever," Jayla murmurs low enough that Cal can't hear. "Thank you."

Her appreciation is already apparent, but it makes me smile nonetheless. "Oh, it's not over."

She glances at Cal as he calls the elevator to our floor, and then shoots me a look. "Austin, don't be ridiculous. I can't leave everything to Brian."

I shake my head, not surprised in the least that she's concerned about leaving her staff high and dry. It's the kind of person she is. But she's earned this small break. Besides, ever since the FBI made an arrest for the bomb in Salt Lake City, we are all breathing easier. "I asked for three hours, and we're taking full advantage."

"It's not even my birthday." She laughs softly.

The elevator opens and Cal holds the door, pressing the button for the top floor as the doors slide shut.

"Well, I've missed too many of them." I take a step closer to her, lowering my voice. "Think of this as a make-up."

"Oh?" Her eyes dance with amusement. "That leaves you twelve others."

She's teasing, but the thought of having her permission to go above and beyond at least a dozen more times brings me more joy than it should. "Done."

She opens her mouth, probably to argue, but Cal interrupts. "This is you. I'll be back when your car arrives."

The doors slide open and we shuffle into the open hallway. Floor to ceiling windows reveal an expansive view of the city.

"Oh," Jayla says, her tone full of awe. Her steps are slow as her gaze drinks it in.

There's something about being above the city this way that I've always loved, but I'm captivated by her. "Beautiful, isn't it?"

She glances over her shoulder. "This is too much."

With just the two of us alone for the first time all day, I grab her hand and tug her loosely into my arms. "There's more." I can't help but brush my lips along hers for a kiss.

"Austin," she reprimands and presses her hands at my chest, but instead of pushing me away, she glances around the empty hall before claiming my mouth with a kiss that awakens every part of my body.

"Come on." I break the kiss and take her hand before we're discovered or things get out of control and we're arrested for indecent exposure. Besides, I can't wait for her to see the next part. With my gaze on her, I push open the ballroom door and walk us inside.

The space is mostly used for weddings and parties, but today there's only one table set for two with our meals hiding under a pair of silver domes. On the stage is the local Motown band I hired. When we were teens and Jayla was in a good mood, she always put her dad's old records on. With one nod from me they begin to play.

I meet Jayla's gaze, expecting a megawatt smile. But her stare is practically unreadable, and her eyes glass over as if she might cry. *Well, shit.* I didn't mean to overwhelm her.

"Jay?" I squeeze her hand to draw her attention.

"This." She shakes her head. "You did all this for me?"

If I could pound my chest and not ruin the moment, I would. Her words, and the way she's regarding me as if I've completely superseded her expectations, makes me feel like the king of New York. "All for you."

"This is too much."

"I have money." I shrug. "Get over it."

"I'd rather you not waste it." The words fly from her lips and she glances at the floor.

"Not a waste." I take a step backward and tug her closer to the band. "Dance with me."

"In here?" She glances around the empty ballroom, a shyness creeping into her usual confidence. "Just us?"

"Please?" I ask her once more, praying she won't turn me down. "Dance with me, Jayla?"

She nods and I draw her into my arms, one hand settling on her hip while the other snakes around her waist. She lets me hold her close, and her hands find the neckline of my T-shirt where her fingers skim the column of my throat. I rest my forehead against hers, content to close my eyes and memorize the feeling. There's nothing indecent about our embrace as we swing our hips to the music, but somehow that makes this more intimate. The band croons about finding lost love, and everything about this moment feels perfect.

This is all I need. I savor it, memorize and capture the beauty. The feel of her curves against me. The way she allows me to lead. Together it feels as if we could take on the world. That we could be forever.

Forever. I swallow back the surge of emotion that tightens my throat and makes it hard to breathe. I don't expect I'll be lucky enough for this to last. Someone as extraordinary as her will eventually come to her senses. I won't be enough. Eventually I'll fuck this up. That truth hurts.

Jayla won't want me forever, but for now I pretend maybe she could.

31

JAYLA

I DON'T KNOW how he does it. Austin has not only made me a liar, but in the span of two hours he steals another piece of my heart. If I'm not careful, he'll have the entire thing. I'm not the kind of woman who's wowed by big, flashy gestures, and I still think it's insane he rented an entire ballroom just for us to dance. But I can't deny everything about this afternoon was sweet, meaningful, and perfect.

By the time Cal arrives to retrieve us, I feel totally pampered and recharged.

"Thank you," I say to Austin after we're tucked into the town car and on our way back to the venue.

"You don't have to thank me anymore," he weaves our fingers together on the seat between us. He lets loose a long sigh and drops his head back on the seat. "I don't want to go back."

I nod, understanding the sentiment. He provided an escape where we didn't have to think about work or life, or anything other than each other. A bubble away from the world. The only other time that happens is when we're having sex. And while I first thought he snuck us to the hotel for just that, I'm glad today was about more than meeting the physical needs of our relationship. Besides, we'll have time for that later tonight.

Lost in my thoughts, his phone buzzes from where it rests on his lap. With his other hand, he picks it up to read the screen. The second he reads the screen his brow tugs into a scowl and his body tenses. A moment later his hand releases mine.

"Everything okay?" I straighten in my seat.

"It's nothing." He smiles, but it's forced and doesn't quite reach his eyes. He taps a few buttons and sets the phone back on his lap, screen down, but doesn't reach for my hand again.

"Austin?" I don't know who he thinks he's fooling, or why he's even trying.

"It's nothing. Promise." He's lying. It's clear as day. He holds my gaze with that fake smile again and I can't tell whether he thinks I'm stupid enough to believe him, or he's protecting me from whatever it is he's not saying.

My stomach churns with unease. *What is he hiding?* The question bounces in my mind as I hold his stare. I won't ask again. If he doesn't want to tell me, he must have a reason. *Right?* My body grows anxious and I give in to the need to tap my heel. Austin glances away, feigning interest at the city outside.

I hate how quickly uncertainty replaces the honest openness between us. Disappointment grows with each passing mile as I realize he's shut me out. *Does he not trust me? What's going on?* A million different scenarios race though my thoughts and none of them bring peace of mind.

Maybe he has a good reason for keeping me in the dark. He better. I grasp the irony, because Austin isn't the only one with secrets. I still haven't told him about my phone call with Vince last week, and I don't plan to. Every time Austin asks to film another video I'm conflicted and filled with guilt, but ultimately it's the right choice. At least for now.

When the car pulls in the secure entrance twenty minutes later we still haven't said a word. I silently beg for him to break the silence, to put my fears at ease, but mostly for him to be honest and real. Only Austin's not a mind reader, and that doesn't happen. Our car stops and the driver walks around to open my door.

"Austin?" I don't attempt to mask the hurt from my tone.

His lips pinch as he meets my gaze, and for a second I think he might acknowledge this shift between us.

My door opens. "Miss Miller?"

I hesitate because I refuse to go back to work when we're on such shaky ground. After everything Austin gave me this afternoon, he can make this right.

"Later." His voice rasps as if he has to fight to push out the words. "We'll talk later, okay?"

I hold his stare, searching for truth, and give him a silent nod. Maybe he's doling bullshit, but his promise to talk later pacifies my worries. At the very least, suspends them for the time being. Besides, we don't have time for this. Not now. We've already had our vacation from reality, and something tells me our crash back down to Earth might hurt.

THERE'S STILL another two hours until we open the doors, but in my absence the security team stayed on task. Everything is ready to go, and after I make my rounds I head over to the green room to see Austin. Our parting was awkward at best and as busy as I've been tonight, I haven't stopped worrying. Even now as I slide inside the room, Austin's stare doesn't quite meet mine. He just sits there, spinning his phone on top of the table as if it's the most interesting object in the room. His quiet rejection hurts.

"How's your birthday?" Sean draws everyone's attention to where I stand. His grin tells me Austin hasn't mentioned anything about the uncomfortable end to our date on the car ride back. Everything changed with that one text, and hell if I can figure out what could have been bad enough to sour our perfect afternoon.

"Oh." I force myself to laugh. "Good, except the security team now thinks I was born on January twenty-first."

Everyone chuckles. Except Austin. I know this because I can't keep my eyes off him. Maybe I should pretend we're good, but I can't stand the distance. Passing everyone, I walk over and pull out the chair next to his. I set my phone on the table and reach across to cover his hand with mine. "Hey, we good?"

He lifts his gaze to mine and for a second I see his vulnerability. Fear. Hesitation. Then my cell vibrates on the table between us and his gaze leaves mine to read the incoming text. His mouth presses together and his brows knit with a scowl. "What the fuck is this?" he growls.

I glance at my cell to the message from Glen, one of the guys I went through the academy with. We're not super close, but he's one of the guys I still meet up with to grab a beer every now and then. It's a one-word text, *hey*, and Austin has no reason to be annoyed about it. Especially with how strange he's been acting.

My jaw locks and I meet his stare with challenge. "That's my phone."

"Yeah, and who's this fuckwad?" He points at my cell.

I came over here to make peace, or at the very least to be understanding of his sudden change in mood, but now he's acting like a jealous little man. I straighten my spine and cross my hands over my chest. "I think you can read."

"Who the fuck is Glen?" He leans forward on his elbows. "And why is he sliding into your DMs with a hey?"

"It's just hey." I glance over Austin's shoulder to find everyone staring, but they all turn around and act as if they aren't. Maybe we shouldn't do this here, with an audience and with tension already at a high. But then I remember how Austin pretty much cut me off when he got a text, and the double standard pisses me off.

"We both know exactly what hey means."

"No." I tilt my head. "Enlighten me."

"When a dude sends a hey, he's looking to get laid."

"Oh, really?" I laugh incredulously. "Maybe he wants to say hi. Talk. See how I'm doing."

Austin scoffs. "Sure, if he wants to fuck you."

"You're a pig." I make a disgusted sound in my throat.

Austin's frown grows with his glare. "Who is Glen?"

"We used to work together. Not that I owe you an explanation." I pick up my phone and my chair scrapes loudly against the floor. "In the future, how about you respect my privacy?"

"Why? You hiding something?" *Hello pot, meet kettle. Aren't we all.* "We agreed no other guys."

I gasp at his accusation. It's completely uncalled for and spiteful. My blood boils and I drag in a breath so I won't yell. I lower my voice so only he hears. "Have a great fucking show." Turning on my heel, I stomp out before he pulls me any deeper into this stupid argument.

I can't believe he alluded to me cheating. All because I received a text from a man! My pulse speeds and I'm still fired up as I stomp through the mostly empty concourse. I don't have anywhere to be or anything to do until it's time to let the public in, but restlessness causes me to pace.

When I've calmed enough to think straight, I pick up my cell to find out what Glen wants. It's most certainly not to sleep with me. *Fucking, Austin.*

Me: Hey, what's up?"

Glen: I was gonna ask if you wanted to hit up Runyon this week, but I see you're on tour . . .

A moment later he sends a screenshot of one of the videos I did with Austin.

Me: Ugh. You saw the video.

Glen: LOL hell yeah I did.

Me: Don't start.

Glen: What? It was good.

Me: AND?

Glen: You always were good at takedowns.

Me: AND?

The stupid bubbles appear and re-appear for what feels like forever before his next message finally comes through.

Glen: Everyone in the department is talking about your ass.

Me: Fucking hell.

Glen: All complimentary.

Me: I'm never coming to happy hour again.

Glen: Oh, come on! Don't make such threats.

Me: My ass is the entire fucking frame!

Glen: Please. You look the best you have in years. Baby got back.

Me: It's HUGE.

Glen: You're thick and you look good. I'm defending your honor as much as I can. I stuck Martinez on traffic stops for the month so they're no longer making lewd comments.

Glen: At least around me.

Me: Thank you.

Glen: One more thing.

Me: Yeah?

Glen: Be careful, okay?

Glen is one of the good guys. The kind of person who considers everyone around him family. But he doesn't need to be worried about me.

Me: That's why I'm on this tour. To keep things safe.

Glen: No . . . I meant with your heart.

It catches me off guard. Completely and totally. Glen's been a friend ever since surviving academy together, and he's one of the few people I still talk with after leaving the force. We meet up for beers on occasion, or to get in a run, but we don't do personal matters and we especially don't talk feelings.

Me: My heart is in perfect condition.

Glen: That rock star. Austin.

Me: Yes?

Glen: Fuck this, I'm calling.

My cell rings a second later and I pick up, wildly curious as to why he's concerned for my heart. "Hey."

"Sorry, I should've called first."

"What's going on?"

He exhales harshly. "I don't trust that Austin guy. Keep an eye on him. Or better yet, stay far, far away."

"What are you talking about? You realize that's impossible." Understatement of the year, but Glen doesn't need to know Austin and I are hooking up.

"I shouldn't be telling you this, so let's forget I am, but a buddy of mine works private sector. He's a retired detective and ex-military. I think I've told you about him."

"Yeah," I say, impatient. "What about him?" And what does he have to do with Austin?

"Austin Jones hires him."

"For what?" When he doesn't answer right away my irritation heightens to severe annoyance. "Glen, stop fucking around. Either say it or don't."

"Sorry, it just pisses me off that you're stuck working to protect a scumbag." He clears his throat. "He pays my friend to find girls."

My gut churns with dread. "Girls?"

"Young ones. Homeless. Prostitutes and drug addicts especially."

"What does he do with them?"

"Does it matter? I can't think of anything chivalrous unless he's operating some program to get young women off the street, and we both know that's not happening. If it was, that'd be all over the press."

He's right. I know he is, but I refuse to believe this about Austin. From my time on the force and in private protection, I know better than anyone that people aren't always who they claim to be. But Austin as a sexual predator? It doesn't sit right with me. "Are you sure it's the same Austin Jones?"

"Positive. We were watching your YouTube video—that's how it came up—and this guy . . . I don't condone his lack of moral compass when it comes to his freelance work, but I'd trust him with my life."

"Thanks, Glen," I say numbly, feeling sick and dizzy all at once. "For looking out. I gotta go."

"Always. Doesn't matter that you quit on me, we bleed blue for life."

My hands shake and I fight back the urge to puke as I process this news. I can't believe this is true. Not Austin. Not the man who comforted me when I told him about the assault I experienced as a young woman. *Oh, God.* My stomach dips. *Did that turn him on?*

"Jayla." Austin's voice catches me unexpectedly and I jump.

I spin around to meet his gaze. I didn't notice him approach. I was too busy freaking the fuck out.

His footsteps slow with caution when he catches sight of my expression. "Everything okay?"

No! It's not okay. *Nothing is,* I want to scream. I want to sit him down and ask him what the hell he's doing hiring a PI to find vulnerable women. But I don't do any of that. Instead, I school my features and harden my heart to the man who's worked his way too close. "Fine."

"You sure about that? 'Cause your face didn't get the memo." It's a stupid attempt at humor but it falls flat, and neither of us give in to a smile.

I work my jaw back and forth, unable to respond without going off or falling apart.

"This have something to do with *Glen?*" Austin asks, but there's no kindness to his tone. He shakes his head as if he didn't mean for any animosity to slip. "I'm sorry I acted like a jealous fuck back there."

I glance down at my cell, still clutched in my hands.

"That was him, wasn't it? So what, did you used to date? Hook up? You can tell me."

I frown and shake my head. "No. He's a friend." But after this call I can't help but wonder whether Austin's jealous or only deflecting. Maybe he's trying to focus my mind on something else so I won't see what's happening. *Fuck.* Has he been doing this to me the entire time?

"What did he want?" Austin shoves his hands into his pockets.

His arms flex and his jaw is tight as if he's angry. He couldn't know what Glen just told me, could he?

I should clear the air. I should ask the hard questions. But I don't. Instead, I spit back the same words he used earlier. "It's nothing."

The air crackles between us, as powerful as the current running through the sound and lighting on tonight's stage. As angry as I am right now, my body tingles with awareness, desire, longing for more of what only Austin gives. I hate myself a little for that.

"So, that's how it's gonna be?" he demands.

"Yeah." My irritation grows. Mostly at myself for not being brave enough to ask him the questions.

He looks as if he's about to argue, but instead of pushing the issue he shakes his head. "Whatever. I've got a show to play."

I bite my lip, holding back the urge to have the last word. He wants to walk away. Okay. Fine. That's how it's gonna be. I have a job to do, too. Arms crossed over my chest and spine straight, I hold his gaze without wavering while I feel as though my insides shatter in a million pieces.

He drops his gaze, and the shake of his head as he turns to walk away is both condescending and disappointed. I should feel relief. Righteousness for not caving to his manipulation. Angry even, for this entire situation and how today went from best to worst. But I don't feel any of those things. Because the trust I was beginning to have in him is tainted. Because a tiny part of me wonders if Glen is right.

In these short few weeks Austin and I have built a connection I never imagined possible. I was the broken one. The one incapable of mixing pleasure with sex. Until him. But if I discover he's no better than a monster? The kind that gets off on young girls? Then he won't only ruin what little hope I have for myself, he'll obliterate it.

With each stride that separates us, my heart cracks further, and by the time he's gone I'm certain I've lost the best thing in my life.

The worst part about it? I still think I made the right choice.

32

AUSTIN

I PUSHED HER AWAY.

As soon as I realize what I accused her of—with no rational basis other than my own jealousy, I race to find her and apologize. Only what do I do? I fuck that up as well. I'm worse than a self-fulfilling prophecy, because I'm the one who pushed her further away. Even if it wasn't my intention, it's what I've done.

And why? All because I'm terrified to admit the truth. To tell her about Brianna and the private investigator and the photos I pay for in my desperate attempt to find her. I'm worried she won't believe me. Or trust me. Or love me enough to see past my failures.

Because I failed Jayla when she moved away. Not intentionally, but she needed me, and what happened to her after she moved . . . she carried that alone for so long. Bri needed me too, but I was hell bent on proving my mom wrong, chasing the dream I always wanted, and in turn I left a little girl to survive amongst wolves.

This is all so fucked up. I stomp back to the green room more torn up than when I left. I can't lose Jayla. Not again. But I don't know how to make this right. How do I make up for so many years? For the missed letters? For the hurt?

My anxious thoughts race at a manic pace through my mind, and my body feels too big for my skin. The urge to erase the surge of panic has me digging in my bag for something to light up.

"Dude, you okay?" Trent puts his hand on my shoulder.

I stop my search to find everyone staring back with concern. Even the hair and makeup girl, Kellie, looks worried.

"I'm not gonna break shit if that's what you're worried about." My hands shake, and my pulse races as if it's going a million miles an hour. "I just need a smoke." *Fucking finally.* Deep in the bottom of my bag is the tiny case that holds a half-smoked joint. I pull it out and look around. "Anyone have a lighter?"

"I got you, boo," Kellie says with all the sass in the world, and an eye roll for good measure. She pulls one out from one of her big makeup boxes and holds it over her shoulder while still managing to trace Leighton's eyes in thick liner with the other hand. "Just bring it back when you're done."

"Care if I join you?" Sean asks.

Of all of these guys, he's the least likely to kill my buzz. "Sure."

He doesn't ask any more questions and keeps up with my brisk pace as I walk in the opposite direction of the stage. I don't know where exactly I'm heading, but when I spot a special restroom marked for families, I go there. Inside the room smells like disinfectant and cleaning supplies, which I guess is a hell of a lot better than shitty diapers.

There's a rocking chair intended for nursing mothers, I realize, and Sean settles in like it's as natural as can be for two dudes to hang out in a family bathroom before a show.

I flip the lock, light up my joint, and inhale a long drag. I haven't smoked this entire tour, which is really fucking strange for me. Not that I consider myself an addict or anything, but I enjoy a buzz every now and again. I've been so wrapped up in Jayla these past weeks that I haven't even thought about smoking.

I exhale a plume of smoke before taking another hit. I glance at Sean, expecting him to say something, even if it's to warn me to take it easy. "What?" I challenge with the lift of my chin. "I know you wanna say something."

He just chuckles, rocking himself back and forth in that damn chair. "I don't have anything to say other than you're being a selfish ass. You gonna smoke that entire joint without offering me a hit?"

"Shit. Sorry," I say and pass it to him.

He takes a long drag and holds his breath as he hands back the joint.

I roll the paper between my thumb and middle finger. "I know you heard us arguing."

"Yeah, everyone did," he says on his exhale and shrugs. "So? Couples argue."

I take another hit and pass it back to him. "I fucked up."

"Of course you did." He grins.

"Thanks."

"And you'll probably do it again. At least a hundred times." He takes one more hit and then snuffs the light out against the side of the trashcan.

I roll my eyes. "You're a real friend."

"Hey, don't get pissed at me for stating the truth. But you do realize you can make it right. That's the thing about fucking up. You have the ability to unfuck it up."

"You're a modern day Aristotle, you know that?"

"Make all the jokes you want, but you know I'm right." He chuckles as if he's so damn smart. He kind of is, though. I set the entire course into play today, starting with the text I received on the ride back from the hotel. Had I taken the time last night to go through the latest images and destroyed the link, my PI would have never followed up. But I was too preoccupied with settling myself inside Jayla's magic pussy, and then later I forgot. Even the fit of rage I had at seeing some other dude's name light up her cell phone had everything to do with the insecurity I was feeling.

Fucked it up.

Unfuck it.

"Fucking brilliant."

"I know I am. You're welcome." He grins, rocking in that chair. Back and forth, back and forth. Damn, that looks relaxing. We should get rocking chairs for the bus. Sean has everything figured out. He's like a voodoo philosopher or some shit.

"Thanks, brother." I shut my eyes and visualize the life I want. The one that Jayla's in and doesn't leave. Tonight, I make a vow to tell her everything. Apologize and come clean. I have to unfuck things. I can't shut her out. I won't let fear win. Maybe I lose her. Maybe she hates me afterward. But I have to try. She's too important, and what we have is too special. I may not be much of a fighter, but I'll fight for her.

Of course, all of that is gonna have to wait until after the show, because right now I'm really fucking high.

33

JAYLA

MY EYELIDS SLAM shut and I press my lips shut so I won't scream. I want to cry. My eyes water, but I refuse to do this right now. A sudden urge to ditch this place, hail a cab, and lock myself in my hotel room for the next twenty-four hours is more than tempting. I need to get my head straight, and space alone to process would help. But I don't have the luxury. I knew it was a risk—getting involved with Austin had the possibility of being messy if things went wrong—only I never imagined it'd go this far south.

Seriously. *What the fuck?*

The more I think about it, I can't fathom Austin being capable of Glen's accusations. The Austin I know has a really big heart, and while yes, he has a history of promiscuity, that doesn't equate to anything other than a high sex drive. After everything I told him about my past and how understanding he was, it doesn't seem possible he would hurt me this way.

But Glen would never lie or start shit without proof.

Real proof. That's what I need right now. Austin's been acting shady at times, like today when he got the message on his phone. Was it a photo of some girl? Is that why he shut me out so swiftly after our afternoon together?

These are the questions I need answers to. Yet the thought of confronting him brings a wave of nausea so fierce I might actually throw up. I hate that I didn't have the strength to call him out. The words stuck in my throat when I should've asked him to explain. Now I'm driving myself crazy running through every possible motive or reason for Austin to be buying pictures of vulnerable girls on the down low.

But none of that matters because right now I have a job to do. I need to shove my feelings aside and focus on filling up this arena and providing a safe show for everyone. The rest will have to wait. Until I'm locked inside my hotel room there's no time to fall apart, scream, cry, or do whatever else I must to deal.

Needing to stay busy for my sanity, I head outside to lend an extra hand with entry. It's a good thing too, because several ticket holders decide to cause havoc. There's one guy who tries to bring his loaded gun to the concert. *Dumbass.* Then two drunk guys get into a fist fight and injure a few innocent bystanders in the process. *Idiots.* That's on top of the normal confiscation of restricted liquids and food that patrons attempt to smuggle in. It all adds stressors to the entry process, and that's not good when the line is already wrapped around the building.

The cops respond to our altercation with the drunk wanna-be fighters and after giving my statement, I check in with Brian. The arena is ninety-percent filled and the opening act is on stage, so I head back to the green room.

One of my regular tasks is to escort the guys to the stage and run point on security until they're safely tucked inside the bus for the night—or rather hotel tonight. This is something I look forward to. I love watching the guys perform and I often catch a few songs from backstage. But not tonight. No. I wish I were headed anywhere else in this arena right now. I feel raw and angry, and unprepared to have any kind of conversation with Austin.

My feet feel heavy in my shoes as I radio to check in with the rest of the team. "Give me updates." *Please, no more problems.*

"Jayla? We've got an unattended bag in section 328. Black backpack. Just outside the restrooms off the concourse," Terrance reports in his low timbre through our secured line.

Shit. This night isn't getting any easier. "Clear the area and check with employees." I head in that direction and tap on my cell to call Brian. "Hey, you get all that?"

"Yes, ma'am. Want me to head over?"

"No." I shake my head even though he can't see. "I'm already close, and if it's a problem I should be there. I need you to get to the green room though, escort the guys to the stage on Casey's lead."

"You sure?" There's surprise in his reply because it's a task I haven't delegated this entire tour.

"If this wraps quickly I'll take your place, but I'd feel better with a backup plan." I may also like the idea of an out. I won't shirk my duties intentionally, but I'm not naïve enough to think spending time with Austin anytime soon will be comfortable.

"Sounds good, boss," Brian says. "Holler if you need anything else."

"You know I will."

I DON'T KNOW what kind of idiot thinks it's okay to park his bag outside the public restroom during a concert while he works his shift in concessions. Probably the same type to yell bomb on a plane as a joke. I'm starting to think there's a full moon or something.

The concession employee whose backpack we recovered once we deduced there were no bombs or weapons inside is back to filling popcorn buckets and souvenir soda cups. Thanks to the photo ID tucked next to his house keys, Oliver Han wasn't too hard to track down. I swear, I don't understand how some people survive in this world.

I walk back through the venue and past the secure checkpoint now that another proverbial fire is put out. If I hurry, I can probably catch the band before they go on. My body hums with anxiety as a war of two differing emotions battles inside my mind. There's a part of me that wants another hit of Austin Jones—his smile, his laughter, and yes, even his kiss—which is so wrong. At least, that's what the other part of me says. She's the piece that guards my heart and is ready to spin on my heel, file my resignation, and fly back home, never to look back.

"Miss Miller?"

"Yeah?" I lift my gaze to find a pimple-faced, wide-eyed young man jogging toward me. He's dressed in the standard concession uniform, and while I don't recognize his face from the staff list, it's been days since I reviewed the employee files for this stop.

"There's an emergency," he demands, his voice urgent. "Someone told me to come find you."

"Slow down," I say. "What's going on? And who sent you?"

"Everyone was yelling. There's blood. It was Austin I think, or maybe Trent. I'm not a big Three Ugly Guys fan." His words fly from his mouth in a rush. "There's something wrong with the baby."

Opal. *No!* My feet move before my mind fully processes the words, and I turn to meet the kid's face. "Where?"

"The green room," the young man yells after me. "Should I call 9-1-1?"

"No. Go back to work," I shout and wave him off so I can run in earnest. The cheers and chants from inside the arena press heavily through the thick, cemented walls. It's time for the band to head backstage. They're on in minutes. Or rather, they should be. Had I not been dealing with that stupid backpack, I would have been escorting them along with the rest of the team.

Guilt creeps along my spine because I should have been there. I can't believe this is happening. Opal looked fine this morning. Hell, she hasn't shown any signs of distress.

As I push my legs to move faster, I offer a prayer that she and the baby are fine. *Please, Lord. Keep them safe.*

I round the corner expecting a commotion or one of the security staff to be guarding the door, but when I yank open the green room door I realize why.

Oh. Shit.

"You're a hard woman to catch alone," says a man I've never met in person, but whose photos and record I memorized long ago. Coy Wright. His hair's a little longer and he's grown a short beard, but it's him. I'd stare longer to be sure, but I'm distracted by the Glock he aims at my head.

"Excuse me," I say and take a step back toward the now shut door.

"Nope," he says, the gun firm in his hand. "You and I are going to have little chat." He stares at my body. "Drop the pack."

It's the small bag I carry during all of my shifts. Inside are supplies, and a gun of my own, but he probably knows that. I want to kick myself for not having that holstered, but because I was out working in the public area tonight, I chose to store it unloaded and inside my bag. I regret the decision now.

I inhale slowly to calm my pulse, and slide the straps off my shoulders. "Here?" I ask, leaving his stare to glance at the floor.

He nods, his eyes glued to my presence.

I lower my arm, not making any sudden movement. If I can catch him off-guard or get close enough, I'm certain I can get the gun from his hands. He's a big guy, but I've practiced these scenarios a thousand times. It's possible to use his strength to my advantage, or talk him out of whatever it is he came here to accomplish. But before I set the bag on the floor, he rushes forward and yanks it from my hands. He backs up again before I have the opportunity to make a move.

Damn it.

"Your cell. Bluetooth. Radio." He's done his homework. "Drop them right there."

I raise my hands slowly and remove each item from my body.

Each device lands on the concrete floor with a resounding thud. Under his watchful stare I'm not able to signal for help; I'll risk his temper if I do. I know way more about Coy than he does about me and I plan to use that to my advantage. I have the training and skillset to take him down, but first I have to make him think he's in control.

"Away from the door," he commands, motioning to the opposite side of the room.

I take measured steps, never giving him my back.

He does the same, keeping the space between us wide, and leaves me no opportunity to go for the gun. Not unless I want to get shot. He approaches my equipment and crushes my in-ear piece with the weight of his boot, then kicks it and the rest of my stuff across the room. The door is at his back, but even if someone were to enter, he'd be able to accost them before they realized any danger.

"Sit," he demands, and points to the same chair Austin sat in only hours ago.

I don't move and instead try to get Coy talking. "What do you want?"

His somber stare lifts with the raise of his brow. His lips twist with a sinister smile. "Don't you want to get to know each other better before we get down to business?"

"I know exactly who you are." I do a poor job of keeping the disdain from my tone.

"Did that piece of shit boy toy of yours tell you how he fucked up my hand?" His chuckle is filled with malice, but that's not what prickles my skin. It's his implication that Austin and I are together. How would he know that? Unless he's guessing because of our videos. His eyes narrow and again he points that damn gun in my direction. "He tell you how he pretended to be my friend? How his buddy fucked my girl behind my back? How they all ruined my life?"

I hold my hands up with my fingers spread wide. "Give me the gun, Coy."

"Right." The vein on his forehead pops as he huffs out a laugh. "You must think I'm stupid."

I do, but I don't trust he's not completely off his rocker. Stress and desperation push rational thought from anyone's mind, let alone this asshole. I keep my voice even, my tone reassuring. "Tell me what you want so we can figure it out together. This doesn't have to be a lose-lose."

"No. It doesn't." His lips form a thin line, his chest puffing as he takes two steps forward. His eyes darken as his pupils dilate. "Not for me anyway. Because those ugly fuckers are gonna pay for everything they took."

I swallow as I'm hit with the very real fear that Coy might be crazy enough to hurt me. No one has reason to come to this green room. Not until the show is over, and that's hours away. Getting out of here alive is up to me, and I better come up with a plan soon.

"Sit," Coy barks. "Now!"

"I'm sitting. I'm sitting." I lower myself into the chair, not willing to spook him any further. I don't know what he's thinking, but he can't pull a gun on me and expect to walk away, which only means one thing. He doesn't. This man has nothing to lose, and that not only makes him dangerous, it makes me screwed.

Sitting on the chair, I force myself to breathe and not fidget under the stress.

For minutes he paces almost manically, cursing under his breath as he takes in the room with wild eyes. "Fuck. This is all wrong." He scrubs a hand over his beard and looks from me to the door, and then back again. "I wanted him to be here," he mutters, and his gaze narrows. He takes a few long strides, closing the space between us.

I consider charging forward off the chair, but I'm not certain I can get to his gun fast enough. Not from this position, and not when he's so much bigger than me. If he would only come a little closer.

"Get comfortable." He grabs a chair from across the table and drags it back against the wall. Positioning it to face both me and the door, he finally takes a seat. He sets my bag at his feet and leans back, his arms crossed over his chest. Unfortunately, he doesn't set down his gun. "We're gonna be here a few hours."

My body tenses and my senses prickle with fear. Maybe I should stay quiet, but I can't help myself from asking, "What happens in a few hours?

He catches my stare and there's no doubt I'm looking directly into the eyes of a man unhinged. One who is capable of ending my life, right here and now. He plays with the clip, locking and releasing it a few times before he lifts his hand and points the gun between my eyes. "I get my revenge."

My pulse beats so loudly I swear I hear it in my own ears. *Is this it?* Is this how I leave the world? I'm not ready. I don't want to leave my family. Or my friends. *Austin.* My heart aches at the thought of never seeing him again, which is all sorts of fucked up given where things stand.

Move! Scream! Fight! The impulse to do all these things bang around in my brain, but rational thought and years of training keep me in my seat. This isn't the time to freak out, or do something stupid. I need to appeal to this crazy man's better judgment. To keep him talking. To build some semblance of rapport so he hesitates before he attempts to kill me. But right now, all I see is the barrel of his gun, pointing straight at me.

34

AUSTIN

GOD, I really fucked up this time. It's almost time to take the stage and Jayla's not here. She never showed up in the green room to escort us as she's done for every single show, and now I'm worried she won't talk to me ever again. *Where the hell is she?*

"Come on, man." Sean clasps me on the back. He's been listening to me whine about Jayla's lack of presence all evening. "The fans wait for no one, especially not a lovesick rock star."

The sound crew hands over my in-ear equipment, and I look over to find Opal and Lexi hanging off to the side. I don't know, this all just feels off. Is Jayla really so pissed? I mean, I take full accountability for ruining the good vibe we had going this afternoon. But Jay isn't petty, and I can't see her skirting her work just to avoid me. That's something I'd do, but not her. She's a bigger person. Professional. She takes pride in her role as director of security for this tour. No way in hell she'd bow out for the night because of some stupid shit I said. My spine prickles with actual worry and I march over to her right-hand man to find out what the hell is going on.

"Yo, Terrance, where's Jayla?"

His frown and glance at his cell do nothing to alleviate my

concern. But before I open my mouth to ask him where I can find her, he's pulling out his radio and muttering into it. I can't hear what he says, but his reaction turns my worry into fear.

The crowd chants from beyond the stage. The audio and lighting crews have cut the interim music and dimmed the overhead lamps, and like Pavlov's dogs, our fans are conditioned for what comes next.

"What?" I ask, stepping away from the entrance to the stage and closer to Terrance. Trent, Lipshitz, and a few others shout for me to come back, but my body is buzzing. Something's wrong. I just know it.

Terrance glances up and meets my gaze.

"Where is she?" I ask again.

"I don't know," he admits, and by the apprehension on his features, he's not happy about it.

"You don't know?"

"She should be back by now. She's not picking up." He holds up his radio and says something again. His cell is ringing and when I glance at the screen I see it's an outbound call to Jayla. It goes straight to voicemail.

"Where was she?"

"There was an altercation in Section 328 near the restrooms, but it's been handled. She should be here, or at the very least, picking up her phone."

I glance around, hoping to catch sight of her, but it's only the roadies and crew. Maybe she's mad at me, but that doesn't explain why she's ignoring her team. I can't go on stage and perform when she's unaccounted for. Fuck this. Jogging back to the guys, I rip out my in-ears and hand them to one of the techs.

"What the hell are you doing?" Leighton's brow furrows. "What's wrong?"

"It's Jayla," I say, my knee bouncing with anxiousness. "I'm gonna go find her."

"Dude." Trent draws out the word, and the chanting from off stage seems to grow even louder. "We're up. Like now."

"So, stall." I shake my head. "Something's not right. She should be here."

"You two had a fight," he says. "I'm sure she just doesn't want to see you right now."

"Maybe give her space?" Lexi adds.

"No. Jayla wouldn't do that. I won't go on until I know where she is."

Sean removes his audio equipment with a nod. "We'll help you look."

"Lipshitz," Trent yells. "Cover for us."

"Cover?" His eyes go wide and his brow scrunches as we start walking away. "Wait. What?"

We don't stay to explain. There's no time.

Without asking or giving us a hard time, Terrance falls into line as we make our way back to the golf carts he drove us over in just a few minutes ago.

"Got any ideas?" Sean asks.

"None," I say and bite the inside of my cheek. Something doesn't sit right, and it's not the weed I smoked earlier or the plate of wings I destroyed afterward. "I'll check the green room. Maybe we missed her. Trent, you search the VIP area. Take the girls. Talk to everyone. Maybe someone's seen her backstage. Sean and Leighton, do a sweep of the halls."

"Take the cart." Terrance throws a set of keys my way and hands the second set to Trent. He nods to Sean and Leighton. "I'll help you cover the halls."

"Keep your phones on. Call when you find her!" I say and shove the key into the cart. Without another glance back, I shift into drive and race back the way we just came.

This is the most rebellious thing I've done in years. I don't bail on shows. Ever. But I can't shake the feeling something is wrong.

Jayla doesn't disappear. Ever. And that only causes my pulse to race as I gun the cart for what little juice it's capable of.

The green room door comes into view and I stomp on the brake, pulling to a sliding stop. My phone buzzes with a few texts and I check the screen to see a group chat's been started as I walk to the door.

Trent: No sign of her. Updates?

Lexi: She isn't in VIP.

I move my cell to my left hand and reach for the door to yank it open. I step inside the room, intending to type out a reply as soon as I check, but instead I'm met with a scene that stops me in my tracks. *Shit.* The door slams shut at my back, bumping my body forward with its force.

"Jayla." Her name flies from my lips in a prayer. Right before dread overshadows my relief in finding her. Fucking Coy is here. With a gun pointed at her head. I want to lunge forward, take him out, scream. But I can't risk her welfare. I lower my hands and take a few tentative steps forward. Working by touch alone, I tap on my cell and hope I'm sending off a warning flare to my friends. We need time and backup, to get out of this situation safely. It's two against one, but Jayla and I could take him if it weren't for that gun.

I think back to the videos we made and a stroke of brilliance hits me. We need a distraction. Enough to catch Coy off guard. Without another glance in Jayla's direction, I step closer to Coy and do what I do best: I bullshit. "Having a party without me?" I force a lightheartedness to my tone and look to the man I once considered a friend. "Not cool, dude."

"On the contrary. We were waiting on you." The smug lift to his lips sparks outrage in my mind. I'd like to knock that look right off his fucking face. But I can't do that without putting Jayla's safety at risk.

I shuffle forward a few more inches. "Aww . . . you miss me?"

"Not at all." He laughs, and there's an edge to the sound that scatters literal goosebumps across my skin. "But it's only fair you're here for this. You did foot the bill for my trip, after all. This gun too." He's still pointing the damn thing at Jay. I need him to move it around, preferably away from her.

"Should've saved your money and stayed home." I *tisk* and shake my head.

"Oh? Why's that?"

"Well, you've got to be breaking a few laws. I'm pretty sure guns aren't allowed in this venue. You know, someone could go to jail for that."

"Good thing we're not going anywhere." With that sure as shit smile and wide crazed eyes, it hits me. Coy Wright is here to kill us all. Which means if I was lucky enough to blindly shoot off a string of random texts, then I just led everyone I love straight to the slaughter.

There's a sound at my back, a lot like the door handle being jostled, but I don't turn to see who it is. I don't have to. Coy's eyes widen with excitement and his smile grows.

Oh, fuck.

35

JAYLA

TRENT BURSTS THROUGH THE DOOR. "What the f—?" His footsteps falter with his words and it takes a moment for him to fully process what's at play. It's not until Leighton and Sean follow that Trent steps back, his eyes wide and fearful.

Through the open door I catch Terrence's gaze. There's a flash of red hair beyond—Opal—and Lexi's platinum blonde too. *Oh, God.* This situation is complicated enough. The last thing we need are more potential victims if Coy decides to hold shooting practice. Terrence can't see Coy, or the gun he's got trained on me, but I hope to God he reads lips because I mouth "run" before the door slams shut. I breathe a sigh of relief when the door doesn't open again.

"Hey, look. The gang's all here," Austin practically shouts. I'm not sure what he's trying to accomplish by rattling the gunman's nerves, but while Coy's attention is divided, I ready myself for a swift and powerful takedown. All I need is a big enough window, and if Austin keeps talking I'll have one.

"This is what you wanted, right?" Austin opens his arms wide and glances at the rest of the guys in the band.

Coy's smile turns to a scowl as he moves the gun to point at Sean. "Where's Jess?"

"Jess?" Sean says as if he's never heard of her. It's a bold move for someone who's got a Glock pointed at his face.

Coy's eyes go wild and his words spill out in anger. "My fucking girlfriend! Where the hell are you keeping her?"

"Jess? Oh, that Jess!" Sean snaps. "And it's ex-girlfriend to you."

"Dude, you need better recon," Trent says in a lazy drawl. "Jess isn't here."

It hits me what they're doing. It's brilliant, actually. Each man shuffles a few steps closer while their friends volley with words to distract him.

"Better luck next time, bro." Austin winces and it drags Coy's attention away long enough that I'm able to stand without him noticing. I swear, if I wasn't so mad at Austin I would kiss him! *After taking Coy down and sending him to jail, of course.* I move back a few steps and attempt to stay out of Coy's peripheral.

"You're lying!" Coy swings the gun around and points it at Austin's chest. "Like you always do. That's why I'm here. To make her see. To make you pay. To make all of you pay!"

Fear bubbles in my gut at all the ways this could go wrong, but I can't think about that. Instead, I inch closer.

"Don't look at me." Leighton holds his hands up in the air. "I wasn't even here."

"What lies, Coy?" Sean's tone is hard and he takes a big step forward.

The gun trains on Sean again.

"You stole Jess." He shakes his head wildly. "You got in her head. Made these two manipulate me so I didn't even see it coming, you piece of shit."

"You hurt her, Coy. That's why she left. The only thing I did was show her she deserved better."

"I can't wait to kill you." Coy's voice lowers, completely void of emotion with his level tone. "I've been planning for months.

Thinking how satisfying it'll be to watch you bleed out in front of her."

Sean's nostrils flare and his hands clench, but his feet stay rooted.

"She's mine. Mine!" Coy laughs bitterly. "Remember this is all your fault when she walks through those doors."

"Uh, someone want to break it to cuckoo brains that his plan sucks?" Austin shakes his head and shrugs as if he were talking to a small child. "Sorry, bud, but Jess ain't coming. She's not here. That kinda ruins your evil payback, doesn't it?"

"N-not here?" Coy sputters.

"She's in Los Angeles. Where she works and goes to school." Austin taps his chin. "Wait, you already know that."

"But she has to be here. She's always here." Coy shakes his head, his words frantic. All I need is two, maybe three steps more and I can tackle him in one jump. "She's here. You're lying. I know she booked the flight, I watched her do it!"

Sean's deep inhalation is the only warning I get before all hell breaks loose.

"You piece of shit!" Sean charges with a guttural roar.

"Sean! No!" Austin shouts and knocks his friend out of the gun's aim. At least, that's what I think happens. My focus is on Coy. He pulls the trigger, but I'm already tackling him to the ground. *Ouch!* We crash with a bang. Or maybe that's the gun. My ears ring and pain rips down my side. Shouts. Groans. Blood. Everything happens simultaneously, and my brain struggles to accept the influx of stimuli.

My legs and arms squeeze with desperate strength as I wrestle Coy. The gun is still in his hand; he's going to shoot us. He shoves at my face, he knees at my body, and his free hand claws at my face. I don't stop fighting. Austin calls my name from somewhere behind us. I can't decipher whether it's a warning or a cheer. I battle for control, and just as I think I've gained it, there's another sharp bang as the gun goes off once more. *Fuck.* I'm pretty sure he just shot me! A burst of anger courses through my veins as I slam my head into Coy's nose and he yelps with pain. Blood floods from his face.

Finally, I gain the upper hand and send the weapon skidding across the floor.

Austin leaps over us both and races to retrieve the gun. In the same second, Trent joins me on the floor and yanks Coy's arm at an unnatural angle. Coy screams, and together we pin him down. Even still, Coy doesn't stop thrashing like a caged wild animal.

"It's over. Stop fighting," Trent shouts as he uses one arm to hold Coy's face against the floor.

"Fucking kill me, then! Do it!" Coy's bravado from before is replaced with anger so shrill, my body shivers in response. This guy is way more fucked in the head than any of us imagined.

"My bag," I grit out through a heavy breath, and point to where it lies. Pain slices so sharp I see stars from the movement and I fear I might pass out. I inhale again, but it's a struggle. "Get my handcuffs."

Coy continues to thrash against us. "Kill me! Put me out of my fucking misery!"

Austin rushes over with my bag and unzips the different compartments. "Jesus! How many pockets does this thing have?" His hands shake, and I'm almost certain it's the adrenaline. My body sags but I refuse to leave Coy until we have him restrained.

"Here!" Austin hands me the cuffs and I make swift work of sliding them onto Coy's wrists. I move to stand but almost pass out, so instead I crawl away. I need space. I don't even want to look at that mad man. And I'm really thirsty.

"Kill me. Fucking kill me," Coy continues to ramble on and on.

"Someone shut him up," I complain and scoot myself to slump against the wall.

Leighton stomps over to Coy, his arm cocked back like he's gonna throw a punch.

"With a gag. Not your fist." I roll my eyes, and try to sit up better but that pain shoots through my body. "*Argh.*"

"Jayla, stop moving." Austin rushes forward. "You're bleeding!"

"Yeah, he shot me!" I almost laugh and press my hand to my side where it hurts the most. My shirt is soaked with blood, but then I catch sight of my nails. My perfect, beautiful, newly-manicured nails. Except they're no longer perfect. Scrapes mar the paint of my ring finger, and my pointer nail is snapped off, broken all the way to the quick. The sight of it hits me with a jolt of anger so fierce my entire body shakes. Coy almost killed me. I almost died. And the fucker ruined my nails!

A sob breaks free, and it's a strangled, guttural sound. I don't want to cry. I really don't. But after today and the emotional yo-yo my heart's played, I'm at my breaking point. The nail is a physical representation of how bad it all is, and I'm tired of holding everything together for pretense. I am not okay. Another cry pushes through my lips and I turn into myself, glancing down to witness blood seeping through my shirt.

"Jayla, baby." Austin's wide eyes zero in on my blood-stained shirt. He pulls his own shirt off in one swift move and presses it to my side. "Don't move."

"Wasn't planning on it," I mutter, and cover his hand with my own to lower the placement.

He regards me with surprise. "Did you just make a joke? Because that's something I would do."

I'm in so much pain and if I weren't sobbing, I might actually laugh.

"Paramedics will be here in five minutes," Terrence says from the door's entrance. "Police too."

I realize everyone's here now, Terrance, Lexi, Opal, and of course, the band. They're all staring, and by their concerned expressions and lack of comment, I must look in pretty bad shape. Someone must have stuffed Coy's mouth; his muffled cries pulse throughout the room. It's infinitely better than his pleas for us to kill him.

"It's just a graze," I say, but don't look down to verify my injury. The fact is, I have no clue how bad it is. I've never been shot before, but I take solace in the fact I'm still breathing, alert, and talking just fine. Hell, two minutes ago I wrestled a madman. I think if he hit anything major I'd be unconscious by now.

Austin's brow furrows and he angles his body closer, using his free hand to cradle me to him while the other still holds his shirt to my side.

I lean into his warmth and take comfort in the strength of his body. The urge to cry again is there, but I fight it this time.

"Hiya—oh!" Casey comes to a sudden stop just inside the doorway. He glances from me to Coy, and then to the others with a gaping mouth. "What happened?"

No one answers for a beat. It's a lot to explain.

The room fills with chatter, murmured conversations between couples, while Sean fills Terrence and Casey in on the CliffsNotes version of what just took place.

"I'm going with you," Austin says. "When the ambulance gets here."

"I'm fine. I promise." Though I do a poor job of showing it. I try to sit up a little higher and bite back the pain. "I'm sorry I scared you."

"Don't apologize. You saved Sean and me. All of us." His eyes dart down to where our hands press his shirt to my side. His face pales a little. "Fuck, that's a lot of blood."

"Just needs a few stitches."

"Jayla, there's something I need to tell you . . . if you don't . . ." He blanches. "If something happens . . . and you—"

"Austin." I cup his cheek in my free hand and draw his gaze to mine. He's sweet, even if it's a little dramatic. The fear in his eyes is real, and I see how scared he still is. "It's over. We're safe. The bullet grazed my skin. I'm not dying. Promise."

"Doesn't matter." He takes a hard swallow and leans forward until our foreheads gently press together. "I can't let another minute pass without telling you exactly how I feel. And Jayla Miller, I'm fucking out of my mind in love with you."

There's agony in his confession, an intimate honesty that makes me wonder whether this is the first time he's ever said those words aloud. The thought that I'm his first for something as big as this fills my chest with so much joy I wonder if it might burst. Any reservations about how I felt before evaporate. Glen's warning from earlier today lingers in the back of my brain, but as I look into Austin's eyes I realize there has to be some logical explanation. Maybe I'm being stupid, or ignorant, but I'm going with my gut. It's never steered me wrong before.

Emotion catches in my throat and I feel as if I might cry. "I love you, too."

A throat clears. "Uh, guys." It's Casey. "I hate to break up this moment, but we have a very excited and impatient crowd out there. One that's been waiting for an hour. Maybe you could take the stage now? Or should we call Vince?"

"We're a little busy here, Lipshitz," Trent still stands guard over the gagged and cuffed Coy.

"Busy? Busy!" Casey's eyes bug out and he clenches his hands into fists before shaking them at all of us. "First you disappear, and right before the show, with no ETA, no information, and leave me to calm thousands of screaming fans. You didn't even give a reason!"

"Sorry, man. That was a shit thing to do," Trent says.

"Meanwhile, I've been putting up with Vince and his verbal lashings! Letting y'all call the shots while my boss chews me out every damn day. Sometimes twice a day!"

"Kinky," Austin mutters.

Casey's face turns beet red, and he might actually pop a blood vessel if he doesn't calm down soon.

"Bro, we didn't know," Leighton's forehead furrows with concern. "That sucks and I'm sorry if we put you in the middle."

"Middle? Middle! Having my parents argue over who got me at Christmas was being in the middle. That was nothing compared to how bad these last months have sucked for me! No one appreciates what I do, and if you did, I'd never know it! Would it kill you to throw me a compliment or invite me to dinner once in a while?" His eyes bug and he throws up his hands. "I don't need much!"

"We appreciate you, Lipshitz," Sean says seriously, but when Casey's eyes go wild I catch him mutter, "Mostly."

"And my name's not fucking Lipshitz! It's Schmitz!"

Sean cocks his head. "Wait, what?"

"I'm tired of your shit, and your nicknames, and everyone treating me like I'm a pain in the ass." Wow. This guy is on a roll. I never knew he had it in him. It's almost impressive, really.

"But you are a pain in the ass," Trent mumbles so everyone hears.

"I'm doing my fucking job! Making sure you do yours!" Casey gestures with his hands, driving his point further and managing to appear one circuit short of crazy. "How difficult is that to understand?"

Trent clears his throat. "Your name's really Schmitz?"

"Sorry, dude," Sean says.

"You should've said something, man. It's not healthy to repress anger like that," Austin adds, and I swear if looks could kill he'd no longer be breathing. Austin recovers before Casey's head explodes. "Dude, I'm sorry. We thought your name was Lipshitz. Why didn't you say something sooner? Now I feel bad."

Casey drops his gaze and kicks at the floor with the toe of his shoe. "I didn't want to start trouble. It's not in my job responsibilities."

"We're sorry, brother." Sean walks over and clasps him on the back. "We only give you shit because we love you. Seriously. You've done an awesome job. You've been amazing on this tour. We couldn't do this without you."

"Th-thanks," Casey stutters, and his face reddens with embarrassment.

Commotion and voices float through the open door and within seconds the room fills with a slew of emergency personnel. The EMTs quickly assess my health and I'm strapped to a board for easy transport to the nearest hospital.

"I'm coming with," Austin announces, walking alongside the

wheeled stretcher. The chants from the crowd in the stadium call out for Three Ugly Guys—fans completely unaware of the chaos.

"You'll have to meet us there," one of the paramedics says. "It's policy. Sorry."

"I'm fine." I reach for his hand and he takes it immediately.

"Jayla, I'm not leaving you."

"I know. I don't want you to." I swallow and suck in a breath. I'm talking about more than a hospital visit, and by the expression in Austin's eyes, he knows it, too. "Come see me after. We'll talk. I promise I'll be in good hands."

"Sir, we're gonna need to take down your statement," a police officer interrupts. "You can meet her at the hospital as soon as we're done."

He hesitates and I see the war within him. He has a responsibility to stay, but he doesn't want to leave my side. He bites at the inside of his cheek as his gaze finds mine. "You're sure you'll be okay?"

"I wouldn't lie to you," I say. "Promise."

There's a flash of hurt in his stare, but I don't have time to question it. He raises his hand in a wave and mouths "I love you" at the same moment my stretcher is wheeled out the doors and into the waiting ambulance.

36

JAYLA

IT'S a whole new experience being on the other end of an emergency. In my time on the force I've sent hundreds to the hospital by way of an ambulance. Most times never seeing them again, and some only for an interview once they were in recovery.

I shouldn't be scared. Logically, I understand I'm being sent for treatment of a wound, and the doctors and nurses are trained professionals. Yet, there's something uncomfortable and overwhelming in watching everyone talk about me, but not to me. There's a moment as I'm rushed to an exam room that I regret not begging Austin to stay.

The exam room is bright, and everyone works so efficiently—doctors bark orders, nurses ask questions—and my mind grows foggy as I struggle to keep up.

Does this hurt? Rate your pain. Do you know your blood type? We're going to take you to radiology for an ultrasound. Only a precaution. Monitor. Internal bleeding. Get some rest. The words pile up in my mind, stacking precariously on top of each other until I can't keep up. I fight to keep my eyes open, but my lids feel so damn heavy. My body no longer hurts, though, and as I finally give in to the urge to sleep, the peaceful darkness is a much needed refuge.

"JAYLA, BABY." Austin steps into my room, rushing to my side to reach for my hand. He leans his hip against my hospital bed, his gaze running the length of my body as if he's worried I might crumble and disappear. His hair falls forward on his brow, casting his features in shadows.

"Good show tonight?" I manage to say through my chapped lips. I'm still a little groggy and I don't know exactly what time it is, but my guess is he came straight from the venue. The pain meds they gave me earlier send me in and out of consciousness, and while I dislike the lack of control, it's also nice to not feel much pain.

"No show tonight. The cops shut it down, what with a crime scene to investigate." Austin attempts to smile, but his eyes narrow with concern. "That's what took me so long. They wouldn't let us leave. I'm sorry. I came as soon as I could. Everyone's outside waiting. They won't let more than one of us in at a time."

"That's good, because I don't feel much like company." I try for a joke but he doesn't laugh.

"The nurse said you're going to be fine." I think he says it more for his own reassurance as much as mine.

My hand goes to my right side and I rest it over the bandage hiding beneath my hospital gown. "I told you, just a graze. A few stitches," I say, but we both know how lucky I am. A few inches more and I wouldn't be alive. Coy would have killed all of us, and that's what I will tell the detectives when they show up to take my statement.

"She said you might have a concussion."

I shake my head. "Just precaution. They want me for observation. I'll be fine." They also want to make sure there's no internal bleeding, but I don't tell him that. The worry etched in his brow is hard enough to witness. The desire to put his fears to rest is almost overwhelming.

Austin grabs a chair and slides it nearer to my bed to sit close. His thumb caresses the skin at my wrist as he holds my hand. "You scared me tonight, baby." He kisses the back of my hand and lays his head gently against my body. His eyes hold a vulnerability and fear that slice to my core. I've been holding it together, but having Austin next to me makes it feel real again.

I almost died.

I was scared, too. Not only for myself, but for everyone in that room. Mostly of losing this love we just found. I clear my throat and with my free hand I brush the hair back from his face. "I know. But everything's fine now."

"I need to tell you something." He lifts his chin and levels me with a stare so serious and so concerned I can only nod.

"Okay," I whisper.

He bites his lip and exhales a rush of breath as he drops his gaze back to where our hands clasp together. "You might not like me much after I do."

This is it. Apprehension and anxiety rush through my body, but there's a steady reassurance in my mind that doesn't believe Austin capable of what Glen inferred. We all have secrets. We all have stories. I need to hear his.

"Whatever it is, I'm not going anywhere." I cup his cheek and lift his gaze back to mine. I blink once and roll my eyes, forcing a smile. "Literally. I can't get up right now."

He chuckles and shakes his head, but sobers as his lips part. "Do you remember Brianna?"

My brain stutters at the name, but then memories hit like a train and I'm assaulted by the little girl's face. "Your mom's boyfriend had a daughter? You had to watch her sometimes."

He nods and his body tenses. "I did. A lot, actually. But when I left home, it wasn't on good terms. I had to leave, you know? They were like a cancer. Toxic, and I had to get out of there for my own sanity. I didn't look back."

I wait. His silence fills the space between us, stretching to an uncomfortable length. Still, I don't interrupt.

"I lost touch, and the band was doing big things." He releases my hand to wipe at his face and I realize he's crying. "Brianna ran away when she was fifteen. I don't know where, but I think to LA. I thought . . . I thought I could make things right . . . I abandoned her when she needed me the most. I was selfish, and she had no one."

"Austin." I hold back my own tears as I brush his from his cheeks.

His gaze holds so much anger. Fear. Agony. It's a side of him I've never witnessed. "It's been over two years now. I can't find her, Jay. I don't know if she's even alive." He sucks in a sharp breath as if it physically pains him. "I hired a private investigator. He's been looking for her for a year."

Everything clicks into place. Glen wasn't lying. He was misinformed. The photos, they aren't for Austin's pleasure, they're so he can find Bri. "It's okay," I say aloud, because I think both he and I need the reassurance.

"No one knows." He slams his eyes shut. "If it got out? The pictures he sends me . . . It would be really bad." I understand what he's not saying, and yet it doesn't make my heart ache any less. His back trembles and he buries his head into my side as he cries.

I stroke his shoulders and hold him the best I can. "It's okay," I murmur over and over again. It's not, though. This is tearing him up inside. I can't imagine for how long.

After a few minutes, Austin lifts his head and his bloodshot gaze meets mine. "They're all on the street, Jay. Homeless. Drug addicts. Working and selling their bodies. There're so many, Jayla. There are so many lost girls."

I nod and hold his hands in mine. My heart hurts for this man, and for all these teenagers nameless and forgotten, lost and broken. "Thank you for sharing this with me."

"I'm sorry I didn't tell you sooner. I'm sorry I didn't trust that you'd understand." He drops his head, shaking it back and forth. "I was scared you wouldn't want me if you found out . . . and I was wrong to keep this from you." He lifts his gaze. "I promise I'll never do that again."

I relax my shoulders into the hospital bed and release a sigh. This feels like a turning point in our relationship. I'd like to believe it would've happened naturally, but there's something about being held at gunpoint that makes a person reevaluate their priorities. I love Austin. I want to be with him, and I'm no longer holding anything back. "I have a secret of my own."

His eyes widen, just the slightest. "Oh?"

"WMI asked me to stop making videos with you." The truth rolls out of my mouth easily. Maybe it's the pain meds, or the belief Austin and I will make it through whatever life throws us, but I'm no longer hesitant to tell him everything.

"When?"

"A few weeks ago. In Chicago." My eyelids feel heavy again, and sleep threatens to pull me under, but I fight through. "I didn't want to start problems for you and the band, and we were in a good place. Besides, I knew if I told you, you'd post another video anyway."

He chuckles and offers me a slight smile. "Yeah, you're probably right."

"It was selfish of me." I snuggle back into my pillow and let my head roll to the side.

Austin rubs his finger against my wrist again, and it's the most soothing touch.

"I didn't want to leave the tour. Not when we'd just discovered something good. I didn't want it to end."

"It's okay. I'm not angry with you."

"But it wasn't right. I'm not someone's pawn." I yawn and my eyes water. *Why am I so sleepy? Apparently, almost getting killed is hard work.* "I manipulated you. Distracted you so you'd stop asking to make videos."

Austin grins. "In your defense, I enjoyed every second."

"Austin." I draw out his name, but smile. When I'm healed and out of this hospital I look forward to 'distracting' him again.

"I'm not mad. I forgive you." He kisses the back of my hand. "That was a shitty thing of WMI to ask of you." His lips press together, his smile gone. "I fucking hate our label. I curse the day Off Track Records got bought out."

"You curse the day?" I can't help it, I laugh.

"Hey!" Austin feigns offense. "Don't poke fun. The injured patient card only works so far."

"I guess you'll be getting a new head of security again." My eyelid flutter shut.

"Yeah," Austin says. "But that's okay with me."

My eyes fly open and hurt seeps through my tone. "Why's that?"

"Because . . ." His lips lift with his smile. "I'd much rather have you as my girlfriend."

I roll my eyes, and even though I do like the sound of being his, I am not about to give up my career simply because we're dating. "I'm so much more than some rock star's girlfriend."

"You're right. You're everything." He stands and leans over me, pressing his forehead against mine a long moment before kissing my lips.

"I don't know how this is going to work," I admit honestly, but my brain is too tired to process the logistics of our relationship.

"Sleep." He kisses my lips again, and then settles back into the chair. "We'll figure it out tomorrow."

"You don't have to stay," I say through another yawn.

He stretches out his long legs and settles back as if the chair's as comfortable as one of the bus's leather recliners. We both know it's not. "Sleep, please. You need to rest," he says. "I'm not going anywhere."

The promise in his words is all I need.

THE NEXT MORNING Austin never leaves my side. Besides a few phone calls and texts, his attention is completely focused on my needs. We navigate my pain meds, more tests, so many different doctors, and the next steps to my care plan.

Terrence hangs in the hallway just outside my door, and I'm not sure whether that's more for my sake or Austin's. Either way, it's comforting.

The only time I leave the room is for tests, all precautionary, and I pass with flying colors. There's no internal bleeding, and I don't have a concussion. The only permanent damage from Coy's attack is the massive scar I'm sure to have once my wound heals. Though, the doctor who stitched me up insists it'll be minimal. A physical therapist comes by and I work with her on basic maneuvers like sitting up, getting to the bathroom, and hoisting myself in and out of the wheelchair they insist I use for another twenty-four hours.

It's late in the afternoon when I'm moved to a different area of the hospital. It's a private room, much nicer than my apartment. "Why does it feel like this room is reserved for celebrity patients?" I say once the transport nurse leaves.

"Because it is," Austin replies. He chuckles and glances down at his cell.

"Austin." I draw out his name, not sure whether I should thank him or reprimand him for this extravagance. I don't need a private recovery ward. I certainly can't afford it, but I don't have to question who's footing the bill.

"Don't." He points a finger and levels his stare. "I need you to get better. Let me do this." His lips lift with the hint of a grin. "I mean, if you're worried about it being fair, we can call it even. I do owe you a solid." He shrugs. "Some might even say I saved your life yesterday."

"Oh, no. Don't even." I shake my head and fight back the urge to laugh, mostly because my side hurts like hell when I do. "I'm not cashing in my favor. Not when I'm the one who got shot!"

"I thought you said it was just a graze," he says with a stupid grin and I can't help but smile back.

There's a buzz from his cell and Austin glances down, checking his phone for about the hundredth time this hour. "I have to leave soon."

I nod, knowing what he means. He has the concert, but he's also leaving New York. There's still another three weeks left on the tour. He taps his fingers nervously at his side.

"Is everything okay?"

"Yeah." He pockets his phone. "Sorry. I would stay if I could, but apparently that'd be a breach of my contract."

"I don't need a babysitter. I'm fine." I already miss him and he hasn't even left. I'm not familiar with the emotion. These next few weeks will be hard.

"I know you are. You're the strongest woman I know." He brushes his thumb over my cheek and along my jaw. "But that doesn't mean I want to leave you." He closes the space between our mouths and captures my lips for a kiss. It starts chaste with the gentle press of his lips to mine, but quickly turns to more. He parts his lips, I brush my tongue along his, and our mouths fuse in a sensual dance that spreads desire in every fiber of my being. Longing. Promises. Love. Fear. Trust. I pour everything into this kiss that feels like both the start of a new chapter and a good-bye I don't want to give.

Austin pulls back, steadying his breath with his forehead pressed to mine. "This tour is going to be torture."

"One month. We can do one month." I'm not sure who I'm trying to convince, him or me. "Then we'll be back in LA."

His grin turns positively wicked. "Get ready because I'm already planning all the sex we're gonna have."

Sex. That's a loaded topic. One we haven't properly addressed. I drop my gaze and fiddle with the edge of my blanket. "Austin, I-I'm not sure . . ."

"What's wrong?" He drops to the edge of the bed and stills my hand in his. His eyes are wide and worried as they find mine. "Shit. I screwed up already, didn't I?"

"No, it's just . . ." I shake my head and will myself to push out the words. I've been to enough therapy to understand how important this conversation is. "You know I have triggers, and I have to be in control." I exhale the fear that I won't be enough for this man and lift my gaze to find his. "I don't know if I'll ever be normal. I don't want you to expect something I can't give."

"Jayla, I only want what makes you happy." His lips pull up with a smirk. "And normal is totally overrated."

"But sex is important to any relationship." With Austin I've been able to explore my boundaries without judgment, but we haven't had much time. He might get tired of dealing with my triggers. My limits. He might want more.

"I'm going to admit something, but you have to promise not to hold it over me." He grins, taking my hands in his. "You are so damn sexy. I loved it when you cuffed me. I want you to hold me down. I like when you lead. I think about it pretty much twenty-four-seven. Hell, I'm confident you could get me off without ever touching my dick."

"I'm being serious."

"So am I." He squeezes my hands. "I promise to respect whatever boundaries you need to feel safe. Whatever gets you off, I'm willing to try."

My body sings with his words. They chase away the doubt and insecurity. They also flame my attraction, and if I weren't in this hospital bed, I would jump his bones.

Austin's gaze heats as if he's reading my mind. His voice drops, low and rumbling in a way that goes straight to my core. "I only have one request."

"What's that?"

"Can we get a new pair of handcuffs?" His brow lifts and his lips pull into a grimace. "Because the ones we used touched Coy, and call me superstitious, but they're tainted now."

A laugh bursts through my lips, and I grip my side because . . . *ouch!*

"I'm sorry," he grimaces.

"Stop making me laugh."

"Can't help it. It's kinda my thing."

We stare at each other, grins painted on our lips like two lovesick fools. We look ridiculous, but I can't seem to care.

A knock sounds at the door and Austin's grin widens. I tilt my head in question, but it only causes him to laugh and I know whatever happens next is all his doing.

He turns to open the door, but it swings open before he reaches it.

Mama. Emotion catches in my throat as I take in the sight of my mother. I didn't call her yet, because I didn't want to worry her or my brother. I knew she'd be torn up about being so far. But this man, *my man*, went and took care of everything. I wonder if there's a day he'll ever stop surprising me with his kindness.

"Mrs. Miller, it's great to see you again." Austin holds out his hand.

But mama isn't having that. "Please, it's Mama Lou." She opens her arms wide and wraps them around him in a tight hug. "Thank you for making arrangements so I could be with my baby."

"It was my pleasure."

Mama pats his shoulder and moves around to come to my bed. "Jayla, he's sweet."

I glance over her shoulder and meet his smile. "He's all right."

She shakes her head and pulls back my covers. "I want to squeeze you, but I don't want to hurt you worse. Where is it?"

I lift my shirt so she can see.

She sucks in a sharp breath. "I can't believe you got shot." Her lower lip trembles and she leans down, cradling me to her side with a hug. "My baby."

It's so good to have my mama here. I didn't realize how much so. Her embrace brings forth a surge of emotion and I cling to her so I won't cry. I can't believe Austin did this. He's amazing, and if my mama weren't here I'd tell him.

Mama releases me from her hug and eyes me up and down. Her lips pinch and her hands go to her hips. "Now, will you please finally put this security career to rest and find yourself a nice man?"

Oh, God. Here it comes. I glance to Austin, a *deer in the headlights, save me please* look in my eyes, but he's already got a foot out the door. I glare.

He just laughs and waves his hand. "Ladies, I've got to go." He gives me a wink. "I'll call you. Later, baby."

I open my mouth to reply, but he's gone.

"Baby?" Mama hums and her eyes light with interest. "I like the sound of that."

Here comes the inquisition. I scowl at the door and swear I hear his laughter from down the hall. I can't believe he just did that. And yet, I can. I'd be mad, except I'm also incredibly touched that he flew my mama in to be with me.

37

AUSTIN

THE NEXT THREE weeks of the tour are brutal. I hate being away from Jayla while she recovers, and no amount of video calls or texting appeases my desire to be by her side. She's back in LA living at home again, and her girlfriends text daily with updates. Between her family and her friends, she's well cared for in my absence, but still it sucks being so far from the one I love.

Love.

It's the only thought on my mind these last weeks. Funny how a dude like me could go from rock's most eligible bachelor to happily off the market in the span of one tour. The guys were right. I fell hard and fast. Jayla's it for me. I know it in my heart of hearts, and while we haven't had the time or space to figure out how our relationship will work, I am absolutely certain we will overcome whatever challenges life throws at us. Hell, she took a bullet for me and my friends. Commitment doesn't get much bigger than that.

I still can't believe Coy blindsided us all. The kicker being the cash I paid him in hopes of getting him out of Jess's life for good, is the same money he used to fund the attack on us in New York. He was behind the incident in Salt Lake too. Apparently, he bribed some woman to purchase and deliver the explosives with an IOU. *Funds he didn't have until I settled the lawsuit.* That's why there wasn't another attack until New York. That's also why the investigators couldn't find a paper trail. They used burner phones and no wire transfers were made around the time of the incident. But all of it's over now. Coy won't be out of jail anytime soon, if ever. I'm okay with that.

"Hiya!" Schmitz pops his head into the doorway and raps his knuckles against the frame. "You guys ready?"

"Let's do this," Trent says, and we make our way out of the green room and onto the stage. I pick up my beloved Lola, and steady the strap over my shoulder. The crowd shouts into the dark stage in anticipation of what's coming, and my pulse kicks up in response. I will always love this feeling. The natural high of being on stage. The fans and the music. Rocking out with my best friends. But now there's a tiny part inside me that can't wait to get home. It's a new and unfamiliar sensation. One I'm learning to like more than I care to admit, and it's because of her.

God, I miss her.

Leighton settles behind his set and counts us off, his sticks crashing down as the house lights blast on. For the next two hours I lose myself in my performance. I have my friends right here on this stage, and we're doing what we love. Later I get to ride home to the woman I love. Life doesn't get much better than this.

It's been a long tour and we're all exhausted, but tonight we bring all we have and lay it out on the stage in Salt Lake City. This is the venue we were supposed to play three months ago, and the one that had the potential to end us all. There's a gravity to the energy of the crowd. This moment is special. Every song becomes an anthem of resilience. Every chord I strike proclaims "We are still here." Every lyric Trent sings says "We will not be silent." It's about survival and not allowing the bad to scare us away from living the life we were meant to live. We feel it. We've been talking about it all day. But this crowd, they feel it, too.

The music fades away and Trent steps closer to the mic. Fans cheer and we all pump our fists in the air. "This is our last song tonight. But before we go, we want you to know how grateful we are that y'all came out tonight," Trent shouts into the crowd. The roar. He wipes the sweat from his face with a towel and stoops to pick up a bottle of water as the arena quiets. Chugging half the contents, he steps back up to the mic. "We thought we'd end things a little differently than we normally do. We usually like to go out with a hard number. Something that rattles your bones. But tonight we're mindful of all that was lost here only a few months ago. Jennifer Kay, the concession worker who passed from injuries. Some of our crew, Darren, Robbie, Jones, and Adam, who've been on the mend recovering." The crowd cheers again, this time in respect.

Trent strums his guitar and our lighting crew dims the lights. "We want to play this last one for them. And also, to you. We realize how scary it must be, coming out to a show and not knowing if something tragic like that might happen again. Yet you all gave fear a 'fuck you' by showing up for us tonight."

The crowd goes wild and I give in to a smile. They love it when Trent says fuck. It's like a golden ticket he can cash out at any time. Which he does often during our shows.

"Thank you. We love you all. We get to do what we love because of your support, and I hope we see you back here real soon." Trent bows his head and turns to meet my gaze. He bobs his chin, counting off, and then our fingers are off, picking out the notes in tandem. It's a stripped down version of one of our older jams and the crowd erupts. Their voices join in with his for the chorus.

Come to the party, come to the show.
This life ain't worth having without a little fun.
Pour me a drink, sing me a song.
The night is for sinners, and lovers, and the dreams that I hold.
I've got no reason to be here, but you, you drag me along,
And baby when you love me, it sure feels like home.

There's magic in the air. That's how it feels. And my bones rattle as we take our final bow on stage. My heart races; any harder and I swear it might beat right out of my chest. I memorize this moment. This feeling. This gift.

As we make our way off stage, my feet move with a lightness from my soul. It'll be another twelve hours until I see Jay, but that's nothing compared to what we've weathered. Lexi, Jess, and Opal wait off stage and greet their guys with hugs and sloppy kisses, ones I used to find pathetic. Now I try not to be jealous. I asked Jayla to come to the show, but her physical therapist didn't clear her for travel and she didn't want to risk a setback.

"You got a delivery from Jayla," Opal shouts to my back. "It's on the bus."

"Sweet." A grin takes over my face, and I walk a little faster. I wonder what it could be. With Jay, I can't even guess. Waving to a few fans and thanking the crew as I pass, I finally make it outside to the bus.

Ace opens the door, and greets me with a big smile as though he knows I'm about to be wowed.

I trot up the steps. "I hear I have a surprise."

"Yes, sir." He points to the living area and chuckles.

I turn, my interest now piqued, but what I find blows any expectation out of the motherfucking water. "Jayla!" Her name flies from my lips. Fucking hell. I can't believe my luck. It's almost too good to be true. I squint again to make sure I'm not hallucinating. I'm not. It's her. Then I run, closing the space between us.

She pops off the edge of the table and leaps into my arms, each of us holding on to the other with so much force we practically trip. My lips find hers, frantic to fuse with hers.

She cups my chin and pushes me back until my ass hits the table ledge. I spread my stance wide and she nestles her body between my legs. She takes my wrists in her hands and place my fingers against the table ledge. "Surprised?" she whispers between kisses.

"I thought—" I pull back, suddenly scared I've hurt her. "You aren't supposed to travel."

"I promised to be careful." She releases a soft chuckle, her hands planted on my chest. "I guess I'm doing a poor job of that."

I smile and take in her beautiful face, her full lips even fuller from my kisses. Her deep brown eyes, so honest and soulful and filled with joy—the same contentedness I feel. Her hair is different. "I like your hair."

She smiles. "Yeah? Kalise and Aaliyah convinced me to get braids. I'm not sure I like it."

"You're always gorgeous."

She grins. "I think you have to say that."

"It's the truth."

"It's all clear!" Trent's voice pulls my attention over Jayla's shoulder. "You can uncover your eyes," he calls over his shoulder as he climbs into the bus.

"All clear?" Jayla turns but doesn't move from between my legs. I'm sort of thankful, since I'm sporting wood. The guys would understand, but they'd also give me hell.

"Jayla! You made it." Trent walks inside, and the rest of the gang follows. "Good thing. He's a sorry son of a bitch without you."

"Pay up." Sean holds his hand out to Leighton, then turns to Trent. "You too."

"What'd I miss?" I say with a grin.

"That you two would be naked."

"Given more time, we would have been," I grumble. "Thanks for the cock block."

Sean laughs, pocketing his winnings and then hugging Jess to his side. "I told them Jayla'd make you work for it. She's classy like that."

"Thanks?" Jayla says, and everyone laughs.

I can't help but be a little disappointed. We have ten hours on this bus . . . with everyone, and I don't think I can wait that long to be with Jayla. By the longing stares she keeps sneaking, she feels the same.

"We're going out for dinner," Lexi announces, and narrows a

glare at Trent. "You're evil, letting these two think they weren't getting any alone time."

I blow out a sigh of relief. "Thank fuck."

"What?" Trent laughs. "It was funny. You saw his face."

"Sorry," Lexi says to Jayla and then turns to meet my stare. "But, um, before we leave you two alone, I have something I want to say." Lexi steps away from Trent and reaches for Opal's hand to gives it a squeeze. "Something we want to say."

Opal's lips part in a wide grin, and she nods to her sister. "You tell them."

"I know these last few months have been challenging, and we've all been adjusting to the management under WMI."

"More like weathering a storm," Trent grumbles.

"A shit storm," I say.

"Anyway, while you guys have been playing, Opal and I have been talking, and planning, and starting our own company." Lexi's lips spread wide with her smile and she bounces on her toes.

"Babe, that's amazing!" Trent says. "What type of company?"

"A music label." She glances at all of us before answering.

"You're kidding." Leighton's eyes widen.

"Nope." Lexi smiles and turns to Opal. "We love music. Opal's going to continue writing, and I'm not giving up my solo career, but we still have our inheritance, and decided on a better legacy than it just sitting there collecting interest."

"This is amazing," Jess says.

"We're starting small," Opal looks to her sister.

Lexi shrugs. "I mean, we only have two bands at the moment."

"You've already signed two bands?" Trent's eyes widen, obviously impressed. "Babe, that's incredible."

"We paid a premium, had to buy them out of their current contracts, but I think they'll be good for business." Lexi shrugs, but I don't think I've ever seen her so smiley before.

"That's sort of risky, isn't it?" Trent's brows knit with concern.

"Who'd you get?" Leighton asks.

Opal's lips press together as if she's holding back her smile. "Some group called Three Ugly Guys, and a solo artist, Lexi Marx."

If a pin were to drop, we'd hear it.

"You're fucking kidding me," Trent exclaims, his hands reaching for Lexi and a hopeful smile on his face. He practically bounces up and down.

"Not even a little."

Our bus becomes an impromptu celebration. Leighton kisses Opal. Jess laughs as Sean whoops with joy. Lexi claps and laughs while Trent breaks out the dancing.

Jayla squeezes my leg and bites her lip, holding in her laughter. My friends are crazy, but she already knew that.

I lean my head onto her shoulder. "Do you think they'll leave soon?"

"Stop." She slaps my thigh, but I catch the hint of her smile. I'm no fool. She wants to get down as much as I do.

"Wait." Trent stops dancing. "Did you really start a label just so we could spend more time together?"

Lexi stares back and blinks several times. "That's your takeaway?"

"You must really love me." His grin is teasing.

Her hands land on her hips and she scowls. "You're very conceited, you know that?"

"So, you won't coordinate our tours and recording times and breaks? That had no bearing on your decision to start a label." He drags out the last word in challenge.

"No. Yes." She pinches her lips together and raises her chin in defiance. "That's not the *only* reason."

"God, I love you." He scoops her into his arms and presses his lips to hers.

I glance away and find Opal's gaze. "Looks like we'll be calling you boss."

She shakes her head, but there's a prideful smile on her lips. "Don't be silly. Not that much will change."

But she's wrong. Everything's about to change. She's having Leighton's child. Lexi and Opal will be running a label. We're all in committed relationships. In no time at all there'll be weddings and more babies, and I've never been more excited for what the future holds.

"All right, I was promised one hour," I say, and point toward the door.

"Good. I'm starving." Sean grabs Jess's hand. "Let's take the party elsewhere."

Soon everyone follows suit, shuffling toward the exit.

"Have fun, love birds!" Trent calls over his shoulder.

"I think I'll go have a smoke," Ace mumbles. "I'll just be outside if ya' need me."

"He totally knows we're about to bone."

Jayla turns to me, her eyes wide and laughing. "I should feel bad, but it's almost been a month, and I want you."

I love the sound of that. "So, what do you say? Bus sex, once more for old times' sake?" I waggle my brows and take a step toward her.

She laughs and shakes her head. "I think bus sex is the only thing on the table right now."

"I'm so excited!" I rub my hands together. "I fully intended to rub one out in the shower, but now this. I feel unprepared."

She crinkles her nose but her eyes dance with humor. "Be careful you don't get too excited. Don't want you to embarrass yourself."

"I might." I grin, but it's the honest to God truth. I look around the empty bus. "What do you think? Bathroom?"

"Actually"—she bites the inside of her cheek and glances down the hall—"do you think Leighton and Opal would mind if we borrowed the bedroom?"

My eyes widen with surprise. "You sure?"

"Yeah." She walks over to the kitchen table, retrieving a handbag from the bench seat.

"As long as we change the sex sheets, they won't care." I shove my hand into my pocket, suddenly a little nervous. Jayla is trusting me to make this good and I don't want to screw it up.

She pauses and lifts her brow. "Sex sheets?"

"Yeah, it's a thing." I chuckle, and meet her stare. "You're sure about this? We don't have to."

"I want to." She closes the space between us and grabs my hand. She walks backward, leading me down the hall and holds up her purse. "I brought ties. I hope you're okay with that."

My dick rises in agreement, my entire body game for whatever she has planned. I don't know what I did to deserve this woman, but I'm never letting her go. "Fuck, I love you, Jayla."

"Don't try to butter me up." She opens the bedroom door and reaches for the waistband of my jeans. With one swift tug she hauls my front to hers. "I'm still planning to tie you to the bed."

My dick gives an excited jump against her core. "Yes, please."

38

JAYLA

"UNDRESS. NOW." I close the door, turn to lean back against it, and flip the lock.

Austin's lips part and he lets out a soft groan. He likes it when I'm bossy. The more forceful I am, the more his eyes light with desire. The more control he gives, the bolder I become. We're a perfect mix of push and pull. I don't think I'll ever get used to it, or stop being thankful for him.

While Austin discards his clothes I move to the dresser and set down my bag. I dig through the contents, producing everything I need. I sync my phone to the portable speaker, and press play on the mix I made. It's mostly throwbacks from our youth, a few Motown faves, and yes, Beyoncé. From the corner of my eye I catch Austin's lips lift appreciatively at the first song to play, "Bring It On Home to Me" by Sam Cooke.

My body tingles with anticipation as I retrieve the padded cuffs and adjustable tethers. I take in Austin's naked form, a beautiful work of body art and taut muscle. I love how he stands confidently, his fist gripping his hard cock, waiting for my next command.

"On the bed. Lie on your back."

He does as I say, leaning back on his elbows.

I drop the restraints on the bed next to his feet, but then step back, swinging my hips to the sensual rhythm of the song. He whispers encouragement as I remove my blouse and skirt. The thong and bra my girls insisted would drive him crazy seemingly do just that.

"Oh, my God. My cock is so hard right now."

"Hands on the bed," I direct, and take one of the cuffs. I climb over his body, teasing as I allow my skin to rub against his. When I get to his chest, I sit off to one side and slide the fabric along his wrist before fastening it to him, and then the attached restraint tie to one side of the headboard. There's still lots of give, but before I move to his other side I make sure he's comfortable. "This okay?"

"It's so good, baby."

"Tell me if it stops," I say, a line he's used on me several times.

He meets my stare with a nod. "I will."

I climb off the bed, grab another tie and run it along the length of his body as I walk to the other side of the headboard. I reach for his hand, but he's already offering it.

"Someone's a little excited," I murmur through my smile.

"Guilty." He grins back, but as soon as I fasten the cuff around his wrist his humor fades and in its place, lust. A thrill works down my spine as I adjust the tie to the bed and step back to assess my work. He arches his back and his muscles strain for my touch. He's beautiful. Exposed. Mine.

I dance for him, this time closing my eyes as I run my hands over my body. His groans of pleasure spur me on, and I remove my lingerie before climbing over his body. I kiss up his abdomen, purposefully avoiding his cock to drag out his pleasure. I kiss the hard planes of his abs, his chest, nipples, and straddle his waist as my lips finally find his.

"I want you. Please" I like that he begs.

"What do you want?" I say between passionate kisses.

His breath is heavy and labored. "I want to taste you. I want you to ride my face."

My legs press together, wetness forming with his request. "You do?"

"Fuck, yeah."

Cupping his jaw between my hands, I kiss him hard. My body grows hotter, my need for him greater. His tongue battles with mine, a fight neither of us loses as we stoke the fire of desire to a point of no return.

"Okay," I say, finally breaking our kiss. With confidence, I scoot up his body until my thighs spread wide over his mouth.

"Give it to me, please," he shudders, completely at my mercy.

I reach for the headboard, finding my balance as I spread my legs wider and lower myself. When his lips make contact with my sensitive skin I gasp in a mix of pleasure and surprise. He licks my center, eating me out like it's his favorite dessert. It's a heady mix, the music, his mouth on me, my thighs straddling his face. He uses his tongue, lips, and face, circling my clit and bringing me to the edge.

I could come like this. I kind of want to. If we had all night I would, but already two songs have played on my mix, and as much as I want to orgasm, I want him inside me more.

Using the headboard, I lift my body off his face. Austin opens his mouth to argue, but doesn't when I grip his shaft. With my back to him, I move down his body as I stroke him, reveling in the softness of his skin and the hardness of his cock.

"Oh, fuck, yeah." He groans.

Spreading my thighs over his hips, I line his thick cock at my entrance and glance over my shoulder to watch his face as I sink down and take him inside, inch by glorious inch. I'm so wet and he slides in deep. We both let loose moans of satisfaction. I grab his thighs for support and arch my back to ride him this way.

"I'm not gonna last," he says. "Fuck, your ass looks so good."

"I want us both to come." I reach between our bodies to find my clit. I'm so turned on. So full of desire and power. It won't take long to meet him at the edge. I swivel my hips, gyrating over his hard length and rubbing my clit in circles. A sheen of sweat covers my body and the entire room smells of sex. Austin doesn't hold back, voicing compliments, praises, and naughty thoughts. Within minutes my body clenches with the onset of my orgasm.

"Fuck, I'm coming." I pant and writhe, over and over again until pleasure rips through my body.

"Yeah, baby. Ride me. Fuck me." Austin lifts his hips and his entire body spasms as he joins me, crashing over the edge. "Oh! Yeah," he shouts.

My sex pulses and my body tingles. So good. My eyes shut tight as aftershocks of my release shudder through me and I work to catch my breath.

"Oh, fuck, Jayla," Austin praises, and I hear his smile before I look over my shoulder to see it. "I think that was the best yet. Damn." His chest heaves. "Fuck."

"You said that already," I tease and climb off his body, unfastening his restraints before joining him on the bed. We lay next to each other, him smiling like a fool and me doing the same.

He turns on his side and slides the back of his knuckles over my scar. "It looks much better."

"It does." I agree with a nod.

"Good call on the music. Nice selection." He catches my hand in his and pulls it to his lips, kissing the back of my palm. His lips lift with a satisfied smirk, and the sight alone makes my heart beat a little faster. He releases my hand and lays his head against his arm, using it as a pillow.

I turn to mirror his position and give in to a smile, my gaze voraciously memorizing his naked body. I already want him again.

"I'm glad you're here." His gaze dips to my mouth and he narrows the space between us. As his mouth moves with mine in lazy, languid strokes, my back presses into the mattress. Except there's no anxiety threatening to ruin this moment. No bolt of fear from the ghosts of my past. His kiss is warm, steady, and my heart races with love for this man. My safe space. My home. He pulls back to meet my gaze. "I lost you before, and I never want to again."

My throat catches at the sentiment. His words are sweet and full of the same truth I feel down to my soul. "Never." I whisper against his lips. "I'm not going anywhere."

"Yeah?" He leans back to study my expression. His eyes flicker with a vulnerability he only shares with me.

"Yeah." I swallow back the surge of emotion, thick in my throat before I can continue. "I used to think I was damaged. Irrevocably changed in a way that meant I could never have this." My hands greedily skim across his body.

He nods, his expression open and inviting.

"I didn't think I could accept love. Thank you for proving me wrong."

He shrugs, a flicker of mischief in his gaze. "I am irresistible."

I push him to his back and roll onto my stomach, shaking my head. "And completely inappropriate, self-absorbed, and entirely too sure of yourself."

He just grins. "You love me."

I do. I really do. "I love you, Austin Jones. I will love you forever."

"Fuck." He scrunches his nose and gives me a wink. "This got really deep. I'm torn between making a dick joke or throwing caution to the wind and asking you to be my wife."

"Your choice." I shrug, the challenge flying from my lips without filter. "How lucky do you feel tonight?"

"Shit." His eyes widen.

Mine do too. *What did I just say?*

"Really?" He coughs as he clears his throat and sits up in bed. "Fuck!" His eyes bug out and he looks as though he might pass out any second. It shouldn't be funny, but it is.

I laugh, letting loose some of my nerves, and shake my head. "Did I just render you speechless? Because I think that's a first."

He moves his mouth open and shut as if he wants to speak, but can't quite decide.

"I didn't think it was possible." I laugh again. "It's too soon. Right?" I'm not sure who I'm convincing more, him or myself. Because we haven't been a couple very long and the logical thing is to wait. Yet there's this tiny voice in my head that says I've always been his. Knows there's no other man in this world I'd rather build a life with.

"Yes." Austin nods, finding his voice. "It's too soon." He stares, narrowing his gaze. "And I can't tell if you're fucking with me or being serious."

I bite my lip, not wanting to admit I was dead serious when the words rolled from my mouth.

"So, I'm going to date you. I'm going to earn your trust. And when I ask you to be my wife, you're going to say yes." His smile is big. Confident. Like he's won a million dollars.

"See. You with the self-assured again."

"Well, this proposal is going to be so over-the-top extravagant you won't even know what hit you." He shrugs. "You'll have to say yes."

"Austin, I don't need grand gestures." I push to my knees and straddle his waist to steal a kiss. I wrap my arms around his neck and gaze into his eyes. "Only you."

He grins. "I guess we'll have to wait and see."

"I guess we will," I say, my lips wide with a smile. My future has never looked brighter. Bigger. Full of possibility, and a love I've always wanted but never thought I'd have. He was my best friend, and though I hate that it took us so long to find our way back to each other, it only makes the love we've discovered more treasured. I've been searching my whole life, but little did I know the key to my happiness was tied to my past. We're meant for each other, because I think Austin was waiting for me, too.

"You know, I was thinking . . . you and I are a lot like a great song."

"How's that?" I thread my fingers through the hair at the base of his neck before meeting his gaze.

"Some songs are so good, you know, but they're even better on the replay. It isn't until you've memorized the lyrics that they become significant. It's not until you appreciate the complexity of the music that it becomes better. The more times you listen, the more you fall in love." He paints his finger between my breasts, down my stomach, and draws lazy circles around my scar and over my hip. "You're my replay, Jayla, and I'm so damn lucky to love you."

EPILOGUE

AUSTIN

"I don't think we have enough food. Maybe you should run to the store." Jayla bites her lip and stares at the spread of dishes taking up the entire square footage of our kitchen island. The last thing we need is more food, but I'm not dumb enough to say that aloud.

"Jay, your mama will be here any second and you know she'll bring more than you asked."

Her hands go to her hips and she sighs. "You're right."

"Have I told you how beautiful you look?" I step up to my girl-friend and capture her lips in a kiss. "And our house." I glance around taking in all the decorations, the spread of food, and the presents piled around the tree. I kiss her again. "You did an amazing job."

"I'm just nervous. I want everyone to have a good time."

"They will. We'll all be together. That's what matters the most." It's our first time hosting anything, let alone a major holiday. Tomorrow everyone is doing their own thing, but we wanted to get together for Christmas Eve, and since Jay wanted her family and friends to feel comfortable and included, she volunteered our home.

Our home. Damn, I love the sound of that. We moved down to

Oceanside a few months after I finished recording the latest 3UG album. We looked all over, but finally decided on this location. She wanted a place close enough we could drive to our friends' homes, but far enough no one was stopping by all the time. I'm pretty sure that mostly included her mother, but I was game. I'm happy wherever Jayla is, and I have to admit I like the chill vibe of this seaside town.

The doorbell rings and Jayla straightens, glancing around the room one last time before she strides over to open the door. I hope she's ready for this.

Shouts of greeting flow through our home. Familiar voices that make this day feel all the more special. I make my way to Jayla's side as Trent, Lexi, Opal, Leighton, and little Axl parade through the door. I've never been one for babies, but damn, that kid's cute.

"Merry Christmas, motherfuckers!" I say in greeting.

Opal narrows her eyes. "You have got to stop doing that. He's gonna start repeating words soon."

"Here," I say, stealing the little bugger from her before everyone else does. "What, no baby equipment today?"

"It's all in the back of the SUV." Leighton smirks.

"Give me that." Jayla scoops Axl right out of my arms. "How's my sweet boy today?"

"Careful. You let your girl hold him too long and she'll start getting ideas," Trent teases, but the joke's on him. I can't wait to start a family with Jayla. "Wait. Hold up." He stops, his gaze bouncing from Jayla to me and then back to Jayla.

"What?" She raises her brows.

"Are you two wearing matching Christmas sweaters?"

Jayla blinks and cocks her head. "Yeah, so?"

"No fucking way!" Trent bursts into laughter.

"Language!" Opal chides.

Trent cringes and shoots the baby a look. "Sorry, little man." He turns to me and his eyes widen. "Are these the sweaters from last year? The ones that light up?"

"Hell yeah," I say and press the button to make mine flicker to life. "They're *freaking* awesome."

"Thank you." Opal blows me a kiss for my effort at censorship.

"Jayla"—Trent shakes his head—"I expect this ridiculousness from Aust, but you lose major street cred. Matching sweaters?" He repeats as if it's not the coolest thing. Okay, so maybe he has a point, but I like being festive, and Jayla likes it too.

"We do a lot for the ones we love, yeah?" Jayla raises her brows. I love that she doesn't take shit from anyone, least of all my bandmates.

"Touché," Trent agrees.

"And what exactly, have you had to do for me these days?" Lexi hands him a bottle of beer from the fridge and twists the top off her own.

"For one, I didn't pitch a fit when you didn't name your label after me."

She rolls her eyes. "Trent Donavan Records was never on the table."

"It should've been. That's all I'm saying."

Opal laughs and joins her sister. The pair make the most unassuming label execs in the biz. You'd never know by looking at them, but Detour Records is setting a precedence for new standards in indie representation. With them, it's all about quality music, equality, and strong relationships with their talent as much as their partners.

"Hey, speaking of work, did we get everything worked out with the Hurley brothers?" Lexi turns to Opal. "I want them signed before someone else gets to them."

"No shop talk today." Trent wraps his arms around Lexi. "This is Christmas."

She tilts her head back to meet his stare. "And what, baby Jesus doesn't care about our company?"

"Please don't talk about baby Jesus like that when my mama gets here," Jayla pleads.

"Okay, okay. No business talk." Lexi holds up her hands.

The doorbell rings.

"Speak of the devil." I wink at Jay and run to grab the door before she yells. For the next hour we welcome a slew of guests. Mama Lou, Jayla's brother Desmond, his wife Lina and their boys Zachariah and Josiah. Aaliyah and her new boyfriend. Kalise. Trent's mom Deb and her boyfriend. Sean and Jess, late as usual. Even our band's Hollywood friend Cora Bentley and her new man pop by for a little while. Our house is full, stomachs fuller, and joy flows readily as the beverage fridge empties.

"WHAT'S WRONG, BUGGERHEAD?" I'm surprised to find Brianna's wide brown eyes peeking up at me as I come into my room. It's way past her bedtime, not that her dad would notice. He's out with my mom at some party.

"Do you think Santa comes to this house? Mom says he won't." She grips her blankie in her hand, and her little lip trembles. It's a sight that always does me in. I hate she even worries about shit like this. Kids her age shouldn't have to, but her mom is probably right. My mom stopped getting me presents after elementary school, and Brianna's dad doesn't think about anyone but himself. The only reason Bri spends every other weekend here is so he doesn't have to pay child support. I know it's so because I've heard him boast about it to my mom a hundred times. I don't know why my mom falls for losers like him. They both disgust me.

"Hey." I tussle the curls on her head and lead her back to bed. I give in to a smile, knowing she'll have at least one present to open, and pleased with myself for swiping one of the stuffed animals left under the giving tree at my school yesterday. Yeah, stealing it wasn't my finest moment, but at least I didn't shoplift. People left those things intending them to go to a child in need this Christmas, and I think Bri fits that bill as much as any other. "I know he will. Promise."

"You sure?" she says through a sleepy yawn.

I stroke her back, lulling her back to sleep. "I'd never lie to you."

"There you are." Jayla slides open the back patio door, balancing two glasses of wine. She passes one to me.

We clink the rims in a silent toast. "Sorry, I needed some air," I say, taking in the horizon from our upstairs deck. The sunset burns through the haze of clouds, creating an array of oranges, yellows, pinks, and blues that light up the sky. "Your family still here?"

"No, Desmond finally dragged Mama from the kitchen." Jayla shakes her head, but there's a trace of a smile on her lips. As much as her mother drives her crazy, she loves her. "I told her she didn't have to help clean, but you know how she is."

I take a sip of the wine and chuckle. "That I do."

Jayla rubs her hand across my back. "You okay?"

"Yeah, just thinking." My gazes goes to the horizon once more, watching as the sun disappears beneath the ocean. Today has been wonderful. Having our friends and family together to celebrate was like stepping foot into a life I always wanted but never expected to have. Being a part of Three Ugly Guys has taught me family isn't always blood, sometimes it's the people you choose. I consider myself a lucky man to be surrounded by so much love. I only wish I had Brianna here too.

"You miss her," Jayla says with compassion and understanding.

"I wish I could find her." I reach for Jayla's hand and take comfort in her touch. "Or know she's safe."

"I do, too." Jayla leans her head on my shoulder. "We'll keep looking."

"Maybe there's another way." I clear my throat and turn to meet Jayla's stare. I've been thinking on this a lot lately, and not only because it's the holidays. "I'm not giving up hope. It's just, I've spent so much money and energy looking for Brianna, and it hasn't done any good."

She takes our wine glasses and sets them down. With both hands free, she kneads the tension from my shoulders. "But you didn't know that. You had to try."

"Yeah." I nod and release a deep breath. "And if I could trade money to find her, I would in a heartbeat. I think it's time to face the reality that it sucks, but this is how life works sometimes." I take a step back and turn to face Jayla. "I want to open a home. With your help."

Her gaze turns earnest. "What kind of home?"

"A place for lost girls. We could provide treatment. Mental healthcare. Teach healthy life skills and decision making. Self-defense, too." The idea pours from my lips, unsure of her reaction, or if a passion project like this would even interest her. Just because it excites me, doesn't mean it's for her.

Jayla wraps her arms around my neck. "I love it."

"It'd be a safe haven, you know? A place full of hope. The kind of place that could've rescued Brianna."

"I love you." Her smile is wide and her eyes are full of unshed tears as she peppers gentle kisses on my mouth. "Your heart." Another kiss. "Your mind."

I wrinkle my nose and press my cheek against hers and make a joke so I won't cry. "My body too? Tell me you love my body."

"Everything." She laughs and steps back to find my gaze. "I love sharing my life with you."

I didn't think it possible, but I love her more now than when I woke this morning. Her capacity to love and accept me as I am pushes me to be the best version of myself. I was planning to wait until tomorrow, but the weight I've been carrying around all day gives me the incentive to do it now. "You hoping for any big presents from Santa?"

Her grin turns rueful as she narrows her gaze. "You think I still have time to write a letter to the jolly old guy?"

"Depends," I tease. "Whatcha gonna ask for?"

"Well"—she taps her finger against her chin—"I was hoping I'd get a rock star under my tree this year."

"I know a guy. I'll make it happen." I reach out and rub my hand along her hip. "But only if you're on the naughty list."

"*Hmm.*" She shakes her head and laughs. "I think you have it backward."

"I apparently do everything backward. Like let the only girl I ever loved get away." My gaze sobers.

"But she came back."

"And I'm the luckiest man in the world." I clasp her left hand in my right and drop to one knee. "Or at least, I hope I will be."

"What?" She gasps, her eyes wide. *Hell, yes.* I've surprised her.

She looks around and then meets my hopeful stare. "Where's the fireworks? The big flashy gesture?"

"I decided you were right. We don't need all that."

She tilts her head, pursing her lips. "Can you repeat that one more time, the part about me being right?"

"Well, we need a *little* extravagance." I chuckle and reach into my pocket, producing the ring I picked out last month with Kalise and Aaliyah's help. I don't know what prompted me to put it in my pocket this morning, but I'm glad I did. This is much more romantic, and the moment feels right. I hold out the diamond band, offering her not only a ring, but my heart. "Jayla Ashanti Miller. Will you do me the great honor of becoming my wife?"

She mashes her lips together, her chin nodding furiously before a smile takes over her face. "Yes, yes, I will."

I slide the ring on her finger and push to my feet, unable to stand the space between us any longer. Pulling her flush to my body, I capture her lips the way she's captured my soul. As our mouths seal together, I vow to do my damnedest to deserve every moment she gives me. Jayla holds my heart. She's my second chance. My home. She's my favorite song on replay, and our future, my greatest album.

The End

THANK YOU

Thank you for reading Jayla and Austin's story. If you didn't get enough of these two, visit my website at www.kaceysheabooks.com and join my newsletter to gain access to a bonus epilogue and a glimpse into their future.

I hope you enjoyed this book! If you haven't read the rest of the Off Track Records novels, they are available now in Detour, Derail, and Hinder. Also, there's more rock stars! Find out what happened to Three Ugly Guys' original drummer in Uncovering Hope.

Please consider leaving an honest review on Amazon, Goodreads, and/or BookBub. Reviews are an excellent way to support the authors and books you love!

ACKNOWLEDGMENTS

I could not write the books I do without the support of my family. Joe, Abby, JD, and G I love you. Thank you for your encouragement, and for being my biggest fans.

When it comes to getting a book ready it takes a village, and I wouldn't be able to do this without the support of mine! To Kerry for reading everything I write, including my text messages when I'm feeling overwhelmed and vulnerable. This writing thing is so much more fun with your friendship. Viv, Rikki, Amy, Rachel, Megan, Amie, and Danielle thank you so much for beta reading. Your insight and feedback helped me get these characters just right. Thank you for loving my Ugly Guys!

To my editor, Brenda, I'm so happy we found each other! Each book you push me, and I think after ten books together we've got a pretty great thing going. Thank you to Chrissy, Erin, and Melissa my fabulous proofreading team who literally find all my flaws. You are amazing and generous.

Najla thank you for the design of Replay and recovering the entire Off Track Records series. I'm in love with these covers and they fit the books perfectly. Thanks to Ellie for being my dealer of this fantastic cover photo of Graham Nation shot by Gilbert Pereda. It's gorgeous and so fitting for Austin's story.

To all the readers and book bloggers who have taken a chance on me, loved these characters, and supported my work thank you. I get to do what I love because of you. Thank you for your time and energy. For reading my books. For the teasers. For recommending my books to your friends. I appreciate you more than I can ever put into words.

ALSO BY KACEY SHEA

Sports Romance

The Perfect Comeback

Firefighters

Caught in the Flames

Caught in the Lies

Rock Stars

Detour

Derail

Hinder

Replay

Uncovering Love Series

Uncovering Love

Uncovering Desire

Uncovering Hope

Uncovering Love: The Wedding

ABOUT THE AUTHOR

Kacey Shea is pen name to a mom of three, wife, and *USA Today* bestselling author who resides in sunny Arizona. She enjoys reading and writing romance novels as much as her son loves unicorns, which is a lot.

When she's not writing you will find her playing taxi cab to her children while belting out her favorite tunes, meeting friends or family for food and to share laughs, or sweating it out in the gym.

She has an unhealthy obsession with firefighters. It could be the pants. It could be the fire. It's just hot. On occasion she has been known to include them, without their knowledge, in her selfies outside the grocery store.

Kacey one day aspires be a woman hand model in a sexy photo shoot. You know, the woman's hand raking across the muscular back or six pack stomach of the male fitness model. Yep, that hand.

Until that day comes she will continue writing sexy, flirty romance novels in hopes to bring others joy!

Sign up for Kacey's newsletter and never miss a new release!

For more information
www.kaceysheabooks.com
info@kaceysheabooks.com

Made in the USA
Columbia, SC
19 March 2019